"The feel-good book of the month. The wonderfully funny, poignant romance has just the right balance of humor, sensuality, and engaging characters to make it a treasure. Ms. Dawson has written a book that gives you that warm glow."
—*Romantic Times*

"Often amusing with plenty of pathos, Western romance that grips the heart and soul. . . . Fans will appreciate this fine tale that holds up quite well, and seek the sequels."
—The Best Reviews

The Bad Luck Wedding Cake

"Warm and delicious enough to satisfy the sweet tooth of any reader. Geralyn Dawson leaves me hungry for more."
—Teresa Medeiros, author of *After Midnight*

My Long Tall Texas Heartthrob

"Delightfully fun."
—Christina Dodd, author of *My Fair Temptress*

"Wow! An excellent, passionate romance."   —*Rendezvous*

"Take a wonderful romance, add some intriguing mystery and a tad of dangerous suspense, sprinkle it liberally with humor, and you have *My Long Tall Texas Heartthrob*."
—*Romantic Times*

Give Him the Slip

GERALYN DAWSON

A SIGNET ECLIPSE BOOK

SIGNET ECLIPSE
Published by New American Library, a division of
Penguin Group (USA) Inc., 375 Hudson Street,
New York, New York 10014, USA
Penguin Group (Canada), 90 Eglinton Avenue East, Suite 700, Toronto,
Ontario M4P 2Y3, Canada (a division of Pearson Penguin Canada Inc.)
Penguin Books Ltd., 80 Strand, London WC2R 0RL, England
Penguin Ireland, 25 St. Stephen's Green, Dublin 2,
Ireland (a division of Penguin Books Ltd.)
Penguin Group (Australia), 250 Camberwell Road, Camberwell, Victoria 3124,
Australia (a division of Pearson Australia Group Pty. Ltd.)
Penguin Books India Pvt. Ltd., 11 Community Centre, Panchsheel Park,
New Delhi - 110 017, India
Penguin Group (NZ), cnr Airborne and Rosedale Roads, Albany,
Auckland 1310, New Zealand (a division of Pearson New Zealand Ltd.)
Penguin Books (South Africa) (Pty.) Ltd., 24 Sturdee Avenue,
Rosebank, Johannesburg 2196, South Africa

Penguin Books Ltd., Registered Offices:
80 Strand, London WC2R 0RL, England

First published by Signet Eclipse, an imprint of New American Library,
a division of Penguin Group (USA) Inc.

First Printing, October 2006
10 9 8 7 6 5 4 3 2 1

For Caitlin,
Fightin' Texas Aggie Class of 2010.
Whoop!
May all your dreams come true.

One

Maddie Kincaid was in trouble. Again.

Trouble caused by a man. Again.

Maybe she should reconsider the convent idea after all.

"There's the sign, Oscar," she said to the fat goldfish swimming in the clear glass fishbowl belted into the mini-van's passenger seat to her right. "The Caddo Bayou Marina. We made it."

The goldfish didn't answer, although the way her world had changed in the last twenty-four hours, Maddie wouldn't have been surprised if Oscar had leapt from the water and belted out "The Yellow Rose of Texas."

Approaching the marina entrance, Maddie gently applied the brakes and flicked her left-turn indicator. Since beginning this long, meandering trip to southwestern Louisiana fourteen hours ago, she'd taken extra care to obey all traffic laws.

It wouldn't do to get pulled over by the highway patrol, not when she had four million dollars' worth of an illegal substance stacked between her dry cleaning and a new sponge mop.

Gravel crunched beneath the minivan's tires as she drove across the lot and claimed a spot between a Dodge pickup and a Chevy Suburban. After shifting into park, she took a deep, calming breath and twisted the ignition key. The engine sputtered and then died. In the sudden quiet, Maddie let out a soft, semihysterical laugh. *Better it than me.*

She sat without moving for a full minute. Her mouth was dry, her pulse rapid. She needed to use the facilities. "Okay," she murmured. "We made it. We handled the crisis. Got here in one piece. We did good. Now we'll have help."

Help. From the DEA. "I must be out of my ever-lovin' mind."

Maddie opened her car door and stepped outside. The summer morning air was hot, heavy, and thick with moisture. She glanced toward the boat slips, then back at the marina's ship store and restaurant. "I'll be right back," she said to Oscar as she grabbed her purse before shutting the door. Then, noting the heat and imagining boiled goldfish, she reconsidered. Moments later, fishbowl cradled in one arm, purse hanging from the other, she headed for the store and its bathroom.

As she walked toward the building, movement at the gas dock out on the water caught her notice. Three pontoon boats filled with people dressed in swim trunks and brightly colored clothing motored slowly away from the dock. Must be one of the swamp tours she'd seen advertised on a billboard on the way in, Maddie surmised. Her gaze drifted over the crowd before it snagged on the man standing at the stern of the trailing boat as he stripped off a sweat-stained T-shirt and tossed it away. He lifted his arm above his head to take a minnow bucket off a hook, and Maddie sucked in a breath.

My, oh my, oh my.

She may be tired, scared, hungry, thirsty, and ready to wet her pants, but abs like those deserved a second look—even if she had sworn off studly men forever.

He wore a battered straw cowboy hat, low-riding Hawaiian-print swim trunks, and grungy deck shoes. Sunglasses hung from a cord around his neck, and a sheen of sweat glistened on his deeply tanned skin. His body looked lean and hard, with long legs and broad shoulders that indicated athlete rather than gym rat.

Yum.

Her appreciative gaze lingered until a good look at his face made her forget about his form. Even from a distance, she could see devastation etched in his expression. Empathy melted through her. Poor man. She wondered what had happened to him.

Then, as if he tangibly felt her gaze, he jerked his stare away from the minnow bucket dangling from his hand and met her gaze head-on. His eyes narrowed, his jaw hardened. He straightened, squared his shoulders, and widened his stance, his aggressive posture a challenge to her for catching him in a private moment.

Whoa. Maddie gave a tentative smile and took a step back. In another moment, he'd be baring his teeth like a wolf, she thought.

A wolf in low-riding swim trunks.

"Oh, for crying out loud," she muttered, deliberately turning away, shifting the fishbowl from one arm to the other. What was wrong with her, ogling a bayou boy when she should be looking over her shoulder for drug-dealing killers? Had she totally lost her mind?

Yes, she was afraid so. This was what an overload of stress and lack of sleep did to a girl.

Dismissing the party barges, Maddie redirected her attention toward the ship store. The place appeared deserted. In fact, other than the pontoon boats now disappearing from view, the only signs of life around the entire marina were a pair of big black grackles pecking at the ground near a lidded metal Dumpster.

Cautious in ways she'd never been before, Maddie slowed her steps and took a second look around.

On the murky water of the bayou, dozens of boats floated beneath the shelter of covered docks. Both the gas pump on the water and the one near the cement launch ramp remained unmanned. She spied an open tackle box and two fishing poles propped against a silver propane tank, but the fishermen themselves were nowhere to be found.

Curious. On a Saturday morning, she'd expect the

marina to be bustling, especially on a warm, windless day. Apprehensive now, Maddie advanced toward the ship store's door.

A handwritten sign was taped to the glass at eye level. "Closed for funeral," she read aloud. "Reopen at 1:00 p.m."

Well, that explained the quiet, and all the vehicles in the lot probably belonged to the swamp-tour people. It didn't solve her need for a bathroom, however, so Maddie turned toward the boat slips in search of the *Miss Behavin' II.*

The woman she'd come to see lived on a houseboat moored at this marina. It shouldn't be difficult to find. If Terri Winston wasn't aboard, then Maddie would backtrack to the fast-food restaurant she'd passed on the interstate. She hoped it didn't come to that. She felt safer here in this out-of-the-way spot than she did in a town or on the highway.

It had occurred to her as she drove through central Texas at three o'clock in the morning that the Brazos Bend police could have issued a BOLO for her van. From that moment on, she'd lived in fear of seeing the red-and-blue flash of a highway patrol car.

Maddie noted two normal-sized houseboats and one huge houseboat that brought the *Queen Mary* to mind among the twenty or so boats berthed in the slips. Since the mansion-boat didn't seem like something a federal agent would own, she made her way toward the smaller vessels.

The name painted across the stern of the first read *Playtime.* Maddie's stomach knotted with tension as she approached the second. It'd be just her luck for Ms. Winston to have up and moved her boat.

"*Bayou Queen*," she read aloud, grimacing. Damn. Maddie blew out a heavy sigh, then gazed at the floating palace. It had to be eighty feet long, with front and rear decks, outdoor ceiling fans, and a spiral staircase to the roof with its fiberglass flybridge and swim slide. A boat like that would be called *Bellagio* or *Shangri-la.* Not *Miss Behavin'.*

Since she was out of other options, she decided to be thorough. To her shock and relief, the sign hanging from the rear deck of the mansion-boat displayed the words she prayed she'd see.

However, the *Miss Behavin' II* appeared as deserted as the rest of the marina.

"Hello?" Maddie called. "Ms. Winston? Is anybody home?"

She heard nothing but the squeak of a rubber boat fender against the wooden dock in reply.

Maddie grimaced. Where could the agent be this time of day? At the funeral? A quick check of her watch left Maddie moaning. If Terri Winston was at the funeral and the funeral lasted all morning, it didn't bode well for Maddie's bladder.

Her teeth tugged at her lower lip and she groaned aloud. Had she made one more mistake in a long line of them by putting her life in the hands of a stranger based solely on the advice of that septuagenarian meddler Branch Callahan? So what if Branch insisted that Terri Winston was a stand-up woman who'd listen to Maddie's story without immediately snapping on the handcuffs? Recent events suggested that Brazos Bend's leading citizen wasn't as knowledgeable as he claimed.

Branch hadn't known about the drug ring operating right under his nose, had he?

Maddie let out a long, shaky sigh. She may well have made a serious mistake, but what other choice had she had? Despite her vow of self-sufficiency in the wake of the disaster that had been her love life, she'd needed help. When she'd swallowed her pride and reached out to her father, he'd been off indulging in one of his new hobbies— wildlife photography in the Alaskan wilderness. According to his latest assistant—his latest twenty-year-old, starry-eyed bed partner, no doubt—he'd be beyond cell phone reach for another week—an eternity to someone in Maddie's predicament.

A predicament growing more dire by the second. She needed a bathroom *now*. Raising her voice, she tried again. "Hello? Ms. Winston?"

Nothing.

Maddie glanced from the houseboat to her van, then back to the floating manse. It was a long way back to that fast-food place. Not a soul was in sight. Even if she tripped an alarm, she'd probably have time to visit the restroom and make herself scarce before anyone showed up to investigate. "Ordinarily I wouldn't think of trespassing," she told Oscar. "But these are no ordinary times."

Besides, Ms. Winston was a woman. She'd understand.

Maddie wiped her sweaty hands on her shorts and then stepped onto the boat and tried the sliding glass door. It slid open easily, and when no alarm sounded, she stuck her head inside, gazing with interest at the luxurious features and furnishings. She hadn't seen a boat this tricked out since she visited her father for a week aboard a Greek tycoon's yacht. "Ms. Winston?" she called. "Terri?"

No response.

Maddie stepped inside. An overstuffed couch and two plump easy chairs faced a plasma TV hanging on a wood-paneled wall finished with crown molding. A wraparound bar separated the main living area from a kitchen complete with granite countertops and a Sub-Zero refrigerator. She spied recessed lighting, brass hardware on the cabinets, and roman shades and padded cornice boards on the windows.

"Wouldn't Daddy love to have one of these," she murmured.

Maddie set Oscar and her purse atop a stylish iron and glass dining table, then made a beeline for the bathroom. With personal business out of the way and fully intending to return to the dock to wait for Terri Winston like a polite un-invited guest, she nevertheless paused when she passed the refrigerator.

She *was* awfully thirsty. Maddie tapped her foot, then sighed. At this point, what was one more sin?

She opened the fridge. Hmm . . . the agent must have recently visited the grocery store. Lots of meat, cheese, eggs. Looked to be a South Beach dieter except for the three gallons of low-fat milk. She spied a twelve-pack of spring water and a six-pack of imported beer. Maddie reached for the water, but somehow, her hand grabbed the beer.

Boldly, she rummaged through Ms. Winston's drawers to find a bottle opener and, after hesitating over a bag of Double Stuf Oreos, grabbed a half-empty package of pretzels from her pantry. She sat at the table, drank her stolen beer, and finished off the bag of pilfered pretzels. When she belched aloud without even trying to smother the sound, Maddie knew she'd lost it.

"Maybe I'm having a heat stroke," she said to Oscar. Or post-traumatic stress syndrome. But it couldn't be that. There was nothing at all "post" about this stress.

Something told her that drug-dealing, crooked-cop murderers wouldn't give up the hunt for her just because she didn't go home last night.

Grabbing her beer, she tossed the empty pretzel bag into a plastic trash can, then walked past one, two, three bedrooms and another bathroom to the front deck. Maddie gazed out at the bayou, where late-morning sunlight strained through the thick green canopy of trees and vines that stretched across the murky water of the swamp. Long strands of Spanish moss dangled from the branches of the live oaks like gray-green tinsel, adding an eerie atmosphere to an already fantastical morning.

"I can't believe I'm in trouble again," she said softly. This time, she hadn't sought it out. This time, she hadn't fallen for a seductive man's line. This time, all she'd done was clean house!

The urge to cry came over her then, but Maddie fiercely fought it back. She'd sworn off crying at the same time she'd sworn off studly men. She was stronger now. She'd survive this.

But as she returned to the kitchen to gather her purse and her pet, despite her best intentions, a pair of big, fat tears overflowed her eyes and slid slowly down her cheeks.

She swayed on her feet, overcome with exhaustion and emotion and the effects of half a bottle of dark ale. Then, feeling like a cross between Goldilocks and Buffy, she chose a stateroom, kicked off her sneakers, found an out-of-the-way spot on the floor for Oscar, and crawled into a queen-sized bed.

Luke Callahan set the plastic bottle of mustard on the ship store counter and said, "That ought to do it."

Perched like a heron atop a three-legged stool behind the counter, Marie Gauthier sighed heavily, her frown deepening the lines in skin tanned dark and leathery. "Ah, it be a sad day, *cher*," she said, ringing up his purchases. "Me, I'll be missing that old coot. I thought the service was fine and fitting."

Luke nodded and cleared his throat. "Terry liked a good party."

"*Mais* yeah." Marie neatly stacked Luke's groceries in a brown paper bag. "That man, he loved a *fais do-do*, and he loved the bayou. It's the right place for his ashes to rest."

Luke agreed. Spreading Terry Winston's ashes was the single part of this god-awful day that had felt right.

"And now, what about you, *mon ami*? My man, he say you're taking the *Miss Behavin' II* away from Caddo Bayou. Are you leaving us for good? The ladies here, they will be brokenhearted."

"I'll be back." Luke lifted the grocery bag into his arms and offered her the first genuine smile he'd managed in a month. "I'm going fishing for a few weeks. One of my brothers just bought a new thirty-foot Grady-White. I'm meeting him in Lake Charles and we're heading out toward the Keys."

"An extended fishing trip? *Mon Dieu*. My man, he be pea green with envy when he hears that. So, it's true, then? You're trading in your gun and badge for a fishing pole and bait?"

Luke's smile slowly died as the sick sensation in his stomach returned. He'd broken the rules when he went after Terry's killer. He'd resigned before they could fire him.

"Beyond fishing for my supper for the next few weeks, I'm not sure what I'm going to do."

Marie Gauthier reached across the counter and gave Luke's arm a comforting pat. "Ah, it's none of my business, anyway. My Pierre, he always tells me I'm a nosy old woman. You take your time, *mon ami*. These are grievous wounds you've suffered. The bullets, they are bad enough, but losing your partner . . . That Terry, he was like a father to you. You give yourself time to heal, Luke. You come back to us when you're whole again."

When he was whole again. Yeah, right.

Luke tried to put the old woman's words out of his mind as he exited the store and made his way across the parking lot toward the wooden pier and the *Miss Behavin' II*. The day had been a killer, and he was anxious to put it behind him. He wasn't scheduled to meet Matt for two more days, but after the strain of Terry's send-off, Luke wanted some downtime, some time alone. Time to decompress.

The months of constant danger during the undercover assignment in Florida had worn him down. Saying good-bye to Terry Winston had damn near killed him.

He'd held up all right in the heat of the moment. The gunfight in the Miami warehouse, stealing the car, the mad race to the ER while trying to staunch Terry's wounds and his own. He'd even managed when, after fighting for weeks in the hospital, Terry called calf-rope, squeezed Luke's hand, and died.

It was the aftermath that did him in. The reality that Luke's mistake had gotten his partner and friend killed was a devastating burden to bear. He'd gone a little crazy bringing the killers to justice. It cost him his job, but he didn't regret it.

What he regretted was losing control of himself last night when Terry's friends set out to honor his memory in a way the old bastard would have appreciated. Terry's farewell had started at sunset with a party the likes Caddo Bayou hadn't seen in years. Lots of food and drink, music and dancing.

Luke had kept it together until the band played a rendition of Jimmy Buffett's "Lovely Cruise." At that point, he'd sat down on a bench and bawled like a baby.

He'd hit the booze hard after that in a misguided attempt to dull the pain, and the rest of the night remained fuzzy in his memory. The festivities had continued past dawn, culminating in this morning's church service and the trip into the swamp to spread Terry's ashes. The remnants of a hangover still throbbed in Luke's head and the lack of sleep dulled his thinking.

A dog's bark jerked Luke back to the present, and his mouth twisted in a hint of a grin as the stray mutt who'd adopted him during the past week came bounding toward him from the woods where he'd been off exploring. A mix of golden retriever, boxer, and who-knew-what-else, the dog must have been dumped on the highway by an uncaring owner. The mutt had made his way to the marina the same day Luke returned to Caddo Bayou.

Luke had tossed the dog a bite of his burger, and from that moment on, the mutt considered himself Luke's. Luke took longer to come around to the idea, but finally, last night, he'd sealed the deal by giving the dog a name.

"Whoa, there, Knucklehead," Luke said as the dog went up on his hind legs, planted his front paws on Luke's shirt, and licked his face. Luke pushed the mutt off him, saying, "The slobber factor is getting out of hand. If you're going on this trip with me, you're gonna have to get some control."

His tail wagged, his tongue dangled out one side of his mouth, and he looked so stupidly friendly that Luke let out a laugh. He reached down and scratched the pooch behind the ears before continuing toward the *Miss Behavin' II*. The dog bounded aboard ahead of Luke, then waited at the door for Luke to let him inside. Like a flash, he disappeared toward the starboard stateroom where he'd claimed the queen-sized bed for his own.

As Luke stowed the last of his supplies for the upcoming fishing trip, he wondered why he'd been a sucker for the mangy hound. He hadn't had a pet in seventeen years. A man in Luke's business had no business owning a dog. Since his job was eighty-five percent travel, he couldn't properly care for a pet.

"Well, that's not a problem anymore, is it?" Luke slammed the cabinet shut with more force than necessary. He didn't want to think about the job. He didn't want to think about what the hell he was supposed to do with the rest of his life. He hadn't felt this lost since the day his father booted his butt out of Brazos Bend.

Well, he didn't have to think about any of that now. For the next three weeks, he'd think of nothing more serious than which bait to attach to his line. Old Marie Gauthier was right. He needed time. He'd give himself time. That's exactly what Terry would have told him to do.

Up at the flybridge helm, Luke fired up the twin Mercruiser three-liter sterndrives, then he struck the lines and pulled away from the Caddo Bayou Marina, headed on a southerly course. He knew his way without consulting a map. He and Terry had made this trip dozens of times over the years, first with the smaller *Miss Behavin' I*, then after their dot-com windfall, aboard this boat. This was the first time Luke had made it alone.

Well, alone but for a mutt named Knucklehead.

Luke cruised for hours before the lack of sleep caught up with him. After guiding the boat into a protected inlet, he sank the anchors, then sought his bed. The hum of the air conditioner drowned out the songs of Mississippi kites and cardinals drifting on the air, and Luke Callahan drifted off to sleep.

He dreamed of a bikini-clad redhead playing topless beach volleyball and awoke to a bloodcurdling scream.

Two

A slurping sound tugged Maddie from the oblivion of sleep, and she opened her eyes to find a hairy monster of a dog with his snout buried in Oscar's bowl, his long red tongue fishing for a snack. Maddie screamed and launched herself at the dog, forcing him away from the fishbowl. Unfortunately, in the process, her knee thumped the bowl and tipped it over. Oscar and water washed onto the wood floor.

"Yah!" she squealed, diving for the flopping goldfish, putting her body between Oscar and the sharp-toothed canine. Oscar flipped beyond her reach and Maddie lunged forward again, going down on her front as she finally trapped the fish beneath her cupped hands. She lay flat on her stomach in the pool of tepid water, trying to catch her breath and calm her pounding pulse.

"What the hell is going on here?" inquired a deep, resonant voice.

Maddie spied the bare feet first. Her gaze crawled slowly upward over moderately hairy, tanned and toned calf muscles, well-defined thighs, and a rather impressive . . . holy hell . . . the man was naked. And armed. Armed and naked.

Naked!

Maddie jerked her gaze away from both his package and his pistol, dragging her stare up his long, lean length all the way to his face. She recognized the features. He was the man from the party barge, the one with the minnow bucket. The shirtless, sweaty, sexy one with the six-pack abs.

Great. Wonderful. Obviously, Ms. Winston had a special guest. Maddie should have considered the possibility, considering the name of the boat, *Miss Behavin' II*. When she'd stepped aboard to pee, she'd never thought she might be boarding the *Love Boat*.

Maddie sat back on her heels and attempted a polite smile. "Hello."

"Who the fuck are you?"

Well. He might be pretty to look at, but somebody needed to take a bar of soap to his mouth. "My name is Maddie Kincaid and you can lower the gun. I'm here to see Ms. Winston."

The gun didn't budge, and when he spoke, his tone was a jagged shard of glass. "Who sent you?"

"Is Ms. Winston here? Ms. Terri Winston?"

"Who. Sent. You."

Were she not so scared, she'd be annoyed by his tone. "A friend of hers. Mr. Callahan. Mr. Branch Callahan of Brazos Bend, Texas."

Surprise flashed in his eyes before fury settled in. He took a threatening step forward. "If that's the case, tell me why I shouldn't shoot you on the spot."

"What!" Maddie pulled her gaze away from the pair of angry red scars on his torso. The marks looked fresh. They looked like . . . bullet wounds. Oh, dear.

He eyed her wet shirt and shorts, and his bayou green eyes narrowed suspiciously. "Are you a hooker?"

She blinked. "Pardon me?"

"How much did the old man throw at you?" he asked, leaning against the doorway, all naked and malicious. "If it's less than a couple grand, you've sold yourself short. That's what he paid the last whore he sent to lure me back to Brazos Bend."

The last whore? Maddie plucked her wet T-shirt away from her breasts. "Wait just one minute. I don't know who you are, and frankly, I don't care. I'm sorry if I've interrupted a romantic encounter between you and Ms. Winston. I know I'm the trespasser here, and that automatically puts me in the wrong. Nonetheless, you can drop the name-calling. And it wouldn't hurt you to put some clothes on, either!"

His mouth worked like a fish, with no sound emerging, until abruptly he backed away and exited the cabin. The dog followed the man, thank goodness, and Maddie climbed to her feet. She quickly returned Oscar to his bowl, then added water from the faucet in the bathroom. After setting the bowl on the dresser out of reach of the dog, she spied dog hair and mussed covers on the far side of the bed. She must have been really tired to sleep through having company in her bed.

"Thank God it was the dog and not the master," she murmured. Although . . . "Don't go there, Maddy. Just . . . think of Oscar."

Oscar was safe, thank God, and she intended him to stay that way. While Maddie recognized that she'd chosen a peculiar time to finally adopt the pet she'd always wanted, and that a goldfish wasn't exactly the dachshund puppy she'd been considering, the moment she'd entered his previous owner's ransacked home and spied the fishbowl teetering on the edge of a shelf, she'd felt a kinship with Oscar.

His owner's death had left them both in a desperate situation.

Maddie dug in her purse for the fish food she'd purchased at an East Texas Wal-Mart, then sprinkled some into the fish bowl. With her pet cared for, she made her way toward the master stateroom.

She rapped on the doorjamb. "Excuse me. Ms. Winston?"

Hearing no reply, she ducked her head into the room. A quick glance around revealed scattered sheets on an empty king-sized bed, and her own disheveled reflection in a mirror. So, where was Terri Winston? Why hadn't she followed on Mr. Naked's heels? Was she not on the boat?

Oh, jeez. Wouldn't that be just her luck? What would she do then?

As much as she dreaded the idea of approaching him, Maddie knew she had to get some answers from the guy. She finger-combed her hair, then scowled down at her shirt—her white, wet, transparent shirt. She again plucked the cotton fabric away from her body and flapped it in the air a few times. Then she wiped her hands on her shorts, drew a deep breath, and went out for round two with Fantasy Abs.

One good look at their surroundings chased all other thoughts from her mind. Marsh grasses, trees, water. Where was the marina? Maddie whipped her head around. All she saw was swamp!

Her stomach sank. They'd obviously left port. How long had she been asleep?

"Um, excuse me? Where exactly are we?"

He raised his pistol and took aim at the stump of a dead tree rising like a ghost from the bayou. Luckily for Maddie's concentration, he'd dragged on his Hawaiian-print swim trunks. Although, now that she considered the question, his broad, bare shoulders proved to be almost as much a distraction as his . . . gun.

He pulled the trigger three deliberate times.

He didn't bother to look at her. "I don't know what you and Branch Callahan are trying to pull, lady, and frankly, I don't care."

O-kay. Fine. Definitely a bit of aggression there.

Bang . . . bang . . . bang.

"It's too late to head back to the marina now. It'll be dark before long, and I'm not navigating the *Miss Behavin'* through the swamp at night. I'll take you back first thing in the morning, provided you don't piss me off enough to toss you overboard tonight."

Bang . . . bang . . . bang.

The dead branch cracked, then broke, and fell into the bayou with a whooshing splash. The motion stirred up an alligator sunning himself on a nearby rock, and after a hiss of irritation, he slipped quietly into the water, then disappeared from sight.

The gator reminded Maddie of the problem at hand, so she cut to the chase. "Look, mister, obviously you're acquainted with Branch Callahan and you have some sort of problem with him. That's understandable. Branch can be a challenge. However, in this case, he's simply trying to help a friend. Me. I really need to talk to Terri Winston. Branch assures me that she can help me."

He glanced over his shoulder, his expression angry and . . . haunted. "That'll be a trick."

What did that mean? Why wouldn't Terri . . . oh, of course. *I'll bet she packed up and left his rude, though spectacular, butt. Great. Wonderful. Now what do I do?*

"Where did she go?"

"She who?"

"Terri Winston."

This time she saw something more in his glower. This time, she saw . . . grief. Bone-deep, gut-wrenching grief. As the dog padded across the deck, then plopped down on one of the stranger's bare feet, Maddie recalled the sign on the ship store. CLOSED FOR FUNERAL. She considered this man's reaction when she mentioned Terri Winston's name. *Oh, no.* "She . . . ?"

"Wasn't a goddamned woman!" he thundered, his scowl murderous. "Terry was the greatest man I ever knew. He was smart and determined and honorable. He knew engines forward and backward, and he could quote box scores going back thirty years. He was a damned fine agent, a damned fine human being, and the world is a poorer place without him in it."

Maddie exhaled a long, heavy breath. "We're talking about the same person? The owner of this boat and special agent for the DEA?"

"Terrence Albert Winston. He and I bought the *Miss Behavin' II* three years ago. Look, lady, I don't know what sort of trick that old Brazos Bend bastard was trying to play on you, but you've wasted your trip. Terry Winston is dead."

The dog gave a whimper and Maddie's stomach rolled. Oh, man. Oh man oh man oh man. What in the world was she going to do now?

"It's against my better judgment to ask, but what made you think Terry was a woman? And better yet, what makes you think that Branch and Terry were even acquainted?"

Maddie stared blankly at the fellow. *Because a man lied to me. Again.* "He told me so. Branch Callahan did."

"Why?"

She recalled the madness of the previous night. She'd fled Brazos Bend with no clear destination in mind, concentrating more on fleeing danger fast than on where to go for help. She'd had the vague thought to lose herself in the wilds of West Texas when her tire went flat. A man had stopped to help her change her tire, then suggested she pay for his labor on her back. When he wouldn't take no for an answer, she'd grabbed a can of hair spray from her grocery sack and shot him in the eyes.

Branch had called just as she'd spun gravel getting back on the road, and she'd treated him to a one-woman rant about the untrustworthiness of men, how they always let her down, how she couldn't forget that the last time she'd found herself in a marginally related situation, she'd trusted a man and been burned. Badly.

In hindsight and based on the circumstances, she wasn't surprised at the lie Branch had told her. Nevertheless, it didn't make her happy.

Based solely on the fact of this fellow's Y chromosome, Maddie shot him a damning glare. "Who are you, anyway?"

He arched a brow. "You don't know?"

"Why should I know? Have we met somewhere?" The only person he reminded her of was one of the Chippendale dancers at Janie Pokluda's bachelorette party.

Ignoring her questions, he set his gun on the deck chair beside him, folded his arms, and studied her, his brow knitted in thought. "Why did the old man send you to Terry? You said you needed his help. With what?"

"Like I'm going to tell you! I don't even know your name!"

He rolled his tongue around his mouth and looked at her long and hard. "I wonder," he murmured.

"Wonder what?"

Abruptly, he took a step forward and stuck out his hand. "It's a pleasure to meet you, Ms. Kincaid, was it? My name's Luke. Luke Callahan."

"Luke Callahan?" she repeated, her eyes widening with surprise. "*Callahan*?"

"Yeah."

"Not Callahan as in . . . Branch Callahan?"

"'Fraid so."

"He's your father?"

"Technically, yes. Though, since he disowned me seventeen years ago, the reality's a little muddy."

"Oh, my God." Her mind spun as she processed this bit of news. "Matthew, Mark, Luke, and John. They still talk about you in town. The four of you set the fire that burned down the boot factory and put half the town out of work. You're the Holy Terrors!"

"No." His eyes went hard and glacial, his voice flat. "Not anymore. My brother John is dead."

Maddie knew that, of course. Townspeople still talked about the scene the surviving Callahan brothers made on their brief return to Brazos Bend for John's memorial service.

Holy Terror or not, this man was still one of Branch Callahan's careless, coldhearted sons. Branch had sent her here. Had he known Luke would be here?

Maddie tucked a strand of hair behind her ear. "I don't understand. What's the connection between you and Ms. . . . uh . . . Mr. Winston?"

"Terry Winston was my partner."

She blinked. "You're gay?" she asked, unable to stop a twinge of regret.

"We *worked* together!"

"*You're* a DEA agent?"

"Not anymore. Now it's your turn. Why did you come looking for Terry?"

"You *were* a DEA agent?"

"Why did you come looking for Terry?" he repeated.

Maddie slammed her mouth shut. She had to think about this. Be hanged if she'd blurt out her story just because he was Branch Callahan's kin.

Considering Branch had out-and-out lied to her regarding the *Miss Behavin' II*'s owner, right this minute, the family connection hurt more than helped.

Was this the same old song? Had Branch Callahan burned her yesterday when he sent her to Caddo Bayou Marina?

Maddie shoved her fingers through her hair in frustration as she tried to make sense of the developments. Ignoring Luke's question, she asked one of her own. "Did your father know you'd be here?"

"Uh-uh." He shook his head. "It's still your turn. I'm still waitin' on an answer. What brings you to my boat, Maggie?"

"Not *g*'s," she corrected, glad for the delay. "*D*'s. Ma*dd*ie."

"All right, Ma*dd*ie. What's your problem? Why did you come looking for a DEA agent?"

She gazed blindly out over the bayou's green water, trying to decide how to reply. She needed more information about Luke Callahan to know how much, or how little, to tell him. She couldn't afford a mistake. Her freedom hung in the balance. She needed time to think this whole matter through.

"Well?" he insisted.

She needed a diversion, and judging by the impatience flaring in his eyes, she needed it fast. But what? She was on a boat in the middle of the swamp. What could . . . the dog? Could she use the dog?

The canine in question let out a snore. Better think of something else.

"What sort of trouble are you in?"

She wasn't about to tell him. Not until she knew a lot

more about him. She was done with giving her trust without weighing the possible consequences.

So, what to do? She came up with but a single, desperate way to delay answering Luke Callahan's questions and give herself the time she needed. *Great. Just great.*

Swallowing her dread, Maddie threw out her hands, waving them wildly as she paced the deck and said, "It's complicated. I don't quite know where to start."

"Pick a place."

"All right. You see, your father is my client."

"So you *are* a hooker."

Maddie tossed him a contemptuous scowl, then continued her tale, walking up and down the deck as she spoke, shifting a little closer to the dog with each pass. "I own Home for Now senior care in Brazos Bend. We provide personal services for seniors who are no longer completely independent, but who prefer to remain at home rather than move to assisted-living centers."

Luke scoffed. "Now I know you're lying. Branch Callahan is the most independent cuss on the face of the earth."

"Yes . . . well . . . working for him is sometimes a challenge. It's been a . . . yeow!"

As she'd intended, Maddie tripped over the dog and lost her balance. She stumbled one awkward step, then two.

Then she hit the boat rail hard and with an extra surge of effort managed to tumble right over the top.

Maddie intended all along to scream as she fell overboard. However, the sight of an alligator slipping into the bayou not twenty feet away added realism to her shriek.

As the cool, murky water splashed over her head, she thought, *What do you want to bet the gator's a male?*

Water splashed up onto the rear deck as the woman entered the water. So much for a quiet, peaceful, relaxing start to his fishing trip, Luke decided with a sigh as Knucklehead bounded to the edge of the boat, planted his paws, and barked. *She falls out of bed. Falls off the boat. Hell.*

Though it had been pretty funny to watch.

"Hush, dog." Luke watched an alligator swim away from the commotion as he waited for the woman to find her feet. According to his depth finder, the houseboat floated in just about five feet of water.

While he watched her head emerge, Luke tried to make some sense of the afternoon's events. He'd handled it poorly in the beginning. Shooting the tree had been a bit much. But in his defense, he hadn't been thinking straight at the time. He'd been sound asleep when he'd heard that initial scream. When he scrambled out of bed, he must have left his brain behind.

He blamed it on the bra. Maddie Kincaid's bountiful breasts had all but overflowed her lacy hot pink demi-cups.

It was an arguable defense. He'd been dreaming about redheads, and there she'd appeared, the sexy woman from the dock, a wet-T-shirt-contest gold medalist sprawled across the floor of his boat. *Of course* he didn't think straight right off.

And what the hell was with the goldfish?

"Yeek!" she squealed when she'd cleared her face of a clump of swamp grass. "There's an alligator!"

"Well, we are in the bayou."

She thrashed toward the *Miss Behavin' II*, her eyes rounded with alarm. "Did you see it?"

"I was too busy looking at the water moccasin," he drawled.

At that, Maddie froze midthrash. The alarm in her eyes intensified to true fear. "Sn-sn-snake?"

Luke felt a twinge of guilt. He hadn't figured anyone who purposefully took a dive into the bayou would be afraid of snakes.

"Swim ladder's over here." He released a catch and metal steps plopped into the water, creating a splash.

The woman remained frozen in fear, barely moving enough to keep herself upright.

"Lady . . ."

"Wh-wh-where . . . ?"

He sighed heavily. "Forget it. I was kidding. I didn't see a snake."

Within striking distance of her anyway.

When she still didn't move, Luke's sense of guilt escalated. It wasn't his habit to terrorize women. In a coaxing tone, he said, "It's okay. There's no snake."

He knelt beside the swim ladder and stretched out a hand. "Come here, honey. Let me help you. Everything's okay."

She focused on his outstretched hand like it was a lifeline. She moved forward, their fingers touched. Luke grabbed her hand and pulled her toward the boat. "Here's the ladder. Put your foot on the rail, sweetheart. There you go. That's good."

Luke grasped her free hand and yanked her up the ladder and aboard the *Miss Behavin' II*.

She shivered, shuddered, and dripped water onto the deck. Her wet, transparent clothes were once again plastered against her abundant curves, and she looked like a drowned . . . beauty queen. Luke sucked in a breath, made himself look away, told himself his hands didn't itch to touch her. That would be a stupid mistake.

The woman had secrets, ones she'd go to great lengths to protect, since she'd obviously taken that tumble deliberately in order to avoid his questions. The last thing he wanted to do was tangle with a woman with secrets, but he figured he'd better find out what Branch Callahan was up to this time. *Damn you, old man. When the hell will you get the message and give up!*

Maybe he should change tactics with the lady, Luke silently mused. Basic interrogation wasn't working. Maybe he should try something else.

"Jerk," she murmured, wringing the water from her shirt. Fury glittered in her eyes. "Lying snake."

Luke smirked, his guilt easing at her snarky tone. "You're lucky you didn't go in head first," he said, grabbing a beach towel from a nearby storage bin. Tossing it to her, he added, "You could have broken your neck."

She caught the towel. As swamp water dribbled down her long, luscious legs, sarcasm dripped from her tongue. "Thanks for the sympathy. And the help. Why, you really put yourself out to drop the ladder, thus saving me from alligators and snakes and God knows what else."

Brat. Luke had to smother a smile. "I try to be courteous to all my trespassers. Speaking of which, I'm thirsty. Can I get you something?" He paused a moment, then added, "Another beer, perhaps?"

She winced, and color stained her cheeks. After a moment's hesitation, she offered him a reluctant, sheepish smile. "I need to apologize for that," she said, a note of sincerity replacing sarcasm. "It was rude of me, trespassing on your boat, drinking your beer. Sleeping in your bed."

Actually, she'd slept in the guest bed. Had she been sleeping in his bed, those redheaded dreams of his might have evolved into something beyond fantasy.

"I'd been driving all night, and everything just caught up with me."

"Hey, no problem." Luke waved a magnanimous hand. "*Mi casa flotante es su casa flotante.* So, you want something to drink?"

"A bottle of water would be good."

Luke ducked into the galley and grabbed a couple bottles of water. As he shut the refrigerator door, movement in the window captured his attention. When he caught the swing of her hips, right at eye level as she twisted to dry herself, he hesitated.

Maddie Kincaid was hot. Long, tall, and centerfold curvy. He'd always had a thing for redheads, and her thick, wavy hair was a rich, vibrant auburn streaked with strands of gold. Those brown eyes of hers were big enough for a man to drown in, and the fullness of her lips gave a guy some downright earthy ideas.

Bet she'd be a firebrand in bed.

Don't go there. Do not *go there.* He dropped his chin to his chest and gave his head a shake. The woman was lying to him. She had secrets. Just because he felt a little bad since he'd unintentionally frightened her didn't mean he should be stupid. He couldn't forget who'd sent her here, or that she'd come looking for a DEA agent—rarely a good sign.

No, he needed to get her to open up, to discover what nonsense his old man had cooked up this time around.

Since interrogation hadn't worked, maybe he should try being nice to her. Maybe he should turn on the charm.

Luke pondered the idea for a long moment, then nodded. Okay, he could do nice. Being nice didn't mean being stupid. Didn't mean he'd start thinking with his johnson instead of with his brain.

That part of him stirred a bit, as if to prove a point to the contrary, and Luke shifted his weight. *No way, pal. Forget it. You are SOL.*

Being nice didn't mean he'd trust her, either. He was smarter than that. He'd keep his gun handy, keep one eye open. He wouldn't get distracted from the goal.

On his way outside, he caught sight of the goldfish once again swimming in its bowl. Had she filled that bowl with water from his system? Must have. Stupid woman. Chemicals in the water would kill that fish. Luke grabbed a jug of distilled water Terry had kept for the battery of his old truck and saved the goldfish's life.

Back on deck, he saw that she'd wrapped the beach towel around herself, and with her bounties concealed, he breathed a little easier. Pasting on a friendly smile, he handed her the water. "Feel free to grab a dry shirt and shorts from the dresser in my room. In fact, you can take a shower if you want. I'm gonna rustle up some supper and it'll take awhile, so don't feel like you need to rush."

"A freshwater shower?" she asked, perking up.

"Yep. I think there's some girl stuff in the cabinet in the other bathroom, too. Fruity shampoo and lotions."

Luke couldn't miss the relief in Maddie Kincaid's eyes as she beat a hasty retreat to the head, and he concluded that his suspicions had been right on the mark. The woman wasn't in any hurry to answer his questions and finish her story. Why?

Why should you care?

The thought came out of nowhere, and Luke blinked in surprise.

Well. Hmm. Why *should* he care?

Staring at the doorway through which she'd disappeared, he blew out a long breath and gave the question serious consideration. She'd come looking for a DEA agent, but she wasn't screaming her innocence. In Luke's experience, an innocent woman would have thrown herself down on the deck rather than overboard, begging for his help and answering any question he posed. No, she was damn sure guilty of something.

He didn't, however, think she'd been sent by a Colombian cartel or the Miami coke ring he and Terry had busted.

Luke turned away and crossed to the railing, where he stared out across the moody bayou, his thoughts in a whirl. So, if drugs and the DEA had nothing to do with bringing her here, could it be that this was simply another one of his father's crazy schemes?

Yeah. Something like this was right up Branch Callahan's alley.

So, the next question was, did he give a damn what mischief his father was up to this time?

Luke watched a heron glide gracefully mere inches above the water. Yeah, he did. He had to. His father was a damned canny man, and if Luke didn't pay close attention, the son of a bitch might slip something past him. That simply wouldn't do.

He let out a long, unhappy sigh. He didn't want to get involved with one of Branch's schemes. Not now, not after a day like today. Not after the bullshit of the past few months. Luke needed peace and calm and a fish on his line.

Instead, he had an uninvited woman on his boat. A woman he didn't know and damned well couldn't trust.

He did need to solve the puzzle that Maddie Kincaid

presented, and he needed to solve it tonight. Because come hell or high water or secretive sexpot, the day after tomorrow he'd rendezvous with Matt, climb aboard his brother's new boat, and head out into the gulf for some serious tarpon fishing. The most important decision they'd make was what brand of beer to pull from the ice chest.

It sounded like heaven, and since he'd spent his recent days in hell, Luke didn't want anything interfering with the plan.

So, he'd turn up the charm. He'd feed her, ply her with wine, and seduce her secrets right out of her. He'd find out the who, what, when, where, and whys of one Ms. Maddie Kincaid while he filled his mouth with a nice rib eye. That way, he could haul her sweet ass back to the marina in the morning and dump her.

"Sounds like a plan," he murmured.

Luke made his way to the galley, where he prepared potatoes for baking, pulled steaks from the fridge, then took a moment over his wine selection. This certainly wasn't a dinner date with a woman he was trying to impress; however, the meat market butcher had bragged of the steak's exceptional quality. Food like this deserved a decent wine. Yet, he shouldn't raid the gold medal bottles he'd laid in for his brother Matt-the-wine-snob, because if they ran short, he'd have to listen to a bunch of griping and whining.

However, when he grabbed a bottle, he chose the best he had on board. It had been a bitch of a day, and he *was* having dinner with a beautiful woman. Tomorrow they'd say their good-byes and he'd probably never see her again.

Unless she's really in trouble, and then what will you do?

The taste in Luke's mouth turned sour. "Nothing," he snapped as he yanked the cork from the wine bottle, trying to convince himself it was true. He was nobody's hero. Not anymore. He wanted to spend his days fishing and his nights getting drunk.

Besides, what were the chances she truly was in trouble and not one of his father's pawns? Slim and none, to his way of thinking.

Luke carried the food up the spiral staircase to the roof bar and the oldest item on the boat—his beloved charcoal grill. He built a fire, then put the potatoes on to bake. He dropped the metal lid shut with a bang when he heard the shower shut off downstairs and a mental picture of a naked and dripping Maddie Kincaid flashed through his mind.

An interesting thought occurred. If she *was* part of one of his father's harebrained schemes, then getting Luke into bed might be part of the plan. He'd need to be on guard against such a ploy.

Though, as an agent for the Drug Enforcement Administration, Luke had been taught to investigate thoroughly and completely.

Maybe he should see just how far she'd go.

•

Three

Clean, dry, and dressed in a Texas Rangers T-shirt and gym shorts, Maddie leaned against the boat railing and gazed out at the otherworldly beauty of the bayou. The last time she'd worn a man's shirt, she'd been with Cade in Rio, leaning against the balcony of their hotel room watching the surf slap against the beach.

A different world, that. She'd been a different person.

All in all, she liked this Maddie Kincaid better.

Before her, tattered gray beards of Spanish moss dangled from branches of live oaks, while red maples challenged tupelo trees and the bowed boughs of willows for patches of solid ground. Green water lurked beneath a deceptive raft of purple water hyacinths, cattails, and lily pads, and from the muddy bank, half hidden by a tangled skein of creepers, a snake, long and thin and as black as a killer's heart, slithered into the water.

The snake made Maddie recall her dip-as-a-distraction, and a heavy sigh escaped her lips. What was she going to do? Terri/Terry Winston couldn't help her. What little she knew about Luke Callahan didn't give her warm fuzzies at the thought of confessing all to the man. Nope, from what she could tell, she was up the bayou without a savior.

Guess she'd just have to figure out a way to save herself.

So, how to do it? She'd pondered the problem while taking her shower, and she'd made a mental note of all her options, ending up with two whole items on her list. She could dump the drugs in the bayou and not go home again. That'd mean giving up her home, her business. She'd probably have to turn to her father for financial support and that would open up another can of worms.

Her other choice was to roll the dice and ask ex-agent Callahan for help. That'd most likely mean spilling all her beans and thus risking her physical freedom.

Which, she wondered, would be worse?

Maddie loved her father, she truly did, but he'd put strings on any help he gave her, and she didn't want to live her life in the paparazzi's camera lenses, not again. She'd done it before, and doing so invariably drove her crazy, which in turn caused her to make bad choices and end up in trouble.

Of course, she'd landed in big trouble now, and the paparazzi had nothing to do with it.

So, was she prepared to trust Luke Callahan? Not without more information. Right now, all she really knew about the man was his reputation in Brazos Bend—and that was all bad. He'd been a hell-raiser, a troublemaker, a bad-boy deluxe.

So how did that James Dean poster child end up a good-guy federal agent? And why wasn't the good-guy federal agent a good guy anymore? Had he gone back over to the dark side or something?

Would that be good for her or bad for her?

The aroma of grilling beef drifted on the air, and Maddie realized she was hungry. For food, for answers. For a solution to her problem.

Apparently, he'd decided to drop his interrogation, and she couldn't help but wonder why.

She made her way back to the stern, where Luke Callahan had traded in his .45 for a spatula. He'd yet to don a shirt, and his swim trunks had worked their way low on his hips again, revealing an intriguing tan line. His feet were bare. He lowered the grill lid, dodged the stream of smoke, and flashed her a grin. "Just turned the steaks. Supper will be ready soon."

The grin did it. From out of the blue came that old, familiar sensation. Maddie tingled. She had one of those nice little boy-girl zings she hadn't experienced in a very long time. A line from an old TV show ran through her mind. *Danger, Will Robinson. Danger.* "They smell delicious."

"A good cut of meat seasoned with my special spice. Mouthwatering good, I promise."

I'll bet.

"So, can I tempt you with a nice shiraz?"

You tempt me by breathing.

"Oh, for crying out loud," she muttered beneath her breath. "That would be lovely."

Maddie accepted the glass, then sipped the rich, full-bodied drink and wondered whether this spike in her libido was a reaction to stress, to danger. That happened in books all the time. Characters would have a brush with death and then want to reaffirm life by going at it like rabbits.

No, dummy. The sizzle in your blood is a reaction to the man. He's drop-dead gorgeous and has a bad-boy history. On top of that, he's nice to his dog. Of course he turns you on. He's just your type!

The type that had caused her nothing but trouble in the past. Maddie swallowed hard.

"The wine is good," she said, sipping from the glass. She listened to Norah Jones croon a moody ballad on the stereo and waited for him to speak.

Luke topped off her glass. "Goes well with steak. I'm glad you're not a vegetarian or something weird like that."

"Not hardly." Maddie told herself to relax. The wine helped. "I'll have you know, I indulge in chicken-fried steak once a month at the Dixie Café."

"The Dixie Café." Luke propped a hip on one of the tall cushioned bar stools, then gestured for her to take a seat beside him. "Oh, man. That brings back memories. Chicken-fried steak, fried okra, best mashed potatoes I've ever had."

"Not afraid to carb load, are you?"

They spoke of Brazos Bend for a time, Maddie catching him up with the changes that had occurred since he left town seventeen years ago while asking subtle questions intended to probe his opinions and beliefs. In the process, they knocked back three-quarters of the bottle of wine.

Maddie was feeling warm and relaxed when Luke pacified a whining Knucklehead by tossing him a pretzel, then observed, "You know, I think I'd remember a girl like you. Did you grow up in Brazos Bend?"

Her gaze rested on Knucklehead as he padded up to investigate the offering. "No. I moved there a little over a year ago."

"From where?"

The dog sniffed, devoured, then whined for more as Maddie hedged, "Southeast Texas. A little town northeast of Houston."

"How did you end up in Brazos Bend?"

This answer was easier. "A friend invited me to visit and I fell in love with the town."

Luke widened his eyes. Disbelief rang in his voice. "With Brazos Bend?"

"Yes. I love it there. Brazos Bend is Mayberry with a Texas drawl."

"And that's a good thing?" Luke gave in and tossed Knucklehead a handful of pretzels.

"Definitely." Maddie used the dog's antics to change the subject. "He's great. How long have you had him?"

"Just a few days. He's a stray who wandered up."

"You must have a soft spot for strays," she said, smiling at him over her wineglass.

His glass halfway to his mouth, Luke paused. "Soft? No. I wouldn't say that."

Then he looked her straight in the eyes, stared at her intently. The air all but crackled with tension, and Maddie felt that zing run through her once again.

"Are you married, Maddie?"

"Married?" she squeaked. "I . . . um . . ."

"Hard question?"

"No. Just . . . well . . . not me. I'm single. Really single."

He laughed softly. "What does 'really single' mean?"

That I haven't had sex in over two years. Her stomach did a somersault. *Don't go there!*

"I've a difficult time believing that a woman like you doesn't date."

"I date. Sort of," she said, her smile shaky. She thought of Mike McDermott, the nice, polite librarian she'd gone to dinner with last week, to the movies with the week before. Members of the Ladies' Seventy-and-Over Tuesday morning bowling league whom Maddie transported to and from the lanes had opined that Mike might be The One for her. "Mike and I . . . we're not . . . we've only had two dates."

"Ah." He sat back in his chair, stretched out his legs, and asked, "So, who is he? Anybody I might know from the old days?"

Maddie dragged her gaze away from the ripple of muscle on his torso. "You might. You and Mike are around the same age."

"Mike Chandler?"

"No, Mike McDermott."

Luke frowned in thought, scratched his five o'clock shadow. "Computer nerd? Skinny with sandy hair and thick glasses?"

"He's into weight lifting now. He wears contacts and he owns a house."

He must have heard something in her voice, because he arched a brow and pursued that point. "That's important to you? The house?"

"Yes." Maddie relaxed a bit, glad to have something to think about other than sculpted male muscles. "I mean, it's not important that Mike owns one, but a house is important to me. A home is important." She thought of those few golden suburban months, then the constant stream of hotel suites and boarding school dormitories. "I'm renting now, but I hope to buy a place by the end of the year. I want to sink roots."

"Hmm." Luke peanut-picked the party mix, then tossed his findings nut by nut into his mouth. "So, you aimin' for a place like my old man's?"

Maddie tore her gaze away from his mouth. "Heavens no. Living in a Country Club mansion isn't my dream at all."

Interest brightened his green eyes. He filled her wineglass yet again. "Yeah? What is, then? Tell me about your dream house, Ms. Maddie."

Maddie turned to watch a heron take flight from its perch atop a rotting log. It skimmed across the bayou mere inches above the surface before lifting to find purchase on a cypress stump. "It's nothing fancy. Three bedrooms, two baths, a big yard in a nice neighborhood with good schools."

"Schools, ah. So the dream includes kids."

Maddie nodded.

Luke topped off both their glasses, then casually observed, "Personally, I plan on driving Vettes the rest of my life."

Maddie picked up on his point right away. "So you don't want children?"

"Nope. I've never found the idea of fatherhood very appealing."

Maddie wasn't surprised by his attitude, considering that his relationship with his own father had been so poor for so long.

"Houses don't hold much interest for me, either," he continued. "That three-bedroom house with a yard would drive me crazy. I'm definitely a footloose kind of guy."

Was he warning her off? Maddie didn't know whether to be insulted or flattered.

"Look at that ol' gator lazin' in the sun." Luke pointed off the starboard bow. "See, over there by that cypress? Gotta be twelve feet long, at least. Makes that little one who scared you earlier look like a toy. Did you know that alligators have lived for nearly two hundred million years with virtually no evolutionary changes?"

Now, that was a typical bad boy's response to a woman's mention of children. He'd gone from asking about her sex life to jawing about alligators. She recalled another time when she'd expressed an interest in children to a man, to her very first lover, in fact. She'd mentioned motherhood, and Rip Tucker started talking about hidden symbolism in the paintings of Michelangelo.

"No evolutionary changes, hmm?" Maddie eyed the alligator and was thankful for the size of the boat. "Reminds me of some of the men I've dated."

Luke ignored that little dig, stretched out his legs, and crossed them at the ankles. He linked his fingers behind his head, elbows out wide. "Gators are top of the food chain in the swamp, of course. They'll eat anything from armadillos to possums to snakes."

Maddie forced herself to look away from those washboard abs. "You are just a font of information, Mr. Callahan."

"Oh, I'm just getting started, sweetcheeks."

I wish.

Maddie swallowed hard, gave herself a mental slap, then drawled a dry, "Sweetcheeks?"

He winked playfully, and she pretended that her feminine muscles didn't clench with lust.

"A male alligator may grow as long as fourteen feet or better. Weigh up to a thousand pounds. He's like a tank in the water." He paused, then added with apparent nonchalance, "You know, I wrestled one, once."

She blinked. "You wrestled an alligator? Oh, come on."

He rolled to his feet and leaned against the houseboat railing, facing her. Then he winked. "It's true. I was down in the Everglades and . . ."

Maddie paid scant attention to his tale of a spring break trip that went awry, because her thoughts were focused on the here and now. The wink had confirmed it. Luke Callahan was flirting with her. And while she didn't quite know exactly where he was going with this alligator tale of his, Maddie couldn't deny that the ride was exciting.

And dangerous.

Obviously, Luke Callahan was no safe, suburban Mike McDermott. Maddie dare not let down her guard and forget that.

If only he didn't appeal to her Wicked Inner Wanton. Maddie blamed her WIW for the sins in her past—namely Rip Tucker, the rebel without a cause who'd swept her off her feet at sixteen; Liam Murphy, the moody Irish poet and, it turned out, IRA supporter, whom she'd fallen for at twenty; and last, but certainly not least, drug-trafficker-in-disguise Cade Ranger, who'd made a fool and a felon of her at the age of twenty-seven.

Her reaction to this man made her feel stupid, made her feel weak.

It shouldn't, whispered her WIW. *The situation is entirely different this time. Mr. Washboard doesn't know who your father is. He doesn't have anything to gain by taking Maddie Kincaid, senior caregiver, to bed.*

You could turn the tables this time. You could hold the power. Rather than being used and tossed away, this time you could do the using. You could do the tossing. This time, you'd be in control.

It was, Maddie admitted, a heady thought.

Luke Callahan is yours for the taking. The wink, the innuendo, told you that. With a little effort you could end your dry spell tonight with a very sexy stranger who, judging by his reaction to your mention of his return to Brazos Bend, you'd probably never see again.

You could end your sexual drought and no one would ever have to know about it. For that matter, what would it hurt if anyone did learn about it? You can handle gossips. You can handle a fantasy man, a barefoot tanned-and-toned temptation. You're not young and naive anymore.

No, Rip, Liam, and Cade had cured her of that.

Wait a minute. Maddie's sense of self-preservation attempted to stand up to her Wicked Inner Wanton. Hadn't she learned that situations aren't always what they seem? She was treading dangerous waters out here in the swamp. She might well be better off taking her chances with the gators than sitting here watching the Big Bad Washboard Wolf busy pouring more wine into her glass. She needed to evaluate the man as a potential white knight, not a bed partner. How had she wandered so far off the path?

Chicken, chided her WIW. *Where has that attitude gotten you in the past? Alone? Broke? Counting tiles in the ceiling above your bunk?*

It is different this time. Your downfall in the past has been falling in love. I'm talking a one-night stand, here. A relationship isn't a possibility. What would it hurt if just this once, you indulged yourself?

". . . eyes peered out from the reeds . . ."

A night of Big Bad Wolf sex with an ex-DEA agent in the middle of the earthy, sweltering Louisiana bayou?

Yum.

"Stop it," Maddie told her evil self.

"Just topping off your glass," the Wolf defended. "No sense leaving just a few sips in the bottom of the bottle."

A simple one-night stand. Who would it hurt? What happens in the bayou stays in the bayou.

Luke continued, "Just a sliver of a moon in the sky, and . . ."

Maddie looked hard at ex-agent Callahan. She recalled the moment he'd burst from the houseboat's master bedroom armed and naked.

Armed and dangerous.

Her blood hummed.

". . . animal's scream sent a shudder up my spine . . ."

Oh, I bet he could make me scream.

". . . teeth right out of Jaws . . ."

Maddie wondered whether he was a nipper. She liked that in a man, those soft little nips that tugged and tested but didn't hurt. *Go for it,* whispered her Wicked Inner Wanton.

Maybe she would. Maddie felt strong and smart and . . . sexy. She'd caught Luke eyeing her legs, sneaking peeks at her breasts. He wanted her. She knew it. She'd bet an entire giant-sized bag of M&M's that somehow, in Luke Callahan's unique way, this alligator tale was leading up to a pass.

". . . whipped his head around and went for my face."

So what are you going to do about it?

For once in her life, Maddie could take advantage of the situation, take advantage of the man. What would it hurt? He seems willing. He seems interested. He seems . . .

". . . about sixteen inches long . . ."

Oh my God!

". . . but it still frightened the bejesus out of me. Sharp teeth on that little sucker, too."

The alligator, dummy. He's talking about the alligator!

"It bit you?" Her throat was as dry as dust.

"Still have a scar." He pointed to a faint white line just below his bottom lip. "See?"

What am I going to do? Maddie responded to her Wicked Inner Wanton. *I'm strong and smart and sexy.*

She pictured herself leaning forward, purring, *Poor baby, want me to kiss it?*

Then she thought one more time of Rip and Liam and Cade. She thought of that town northeast of Houston and of a country house estate in England. She told her Wicked Inner Wanton, *I'm taking charge.*

She looked ex-agent Callahan right in the eyes and asked, "Would you like some mushrooms with your steak?"

Four

Mushrooms?

Halfway through the first bottle of wine, Luke had decided that as long as he went into the event with his eyes wide open—as if any man in his right mind would shut his eyes when Maddie Kincaid was naked—it wouldn't matter what his father may or may not have intended when he sent her to Caddo Bayou. So what if seduction was her plan all along? As long as he made sure his big brain stayed engaged, what did it matter if his little brain had a good time?

Okay, maybe in his heart of hearts he knew he was making excuses, making justifications, but the wine and the woman and the bayou by moonlight had gotten to him. Judging from a few of the looks she gave him, he suspected Ms. Maddie Kincaid was feeling the tension, too.

Luke had been working up to suggesting they indulge in a little no-strings sex.

He thought he'd just float the idea. If she wasn't interested, he wouldn't press it. He was a nice guy. Most of the time. And, if he could end this sorry, suck-ass day by making love to a beautiful woman on a moonlit night aboard the *Miss Behavin' II*, well, looking down from heaven, Terry Winston would smile with pride.

So he'd turned on the charm, ratchetted up the romance, and for a while, he thought he'd been getting somewhere. But mushrooms? Usually when he told his scar story, women asked whether he wanted them to kiss it. This was the first time he'd elicited a mushroom response.

"Mushrooms?" he finally said aloud.

"I had a sample in my purse, but I must have lost it."

He rolled his tongue around his mouth. "You carry mushrooms in your purse?"

"Only when I'm running away from killers."

Oh, hell. Luke went still. "Killers?"

"Yes."

He briefly closed his eyes. So, did this mean she was a damsel in distress for real? Not his father's lackey, after all? Well, shit. Guess that hosed the sex.

"This is about why you came to see Terry, isn't it?"

At her nod, what was left of his fantasy of no-strings sex sizzled away to nothing, like grease dripping onto hot coals. "And you decided you just had to share this tidbit *now*?"

Maddie took an extra-large sip of her wine, then babbled, "You were flirting with me, and I was thinking about it, and I realized that if I trusted you enough for sex after Rip, Liam, and Cade, then I obviously trusted you enough to tell you about the mushrooms."

Luke's thoughts bounced back and forth like a pinball, then locked in on the sex. She'd been thinking about it? But now she's not? And who were Rip, Liam, and Cade? And . . . well, hell. "Mushrooms. Let me guess. Mushrooms and the DEA, so you're talking psilocybin mushrooms."

"If that's what you call the ones that make you high, then, yeah. I'm afraid so."

Luke sighed heavily, then opened the lid of the grill. Smoke billowed into the evening air. He picked up his spatula and shifted the steaks over the fire.

A dozen questions hovered on his tongue. He wanted to know where she got the shrooms. He wanted to know who'd been killed. He wanted to know why she didn't go to the local cops for help, why his father sent her to the *Miss Behavin' II*, and why he'd led her to believe that Terry was female.

Rather than voice the questions, Luke bit his tongue. He wasn't going to get involved. Absolutely, positively not.

After a moment of waiting for him to speak, Maddie said, "Uh, I was kidding about putting the mushrooms with the steaks."

"I figured that."

The silence dragged. Maddie shifted anxiously from one foot to the other. Luke whistled beneath his breath and concentrated on the meat, doing his level best not to think about his guest's revelation. "How do you like your steak cooked? I'll do anything from rare to medium well. It'd be criminal to cook this piece of beef until it's well done."

She let the moment hang, and he watched her eyes light with annoyance. "Medium is fine," she finally replied. "I wouldn't want to do anything"—she drawled the word—"*criminal.*"

Luke snorted. Okay, maybe he couldn't keep the subject entirely off his mind, but that didn't mean he had to pursue anything. "They're just about ready. You want to eat up here or inside downstairs?"

"You're just going to ignore me? You don't care that a nice old man may have been murdered? That his killers are now after me?"

A nice old man? Who . . . ? No. Don't. "You're safe, Maddie. We're in the middle of a swamp. There's not much either one of us can do now but eat. Personally, I'm looking forward to it. I'm hungry."

She finally took his not-so-subtle hint, and Luke breathed a sigh of relief when she disappeared down the spiral staircase. Moments later, the bang of dishes against the table made him smile. Yep, he bet she would have been a firecracker in bed.

Dinner turned out as delicious as he'd expected—he did know his way around a grill. Maddie did more playing with her food than eating, something Knucklehead was bound to appreciate. While the food was outstanding, conversation proved to be downright stilted.

He tried small talk, but she wouldn't discuss baseball or college football or even golf. The woman was as angry as hell that he wouldn't listen to her tale of mushroom, murder, and mayhem.

Why was it women always had to sulk?

Finally, Luke got tired of it. Having finished his meal, he opened another bottle of wine and filled their empty glasses. Then he sat back in his chair and attempted to explain. "It's been a long time since my brother and I spent any time together. This fishing trip is important to us both."

Maddie stabbed a piece of steak with her fork. "You don't want anything to interrupt it."

"Exactly."

"You don't feel obligated to help me because you no longer work for the DEA."

"That's true."

Maddie placed the bite of meat into her mouth, chewed, then swallowed. "You don't trust me because I'm here because your father sent me."

Luke considered it, then nodded. "Can't argue with a word you said."

She set down her fork. "When's the last time you talked to Branch?"

His lips made a sour twist. "Don't go there."

She opened her mouth, then wisely backed off when he shot her a fierce warning glare. Shrugging, she picked at her baked potato for a few minutes, then asked him a question about the fishing tackle a man used when going after tarpon. Happy with the change in subject, Luke responded in detail and at length. By the time they'd finished the meal, fed the dog the scraps, and loaded the dishes in the dishwasher, Luke believed the topic of magic mushrooms put to bed.

Therefore, he wasn't the least bit suspicious or defensive when she shifted the conversation back to Brazos Bend. She asked him whether he remembered Mrs. Hart, the principal of the elementary school in town, and Mr. Warrington, the former fire chief, who'd retired to a cabin out at Possum

Kingdom Lake. Luke did recall the pair, and Maddie gave him an update on their recent activities.

She reached down and rearranged the plates in the dishwasher. "What about Gus Grevas? Do you remember him?"

"Gus Grevas?" Luke repeated, frowning. What was wrong with the way he'd loaded the machine? "Grevas bought flowers for his wife every Thursday afternoon at the flower shop across from the high school football field. We could time our watches by the man. Practice always ended ten minutes after Gus showed up."

Maddie smiled wistfully. "He was the most romantic man. Some of the stories he told about romancing his wife, why, they left me breathless. I've never had that in a lover, but now that I know romantic men are not just a fantasy, I'm thinking I might hold out for one." She paused for a moment's reflection, then added, "I guess that's a bright spot in this nightmare. Gus gets to be with his Sue-Ellen again. I'll bet he's romancing her in heaven right this minute."

Luke frowned. "He passed away? When?"

"Yesterday. He's the man I told you about. I think he might have been murdered."

Luke's arm jerked, accidentally knocking a fork to the floor. "Wait a minute. You're telling me this murder and mayhem happened in Mayberry? In quiet little friendly Brazos Bend? That Mr. Grevas was a drug dealer?"

"Yes! Well, except for the bit about Mr. Grevas. That I just won't believe. He wouldn't have sent me to clear out his lake house if he knew it was chock-full of an illegal substance. I think he found out yesterday and that's what upset him. He thought he was having a heart attack, but when he went to the hospital, the tests ruled out heart trouble. The doctors said his heart was fine and he'd had a panic attack instead."

Maddie paused long enough to fiddle with the way he'd loaded the silverware basket. "Because he was such an emotional mess, they decided to keep him a couple of days for observation—mostly to calm him down. When I visited him, he told me the mushrooms were worth six million dollars, and I needed to get rid of them. He said the killers are looking for me and not to trust the police. Then I discovered his home had been ransacked and neighbors who also happen to be cops visited him in the hospital shortly before he died."

Oh, shit. Dirty cops? In Brazos Bend?

Luke scooped the fork off the floor and dumped it into the dishwasher, then slammed the damn thing closed. He didn't want to hear another word. Yet he asked, "What makes you think he was murdered, Maddie?"

"He was fine! It was just panic. I honestly don't know, but my suspicions are enough to scare me silly. I have their mushrooms, after all. Gus was another client of mine, and he'd asked me to clean out his lake house before he listed it with a real estate agent. Gus is . . . or was . . . an avid gardener, so I didn't think anything of finding all the mushrooms."

Luke's stomach did a slow, sickening turn, and it wasn't a result of bad food. "Stop. Just stop it. I'm going fishing. Remember? Fishing. Save the rest of it for someone who can help you."

"But—"

"I mean it, Maddie. I'm not getting involved in this. I can't. I'm sorry about old Gus, I truly am. But I don't have the creds anymore. I'm not on the job. Save your story for someone who is."

Maddie's mouth flattened into a grim smile, but she hand-washed and dried the wooden-handled barbecue tools in silence. For a time, the only sound to be heard was the night sounds of the bayou and Knucklehead's peaceful snores. Thank goodness.

With the galley put to rights, Luke decided to call it a day. Never mind he hadn't gone to bed this early in months. Years, even. He couldn't stand here a minute longer looking at her sad, angry eyes. "I'm whipped. Feel free to stay up as long as you want, but I'm hitting the sack."

His door was halfway closed when her voice floated on the air like a discordant melody. "They're cops, Luke. What if they kill me, too?"

Luke snarled and slammed the door hard.

"Not gonna go there," he muttered. "Dirty cops are not my problem."

He shucked off his swim trunks and climbed naked into bed. He yanked the midnight blue sheet over his hips and put his arm over his eyes. *Think about tarpon, Callahan. Think about the pull on the line when he takes the bait. The fight.*

He thought of what drug dealers do to people who cross them. Especially those bastards with the benefit of a badge.

Think about Matt and imported beer and the gentle sway of the boat at dusk.

He visualized a waterfall of red hair soaked in a pool of blood.

"Son of a bitch." He flipped over onto his stomach and buried his head in his pillow.

Think of turquoise water. Think of sugar-sand beaches.

He thought of chocolate brown eyes, wide and lifeless.

Luke muttered a string of curses and rolled onto his side. He pulled the pillow over his head and mentally inventoried the fishing lures in his tackle box. He worked his way to the bottom, envisioned the boning knife nestled in a leather sheath, and gave up. "Damn me for an empty-headed idiot."

He rolled out of bed and headed for the door, pulling on his swim trunks as an afterthought.

Luke found her sitting cross-legged on the floor beside her bed, rubbing an ecstatic Knucklehead's belly. She looked up in surprise as he burst into the room. "Tell me."

Her tongue slipped out of her mouth and ringed her lips. "You want to know . . . ?"

"Everything. The drugs. The murder. Your involvement."

"And you'll help me?"

"I'm not promising anything. I have to hear your story first."

She glanced down at the dog, then back up at him. "Then can I at least have your word that you won't do anything that could hurt me?"

Affronted, his body stiffened. "Hurt you? I'm not the bad guy here. You came to me, remember? What do you think I'd do to hurt you?"

Maddie's teeth tugged at her lower lip. "Talk. You could tell the wrong somebody something I'm going to tell you, something that could get me in trouble. Will you promise me you'll keep this between the two of us, Luke?"

"All right."

"Oh, jeez," she muttered. "What am I doing? About to put my faith in a man? Again? You swear it, Luke Callahan? You swear you won't tell anyone what I'm about to tell you? On . . . on . . . on Knucklehead's life?"

Luke sighed heavily and rolled his eyes. "Oh, for God's sake, Maddie. Just tell me what happened, okay? I won't make trouble for you. I'm going fishing, remember?"

She rose from the floor and sat on the edge of her bed. She wiped her palms on her bare thighs. "Okay. Well. Like I said, it all started yesterday morning. I can't believe it was only yesterday. It feels like a year ago."

Luke thought it might take a year for her to tell her story at this rate. The golden highlights mixed among the red of her hair glistened in the lamplight, and even in the seriousness of the moment, he couldn't help but notice just how damned beautiful she was.

"Early yesterday morning, I cleaned out Gus's lake house and found the mushrooms. I decided to take them to the farmer's market to sell."

Now, that dragged his attention back to matters at hand. "You were going to sell psilocybin mushrooms at a farmer's market?"

"I didn't know they were . . . well . . . the magic kind. I thought they were shiitake or some other gourmet variety."

"Jesus." He raked his fingers through his hair, amused despite himself as he pictured the likes of sour old Mrs. Moody high on magic mushrooms. "What did the mushrooms look like?"

She bit her bottom lip, then said, "Little penises."

Luke made a strangled sound in his throat.

"Well, that *is* what they look like." She tucked a loose strand behind her ear as she considered it. "Most of them were tall and skinny, but I did see some short and fat ones."

"Colors?"

"A bunch of different ones. The ones in the jars were mostly dark, sort of a dark olive brown, but others were a chestnut rusty color. Some even had kind of a blue edge or ring. The dried ones in the burlap bags were sort of yellowish."

"Jars *and* burlap bags?" He braced his hands on his hips. "Jesus, how much do you have?"

"Lots. All that would fit in my van. I threw away the rest."

His jaw gaped. "You realize you threw away evidence, don't you?"

Her eyes flashed with indignation. "I didn't know it was evidence then! I'm no mushroom expert. The dried ones didn't look any different from ones for sale in the produce section."

He dismissed it with a wave. "Fine. All right. Then what happened?"

"I went to another client's home, and then to your father's. He's been having an awful time with his knees, so in addition to writing the letters he dictates each day, I've started overseeing his exercises. I make sure he does them and does them right. I confer with a physical therapist, mind you, so—"

"Is this relevant?" He didn't need to know a damn thing about Branch Callahan's daily life.

She let out a huff. "I brought him some mushrooms. I thought your father's cooks might have a use for them, but the Garza sisters didn't like the looks of them, so they threw them away. I was in Branch's kitchen when a friend of mine, a nurse, called me from the hospital, and said Gus had been admitted and was asking for me."

Maddie repeated Gus's cautions to her and explained how he'd become so worked up, his blood pressure skyrocketed and the nurses chased her away. "I went to his house to pick up his robe and toiletries, and that's when I found it ransacked. I was trying to decide what to do about it when my cell rang again and my friend told me Gus had died."

"Of a heart attack," Luke clarified.

She nodded. "The doctors were shocked, but when I asked my friend if they were sure it was natural causes, she assured me it had to have been. But he'd had visitors, Luke. What would have stopped someone from giving him something to cause a heart attack?"

"That's a stretch."

"Maybe, but I don't think I want to risk my life on it."

Luke grimaced and raked his fingers through his hair. "So, how did you end up at Caddo Bayou Marina?"

"I left Brazos Bend on the run just to get out of town. I'd been on the road for hours, pretty much driving aimlessly, when Branch called and suggested I come to Terry for help."

What a mess. Luke smothered a sigh. "Where are the mushrooms now?"

"In my trunk. Well, not the trunk. I don't have a trunk. I drive a minivan because of my work. I think you saw it in the parking lot. They're in the back of my van." After a moment's pause, she frowned and added, "You know, they're liable to cook in this heat. I probably should have cracked a window."

He stared up at the ceiling. "So, let me see if I have this straight. Yesterday morning you loaded your minivan with mushrooms from Gus Grevas's lake house, then you went about your workday until Gus summoned you to his hospital room where he warned you about the cops."

"That's right."

"Then you found his house searched, Gus died, and you took off headed . . . where?"

"Just away. I told you all this already. I didn't have a destination in mind until your father called and told me to go to Caddo Bayou."

"And you drove all night, parked your car at the marina, trespassed on my boat, and fell asleep."

"Basically, yes."

Luke rubbed the back of his neck. "So the minivan back at the marina is filled with six million dollars' worth of sun-cooked psilocybin mushrooms?"

Maddie shook her head. "Not six million. Remember, I threw some of them away. I'm guessing four."

"And the growers just might be cops who may have murdered a helpless old man in Brazos Bend and who are now after you."

"That's right."

Wrong. Her story was unbelievable, like something out of a bad B-movie. Like one of the scenarios Branch Callahan had cooked up in his futile efforts to reconcile with Luke, Matt, and Mark. It reminded Luke of that time Branch sent a gorgeous hooker disguised as a kindergarten teacher to Matt's place with some cockamamy story about Matt's providing the prize for the teacher-of-the-year winner. Or his salvo at Mark, some complicated scenario involving stolen family jewels and a lady detective wanting to check those of his brother.

No, Maddie's story was just another Branch Callahan fantasy tale.

Luke's gaze swept her from head to toe once again, lingered on her bosom once again; then his features flattened into a grim expression of disgust. Mushrooms and murder. Crooked cops and a runaway damsel in distress. It was simply too damned far-fetched for a sleepy little place like Brazos Bend, Texas.

Branch must have been watching the afternoon soaps again to come up with a fairy tale like this one.

The fact that Branch had conned Maddie into weaving a story about a dead Gus Grevas, though, was over the top even for his old man. The rotten old bastard. Wouldn't he ever learn?

Now Luke was really pissed. He'd almost fallen for it, dammit. Fallen for her act. "Oh, this is rich. The old man is really reaching to think he'd put this over on me. Instead of a hooker, he sends a fake damsel in distress to pull on my heart-strings. Well, guess what, babe. I don't have a heart. Good night."

Luke turned and left her and, seconds later, slammed his bedroom door. Again.

Maddie's mouth gaped in shock. In all the scenarios she'd imagined regarding Luke Callahan's reaction to her story, she'd never considered that he might not believe her.

Considering her previous experience with law enforcement, that had been a stupid oversight on her part.

How foolish of her to think a man the likes of Luke Callahan would help her. After all, he'd been estranged from his father for a very long time. Sure, Branch was difficult, even ornery, but Maddie knew all about difficult fathers. Shoot, she had the king of difficult fathers, but she didn't let his bad behavior ruin their relationship.

The fact that Luke hadn't tried to repair things with his father didn't speak well of Luke Callahan's character.

No, she'd done it again. She'd listened to her heart and her hormones instead of her head. Good God, would she never learn? Luke Callahan had been a hell-raiser in high school. He remained to this day the role model for bad-boy wannabes in Brazos Bend. He was Rip and Liam and Cade all over again.

After the fallout from Cade, Maddie had believed herself cured her of bad-boy-desire disease forever. Well, she'd been wrong. Dead wrong. And worse, she'd been stupid. *For crying out loud, Maddie. When will you ever learn?*

Anger roared through her, furious and hot. Luke Callahan was nothing more than a jerk. A class-A, number one jerk!

But, by God, she wasn't the only one who could lay a

claim to stupid. She pushed to her feet and stomped toward his cabin, not pausing to knock. She shoved the door open.

He lay naked on his back on the bed. On top of the sheets. His pillow over his head. It was a sign of the intensity of her anger that her gaze barely lingered on his crotch. "You know, Callahan, your father told me you were stubborn, but he never mentioned stupid."

He jackknifed up. "Excuse me?"

"Well, somebody's being stupid here." She lifted her chin, letting him know that "somebody" wasn't her. The dog sidled past her and leaped onto the bed, then stretched out beside Luke. Of the two, Maddie thought, Knucklehead had more sense. "I guess the truth will tell. If I'm inventing this story, then I won't be able to produce the cache of mushrooms, now, will I? I don't suppose you'd like to make a bet on the outcome, would you, ex-agent Callahan? I've got my eye on a pretty little purse at the Brazos Bend Boutique."

A muscle worked in Luke's jaw and a chill entered those gorgeous green eyes. Maddie glared right back at him. She wished he'd put on some clothes. Cover up, at least. Unfortunately, his lack of character didn't distract from the appeal of washboard abs and a substantial package.

Maddie was tired, desperate, and scared. She held on to her patience by a string. Why did Branch Callahan have to go and lie about Terry Winston? For that matter, why couldn't Branch have had girls rather than boys? If he'd had an ex-DEA agent daughter, she'd have helped Maddie rather than let her down. Women didn't let Maddie down.

A sense of hopelessness washed over her. Tears threatened, but she fought them back. "Look. Never mind. Maybe it's best we just forget about it. I'll find someone else to help me."

He muttered something under his breath that she couldn't quite catch, then said, "If by some wild chance you're telling the truth—and I'm not for a minute saying I believe you—do you have a clue of the kind of trouble you're in?"

Maddie's spirit came roaring back at that. She rolled her

eyes, then dramatically clapped a hand to her chest. "Trouble? Me? Do ya think?"

When he lowered his brow and scowled at her, Maddie sneered right back. "Welcome to this week, Agent Callahan. Yes, I know I'm in trouble. You see, in addition to having millions of dollars worth of a controlled substance in my vehicle and killers on my tail, I have another little worry."

His scowl morphed into a grimace. "Don't tell me you're pregnant. The hooker tried that one when I wouldn't cave."

"I'm not pregnant, G-man." She lifted up the left side of her T-shirt and tugged down the waistband of the gym shorts she wore, revealing a small, artistic tattoo on her hip. "I'm on parole."

Five

"That's a prison tat!" Luke's appalled gaze zeroed in on the figure on her hip. He recognized the style. The artist. "That's Wanda Jarrell's work."

It was a stylized version of a Texas Department of Corrections number about as big as his thumb in colors of green, blue, and red.

"I thought you might recognize it. I understand Wanda's work is very well known among law enforcement officials as well as inmates."

Luke managed little more than a nod. Wanda Jarrell had made a name for herself with her creative designs utilizing a person's Texas Department of Corrections number.

"I firmly believe that had Wanda's family circumstances been different, her work would be hanging in museums rather than on convicts' biceps and butts," Maddie added.

"Why . . . ?"

She sighed and let loose her T-shirt. Luke knew a small sense of loss as the sexy little scroll was covered. "I did it on a dare," she replied. "That and to serve as a permanent reminder of my stupidity. Plus, I truly like her artistry."

He shook his head. He'd not been asking why the tattoo, but rather why the DOC prison number. "Who the hell are you, woman?"

"It's complicated. I—"

His lawman's senses on high alert, Luke reached beside

the bed for his gun. He didn't know who sent her, or why she was there, but he wasn't taking chances with this sort of thing.

"Who sent you?"

"Oh, for crying out loud."

"Who sent you, Maddie? Goddammit, I can't believe I almost let a piece of ass—"

"Hold it right there," she snapped, dismissing the weapon in his hand, folding her arms, and lifting her chin. "No need to be snotty."

He mouthed the word "snotty," then grimaced and shoved his fingers through his hair. "Start talking."

"Would you put the gun away? I swear. You wave that thing around as if it were a second penis."

Luke narrowed his eyes and glared at her, then lowered the gun. He did not, however, return it to his nightstand.

Maddie nodded, then asked, "What do you want to know?"

"Oh, I have quite a list. Who you are, why you're here, why you have one of Wanda Jarrell's prison tattoos on your ass, to name a few."

Maddie wrinkled her nose. "It's on my hip, and as a point of fact, it's not a prison tattoo. I've never been to prison."

"I recognize—"

"I was in state jail. There's a difference. It might not be significant to you, but it is to me. I really am Maddie Kincaid. I really do own a senior care business in Brazos Bend, and your father really is one of my clients. Everything I told you is the truth."

"You're telling me Branch Callahan hired a convict to wash his socks?" Luke asked in a scathing, disbelieving tone.

She lifted her chin. "He likes my pesto."

"I just bet he does."

He could tell by the look in her eyes that Maddie wanted to tell him where he could stuff his suspicions, but she must have decided that doing so wasn't in her best interests.

She visibly tamped down her pique. "I write letters for him. His penmanship is no longer legible, so every day, I go to Callahan House and he dictates three letters to me. You're right that your father didn't know about my record when he hired me. Before yesterday when I explained my troubles to Branch, the only person in Brazos Bend who knew about my past was Kathy Hudson."

"The lady who owns the Dairy Princess?"

Maddie nodded.

He recalled the woman, who'd be in her late fifties or early sixties now. She'd kept the jukebox at the Dairy Princess playing nonstop. "She started a riot in downtown Brazos Bend the day the Beatles announced their breakup."

"She makes a pilgrimage to Graceland every year."

Luke eyed Maddie's features, searching for a resemblance to the woman he remembered from his youth. "Whoa. Are you her daughter? The one who ran away?"

Maddie shook her head. "I'm not Sparkle. Kathy and I aren't family. She's my friend."

"Why? How? How about you tell your story in one piece so that it makes some sense? How did you get to be friends with Brazos Bend's queen of rock and roll? What? Are you Ringo's lost love child or something?"

She blinked. After visually weighing her words, she said, "Kathy wrote to me in jail. We became pen pals, and she invited me to live with her when I got out."

Luke could tell there was more to that part of the story, but he pursued what he considered to be a more important path. "So what were you in for?"

She closed her eyes. "Possession of a controlled substance."

Luke's mouth curled and he shook his head in disgust. "A goddamn doper."

"I've never taken drugs in my life!"

"No? I suppose you sold them. Like seeing little crack babies, Maddie? Like how they scream for a fix?"

"I don't deal, either!" One of Knucklehead's plastic chew

toys lay on the floor, and she gave it a swift kick. "It was my boyfriend. He planted the grass on me and it was only a small amount. Less than an ounce. It was my first and only arrest."

Grass? Brows arching in disbelief, Luke scoffed, "And they sent you to jail for that? Sorry, hon. I know the way the system works. I know better."

"I'm telling you the truth. I wasn't dealing. It was possession, and the evading arrest charge was just bogus. They made an example of me because of who I am."

Evading arrest, too. This just got better and better. He held up his hands, palms out. "And you're who? The queen of Sheba?"

She opened her mouth, then abruptly shut it. "Oh, just forget it. Forget everything. I was a fool to think you might help me. You're a man! How could I have forgotten that? You dangle the evidence in front of me every chance you get. Just take me back to the marina tomorrow, and I'll go on to plan B."

"My evidence doesn't dangle," he fired back, setting his gun into the nightstand drawer. "It . . . presents."

Maddie snorted.

Ignoring that reaction, he asked, "What's plan B?"

"I don't have one yet, but I'll think of something."

She turned to leave, but Luke lunged forward and grasped her arm. "Wait. Back up a minute."

"Would you put on some clothes!"

"Tell me the rest of it, Red. Start from the top, and tell the truth this time."

"Don't call me 'Red.' I've always hated it."

"So who are you, really?"

She rolled her eyes in frustration, then pursed her lips and thumped them with her index finger a moment before saying, "I was born a poor coal miner's daughter in the Black Hills of—"

"Oh, for God's sake. You are such a brat." He grabbed his trunks and tugged them back on.

"Forget about it, Luke. Just go fishing."

"I will. Don't worry." First, though, he wanted answers, answers she suddenly didn't appear willing to give. Brushing past her, he crossed to her bedroom and scooped up her purse.

"Hey," Maddie protested. "Stop it. That's private."

He ignored her completely and dropped her keys on the table, then a compact. When he tossed her plastic tampon case next to her keys, he saw her cheeks flush with embarrassment.

Next Luke pulled her wallet from her purse. He flipped it open to her driver's license. Then he opened a drawer beside the galley sink, dug out a cell phone, and thumbed the power button. "Damned roaming charges."

"This from a man who owns a floating palace."

He held Maddie's gaze as he punched in a number, then said, "Hey Deidre, it's Luke."

After listening a moment, he replied, "Fine. It was nice. No, Terry would understand why you couldn't make it. He loved your kids."

He paused again, grinning at Deidre's mention of Terry's horrible singing voice, then said, "You're right. I swore the whisky glasses were gonna break last time I heard him sing 'The Yellow Rose of Texas.' Listen, I need a favor. See what your system pulls up on a . . ." He read her name and address off the license, then added, "Yeah, I'll hang on."

"Fine," Maddie snapped. "Be a show-off. Use your connections to ferret out every last kernel of information about me. Then what are you going to do? You promised you wouldn't cause me trouble. Will you break your word? Sworn on Knucklehead's life, I might remind you?"

Actually, he'd dodged that particular promise, but Luke doubted she'd see it that way.

"Or will you delay your fishing trip and help me? Hmm?" She folded her arms. "Men. What's that saying? Can't count on them, can't shoot them?"

Deidre came back on the phone and began relaying salient facts about Maddie's record. Hmm . . . looked like she'd told the truth. So far, anyway. Luke grabbed a pen and made a note of the name and phone number of Maddie's parole officer.

Maddie watched him write the name Jennifer Thompson and winced. A nerve there. She obviously didn't want him talking to the woman. What else was she hiding?

"May I remind you that you're not official anymore, Mr. Callahan? My parole officer doesn't have to speak to you. Surely I have some privacy rights."

"Thanks, Deidre. Yeah, you, too. Bye." Luke stared her straight in the eyes as he set the phone on the table. "What did Branch Callahan say when you told him you got busted for dope? He about split a gasket when he caught Matt smoking a joint when he was a high school freshman."

Calmly, quietly, Maddie said, "I've already told you what happened. Believe what you want. Your kind always do. Now, if you'll excuse me, I'd like to get some sleep."

His kind? Luke wasn't about to excuse her. Though he'd tried hard to let this whole thing go, his gut wouldn't let him. Not now, anyway. Something about this entire business was screwy, and he by God wanted to know what it was all about.

First she wants his help; she tells him secrets that could land her in jail. Then, abruptly, she changes her mind and shuts up? What other secret could she have? She had no outstanding warrants. No criminal history except for the one arrest. She'd blamed her punishment on her identity.

They made an example of me because of who I am.

So, who was she? What was so special about Madeline Kincaid?

"You're driving me crazy, you know." He folded his arms and leaned against the door frame just as his cell phone began to ring.

Luke checked the number. Deidre? "Hello."

The voice in his ear said, "Hey, Luke. Listen, we no

sooner hung up than I realized where I'd heard her name before."

"Oh?" His gaze locked on Maddie's. "What else do you know about her, Deidre?"

"She changed her name legally when she got out of jail. They've kept her new name real hush-hush. Maddie Kincaid's record is real, but the name has definitely been changed to protect the not-so-innocent. I only found out because Jennifer Thompson missed the change on one report. Up until then, I had no clue she'd stayed in Texas. I figured her father would have pulled some strings. Luke, Madeline Kincaid was born Madeline Connaught."

Madeline Connaught. Didn't ring a bell. "So?"

"Don't you know your rock music trivia? The Swords? She's Blade's daughter, Callahan. Madeline Kincaid is Baby Dagger."

Maddie watched awareness enter Luke Callahan's eyes. So, now he knows. She was Baby Dagger, the most hated child in the Western world. The despised person responsible for breaking up the Swords, the greatest rock group since the Beatles. As a third grader, Maddie had been the Yoko Ono of the elementary school set.

She really didn't want to go over that part of her life with the likes of Luke Callahan. While he was still on the phone, she pushed past him, running away from both past and present. She fled to the flybridge, where she plopped down on the deck, gazed up at the stars, and wished herself miles away.

Maddie knew how to wish. She'd been eight years old when she begged her parents, British rocker Blade and his American, vocal-lead wife, Savannah, to give her a normal childhood. Even then she'd wanted Mayberry. She'd dreamed of a *My Three Sons* house and a teacher the likes of the Beaver's Miss Landers. She'd craved a real-life bedtime and brownies made from scratch by her mother.

Her parents loved her and they listened. At the end of a concert in Barcelona, Blade announced to the crowd that he and Savannah were leaving the band—because that's what Baby Dagger wanted.

It proved to be a poor choice of words. A riot broke out in the stadium. People were nearly trampled to death. Someone started a fire in a trash can, which then spread to a concession. One woman had a stroke. Headlines across the world picked up the quote, and overnight, Baby Dagger became a synonym for spoiled brat.

Nevertheless, her parents persevered and chose for their home a suburb in Middle America, looking for picket fences. Instead, they got picket lines and paparazzi. In Kansas.

The townspeople didn't appreciate the fuss, and Maddie's dream was spoiled. They'd had to replace pretty white pickets with an iron fence and gate, intercoms, and cameras. Neighborhood games of tag didn't happen. Baby Dagger couldn't walk to and from school without a bodyguard, and no matter how much she wished it, she could never be just another kid hoping to be chosen for a softball team or to play red rover on the playground.

Luckily, except for a few diehards who refused to go away, the press's pursuit faded as the months went on, and for an oh-so-brief amount of time, Baby Dagger caught a glimpse of Normal, USA. Oh, she never quite managed to ride that school bus, and she wasn't chosen to play Mary in the Christmas pageant, but she did get to go trick-or-treating door-to-door. The Halloween when she was nine was the absolute best day of her life.

Then, the next day, she asked Savannah to make brownies.

It was a freak accident. No one knew for sure what happened, but the detectives suspect Savannah spilled the batter, then slipped and hit her head on the edge of the kitchen table. Savannah had been dead for about an hour before father and daughter found her.

The press went wild. Blade went crazy. Like a violent black tornado, he scooped Baby up from Kansas and dropped her back into his version of Oz—the world of sex, drugs, and rock and roll. Only this time, without the settling presence of his beloved Savannah, for the better part of a decade Blade got lost.

A warm night breeze swirled around Maddie as sorrow welled up inside her at the memory. Such sad years. Such lonely years. There'd been one stretch of time when Blade left her on the estate in England and didn't return for more than twenty-six months.

Maddie heard Luke's footsteps climbing the stairs to the flybridge. She drew a deep breath of damp, earthy air, then her sigh joined the whispering of leaves in the trees. "I should have just told you," she said as he stretched out beside her. "I was stupid to think I could get through this mess without that bit of news coming out. I've never been that lucky."

"You certainly are full of surprises."

From somewhere below them, Knucklehead let out a whimper. Luke responded with a soft whistle, and moments later, the dog padded up the steps and plopped down beside Maddie, laying his head in her lap. She scratched him behind his ears and waited for Luke to bombard her with questions.

First, he'd ask her about her parents' decision to leave the Swords. Then he'd want to know about her mother's death and her father's drug addiction. After that, he'd pepper her with questions about the Infamous Comeback Interview of her father by Barbara Walters, and Luke's voice would drip with the scorn that invariably accompanied any sentence that included the words "Baby Dagger."

But Luke surprised her. Rather than lashing her with the usual vitriol of angry fans, instead of asking about her parents and all the trials and tribulations associated therewith, he focused his interest in a different direction. "So, you've only had the one arrest."

"Yes." Officially. There had been a few other close calls, but her father had managed to buy Maddie's way out of those.

"What about that incident at the Le Mans race?"

That had been twelve years ago when she'd been with Rip. "I was totally innocent. I didn't steal that car."

Luke's eyes glittered like a cat's in the milky moonlight, his gaze drifting down across her chest. "I heard the idea for that Super Bowl halftime stunt a few years ago came from your wardrobe malfunction at the MTV awards."

"Mine *was* an accident." Liam, the blighter, had gotten amorous in the limo on the way to the awards, and neither of them noticed the torn seam. "I didn't get arrested for that."

"Hmm . . . I seem to recall something else." He paused a moment in thought, then snapped his fingers. "Bad checks. Didn't you rack up some ridiculous amount of bad check charges a few years back?"

Maddie tossed her head, sending her strawberry locks flying. "That was a lie. A bold-faced lie. Tabloids didn't have anything to report on me, so when they saw me shopping in London, they made it up. All of it."

"You didn't sue?"

"What's the point?" Bitterness soured her tone. "With my reputation, I'd look even worse. It's easier to let it go. Frankly, Callahan, I'm surprised a DEA agent would lower himself to read tabloid trash."

"Hell, I once read a telephone book while sitting on a stakeout."

"Aren't you going to ask about Blade's drug addiction? His next album? His hit single 'Baby's to Blame'?"

"No, don't think I will."

She studied him, a faint smile playing across her lips. "You're not a rock music fan?"

"I wouldn't go that far. I think the Swords' 'Honey' is one of the best rock ballads ever written. I'm more a blues and Buffett guy. As far as your father goes . . ." He shrugged. "Not to be insulting, but celebrities don't interest me. I learned long ago that too much money tends to get folks in trouble. I'll listen if you want to talk about your father and his peculiarities, but to be honest, what I'm really interested in is you."

He couldn't have said anything more perfect, and Maddie melted. "Thank you," she murmured, then she leaned over to give him an affectionate kiss on the cheek.

Somehow, her lips landed on his mouth.

He didn't let them leave.

Maddie knew almost immediately that she'd made a huge mistake as Luke took control of the kiss. Her pulse leapt, her blood hummed. Desire washed through her like a warm summer rain. He tasted of moonlight and man, and he made Maddie yearn. She wanted to press herself against him, to experience the sensation of a firm, hard body molded to hers. She wanted to lose herself in the magic of the moonlight, the mystery of the man, and the marvel of his mouth that even now took control.

So she did.

At her surrender, Luke Callahan's kiss turned hot and hard and merciless. He captured her head in his hands, sinking his fingers into her hair, and drank from her lips like a drowning man. The intensity of his reaction sent a giddy sense of power sizzling through her.

Oh, how she'd missed this—the heat, the wonder, the delight. Tension curled in the pit of her stomach and she shuddered with pleasure. He muttered words against her mouth, but they sounded more like curses than compliments.

Suddenly, he shifted and she was under him on the hard deck, her hair a copper halo around her, his hands impatient, sweeping her farther into the madness.

Madness.

Oh, God. What was she doing? Had she lost her everloving mind?

It ran through her mind that she was completely within his power. They were alone in a secluded spot. He was strong, much stronger than she. He could take whatever he wanted and she couldn't stop him.

A shameful part of her thrilled to the idea. She could indulge herself guilt free. She could satisfy this deep, delicious ache without responsibility. She could . . .

"No. Please." She could hear the needy whimper in her voice. "Please, Luke. I can't do this."

He went still. For a long, tense moment, he didn't move,

yet she could feel the pound of his pulse, the hard ridge of his arousal against her. Maddie moved her hand, which had been clutching his shirt, and ever so slightly pressed against his chest.

Luke Callahan rolled off her with a curse. *So much for being forced.*

Gulping air like a diver down too long, he lay on his back on the houseboat's deck with his arm slung over his eyes. Above, a dark cloud drifted across the moon's silvered light, and the night turned inky. The sounds of the bayou seemed to swell in the sudden darkness—the constant chirp of crickets, the repetitive croaks of frogs.

The rapid breathing of two people in the moments following thwarted lovemaking.

From somewhere behind them came the bellow of an alligator. Luke, however, didn't speak.

Maddie didn't know what to say. Despite the fact that sexual attraction had hummed between them all day, this inferno had caught her by surprise. How had a simple thank-you kiss evolved into something so . . . intense?

"Luke, that shouldn't have—"

"Don't ask me to apologize, lady. You're the one who started it." His voice vibrated with frustration as he added, "I guess I missed the tabloid story about Baby Dagger being a tease."

Hurt by his anger, she sucked in a breath. "I'm . . . going downstairs. Good night."

She scrambled away from him and fled down to her cabin, where she dove into bed and yanked the covers over her head, trying to hide from herself. *Oh, Maddie. You're such a mess.*

The events of the day and of yesterday rolled through her mind like a bad movie. She lay for a long time before finally drifting off to sleep.

She never did hear Luke come down from the flybridge.

Six

Dawn crept like a thief across the bayou, stealing the shadows and songs of the night and leaving an anticipatory quiet in its wake. Luke stood at the wheel, waiting for the moment that sufficient light filtered through the trees to illuminate the surroundings.

His eyes felt gritty from lack of sleep, and his head ached from a night spent doing too much thinking while arriving at too few answers. He'd had trouble wrapping his mind around the idea that an honest-to-God rock princess had managed to get herself involved in mayhem and murder while hiding out in Brazos Bend, Texas. It was so far-fetched, so completely unbelievable, that he had to believe it might be true.

However, he couldn't rule out the possibility that his father had orchestrated the entire thing. Branch Callahan was the King of Conspiracy, and Maddie could easily be working with him. Or she could be his innocent pawn. Either way, if Branch Callahan was acting the puppet master, damned if Luke wanted to dangle on his strings.

Which left him balanced on the old horns of a dilemma. He'd tossed and turned for hours trying to decide what to do with Maddie "Baby Dagger" Kincaid. He'd considered easing the *Miss Behavin' II* up to the dock at Caddo Bayou Marina, and stopping only long enough to kick her and her goldfish off his boat before heading right back toward the gulf. He'd pondered hanging around long enough to check the back of her minivan and verify the existence of the shrooms. If all was as she claimed, he could then wash his hands of her and her problem by calling his old boss and dumping the problem in his lap.

Then there had been a third possible course of action that had flitted through his mind like a sin off and on throughout the night. He could tie up the *Miss Behavin' II*, blow off his brother, and devote himself to solving his houseboat guest's problems. It'd screw his fishing trip, but chances looked good that he'd get seriously laid. Judging by the heat of their kiss, Luke doubted they'd last another day together without going at it.

He'd been tempted. Oh, he'd been tempted. Which is why he'd reached for his cell phone at three o'clock in the morning and made arrangements that should send Maddie safely back to Texas and have him back on his boat on the bayou by noon.

Now able to see his surroundings, Luke fired up the engines on the *Miss Behavin' II*. Then he hoisted the anchors and pointed the boat toward home.

They'd been under way almost an hour before Luke heard Maddie stirring below. Knucklehead plodded down the stairs, deserting him for feminine cuddles and coos. Luke didn't hold it against the dog. Hadn't he been thinking about those cuddles half the damned night himself?

Luke let her hide in her room until the houseboat rounded a curve and Caddo Bayou Marina came into view. He scanned the parking lot for a familiar car, and upon seeing it, blew out a heavy breath. "Okay, princess. You better hope you were playing me straight." He shifted the boat into neutral, released the wheel, and walked to the edge of the flybridge. Leaning over it, he called, "Maddie? The marina's right up ahead."

Moments later, he eased the *Miss Behavin' II* up to the marina's gas dock. While an attendant secured the bowline, placing a plump white fender between boat and dock,

Maddie stepped off the boat, fishbowl in one hand and purse in the other. She set the fish and her bag down, then secured the stern to a piling with a competent double half hitch.

Surprising talent for a rock princess, Luke thought. But then, surprises seemed to be what Maddie Kincaid was all about. *Well, I hope she's happy with the surprise I have planned for her.*

She picked up her fish and her purse, then visually braced herself as, for the first time since last night, she met his gaze. *She's nervous,* he realized. But was it because of the killers or the kiss?

Maddie lifted her chin. "So, what next? We just go our separate ways?"

"In a bit." A quick glance around suggested that the person Luke had summoned to Louisiana awaited them inside the air-conditioned ship store. He recognized the logo on a truck in the parking lot. "Why don't you show me your contraband first."

"All right." She nodded, then shoved the fishbowl at him. "Hold Oscar, would you, please? And be careful. He's had a rough couple of days, poor baby."

Luke frowned down at the goldfish. He kind of had that dying-fish look to him. How else had she mistreated the poor thing?

As Maddie dug in her purse for her keys, Knucklehead bounded off the houseboat, gave a quick bark, and loped off toward the Dumpster behind the ship store. Maddie led Luke in the opposite direction toward a maroon minivan. She clicked a button on her keyless entry remote, and the release on the van's back door clicked. The door cracked open.

Maddie tugged it all the way up, and the moldering scent of decay wafted from inside the vehicle. "Son of a bitch," Luke muttered as he got a gander at the contents. He shoved Maddie's goldfish back into her arms, then turned close attention to the minivan's cargo.

A bundle of dry cleaning hung from a hook on the left side,

a sponge mop was propped against the backseat on the right. Between the two sat bags, jars, and even a crate full of what Luke recognized as psilocybin mushrooms. Lots of them. Many well on the way toward rotten. "You say you threw some away?"

"About a third of them."

"Where?"

"The Dumpster behind Kroger in Brazos Bend."

Jesus. Luke's mind raced. "What day do they pick up trash in that part of town?"

"The trash truck drove up just as I was leaving."

He shook his head. The woman dumped probably two million dollars' worth of magic mushrooms into Kroger's trash can. Leaving town had been a damned good decision.

He hoped like hell he'd made the right decision in how he'd chosen to help her.

"Okay," he said. "Let's head for the ship store. There's someone I want you to—"

"Sin!" The feminine shout ended on a squeal.

Luke and Maddie both turned to see a tidy, attractive sprite of a woman rushing toward them in strappy yellow high-heeled sandals. "Oh, my gosh. Sin Callahan, just look at you! You're even more disreputable than ever. Still sexy as sin. C'mere, hot rod. Gimme a kiss."

"Sin?" Maddie grumbled. "Of course he's called Sin. Had to be either that or Devil."

"Devil's my brother Mark."

Sara-Beth Branson launched herself at Luke with a laugh, and as he lifted her and twirled her around, she planted a big, fat kiss on his mouth. "Hi Sara-Bee," he said against her ear as he hugged her hard, then returned her to her feet.

She smiled wistfully up at him and said his name with a sigh. "Luke."

Sara-Beth was still no bigger than a minute, and he knew from reading the editorial page of the Brazos Bend newspaper that she still had the fire that had attracted him in high school. "It's good to see you."

She gave him a thorough once-over, then clucked her tongue. "And you still make my mouth water, Sin Callahan. However, I didn't leave my comfy bed in the middle of the night and drive for hours for nostalgia's sake. Where's the story you promised?"

Luke winked at Maddie, whose expression had gone downright sour.

Sara-Beth smiled at her. "I don't think we've ever been introduced. I'm Sara-Beth Branson with the *Brazos Bend Standard*. You're Maddie Kincaid, right? You run the new senior care business in town? My colleague Bill Stevens has helped you with your ads, I believe. I suppose Sin's big story has something to do with you?"

Maddie turned to Luke, her big brown eyes round, stunned, and brimming with hurt. "A newspaper reporter? You called a *newspaper reporter*?"

Preferring to lay all his cards on the table, Luke nodded. "Supposed to be a cop on the way, too."

A reporter. A cop. Betrayal was a punch to the gut, and Maddie fought to draw a breath.

"Maddie—"

She closed her eyes, held up a hand, and shook her head. Her thoughts spun wildly. It was over. Her nice, calm, pleasant life. She'd go back to jail, only this time they'd probably send her to prison.

She wondered who'd show up in Brazos Bend first. The *Globe*? The *National Enquirer*? Imagine the headlines: BABY DAGGER DRUGGER—AGAIN. She swallowed hard. "My fault. I should have known. You are a man, after all. You're just like . . . all of them."

He touched her arm. "Now, hold on a minute."

Maddie jerked away, then slammed the minivan's back door closed. She walked around to the driver's door. "Thanks for nothing, Callahan."

"Dammit to hell. I figured you might be difficult about this, but I didn't expect you to pack up your mushrooms and leave before I explained. Just slow down, Red. You came to me for help, so let me help you."

"Do *not* call me 'Red.'"

Sara-Beth watched the interchange with interest in her eyes and a smirk on her lips.

Luke shot her a scowl, then said, "Bee is an old friend, Maddie—"

"Obviously," she drawled.

Frustration flashed in his eyes, but she didn't care. She didn't want to hear his excuses. Didn't want to listen to his lies. A reporter. He'd called a lousy reporter!

"You want to go home, don't you?" Luke demanded, bracing his hands on his hips. "Well, Sara-Beth can fix it so you can."

Right. Home to paparazzi hell.

"I trust her, Maddie." Giving her a pointed look, he added, "The woman can keep secrets."

"That's right," Sara-Beth piped up. "I've never told anybody about the time Luke took me to Fort Worth and we—"

"Hush, Bee." Luke scooped the fishbowl out of Maddie's arms and pointed toward a trail leading into the woods. "There's a picnic table a hundred yards or so into the trees. It's private. We can talk there."

"Don't we need to wait for your cop?" Maddie asked, her voice dripping with poison.

"He'll show when he's ready."

Indecision gripped Maddie. Should she stay or cut her losses and leave? Make a run for it? Go on the lam?

Oh, God. She was sounding like a bad fifties movie.

When her gaze dropped to Oscar, Luke made the decision for her by tightening his hold on the fishbowl, then started walking toward the trees. Sara-Beth scampered right after him. Maddie hesitated, then when Luke glanced over his shoulder, she fell in behind them.

Sara-Beth chattered at Luke, asking about his brothers, sharing the story of how she'd bumped into Mark at a hill-country Dairy Queen last October. Maddie muttered about the perfidy and treachery of men, making sure she spoke loud enough for Luke to hear her.

Upon reaching the picnic table, Luke set Oscar's bowl in the center, directed the women to take a seat, then made a quick check around. "You here?"

As quiet as a wraith, a figure slipped from the woods and stepped out of the shadows. As she got a good look, Maddie's mouth gaped. She looked from the newcomer to Luke, then back to the newcomer again. Not just twins, but identical twins. Bet the daddies of Brazos Bend trembled with fear for their daughters when the Callahan brothers lived in town. "Mark Callahan, I presume?"

"Devil!" Sara-Beth squealed, then she launched herself at Luke's brother just as she had at Luke. They did the hug, twirl, and kiss thing. "I can't believe you're here. Look at you, you and Sin. You're still two peas in a pod, only . . . hunkier. So, Luke said he'd called a cop. Is that you? I thought you were in the army."

The Callahan brothers shared a brief but significant look before Mark said, "Not anymore. Darlin', I can't give you details. Let's just say I have federal connections, and I trust you'll forget you ever saw me here."

"I guess I owe you that, considering . . . ," she said with a sigh. To Maddie, she explained, "I was a bit of a wild child. These two saved my bacon a time or two."

Despite her best intentions—was she really going to put her faith in a man, in two men, again?—hope kindled within Maddie. Addressing Mark Callahan, she asked, "You're here to save my bacon?"

He grinned at her, the same boyish, sexy, knee-melting smile she'd seen on his brother's face, his eyes alight with the same devilish twinkle. "Honey, I'll be happy to handle your bacon any way you want."

Luke took a step closer to her. "You're here to deal with mushrooms and maybe murder. Bacon is my territory."

Maddie rolled her eyes as Sara-Beth croaked, "Murder?"

Luke turned to Sara-Beth and said, "Tell me what you know about Gus Grevas's death."

"Mr. Grevas?" Her brows arched; her eyes registered the connection. "You think he was murdered? That's crazy. He had a heart attack. Or maybe it was a stroke. Anyway, he was in the hospital when he died."

Luke shot a glance toward Maddie. "So it was natural causes?"

Sara-Beth shrugged. "Well, yes. I guess. He was at least in his seventies, maybe over eighty. No reason to question it."

Maddie gave Luke a pointed look. "I'm sure the cops wouldn't have requested an autopsy."

"Why would they?" Sara-Beth asked. "What's going on? Why does Maddie here need help from a reporter and a cop?"

Maddie watched Luke's eyes while he thought it through. Now that he'd seen the mushrooms for himself, he had to believe her. Would he or his brother pull some strings and have an autopsy ordered to prove Gus was murdered? If Mark Callahan was some sort of hush-hush government muckety-muck, and Luke was very-recently-former DEA, surely one of them could do that.

If Luke trusted she'd told the truth about everything. *If* he didn't believe her to be a pawn in one of his father's schemes.

The problem was that Maddie could see it from his point of view. She could understand how Luke might think that Branch Callahan was using her. Branch wouldn't go so far as drug dealing and murder to get his sons back to Brazos Bend, but the conniving old son of a gun wasn't above seizing the opportunity presented by the whole sordid mushroom mess. He hadn't sent Maddie to Terry Winston; he'd sent her to Luke. Had he hoped Maddie would appeal to his son's sense of duty? Appeal to his senses, period? Had Branch thought she might somehow be the lure he'd been looking for to get at least one of his boys back to town?

Maybe. Maddie wouldn't bet against the idea.

"I want to know the truth about Gus," Luke finally said.

"When's the funeral?" his brother asked.

The reporter shrugged. "I don't know."

"Can you find out for us?" Luke held his cell phone out to her. "Now?"

Now Sara-Beth folded her arms. "What's this about?"

"All in good time, Bee. We need to take it one step at a time, if you don't mind."

"I do mind. I want to know what's going on before I call anyone."

He offered up that charming smile that Maddie had come to be suspicious of. "Don't be difficult, please? Just make the call?"

Sara-Beth wrinkled her nose and stuck out her tongue at him while she pulled a cell phone from her shoulder bag and punched in a number. Maddie turned a belligerent look his way but kept quiet.

"Great," he observed to his brother. "Now they're both pissed at me."

It made Maddie's heart feel good.

Mark Callahan smirked and leaned against a cottonwood tree.

"Sure. Thanks, Ben," Sara-Beth said a few moments later. She thumbed the power button on her cell phone and said, "Well. I'm surprised. Apparently, there's a memorial service scheduled for this afternoon."

"That's fast," Luke said, frowning.

The reporter's instincts were on obvious alert as she added, "The body's already been cremated."

"That's real fast," Mark said.

"And real unfortunate." Luke dragged his hand down his whiskered jaw. "Without a body and short of a confession, murder can't be proved."

Maddie's heart sank. She'd been afraid of that.

"Uh, murder?" Sara-Beth's purse slipped from her shoulder.

"It would have been nice to have proof." Mark waved

away a yellow jacket circling around Sara-Beth's head, then handed her her purse. "However, the manner of Gus Grevas's death doesn't really affect our current business, does it?"

"What business, Devil?" Sara-Beth asked impatiently. She turned to Luke. "What does Gus Grevas have to do with your middle-of-the-night call to me?"

Luke shot Maddie a quick look, then said, "Someone was growing magic mushrooms in Grevas's house out at the lake. Maddie found them the day before yesterday. They're worth a lot of money."

"Which accounts for your earlier mention of mushrooms. So, how much is 'a lot'?"

Luke rolled his tongue around his mouth. "Millions."

"Really!" Sara-Beth drummed her acrylic fingernails on the picnic table and thought for a moment. "Whoa. You think there was something suspicious about Gus's death, don't you? You think that sweet old man was dealing drugs and somebody killed him? Come on, Luke. We're talking about Gus Grevas. He volunteered to cut the lawn at First Baptist Church once a week until his knees gave out on him just last year."

Maddie opened her mouth to answer, but something in Luke's expression stopped her, a patience that she hadn't seen from him herself. The reporter drummed her coral-colored nails some more. "Bee likes puzzles," Mark said to Maddie. "She's always been sharp. Top ten percent of our class. I expected her to end up working as an investigative reporter at a big-city newspaper."

Luke nodded. "Instead, after I broke her heart by leaving Brazos Bend, Jeff Branson caught her on the rebound and tricked her into marrying him. They now have three children, and she works part-time for the local paper."

"You're so full of it, Callahan," Sara-Beth murmured. "And you almost got me. You shouldn't have mentioned my kids. Look, I don't know what you have planned, but I don't think I want to get involved. I'm happy writing family fluff for the *Standard*."

"How old are your children?" Maddie asked.

"The boys are six and four. My little girl is two."

"Wait a minute, Bee," Luke chastised. "I told you I had a real story for you when I called. You wouldn't have left ol' Jeff in the middle of the night if you weren't willing to stir things up a bit at the *Standard*."

"I was mad at him," she said with a sniff. "You're his biggest hot button, and I was in the mood to push it."

Luke's lips twisted in a smirk. "Some things never change. Sara-Beth, I wouldn't propose anything that might harm you or your family. You should know that. What I propose is intended to keep everyone safe."

"Explain it to me."

To his brother, Luke said, "You'll find some jars in the back of Maddie's van."

"You want me to check for prints?"

"Yeah. If we're lucky, our grower will be on the jars and in the system."

"Priority?"

"Immediately. Plan A hinges on an ID."

"I'm on it."

Mark Callahan faded back into the trees, disappearing so quickly and quietly that he caught Maddie by surprise. "My car keys . . ." she began.

"He doesn't need them."

"Wow," Sara-Beth murmured. "You know the curiosity is going to kill me. What is he, Luke? Just give me a hint. Three little letters. FBI? CIA?"

"NYB."

None of your business, Maddie translated. Then, more interested in her own concerns than Mark Callahan's professional pedigree, she asked, "What's plan A? You said you intend to keep everybody safe, but I'd like to know, safe where? Brazos Bend? Or am I going to have to do this again?"

By "this" she meant disappear again. Did he intend to reveal her identity or not?

"Home to Brazos Bend," he said, the look in his eyes conveying the message that he understood what she was asking. "Now, let me tell Bee what's going on."

Luke explained how the mushrooms came to be in Maddie's possession. "At this point, we can't concern ourselves with the hows and whys of Gus's death. Our only goal is to fix it so that Maddie won't have drug dealers waiting for her when she goes home. Hopefully, Mark will get us a name and we can have him picked up before you cross the state line."

Sara-Beth turned to Maddie. "Why did you bring the stuff to Sin? Why not go straight to the Brazos Bend police?"

Luke didn't give Maddie a chance to answer. "My father told her to bring it here."

"Why? To meet up with Devil? I'll bet that means he's DEA. Am I right?"

"No." Luke shooed away a fly that buzzed around Oscar's bowl. "Remember that biker bar south of Miami?"

"I'll never forget it," Sara-Beth replied, wincing. "I've never been so scared in my life."

Turning to Maddie, she explained, "Jeff and I were on a second honeymoon headed for Key West when our car broke down somewhere south of Miami. We couldn't get a signal on our cell phone, so we walked until we found a bar. We went inside and . . . well . . . we knew right off we'd made a mistake. We were getting ready to make a run for it when Sin walked out of a back room."

"Bee, you need to know that I wasn't there to play pool with my friends like I told you," Luke said.

Her blue eyes widened. "Oh, God, Sin. Don't tell me Jeff was right. Tell me you're not a drug dealer!"

Luke couldn't help but laugh. "Your husband really doesn't like me, does he?" As an aside to Maddie, he added, "They'd wandered into the middle of an operation, and I had to talk fast to get them out of the bar and on their way without blowing my cover."

"Your cover?" Sara-Beth asked.

"I was working undercover that day, Bee. Mark's not DEA. That was my job."

"You?" The reporter's jaw dropped. She swayed away from the table. "As in the Drug Enforcement Administration?"

"Yeah, me."

"But you're . . . I don't . . . Wow." She shook her head. "That one I never expected. Your brothers, I can buy. They never seemed quite so . . . rebellious, I guess. But you?"

Sara-Beth folded her arms and studied him, her mind obviously working, until finally, she nodded. "So your father knew, of course. He's kept tabs on you and your brothers all this time. What surprises me is that he never bragged about it around town. He certainly never hesitates to boast about Matt's accomplishments at the Treasury Department. But I guess with you and Devil both working undercover—which I'm going to assume since no one's talking—Branch didn't want to put you at risk. And now his caregiver is at risk . . ."

Sara-Beth paused and flashed a smile toward Maddie. "A caregiver all her clients appear to adore, and Branch wants the best help available for her, so he sends her to you."

"It's one possible scenario," Luke agreed. "Only problem is, Branch's information isn't quite up-to-date. I quit the DEA earlier this month. I'm not in a position to help Maddie."

Sara-Beth frowned. "Why not?"

Maddie folded her arms and gave him a *yeah, why not?* arch of her brow.

"I have no authority to investigate this case. It's not my job."

"But it's your hometown."

"Which is why I called Mark. Look, between the two of us, we can make all the arrangements for Maddie to turn over the mushrooms."

"And promptly be hauled off to jail?" Maddie snapped.

He held her gaze with a steady stare. "No. Explanations will be made ahead of time. There won't be any trouble."

Sara-Beth dug a notepad and pen from her purse. "What's my part in this plan of yours, Sin? If y'all can do the legal thing, why do you need a reporter?"

"Insurance. I want you to take pictures and publish a front-page story about Maddie's part in the haul. If you'll make it clear that she"—he ticked off the points on his fingers—"no longer has the mushrooms, doesn't have a clue about how they came to be in Gus's lake house to begin with, and has no plans to pursue the question any further, that should make it safe for her to go home whether we arrest the grower or not. With everything out in the open, I seriously doubt anyone will give her any trouble."

"Seriously doubt!" Maddie exclaimed. "You want me to risk my life based on serious doubt?"

"Maddie, considering what we all know of Brazos Bend, it's a fair assumption that we're not talking about folks like the Mendoza cartel, who wouldn't think twice about slitting your throat if you touched their property."

"I don't think that helps, Sin," Sara-Beth observed.

"If your suspicions are correct and the cops are involved—"

"Cops?" Sara-Beth squeaked.

"—I think that only makes you safer. Unless you go back to Brazos Bend and start snooping around and getting in the bad guys' way, they'll leave you alone."

"So we're just supposed to let the murderers get away with it?" Maddie demanded.

"Cops?" Sara-Beth repeated.

"There'll be an investigation into the drugs, Maddie. We will see to it. Maybe these guys won't go down for murder, but they'll go down."

"What about Gus's warning? If the cops are dirty—"

"Wait just one minute!" Sara-Beth exclaimed. "No more until somebody clues me in to the cop comment. Are you saying that the Brazos Bend police are involved in this? On the *wrong* side? Oh, wow. This *is* a story." After a moment's pause, she added, "Too much story. Murder and cops in Brazos Bend. This could be big. Huge."

"Dangerous," Luke warned.

She frowned at him a long moment, then sighed. "Yeah. Dangerous. Not where I want to go at this time in my life. Besides, I work for the *Brazos Bend Standard*, not the *Washington Post*. The only investigative reporting I've done involves the ingredients of the secret sauce Wilson's puts on their hamburgers."

"You have that recipe?" Luke asked, interest lighting his eyes.

"I can't do anything that might put my family at risk."

"You don't need to, Bee. I'm not asking for an investigative piece. In fact, I'm specifically asking you not to do an investigative piece. Make it a strictly general interest story with no mention of Maddie's suspicions or Gus's wild rambling or the Callahan brothers' involvement. That way, everyone stays safe."

"It goes against everything I learned in journalism school," Sara-Beth muttered.

Luke gave her hand a quick squeeze. "Maybe so, but you'll get an A-plus in mommy school. Tell you what, I'll do what I can to make sure you get the scoop when they bust these bastards. Hell, maybe you can write a book."

Maddie rolled her eyes. Sara-Beth smiled. Luke gazed from one woman to the other. "This will work. I'm sure of it."

Sara-Beth studied her fingernails. "I should be thrown in journalism jail even for thinking about doing a puff piece about this."

"But you'll do it?"

"I'll do it. Only because I love you, Sin Callahan. And I owe you for not telling Jeff about . . . well . . . you know."

"So, it's settled? Maddie? Are you on board with this plan?"

Did it really matter whether she was or not? She had no other choice. At least he hadn't told his girlfriend who she was. She leaned over, tapped her forehead against the table once, twice, three times. "I can't believe this is happening to me."

Luke reached out and stroked her hair as Mark Callahan came strolling toward them on the trail. "I have a name."

"Already?" Sara-Beth gave her dark hair a toss. "I don't believe that. Nobody gets information . . . whoa . . . are you Homeland Security?"

"Who is it?" Luke and Maddie demanded simultaneously.

"I printed two jars and found two sets of prints on both. Maddie's, and Gus's son, Jerry's."

"Jerry Grevas!" Maddie exclaimed. "But he's an accountant."

"With a record, apparently?" Luke asked his brother.

"One arrest for pot when he was young. Apparently he liked to grow things even then."

"I can't believe it's Jerry." Maddie massaged her brow. "He's really a nice guy. He loved his father. He treated him so well. Why would he murder his own father?"

"What about the cops?" Sara-Beth demanded. "How are they involved?"

"Maybe they're not," Maddie said, a great weight lifting from her heart. "Gus was babbling, panicked. When he said don't trust the cops, rather than meaning they're involved, maybe he was telling me not to get them involved. Maybe he was trying to protect Jerry." She met Luke's stare. "I wasn't in danger, after all."

That observation hung in the air for a long minute.

"Maybe not. Unless things have changed a whole lot in the years that I've been gone, that makes more sense than the existence of a drug ring in the BBPD. But you were running on adrenaline, and you had good reason to worry. Didn't help that you were egged on by my old man."

"So I can go home."

Luke addressed his brother. "They're picking him up?"

"I understand Chief Harper has a car on the way even as we speak."

"How did you do that so fast?" Sara-Beth exclaimed. "I'm not sure I like that, to be honest. This has a real Big Brother feel."

"You can go home," Luke told Maddie. "After we take care of the little detail of disposing of millions of dollars of psilocybin mushrooms in such a way that keeps you square with the law. And, to be on the safe side, I'd like to see you give Bee a chance to publish her article before you return— without mentioning me or Mark, by the way—just in case Jerry had a helper we don't know about."

"I've been needing to make a shopping run to Dallas anyway. I could take a couple days."

"That'd be a good idea."

"Have you been to the import district on Harry Hines Boulevard recently?" Sara-Beth asked her. "You won't believe the upgrading they've done in that end of town."

The brothers discussed arrangements for a few minutes, then both men stepped away and spent some time making private calls on their cell phones. When they finished, they conferred another few minutes, then Luke turned to Maddie. "It's all set. You're to take the contraband to a field office in Tyler. Agent Flores will meet you. He's a good guy, photogenic for your shots, Bee. Flores will make sure all the *i*'s are dotted and *t*'s are crossed so that none of this will come back to haunt you."

"Aren't you coming with us, Sin?" Sara-Beth asked.

He hesitated and Maddie's heart took a dip. *No, he's not. Of course he's not.* What had gotten into her, thinking that he might go along? He'd made it perfectly clear that he was going fishing come hell or high water or magic mushrooms.

At least she hadn't slept with him. She still had that bit of dignity.

She lifted her chin and pasted on a smile. "I'm a big girl. I can handle it from here. Luke's been a tremendous help to me, though, and I do appreciate it." She paused a moment and added sincerely, bravely, "I do."

The look in her eyes damn near broke Luke's heart. He glanced at his brother and Sara-Beth. "Give us a minute?"

"Sure," Mark said. "I wanted to get a look at the *Miss*

Behavin' II before I headed out, anyway. Bee, you want to come with me?"

The reporter shook her head, her eyes alight with that feminine gleam of nosiness that reared its head whenever romance floated in the air. "No, thanks. I need to duck into the ship store. When I was in there earlier I noticed some rubber alligator toys my kiddos will love. Since I left in the middle of the night without saying good-bye, I know better than to go home without peace offerings in hand."

Luke waited until the pair had disappeared from sight before moving to take a seat beside the woman who'd blown into his life like a springtime tornado. Unable to resist the urge to touch her, he played his fingers through her hair. The fiery strands flowed across his fingers like silk. "Maddie, when you came looking for Terry, what sort of help did you expect?"

"I don't know. I wanted her—well, him—to fix it. I don't know how. Everything was such a mess, a panic. I hadn't thought it all through. It's just . . . I really like it there. It's finally home. A real home. You can't understand what it's like for me. How much it means."

"I know what home is, Maddie. I've not forgotten. But Brazos Bend isn't my home anymore, and this isn't my job anymore. I can't do it anymore. I'm toast. Terry . . ."

"I'm sorry about your partner." She smiled sadly and added, "For both our sakes."

"You really thought he'd return to Brazos Bend with you?"

She nodded. "I did. Branch said . . ." She stopped and shook her head. "I'm still learning to be independent. It's not something I was taught since birth. I guess I wanted a white knight riding to the rescue. Wearing a skirt, of course."

"If Terry had a grave, he'd be turning in it after hearing that one," Luke observed with a smile. "Not over the white knight bit. That fit him to a tee. The skirt is something else entirely."

After a moment's pause, he added, "I'm different from Terry, Red. I'm not your knight. I don't ride a white horse and armor makes me itch. I won't go back to Brazos Bend."

"But—"

"Branch spotted an opportunity and tried to use it to his advantage. He tried to manipulate us both. I can't let him do that to me. There's too much water under our bridge."

"Too much male pride, you mean. Too little forgiveness."

"Maybe so."

Silence hung between them like a black cloud in the wake of that concession. Luke didn't know what else to say to her, and yet, he wanted to say something. He wanted to say that he wished he'd met her at another time, under other circumstances. He wanted to tell her . . . hell . . . he didn't want to tell her good-bye.

Hearing a crashing sound approaching from the direction of the marina, Luke looked up to see Knucklehead bounding toward them, a mangled athletic shoe in his mouth. He dropped the shoe at Luke's feet. Good dog. Good distraction. "You looking to play fetch, boy?"

He threw the shoe and Knucklehead galloped after it, then brought it back. They played the game twice more before Maddie pasted on another one of those damned fake smiles and took a step toward the path. "Well. We probably should go looking for the others. Your brother likely has a country to go save, and Sara-Beth might need help carrying all her loot from the ship store."

"Yeah. Yeah. In a minute." He took her by the arm to stop her. "I want to say . . . I need to tell you . . . Ah, hell."

He raked his free hand through his hair, scowling in frustration. "Goddammit. I wish you wouldn't stand there looking like Bambi's mother. I have no reason to feel guilty here."

"No, you don't."

"I didn't tell the others about the rock-and-roll stuff," he pointed out.

"I noticed and I do appreciate it, Luke." Maddie again gave that plastic smile. "I finally have a home in Brazos Bend. A real home. Thank you for helping me to keep it."

He waited to feel a sense of satisfaction, but instead came the certainty that he was fucking up. Ruthlessly, he quashed that. Fucking up would have been sleeping with her. He had the sneaking suspicion that had he done that, she'd haunt him for a very long time, if not forever.

Then Maddie, damn her, extended her hand for a handshake. A handshake! "Good-bye, Luke. It was nice to meet you, and I do appreciate your assistance. I hope you and your brother have a wonderful fishing trip."

He stared at her hand, his heart pounding. He felt as if he stood at the edge of a cliff and he wanted—God, he wanted—to take a flying leap off into the madness.

Self-preservation won, to a point. He didn't leap, but he did lean. He took the hand she proffered and tugged her into his arms, then captured her mouth with his, telling her good-bye without words, words he felt but couldn't form.

He sank his fingers into her hair and let the emotion flow. He wanted her desperately, but he couldn't cross that line. If only he'd met her somewhere else—a different time, a different place.

If only . . .

She moaned into his mouth and he growled low in his throat in return. Finally, when he reached the point where he considered laying her back upon the picnic table, he broke off the kiss with a curse.

He took a step back, clenched his fists at his sides, and stood staring at her, breathing heavily. "Maddie, I don't . . . I wish . . . oh, hell."

Her breaths weren't all that steady, either, and the glimmer in her eyes told him she had wishes, too. But the woman proved stronger than he. She managed to gain control, and this time, Maddie Kincaid was the instigator of the kiss. A quick, up-on-her-tiptoes buss on the cheek. "I'll think of you. Good thoughts. You didn't lie to me. You didn't use me. That's a first for me, Luke Callahan. It's a gift. Something I can take into the future. Who knows, maybe there's a knight out there for me, after all."

Son of a bitch.

Seven

In a parking lot outside a nondescript office building in Tyler, Texas, Maddie gazed with satisfaction at her mini-van's empty cargo space, then slammed the back door shut. "Well, that's it, I guess."

Sara-Beth Branson tucked her camera and notepad back into a canvas tote bag while frowning at Maddie's van. "I hope that rotten vegetable smell doesn't linger."

"I plan to stop at the first store I see to buy air freshener. Think I'll drop my clothes back at the dry cleaners before I take them home, too."

"You might as well throw away that mop head while you're at it, I'm afraid. But I'll bet if you drive with the windows down, it'll be all right by the time you hit Dallas."

Maddie nibbled her bottom lip, then said, "Man, I hope so. That drive from Caddo Bayou almost killed me."

Sara-Beth studied her fingernails. "Or was it leaving Sin that put those tears in your eyes?"

Ugh.

"I wasn't crying," Maddie defended. "Really. I wasn't."

"Wistful" was a good word for her state of mind when she pulled away from Caddo Bayou Marina, Mark Callahan saluting from the flybridge of the *Miss Behavin' II*, his twin brother staring moodily from the edge of the trees. Sin and Devil. Pure temptation.

"I wouldn't blame you if you did weep a bit. I certainly

did when Luke and I parted ways. I thought my life was going to end."

"How long were you together?" she asked, trying to rise above the stab of envy she felt. Not that she truly wanted to hear about Luke and Sara-Beth's romance. She simply couldn't resist . . .

"Nine wondrous months," Sara-Beth replied on a sigh. "My freshman year in high school. I'm telling you, I was the envy of every freshman girl. My father was fit to be tied. He used to get really bad gas every time Luke came to pick me up for a date. Fathers." She rolled her eyes. "I swear that Jeff will be just the same when our Kristen grows up. You know how fathers are."

Actually, she didn't. Blade had made a stab at acting like a traditional father during those sweet months their little family lived in Kansas, but even giving it his best effort, he never quite pulled it off. Not even Maddie's mother could convince him that offering Maddie's elementary school principal a toke on parent's night wasn't the thing to do.

Curiosity pricking like a thorn, Maddie fished in her purse for her keys as she asked, "So, what broke you and Luke up?"

"He refused to sleep with me."

Maddie's keys slipped from her grip and clunked to the hot asphalt of the parking lot. "Sin Callahan?"

Sara-Beth's eyes sparkled. "Not what you'd think, is it? He had such a reputation. Do you know that he and his brothers kept a rented party house out by the lake? No adults knew about it. Then there were the road trips. The Callahan boys would load up their friends and drive to Mexico and the whorehouses almost once a month. My best friend's sister's boyfriend told her they all were having sex by the time they were fourteen. And Luke was sixteen when he dated me. Everyone thought we were doing it, of course, and they asked me about it all the time. I had to lie. It's hard for a virgin to lie about sex, I'll have you know. Well, a fifteen-year-old virgin. That's why he wouldn't do it. Said I was jailbait and he'd wait. Except, he wasn't waiting—those trips to Mexico, you know."

"He cheated on you." Disapproval mixed with a measure of disappointment rolled through Maddie on a wave. She hated cheaters. Despised them. For all the harm the Terrible Trio had done to her, that's one sin they'd never committed. Of course, they hadn't been named Sin, either.

"I don't think it's fair to say that," Sara-Beth replied. "We weren't going steady. I dated other guys, too, but I was a heartless girl and if Luke asked me out, I'd break my other date to be with him. I did that a couple times with Jeff, in fact. That's why Luke is such a touchy subject with him, even after all these years."

Maddie felt a twinge of sympathy for ol' Jeff. "He won in the end, though, didn't he?"

Sara-Beth beamed. "That's what I tell him."

The office building's front door opened and Hector Flores walked outside carrying a fistful of papers. A Hispanic man in his midfifties, Hector was small, round, and jolly, and in his flashy red vest, he reminded Maddie more of Santa Claus on a tropical vacation than of a federal agent.

"You're all set, missy," he said, handing her the processed forms. "Next time you see Callahan, be sure and pass along my thanks. I don't know who he contacted in what part of the government, but I've never seen anything get shoved through the system so fast. Not only is all the paperwork done, but the Brazos Bend police already have the subject in custody, too."

At that piece of news, a weight rolled off of Maddie's shoulders. "I'm *so* glad to hear that."

"Me, too," Sara said. "That'll be a great way to end my piece, then I can do a follow-up once I've returned to town." She extended her arm for a handshake. "Thanks, Hector. You've been a joy to work with. I've never known law enforcement to be so cooperative with the press."

"I wanted to make sure you got a flattering picture of me to put in your paper."

"I'm certain I have that one covered."

Maddie glanced through the papers she'd been handed. Spying something from the Board of Pardon and Paroles, she paused and read the paper more carefully. *Oh, my God.* Her gaze jerked up to meet the agent's. She'd been released.

"Friends in high places apparently decided one good turn deserves another," he said.

"I don't have any friends in high places."

He nodded toward the papers. "You do now."

"What good turn?" Sara-Beth, ever the reporter, demanded.

Maddie tensed and she shot a pleading gaze toward the agent. *Please don't blow my cover, not now!*

She held her breath as Hector Flores nodded toward the documents. "Texas has a program that offers rewards to those who turn over contraband. Maddie's getting five hundred dollars."

"That's cool." Sara-Beth grabbed her notepad and jotted a few more notes.

Sure enough, Maddie flipped through the papers again and spied the reward authorization, too. "Hector, you're a doll. I can't tell you how much this all means to me."

"And I can't tell you how nice it's been to work on a positive project for a change. Now, you both have my number. Feel free to call if you have any problems."

As Hector Flores returned to his office, Sara-Beth hit the remote on her key chain. In the next row over, a horn beeped on a huge pickup truck. "I'm going to hit the road. I need to be home in time for Jeff's slow-pitch game. We're playing the Rattlers tonight and I want to be there to watch my team beat their butts."

"Sara-Beth, I can't tell you how much I appreciate your help."

"Happy to do it. I've enjoyed the whole thing. I haven't seen Mark and Luke since John's memorial service, and it was a real pleasure to see those Callahan boys again. Don't you know I'm going to spend hours on end trying to solve the puzzle of who Mark works for? And I've been worried for years that Luke was dealing drugs in south Florida. It's nice to know I can let that one go. Plus, I got to know you and I'm happy as a clam about that. I like you, Maddie Kincaid. I'm glad you've settled in Brazos Bend. Want to meet for lunch one day next week?"

Happiness put a warm smile on her face. "I'd love that."

Maddie watched Sara-Beth climb into her truck, and she smiled again at the incongruous sight of such a petite woman driving such a monstrous vehicle. They shared a wave as Sara-Beth drove off, then Maddie got into her own car and started the engine.

She was on the interstate before it all sank in. She was free. No more trips to Fort Worth to meet her parole officer. No more reason to fear every time a policeman met her eyes. And just maybe, no more middle-of-the-night flashbacks about Leering Lurk, one of the guards at the Woodman unit.

All because of Luke Callahan.

As Maddie blended into the constant stream of traffic traveling between Tyler and the Dallas–Fort Worth metroplex, her mind was back in the bayou.

She'd misjudged the man.

It was true. Maybe he was Sin and all of that, and he probably was the love-'em-and-leave-'em type, but at least he didn't use her for who she was, rat her out to the press—or worse, the tabloids. He didn't try to cozy up to Blade's daughter to meet the rock star. In fact, he didn't seem all that impressed with the whole rock scene. He wasn't after her money, and even if he hadn't been wealthy in his own right—a result of a technology investment recommended by his brother John, according to Branch—Luke didn't strike Maddie as the type to live off a woman. Apparently, there was more to Luke "Sin" Callahan than a sly grin and bedroom eyes.

A bad boy with layers. Who would have thought?

When her cell phone rang, she almost didn't look to see the number. Already, the missed-call message listed forty-seven calls. Today. All from the same number. Today. That didn't count the fifty-three that accumulated yesterday.

Branch Callahan could stew a little longer. Despite the fact that everything turned out fine—all right, wonderful—in the end didn't mean that she was ready to forgive him for the lie about "Terri" Winston.

Yet, part of her couldn't ignore the ring. What if . . . No, Luke wouldn't call. He'd said good-bye. Wow, had he said good-bye.

Her ringtone continued to sound the Swords version of "Born to be Wild." She picked up the phone and checked the number. With a smile in her voice, she connected the call and said, "Hi, Dad."

"Baby D!" crooned a voice through the phone. "How's my girl?"

Maddie laughed. "You wouldn't believe me if I told you."

"What's going on, love? My people said you called."

She decided this story could wait until circumstances were more conducive to relaying a long, involved tale. "It's nothing, Dad. Just a little excitement in Brazos Bend I thought I'd share."

He gave a disinterested snort, just as she'd anticipated. Her father didn't understand or approve of her decision to "bury herself in a boring little backward Texas town." He was insulted that she preferred to "putter around about blue hairs and old billy goats" than live with him and share his lifestyle.

"How was the photo safari? Did you get some good shots?"

He launched into a tale of beavers and bear that promised to last awhile, so Maddie exited the interstate and stopped her car in a fast-food restaurant parking lot, then settled in to listen. The man had always had a way with words, and Blade painted a picture of Alaska that put her right in the middle of it. So caught up was she in the wilderness that it came as quite a shock when he abruptly said, "Want to meet me for dinner at Nikki's? I'm in the mood for Italian."

Nikki's was Blade's favorite Italian restaurant in Tribeca. "Where are you, Dad?"

"Somewhere over Canada. We're due in at LaGuardia in a couple of hours. Say you'll meet me, Baby D. I'll call for a plane for you the minute we hang up. It's been too long since I've seen you."

The offer tempted her. She couldn't go home yet and she did miss her father. He'd pamper her, ply her with gifts. He'd sponsor a day at a spa if she asked.

Surrounded by the stench of rotting mushrooms, mindful of the grilling she'd get from Branch and Kathy and the clients who didn't like substitute caregivers, Maddie thought the idea of escape sounded especially sweet.

It wouldn't be running away. Okay, maybe it would be. A little bit. Mainly, though, it'd be a quick trip to see her dad. That, and to try and forget Luke Callahan.

Right. Like that would happen. Nevertheless, a little getaway might be just the thing to repair the little chip Luke had carved out of her fragile heart.

Maddie decided she was of a mood to ask for that day at the spa. She was ready to spruce herself up, to pamper herself. She was ready to celebrate her freedom. "Just dinner, Daddy, or could I talk you into spending a few days in the city with me?"

"You'll come?" he responded, delight obvious in his voice. "Ah, Baby, that's fabulous, just fabulous. I'm thrilled."

They discussed the arrangements for a few minutes, including a surprise her father said he'd have waiting for her. Maddie disconnected the call with a light heart and anticipation singing in her veins. This was good, just the distraction she needed.

Surely a few days in New York City with her father would wipe all thoughts of a bayou boat cruise with a hardbodied skipper from her mind.

"For God's sake, he's doing it again." Matt Callahan stretched out his long legs from his captain's chair aboard the *Siren Song*, then propped his canvas deck shoes atop the nearby beer cooler and crossed his feet at the ankles. A strong southwesterly breeze kept the boat rocking and threatened to blow the Texas Aggies baseball cap off his head as he observed, "Mark, did you ever think you'd see the day that our little brother would rather brood about a broad than fish?"

Mark Callahan checked the tension on his line, frowned, and adjusted his reel. "Never. I wouldn't believe it if I wasn't seeing it with my own two eyes."

Standing at the stern of the boat gazing at the muddy swells of the Gulf of Mexico, Luke flipped his brothers the bird.

"Although," Mark continued. "I can't really blame him. You should have seen the broad, Matt. A real looker, that one. Redheaded and built like a brick shithouse. Her eyes went all bedroomy whenever she looked at Luke, too."

"Now, that I believe." Matt scratched his chin, bristled from a four-day-old beard. "He always did attract the easy lays."

"Shut the hell up," Luke snapped. "Maddie's not like that. She's . . ." His voice trailed off when he spied the knowing look his brothers exchanged. "Oh, bite me, assholes."

Unable to leave it alone, Mark leaned forward, propping his elbows on his knees, and asked, "She's what? How did she do it? You spent, what, a day and a half with her, and you're suddenly calling in markers I thought would never see the light of day? We spent a lot of political capital on Maddie Kincaid. The governor was my ace in the hole."

"Get over it," Luke snapped. "It wasn't any skin off your nose to do a few favors for me. Besides, the governor is still in our pocket. Between that problem you handled with his wife and the fact I got his stupid kid off an ecstasy rap and into rehab, he still owes us plenty."

"True." Then, to Luke's surprise, Mark turned serious. "I know we all decided a long time ago that we wouldn't keep score, but that doesn't mean I don't realize how much I owe you. I'm in the unit because of you. This work . . . well . . . you know how much it means to me."

Matt gruffly cleared his throat. "It means that much to all of us." He lifted his beer bottle. "For Johnny."

For just a moment, their missing brother's spirit was alive and strong among them. Then Mark continued, "But you've never asked for help before, Luke. Not even during the worst of the Miami mess. Why now? Why with rock-and-roll royalty, for God's sake?"

Luke turned away from the water and shoved Matt's feet off the cooler. He flipped open the lid and pulled a bottle of water from the ice. "That's just it. She doesn't want to be a princess. She wants to be a girl next door."

"Ahh. Now I understand. She's a rebel. No wonder she appeals to you."

"Not a rebel. She just wants to be left alone. Hell, you read the papers. She's had some hard knocks."

"Knocks she brought on herself," Matt put in. "Bad checks. Bad decisions."

"Bad asshole boyfriends," Luke said. "I made some calls, and from what I learned, that's a big part of her problem. She got herself talked into all kinds of stuff by three dickheads."

Mark fished in the cooler and brought out a bottle of water and a beer. "You know, I never really thought about it before, but it's kind of sad. Hell, her father wrote a song giving her grief for everything wrong in the world. Christ, she was just a kid."

"'Baby's to Blame,'" Matt mused. "Number one hit, wasn't it?"

Luke twisted the cap off the water bottle and took a long pull. "Look, you're making this into a bigger deal than it is. The woman was in trouble and I decided to help her. Now, what do you say we get the grill fired up? My mouth's been watering for that snapper ever since Matt yanked it aboard."

His brothers let the subject drop while they prepared their meal. Mark and Matt argued over seasoning the fish while

Luke cut up vegetables to grill. Once the food was on the fire, he broke out one of the special bottles of wine he'd brought and conversation degenerated into general sibling bickering.

All in all, it was a damned fine time. The brothers laughed and joked and verbally jabbed at one another as they enjoyed their meal, then listened in companionable quiet to the satellite radio broadcast of an exciting eighth inning between the Rangers and the Yankees. A balmy, easy sea breeze kept the temperature comfortable, the boat rocking gently as the sun sank toward the sea, painting the sky in swaths of vermillion and gold.

As the lower edge of the sun dipped below the watery horizon, Matt reached over and switched off the radio. He cracked open a bottle of the Macallan and poured four glasses. Then the three brothers stood shoulder to shoulder, silent and somber, and watched until the last bit of light winked out.

They tossed back their whisky, then each took a sip from the fourth, Matt going last and polishing it off. He handed the empty glass to Luke, who reared back and threw it as hard and as far as he could.

Luke exhaled a heavy sigh.

Matt muttered, "This sucks."

Mark murmured, "It doesn't get a damned bit easier, does it?"

"Actually, it does," Luke said. "Having you here this year makes it easier." Last year on the third anniversary of their brother John's memorial service, Mark had been on a mission on the far side of the world and unable to join Matt and Luke on their "family" day. He hadn't been sure he'd be able to hang around this year until he got a call the night before the *Miss Behavin' II* rendezvoused with the *Siren Song*.

The tradition of getting together to make a stab at a family holiday of sorts dated back to their fifth year away from Brazos Bend. That's when John used his computer skills to track his siblings down and reunite them. Unable to spend any traditional holidays together, they'd decided to designate a summer weekend each year when they'd do their damnedest to show up. Over the years they'd done a decent job of keeping the date. Assignments caused Luke to miss twice, Mark three times. Matt made it every year, as had John, up until his death. It'd been at his memorial service, the first and only time the Callahan brothers returned to Brazos Bend, that the three surviving siblings decided to hold their holiday that same time every year.

Their father specifically wasn't invited.

"With this day coming on top of Terry's funeral, I admit I was dreading today," Luke added, throwing his own glass out into the gulf. "But it turned out okay. Considering that it sucked."

Mark chucked his glass overboard. "Considering that."

Matt lobbed his after his brothers', then dropped a little bomb. "Langley thinks they have a lead on Ćurković."

Mark and Luke both went as stiff as fence posts. About a year ago, the CIA had identified Ćurković as the sick son of a bitch who'd ordered John's kidnapping and subsequent murder. "Where?" Luke demanded.

"Pakistan."

"You in on this one, Matt?"

Matt scowled. "They're telling me no. The leg's still not worth a damn. The bullet did more damage than I realized. I'm holding out hope, but I suspect my bosses will try to make my Treasury Department job fact rather than fiction."

Mark rubbed the back of his neck. "Who could I contact to . . . ?"

"Won't happen." Matt shook his head. "The politics of this one make it dicey. This team will be strictly official."

Knucklehead emerged from the cabin where he'd been sleeping, padded over to Luke, and plopped down beside him. Scratching the dog behind the ears, Luke said, "Does the old man know?"

"Branch?" Matt asked. At his brother's nod, he shrugged.

"Honestly, I haven't a clue. I've been trying to figure out his source for years."

"What does it matter if he knows or not?" Mark said with a sneer. "He doesn't do a goddamned thing with his information, now, does he?"

Mark didn't have to explain his remark. Matt and Luke knew just what he was talking about. The ransom demand arrived by e-mail the same day John was taken hostage. Rather than contact the son who was on the CIA's payroll, or the son who at the time was working in military intelligence, or even the one who hung with bad-ass South American drug dealers who could teach political terrorists a trick or two, Branch Callahan called his inept congressman for help.

Three weeks later, John was dead, and Matt, Mark, and Luke learned about the debacle after the fact. The Callahan brothers had come to understand and even accept their father's reasons for cutting them off financially after the boot-factory fire. They'd been worthless, rich-kid a-holes who hadn't had a clue about the real world until forced to deal with it on their own. They wouldn't argue that by making them make it on their own, Branch had made men out of all four of them.

However, they'd never forgive him for failing to turn to them, to trust them, when it counted. They'd never forgive him for ignoring the men they'd become, men who had the tools and connections to give John a fighting chance.

Instead, he'd listened to a good-old-boy congressman from Odessa, Texas, and John, the best of all of them, had paid the ultimate price.

"How about we change the subject," Luke suggested. "If I have to think about Branch Callahan too much longer, I'm liable to lose my dinner, and that fish was too good to waste."

His brothers shared a look and a shrug, then Mark said, "Fine by me. I was hoping to take the conversation back to the girl, anyway. I've been thinking about this all day. So which is it? Are those perky, plump boobs of hers the real thing, or are they plastic?"

Luke recalled the feel of her breasts crushed against his chest. He knew he was being a pig to answer the question, but these were his brothers, after all, and they'd been talking about girls this way as long as he could remember. "Oh, they're real."

"So you *did* sleep with her!"

"Nope." He gave a slow, wistful smile. "Came close, but . . ."

"Close only counts in horseshoes," Matt observed.

"Tell me about it."

Mark shook his head and clicked his tongue as he reached down to pet Knucklehead, whose tail thwapped against the fishing boat's deck. "My sympathies, bro."

"She's that fine?" Matt asked.

The twin brothers shared a look, then both nodded.

"What about her legs?"

Mark considered. "Showgirl quality. Even better than her boobs."

"Damn, boy." Matt shook his head at Luke. "What the hell are you doing here with us?"

Luke frowned. It was one thing to give his brothers a hint of Maddie's appeal, but another thing to discuss it in detail. He didn't like it. Didn't like hearing them talk about her like, well, like guys.

This was something new for him.

Luke rubbed the back of his neck. In the past, he'd have given them play-by-play from first base to home. This time he didn't want them knowing a damn thing. He didn't want them thinking about Maddie that way. The woman was . . . special. She was . . . his.

Well, hell.

"Hmm . . ." Matt scratched his whiskers. "Okay, then, here's the deal breaker. What about her butt?"

"Her butt!" Luke exclaimed. "Now, hold on just a damned minute."

"She's got a fine ass," Mark contributed helpfully. "Nice and rounded but not too big. A good handful."

"Excellent." Matt sat back with a satisfied smile. "Nice image to take to bed. My fantasy life has needed some new material."

"You two peckerheads need to keep your dirty minds off of Maddie Kincaid's . . . attributes."

"Why?" Mark asked, his expression full of innocence. "You might have had first dibs, Luke, but you released her back into play. She's a Brazos Bend girl, and you're not going back there. Remember?"

"Neither are you."

"I am," Matt piped up. "I plan to go back regularly."

"The hell you say," Matt's brothers simultaneously chimed.

Mark added, "What the hell for?"

"Business. I visited Brazos Bend just last week, in fact. Under the old man's radar." While his brothers tried to wrap their minds around that bit of betrayal, Matt dropped his second bombshell of the day. "I bought land there."

"What!"

"Wait a minute." Luke held up his hand and gave his head a shake. "Hold on just a bit. I know you enjoy jerking me and Mark around, but how about you take this from the top? What have you done, Matt?"

For a few seconds, it was a toss-up whether he'd continue his infuriating teasing or offer up the truth. Luke saw Matt's decision in the gleam of his eyes, then heard it in his voice when he said, "I need a home."

"In Brazos Bend?"

"Near Brazos Bend. I bought the Double R ranch. Les Warfield and I are well on the way to establishing a vineyard and winery there."

The Double R ranch was owned by Randolph Rawlings, Branch's number one rival back in the day. Their father hated Rawlings with a passion. Positively despised him. They'd wrangled over oil leases and political races and horseflesh, to name a few points of contention. As a rule, Branch came out on top, but the one thing he couldn't win, couldn't wrestle away from Randolph Rawlings, was the prettiest section of land in Palo Pinto County.

Mark laughed. "Holy shit, that'll drive the old man crazy."

"Especially when he learns Randolph wouldn't sell it to me until I signed a sworn affidavit that Branch Callahan wasn't allowed to step foot on the property."

"I can't believe he'd sell it. Figured he'd keep it in the family for his son."

"Austin inherited his wife's property along the Pedernales when she died a few years back. Since his interests lie in politics and law rather than land, he didn't care that his father kept this property. Honestly, I doubt Randolph would have sold it to anyone but me. He did it just to chap Branch's hide."

"I always liked old man Rawlings," Luke observed. Then he grinned. "It's perfect, Matt. Suits you to a tee. A farmer."

"If I can't be a spy . . ."

Luke understood both the tone and the sentiment. "Hey, I'm retired now, myself. If you need an extra pair of feet when it comes grape-stomping time, I'm your man."

"So, you'll go back to Brazos Bend?"

"I'd go to your ranch. Hell, I'd have to see it for myself. Matt Callahan's grape ranch."

Mark snorted at the term, then the three brothers spent some time discussing Matt's plan for the vineyard, Luke's post-DEA plans, and Mark's concerns about his upcoming assignment. Eventually, talk turned to recent events in Brazos Bend and Ms. Maddie Kincaid.

"I wonder what got into Jerry Grevas," Mark mused. "He never seemed the type to get into drugs."

Matt nodded. "I'll bet it hit Gus by surprise. Poor old guy. He doted on that boy."

"I figure I'll give the Brazos Bend Police Department a

call in a week or so, see what, if anything, they'll tell me about the case," Luke said.

"Checking up on your woman?"

Luke opened his mouth to deny that Maddie was his anything, but the words wouldn't quite come. He hated feeling this damned uncertain. "I always follow up on my cases."

"You have a case all right." Mark smirked. "A case on Baby Dagger."

Suddenly bored with the conversation, Luke ended it like he'd begun it. He gave his brothers the middle-finger salute.

Eight

After landing at DFW Airport, Maddie took a cab to the Fort Worth auto dealer where she'd left her van for mushroom detox. She breathed deeply of the fresh, new-car smell and decided she'd have her car detailed more often. She tossed her purse onto the passenger-side floorboard, belted Oscar—now back in his fishbowl after making the plane trip from New York in a plastic bag inside a small cooler—into the passenger seat, and set her cell phone and a bottle of water in the console beside her, then headed west. She experienced a déjà vu moment when her phone rang before she'd cleared Fort Worth.

Again she debated. Again curiosity got the best of her. She picked the phone up, checked the number. "Branch Callahan. Imagine that."

She had to give the man points for dogged determination. He worked the redial button on his phone better than he did his TV remote.

"Well, you can just wait, Branch Callahan," she murmured, checking the display of missed calls. Twenty-seven. The first screen showed two different numbers. Branch's and Blade's. She dropped the phone back onto the console without checking the numbers further. "You and my father, too."

What was it about fathers? Did they all meddle like Branch and Blade? Blade had pulled a number on her in New York.

The big surprise he'd promised her had turned out to be a big nightmare.

"Why would he think I'd possibly want anything to do with Liam Murphy?" she asked Oscar. "He knows about Liam's IRA connections. He knows the man stole from me, put me through hell. What in the world made him think I'd be interested in picking up where we left off years ago?"

She couldn't believe her father really bought into Liam's just-happened-to-bump-into-Blade-in-Fairbanks-Alaska fairy tale. No, her ex was after something, but she'd yet to figure out exactly what. She'd done her best to warn Blade. She'd made certain he understood she didn't want Liam or anyone else from her past to know anything about her present life.

Despite her father's assurances, she'd have sworn she saw Liam at the airport today before she went through the security checkpoint. It left Maddie feeling more than a little nervous and insecure.

"Probably just leftovers from the whole mushroom mess," she said aloud. It's only natural she'd be a little on edge following that entire trauma. She had trouble forgetting the fear.

She had trouble dismissing Luke Callahan from her mind.

It was quite infuriating. Thoughts of the man popped into her brain at the most disturbing times. When she chose her lingerie in the mornings. Just as she drifted off to sleep. In the shower.

"Stop it." She punched the power button on the radio and surfed the stations. Country. Pop. Country. Talk radio. Cajun music.

Bayou music.

Bayou boy.

Slow, seductive, sensuous kisses. A hand trailing soft and slow like the sluggish current, a finger tracing a whirlpool around the tip of her br—

"Ahh!" she cried out and jabbed at the radio button until she found some mood-breaking mariachi music, which she turned up high.

Maddie sang Swords lyrics to Spanish songs she couldn't translate all the way to Brazos Bend. As she passed the city limits sign listing the population at a generous eighty-six thousand, Maddie grabbed her cell phone. When she pulled into the tiny rest stop, which featured a statue of the town's founding father, Branch Callahan's namesake, she finally returned his call.

The old goat put her on hold.

Maddie looked up at the statue. "I'll bet scientists would have a field day with your genetic line."

As she debated hanging up, she studied the statue's face, looking for a resemblance to Luke. Hmm . . . similar nose, maybe. A dead ringer with that arrogant stance. Maddie knew the history behind the man and his town because Branch liked to lecture her about it while she cleaned his study.

A former colonel in the Confederate Army, the first Branch Callahan came to Texas as a shareholder in the Texas Emigration and Land Company in the early 1870s, and he established a saltworks in the northernmost section of the hill country on Bluff Creek, five miles north of its confluence with the Brazos River. When Colonel Callahan noted that the large buffalo population seemed to prefer the surrounding lands over other North Texas areas, the idea occurred to him that this territory could be one of the finest cattle-raising districts in the entire state of Texas.

For that reason, in 1872 he founded a town in the Brazos Bend Valley adjoining his saltworks. He surveyed and plotted a town site with unusually wide streets, large blocks, and spacious lots. The colonel resisted the egotistical urge to name the town after himself, although his town map did include a Callahan Square, Callahan Boulevard, Branch Street, and Hannah Avenue, in honor of his bride.

Brazos Bend prospered and by 1877 boasted more than one hundred buildings. The Callahan family flourished financially right along with Brazos Bend. Personally, they suffered significant tragedies. Only one of the six children born to Hannah and Branch lived to adulthood. That son, John Ross, displayed the same entrepreneurial spirit as his father, and by the time the boomtown twenties rolled around, J.R. had the family well established in railroads, agriculture, ranching, and oil.

J.R. married late and died young, siring only one son, whom he named after his father. The second Branch Callahan, the same old goat who still had Maddie on hold, had entertained dreams of a dynasty when he started looking for a bride. He went looking for a wife from among the first families of Texas—the Kleeberg cattle and oil clan, the scions of the Spindletop oil bonanza, the luminaries of Houston's stables set. He never expected to fall head over heels for the redheaded woman who'd moved next door to his widowed mother.

Margaret Mary McBride wasn't overly impressed by Branch number two's wealth. Nor was she affected by his handsomeness or his quick wit or his boyish charm. After all, such was the norm in her family. McBride men had cut a swath through Fort Worth since the 1870s.

What won Margaret Mary's heart was Branch's devotion to his invalid mother. After all, a man who displayed such gentleness and care to a mindless woman had to be a man of the truest heart.

Branch and Margaret Mary wed in Saint Michael's Catholic Church and waited for the babies to arrive. They waited and waited and waited. After eight years of marriage and no booties for the crib, Branch's dreams of dynasty waned. Margaret Mary despaired and turned to her faith for comfort and support.

Her first pregnancy came as a shock, Matthew's birth an occasion of great joy. Her second pregnancy, almost on the heels of the first, was a blessed surprise. When she gave birth to twins, she gave thanks to God and named her sons for saints. Four years passed before she missed a period again, and when another son arrived, the natural name for him was John.

"Madeline?" boomed a voice in her ear, jerking her from her reverie. "Madeline, where the hell are you?"

"Nice to hear from you, too, Branch," she dryly replied. "And so nice of you to inquire about my health. I'm safe. I'm well." She paused significantly, then added, "I'm furious with you."

She could almost hear his wince. "Uh, sunshine, now, um, there's no reason to . . ."

"To?" She tapped her foot against the gas pedal.

"Yeah, um . . . it's awful nice to hear your voice."

"Uh-huh."

"I . . . uh . . . heard from Kathy Hudson that you spent a few days in New York with your dad. That's real nice, honey. Glad you had the chance to get together with him. That's real important for a father and his child."

"Right."

She let the silence drag out.

"Um, Madeline?"

"Hmm?"

"Speaking of children . . ."

"I called to tell you I'm making supper for you tonight."

He hesitated a moment. "You are?"

"Yes. So if you and the Garza sisters are planning to watch reruns of *Murder She Wrote*, you need to cancel. I'm making Alfredo. I'll be there at six."

Which gave him an entire afternoon to fret, she thought with a touch of evil glee.

"Supper sounds good," Branch replied. "I'll give Juanita and Maria the night off."

The false cheer in his tone put a smile on her face as she drove to her next destination—the Brazos Bend Dairy Princess.

Five minutes later, when the red gambrel roof of the Dairy Princess came into view, Maddie had her usual reaction—she craved a dip cone, soft-serve vanilla ice cream dipped in chocolate sauce that hardened into a sweet, crisp shell.

The dip cone and the Dairy Princess represented small-town life to her. Originally a Dairy Queen franchise owned and operated by someone out of Dallas who'd abandoned their small-town-living dream, the restaurant sat empty for two years during the seventies before Kathy Hudson purchased the property and turned it into her notion of paradise—a combination ice cream parlor and rock-and-roll museum.

Maddie turned into the Dairy Princess lot, then parked in her usual spot. Not wanting to leave Oscar in the heat, she gathered up the fishbowl and her purse, then grabbed a sack from the backseat and headed inside.

An electronic chime sounded the first strains of Elvis's "Jailhouse Rock" when she opened the shop's door, then strolled toward her usual booth, finger-waving at Kathy, who stood behind the counter mixing a milkshake for a waiting teenager. The aroma of fried onion rings lingered in the air like a temptation.

"Well, look who's here!" Kathy called, her round face lighting with pleasure. "Be with you in a minute, hon."

"No rush." Maddie snuggled back into the well-worn comfort of the booth's red vinyl seat, closed her eyes, and listened to Janis Joplin sing about Bobby McGee on the jukebox.

Janis was still crooning when Kathy plopped down in the opposite seat. She wore her bleached blond hair long and straight, her dangling earrings, makeup-free face, and signature home-sewn granny dress signaling that she'd never quite left her hippie days behind. The smile on her face and the warm welcome in her eyes were pure Brazos Bend, however, and upon seeing them, Maddie knew she'd come home.

"I don't ordinarily allow pets inside the Dairy Princess, but I'll make an exception on Oscar's behalf on account of he's grieving for Gus." Kathy handed Maddie one of the two dip cones she carried, then sat back and gave her a thorough once-over. "Well, now. Aren't you just a sight for sore eyes! You had me worried, girl. So, tell me everything. I want all the details you couldn't fill in over the phone. Is Sin

Callahan as handsome as ever? Does he still have that bone-melting grin? And what about your father? Did he enjoy his photography trip? What did the two of you do in New York? Did he do any singing?"

She paused to take a breath, then leaned forward. "Did he mention anything about making a visit to Brazos Bend?"

Maddie grinned at her friend, then licked her ice cream cone. *It's so nice to be home.* "Luke Callahan is gorgeous and his smile will make you melt. He'd hate to hear me say it, but he's a lot like Branch. Stubborn. Smart. Trouble."

"Hmm." Kathy licked her cone. "Those boys always did take after their father. That was part of the problem after Margaret Mary died. Not a one of them knew how to handle their grief, and any time Branch tried to take control, it was World War Three. It was easier for him to give up trying, and that's what led to all the trouble. I've always said it was as much Branch's fault as the boys'."

"Branch is no innocent in anything." Maddie tugged a white paper napkin from the metal dispenser and wiped her mouth. "And I intend to tell him so tonight at supper."

"My, oh, my, don't you know I'd love to be a butterfly sniffing the centerpiece flowers in the Callahan House dining room tonight!" Kathy said with a grin. "Enough about that. Tell me about Blade. Did you bring me any pictures?"

Maddie reached into her purse and pulled out a small digital camera. The two women spent the next few minutes discussing Blade, the band, his recent travels, and their week in the Big Apple. Kathy oohed and aahed and her eyes lit with yearning. "How exciting. I'll bet you had just the most wonderful time. New York is one place I've always dreamed about visiting, and to do it on the arm of Blade . . . well . . ." She ended on a sigh.

For perhaps the hundredth time since she'd met Kathy, Maddie said, "Blade can't come here without blowing my cover, but if you'd like to go with me to visit him, you know I'd be happy to arrange it."

"No. No. I can't leave Brazos Bend. Sparkle might come home and . . ." Kathy shrugged.

Sparkle Hudson had been only fifteen years old when she disappeared from Brazos Bend. She and her single mother had been having the typical teenage problems, nothing too terribly serious, and everyone assumed Sparkle had run away and would come home once she came to her senses. The assumption proved wrong. Days passed, then weeks, then months without so much as a postcard from Sparkle. By the time the six-month anniversary of her disappearance arrived with law enforcement and private investigators coming up dry in their investigations, most of Brazos Bend believed Sparkle must be dead.

Her mother never gave up hope. Two decades later, Kathy still left the porch light on for Sparkle, and she never, ever left Brazos Bend.

Sparkle had vanished before Amber Alerts, before DNA analysis, before twenty-four-hour cable news brought missing children to national attention. But after so many years . . . everyone knew that Sparkle was probably the victim of a hitchhike gone bad, but Kathy just couldn't accept it, wouldn't accept it. No matter what anyone said, she believed her Sparkle would come home one day.

Maddie knew she'd never be able to understand Kathy's pain, so she didn't try to force the issue. She simply offered. If Kathy ever broke down and said yes, she wanted to visit Blade, Maddie would have her on an airplane before the day was out.

Sensing the need for a change in subject, Maddie asked what happenings she'd missed in Brazos Bend while she'd been gone. Kathy entertained her with stories of children's antics at the public pool, gossip about Mrs. Tillman's new boyfriend, and news about the unfortunate sickness spreading through Larry Larsen's herd of cattle. Maddie finished her ice cream cone long before Kathy finished her tale.

Yet, despite Kathy's verbosity, Maddie sensed there was more coming, that her friend had something more to tell her.

Something she didn't want to hear. Finally, when the older woman launched into a tale of her bids on an online auction for Rita Kimbler's Hummel collection, Maddie interrupted. "What is it you're trying to avoid, Kathy? Is one of my clients ill? Is there trouble with the business? My house? Did Mike McDermott go off and get engaged to a woman over the Internet or something?"

Kathy heaved a sigh. "I don't know how you do that. You read me like a book. I didn't want to tell you."

"Obviously."

"It's about Gus."

Warily, Maddie repeated, "Gus?"

"Well, not Gus, exactly. About his boy. About Jerry."

Maddie licked her lips, suddenly tense. "The police arrested him on drug charges."

"That's true."

"They told me he'd been denied bail."

"That's true, too."

Okay. "So, then, what's the problem?"

"I guess Jerry hired a new lawyer. Some hotshot out of Fort Worth. I don't know how he did it—you know what a grumpy old cuss Judge Harrison is—but anyway, this new lawyer got Jerry released. He's out on bond, honey. I don't think he'll cause you any trouble, but you might want to be careful."

The news rolled around her stomach, then settled like a bad burger. She cleared her throat. "He knows I don't have the mushrooms, though, right? He has to know that I turned them in."

"Oh, for certain. Sara-Beth ran her article about you with the picture of that nice-looking fed from Tyler, then she did a follow-up with Jerry's lawyer. Here, let me get it for you." Following a quick trip behind the service counter, Kathy handed Maddie the paper.

The attorney was quoted as saying, "Mr. Grevas is innocent of all charges and shall be vindicated. As for Maddie Kincaid, he offers his sincere sympathy that a Brazos Bend citizen was caught up in such a terrible crime, but he had absolutely nothing to do with it."

"What's Jerry Grevas doing now?" she asked Kathy.

"I'm not sure. He's not supposed to leave town until his trial date, though, so you're liable to run into him."

"Does anyone think he had anything to do with his father's death?"

The question obviously shocked Kathy, which gave Maddie a measure of comfort. "Gus!" Kathy exclaimed. "Jerry? You mean, as in murder?"

"No . . . yes . . . I don't know. It all just seems so strange."

The little balls on the ends of Kathy's earrings swung and clattered against each other as she reached across the table and patted Maddie's hand. "Don't go there. Gus might have died of a broken heart if he found out his boy was growing shrooms, but Jerry didn't out-and-out kill the man. I've known that boy all his life and he's not a killer. Stupid, yes. A doper, sure, but you know I don't hold that against anyone. But a killer? I just can't see it. You're being a bit paranoid, there, honey."

"Okay." Maddie recognized that Kathy knew Brazos Bend better than just about anyone in town. "Yes, I'm sure you're right. I'm sure it will be fine. My adventure is over and I'd better get home. I imagine I have a few customers who'll be wanting to talk to me."

"A few? Try every last one of them. Since they know we're friends, they've been calling me to complain, to demand to know when you're coming home, to ask ridiculous questions like how to program the TV remote. Martha Hartford even wanted me to come clean her dog's ears. Do you do that, hon?"

"Yeah."

"Wow." Kathy shook her head. "No wonder you're in such demand. Anyway, Pauline and Polly Perkins have done a good enough job filling in for you, and Sandy runs the office fine, but your customers are ready to have you back.

They want you, Maddie. They need you. That should make you feel good."

"It does." It did. Kathy might not understand it—her father certainly didn't—but Maddie loved helping her seniors. She'd missed them.

"I'd better be going," she said, inching toward the edge of the booth. "I'm sure I have bills waiting for me at home. I'd like to get caught up on my paperwork before I jump back into service tomorrow."

Reaching for Oscar's bowl, she spied the sack she'd brought in with her for Kathy. "Oh, I almost forgot." She handed the sack to her friend. "These are some things from Gus's place. I thought you might like them."

"They're not roach clips, are they?" Kathy asked opening the bag. "I gave up that stuff back in ninety-seven, you know."

"Not drug paraphernalia," Maddie said with a laugh. "There's an eight-track of Jefferson Airplane, an old *Time* magazine with an article about Elvis, and some jewelry."

Kathy's eyes lit up. "Jewelry, too?"

"A few costume pieces that had your name written all over them."

"Big and gaudy, in other words." Kathy reached inside and pulled a strand of alabaster beads from the bag. Her mouth dropped open at the sight of them.

"My God."

Maddie grinned. "The clasp is broken, but I knew you'd like them. Keep whatever you want from the bag, then give the rest away, okay? Now, I'm out of here."

Kathy was still seated at the booth, her gaze fixed on the gifts, when Maddie exited the Dairy Princess. She glanced around the parking lot, checking for any sign of Jerry Grevas, then told herself she was being foolish. The man had no motive to pester her. None at all.

She made the drive home in less than ten minutes. Maddie lived in a modest cottage-style rental in an older, centralized neighborhood in Brazos Bend. Noting that her yard had turned a bit brown during her absence, she winced. She hadn't thought to arrange to have the grass watered while she was gone.

"I need to hire a yard guy, Oscar," she said to the fish as she pulled into her driveway and switched off the engine. As much as she enjoyed doing her yard work herself, she wouldn't have time for it during the upcoming weeks as she played catch-up at Home for Now.

With her mind on her business when her cell phone rang, Maddie answered without checking the number. "Hello," she said, expecting the Brazos Bend grapevine to have passed word of her return to her customers.

"Baby, don't hang up."

Liam. Her stomach sank. Just what she needed. "How did you get my number?"

"It doesn't matter. Listen, honey. I need you to—"

When call waiting on her phone beeped through, she switched to it automatically. "Yes?"

"Where the hell have you been?"

Branch? Hadn't they had this conversation already? "Excuse me?"

"I've been calling you for days. Don't you ever check your messages?"

Not Branch. Sounds like Branch. Maddie's heart lifted. "Who is this?"

"You don't . . . ? Hell. It's Luke. I'm Luke."

"Callahan?"

"How many Lukes do you know?"

Luke Callahan. Maddie's brows arched in surprise, then she smiled. "Hi. I didn't expect to hear from you."

A moment of silence dragged by before he said, "Well, yeah, I just thought I'd check to see that everything went okay, but you never answered your goddamned phone, and Sara-Beth said you never made it back to town."

He checked up on me? He called Sara-Beth? "You were worried?"

Her toes curled inside her sneakers.

Another silence. "I always follow up on my jobs."

From offshore fishing trips? Warmth stole into her heart. "So, where are you?"

"I'm in my driveway at home. I just got here. Rather than spend a couple days in Dallas like I'd planned, I met my father in New York for a week."

"Oh."

The phone clicked with another call, and figuring it was Liam, Maddie ignored it. She slipped the keys from the ignition and opened the car door, then slipped her purse strap over her shoulder and reached for Oscar's bowl. "How's your trip going? Have you caught lots of poor fish?"

"Uh . . . yeah. Look, Maddie, there's something you need to know. Grevas is—"

"Out on bond. I heard. Believe me, I plan to stay far away from him."

"Sara-Beth's article ran."

"I know. But Jerry's an accountant, not an oil-field roughneck. He's a nice guy, Luke. I think he just got mixed up in something he shouldn't. I'm not really worried about him."

Liam Murphy, now, was another matter entirely. Part of her wanted to mention her ex's sudden reappearance to Luke, but something held her back.

Maddie climbed out of her van and shut the door with her hip. The fragrance of Mister Lincoln roses drifted in the air and welcomed her home.

Luke muttered a curse, then said, "It never hurts to be cautious, Red."

"I won't argue that." In fact, she gave the front of her house a thorough look for any sign of intrusion, but all appeared as it should. Her neighbors had hidden her newspapers behind the hedge, and a sack full of mail was tucked behind the geranium planter. Then, because she wasn't in any hurry to get Luke off the line, Maddie said, "Tell me about your trip. What kind of fish did you catch?"

He started telling her about the frisky sand shark they'd

pulled aboard his brother's boat as she set Oscar on the porch, fitted her house key into the lock, and opened the door.

Maddie gasped at the sight that met her eyes. She dropped the phone as she exclaimed, "Oh, my God!"

Her home had been ransacked—cushions ripped from the sofa and chairs. The contents of her bookshelves lay strewn across the floor. The drawers from her end tables had been dumped.

"Maddie? Maddie!"

She heard Luke's voice through the phone as if from far away. Her heart pounded. Her breath came in shallow pants. Fear had a stranglehold on her throat.

She wanted to search the rest of her home, but she knew the smart thing to do was to get out of the house immediately and call the police. She bent to pick up her phone, and spying one of the brass bookends that belonged on the bookshelves, she grabbed that, too, to use as a weapon, just in case.

"Maddie? Dammit, Maddie, answer me!"

She brought the phone up to her ear, but before she could speak, a strong arm grabbed her around the neck from behind. A gruff, raspy voice murmured in her ear. "Hang up, bitch. You're talking to me now."

Nine

Luke double-checked Maddie's address on the sheet of paper lying on the seat beside him, then pressed his gas pedal a little harder. He'd known better than to let her go back by herself, but he'd ignored his instincts. Ignored the knowledge he'd learned in almost a decade with the DEA. "Damn me for a fool."

Guilt and fear and fury had him driving like a madman. What if he didn't get there in time?

He'd known in his gut that the woman was in trouble. The feeling had plagued him on the boat, annoying his brothers to the point that they threatened to abandon him on a sand shoal if he didn't break down and call her. So he'd called. And got no answer. For three straight days.

They'd put him ashore at Biloxi. He'd scrambled for transportation, finally buying a brand-new Ford F-350 right off the lot, and headed west. He spent nearly the entire time on the phone. The news of Grevas's release cost Luke a speeding ticket in Louisiana. Listening as Maddie was attacked in her own home damn near gave him a heart attack on the outskirts of Brazos Bend.

He'd called 911, but he expected to beat them there. From his experience with the police in Brazos Bend—and he'd had plenty of it—they seldom were in a hurry to do anything.

It helped that Luke knew the town like the back of his

hand, and he roared onto her street less than ten minutes after she'd dropped the phone.

Ten minutes was plenty of time to hurt someone. Plenty of time to rape. To torture.

Plenty of time to kill.

"No." He homed in on her minivan parked in a driveway halfway down the block, and while he wanted to rush in with guns blazing, training made him stop his truck a few houses away and take a stealthy approach.

As he closed in on her house, he drew his gun. He sidled up to a window and peered inside. Kitchen. Torn to ever-lovin' hell. No blood. No body. Good.

No sign of life. *Dear Lord, please.*

He listened for sirens, to no avail. Check the back next? Or the front? His gut sent him sneaking toward the front door.

"Oh. Oh, shoot." Maddie's voice drifted through the open window. "Oh shoot oh shoot oh shoot oh shoot."

"Red?" Luke could breathe again. He strode toward the door. "Maddie? Where are you—?"

He saw her. She lay on the floor, black and blue and bloody. Luke's stomach dropped and a dozen more epithets tumbled from his mouth. "Is he still here?"

"No." She struggled to sit up. "Luke. You're here. How did you get here?"

Ignoring her question, he kneeled on the floor beside her, reached to support her. "Where are you hurt? Where's the blood coming from?"

"Jerry Grevas's nose, for the most part."

Luke blew out a sigh of relief. His blood, not hers. "Is he still here?"

"No. He ran out through the back." She attempted to rise, but he shushed her and told her to be still, to wait for the paramedics. "He was a wild man, Luke. Crazy-acting. I'd never seen him like that." She paused a moment, grimaced, and said, "He wanted a box. Kept asking what I did with the box."

"What box?"

"That's what I wanted to know. I guess it was something of his father's, but I don't know what. I got rid of a lot of boxes for Gus. When I told Jerry that, he hit me." She shut her eyes. Shuddered. "Kept hitting me. I think he might have broken my rib."

His mouth set in a grim line, Luke looked at her injuries and tried to keep his voice steady. Visualized what he'd do to Jerry when he found him. "I'll kill the son of a bitch."

Her chin came up and she attempted to smile. With her complexion pale, her expression pained, her body bloodied and beaten, she managed to sound almost Amazonian as she declared, "I hit back. I'm pretty sure I broke his nose. He never saw it coming."

She sounded damned proud of herself, Luke observed.

"Good girl." Luke fell just a little in love right then.

The sound of a siren intruded on the afternoon and Luke muttered, "About damned time."

From that point, the situation became a flurry of activity. Two policemen Luke didn't know entered the house and tried to arrest him until Maddie told them they had the wrong guy. For the first time since he'd turned it in, Luke truly missed his badge.

Maddie tried to stand and at that point, fainted. Luke called for an ambulance himself rather than wait for the Keystone cops to do their job, and when it arrived, he followed on its tail the entire way to Brazos Bend General.

Fear was a copper taste in his mouth. He'd seen this happen before; a guy takes a few whacks to the head, seems to be fine, then keels over with an aneurism. He wondered whether this podunk town had a doctor worth a damn and whether the hospital had the kind of equipment it needed. Surely Branch had seen to that over the years. It'd be in his best interest to make sure competent doctors were around to take care of him should he need it.

Maddie came to as the paramedics wheeled her into the emergency entrance, which relieved him greatly. This time, no amount of browbeating got him access to Maddie once they wheeled her into an examining room.

So Luke spent his time pacing the hospital hallway and making demands upon any law enforcement official he could connect with in order to expedite the apprehension of Jerry Grevas. "I've sent a patrol car out to his place," Luke's old nemesis, Chief Harper, said. "We'll pick him up and find out what happened. Probably a domestic situation."

A domestic situation! For Christ's sake. Luke about went through his phone after the stupid old geezer.

"Why was Grevas let out on bond?" he demanded of Sheriff Drake, a contemporary of his father's.

"Back off, Callahan," the sheriff replied. "I can't believe that you, of all people, would get your panties in a twist because somebody bonded out of jail. And aside from that, what the hell are you doing back in town? Does your father know you're here?"

Luke actually bared his teeth and growled.

A call to the judge in the case, someone new to town since Luke's departure, elicited a referral to the district attorney's office. When Luke learned the identity of Brazos Bend's current DA, he wasn't surprised. If the Callahan brothers had been the Holy Terrors of Brazos Bend, Austin Rawlings had been the town's Golden Boy. And yet, Luke had always liked the guy. Felt a little sorry for him, too, since Randolph Rawlings was an über-controlling father who'd kept him on such a short leash that Austin never had any real fun.

It took three tries for the district attorney to take Luke's call. Rawlings answered the phone saying, "Did my secretary get your name right? This is Sin Callahan?"

Focused on the red fire extinguisher hanging on the hospital wall, Luke grimaced at the name. "Yeah, it's me. Have you heard that Maddie Kincaid was attacked in her own living room this afternoon by Jerry Grevas?"

There was a moment's pause before Austin said, "Oh, no. How bad is it? Will she be all right?"

"She'd damned well better be. Look, I want some answers. Why was Grevas released on bond?"

Rawlings sighed and sounded more than a little defensive when he replied, "He only had one prior on his record, Sin. A possession charge back in high school."

"This was a six-million-dollar seizure. Didn't the feds want him held?"

The note of friendliness disappeared from Rawlings's tone. "It's my town, Callahan."

Actually, it was their fathers' town, but Luke wasn't going to quibble the point.

"Besides," Rawlings continued, "who are you to come asking questions? And how do you know about Grevas and his mushrooms at all?" When Luke took a second to formulate his answers, Rawlings launched into a different direction. "Are you part of this? You're his drug connection?"

Like Luke would admit that to a district attorney even if it were true.

However, he wasn't ready to reveal his DEA ties to anyone in Brazos Bend. "I'm a special friend of Maddie's."

Absently, Rawlings said, "I thought she was dating Mike McDermott."

"Not exclusively." Luke's hand gripped the receiver hard and spat out his demands. "Look, Austin, I want Jerry Grevas off the streets before dark, and I'd appreciate your help in lighting a fire under the cops to bring him in. I want to know why he went after Maddie, and what he was looking for when he trashed her house."

"Her home was vandalized?"

"Looks like an angry wildcat went through it. He was looking for something—a box—and when he didn't find it, he took it out on Maddie."

"The bastard." Austin Rawlings's voice vibrated with anger. "We're not going to put up with behavior like that in our town. We'll bring him in, and with an assault charge, we can hold him this time. Don't you worry."

"We have to know what he was looking for, Austin, if only to make sure nobody else will come looking for it, too."

"Yes, I see what you mean." The DA thought for a moment, then said, "We can't have Maddie looking over her shoulder all the time. Tell you what, Sin, I'll give Chief Harper a call right now. We'll make sure our citizens are protected. You have my word."

"Thanks, Austin. I'll owe you one."

"And, Sin? I won't take time now under the circumstances, but I'd sure like to visit with you, catch up on what you've been up to since high school."

"Sure. We'll get a beer or something."

"One thing I have to ask, though. Does your father know you're back in town?"

Luke sneered at that and an orderly walking past him in the hallway gave him a wary look. "I expect Branch has heard the news by now."

The DA ended the call by repeating the assurances Luke wanted to hear, and Luke resumed his pacing until a nurse called his name. "You're with Ms. Kincaid?"

"Yeah." Luke took two long strides toward her. "What's wrong?"

"Nothing's wrong. She's getting dressed. The paperwork is all done, and she'll be ready to leave in a few minutes. Do you want to bring your car around?"

"Yeah." Lowering his voice, he said to himself, "Now I just have to figure out where to take her."

"That's easy. Bring her to the house." The voice sent a shudder down Luke's back as Branch Callahan added, "Welcome home, son."

Whoa. If they're not two peas in a pod.

Maddie had recognized it before, but seeing the proof right here before her eyes drove the point home. Branch was

how Luke would look in thirty years, while Luke was his father thirty years ago.

Except that right now, Luke looked more like that bronze
statue of his great-grandfather than anything. He stood that
stiff, that silent. His expression was as hard as iron.

His father, on the other hand, had a puppy-dog look to
him. She'd never seen Branch's blue eyes look so soft and
pleading. She almost expected him to stick out his tongue
and hold up his paws and whimper.

Maddie's head hurt too badly to play referee, so she decided to do invalid instead. She slumped against the wall
and said, "Hi."

"Madeline," Branch said, a catch in his voice as he gave
her a quick once-over. "Look at you, you pitiful thing."

Luke's gaze zeroed in on the Band-Aid on her head.
"What's the verdict?"

"Various cuts and contusions. One on my head I hadn't
noticed. A concussion."

"The ribs?"

"Just bruised. I ache, though, Luke. I want to go home."
She glanced from son to father. "Will you just take me
home?"

"Come to Callahan House," Branch stated. "I'm told your
house was ransacked. You can't go back there."

"Not until they pick up Grevas," Luke reluctantly agreed.
"You need someone with you tonight, too. Concussions are
nothing to ignore."

Maddie wasn't about to argue with them. Playing the invalid was more truth than acting. Branch's home sounded
like a real nice refuge at the moment. "Callahan House will
be fine."

"Good. Excellent." A smile bloomed on Branch's face.
"Let me go get my truck and I'll take you home."

Luke looked like he'd swallowed a lemon as he brusquely
said, "I'll take her."

Branch's smile grew even bigger. "I'll meet you there,
then, son."

While Branch shuffled happily down the hall toward the exit, Luke busied himself looking around for a wheelchair. "Shouldn't you be sitting down?" he snapped at Maddie. "I thought it was a rule a person had to leave a hospital in a wheelchair."

"I wasn't admitted, and besides, this is Brazos Bend."

"Tell me about it," he grumbled beneath his breath.

Maddie had a dozen questions she wanted to ask him, a variety of topics she wanted to cover, but the headache prevented her from giving them voice. Despite her aching head and ribs, she felt . . . happy. He'd come. Luke had come to Brazos Bend.

He wrapped his arm around her to support her, and she felt safe and secure and protected. *And he said he wasn't anybody's white knight.*

"You won't just leave, will you? You'll stay with me? Keep me safe?"

"At Callahan House?" He shut his eyes and grimaced. "God, can this day possibly get any worse?"

She might have been offended had she the energy. The adrenaline that had flowed through her blood in the wake of the attack had dissipated. She wanted to curl up in Luke Callahan's arms somewhere and sleep. She was just loopy enough to tell him so, then added, "Maybe you and your father will use the opportunity to talk."

"Right after hell freezes over."

She started to protest, but then she swayed a little and Luke muttered another curse. He lifted her gently into his arms and carried her toward the emergency room entrance and his truck. "No more talking," he ordered.

An extended-cab pickup pulled past the circular driveway just as the automatic doors slicked open and Luke walked through. Branch gave a little wave from behind the wheel. "Son of a bitch," Luke muttered. "It's the same model I'm driving. Same color, too."

Maddie smiled softly and rested her head against Luke's chest.

Tension sizzled in the air in the cab of the truck on the short drive through town to Branch's house. The painkillers had kicked in, and though Maddie's thoughts grew fuzzy, she still felt sorry for both Luke and his dad. All her life she'd wanted family, and here was one that simply refused to repair itself.

The truck turned into the neighborhood of two- and three-story estates built back in the forties and fifties with money made from ranching and the oil fields. One of Maddie's clients had told her that Brazos Bend had more millionaires per capita than did any other town in the United States. She wasn't sure whether she believed that or not, but there was no denying that Brazos Bend's Country Club estates would fit right in among any of the old-money parts of the country.

Branch arrived at Callahan House before them, and as Luke pulled into the long circular drive, his father made his way up the walk to unlock the front door. Luke threw the gearshift in park, then, with his mouth set in a bitter line, strode around the front of the truck to help her from the cab.

Maddie twisted her torso a little too quickly and gasped in pain. Luke's expression became even more grim.

"Hold on." He carefully scooped her up into his arms and carried her toward the house. "I can't believe I'm doing this. Swore it would never happen."

Amidst the aches and pains, Maddie felt a stab of guilt. She understood personal oaths and promises, even if she didn't agree with this one. "I can walk on my own."

He ignored that just like he'd ignored his father.

Luke swept into his childhood home and headed straight for the stairs. On the second floor, rather than turning right toward the guest room, he went left, carrying her without hesitation to the bedroom that once had been his.

It still was. Maddie detected a slight hesitation on his part as they entered the room. Was he surprised that it remained exactly as it had on the day he'd left all those years ago?

Branch had told Maddie he'd kept all the boys' rooms

just the way they were when he'd sent them from Brazos Bend. He'd never intended they stay away forever. He'd thought a year or two of hard work and independent living would make men of them, that they'd then return home and live the lives he'd envisioned for them as fine, upstanding members of the Brazos Bend community.

It hadn't quite turned out the way Branch had hoped. Oh, his boys became men, all right, the kind of men to make a father proud. Only, they weren't proud of him. Branch's voice had cracked, and tears pooled in his eyes the day an early start on his bourbon had loosened his tongue to the point where he confessed that his sons wouldn't even come home for the bereavement meal following John's memorial service.

Luke set Maddie on her feet, then yanked back the bed-spread. "Hope to hell he at least changes the sheets from time to time."

"Every other Tuesday," Maddie said. "I do it myself."

"You change my sheets?"

"Yes."

"You clean his house? Did he fire the Garza sisters?"

"No, but they're getting on in years and it's difficult for them to get up and down the stairs. I see to the second floor. No one ever comes up here—Branch can't climb the steps, either—so it's an easy job."

"Hmm." Luke motioned for her to lie down. "So do you do any of the Garza sisters' other work?"

Maddie shrugged and toed her shoes off. "Your father has offered them a pension, but they're not ready to retire. I think they'd be just as lost without him."

Luke just shook his head and tugged the sheet up over her. "You better get some rest."

"You'll be here when I wake up?"

He picked up a framed photograph of the high school football team from the bedroom's built-in bookshelf. "I'll call Bee and see if she'll do the 'wake you up every few hours' thing."

He wasn't staying. Maddie tried to swallow her disappointment, but it hung in her throat. "Why are you here, Luke? Why did you come if you're going to leave right away?"

"I just intended to check up on you."

"So now you've checked, seen I'm in sad shape, and you're going to leave?"

"I'm gonna make sure the SOB who did this to you understands he'd better never show his face within a hundred yards of you again."

"And then you'll leave."

"I can't stay, Maddie."

She wasn't buying it. For him to be here now meant he left his fishing trip early and traveled hundreds of miles to follow up on the mission she'd begun by boarding the *Miss Behavin' II*. A man didn't do that on a whim.

No, he'd wanted to be here. Whether because of her or because of his father or because of the need to make peace with his past, she didn't know, but she was certain that Luke's motive for visiting Brazos Bend ran deeper than a need to "check up" on her.

So, what should she do? Make it easy for him to go? Make it difficult for him to stay?

She should probably shut her eyes and go to sleep. Her mind was working as slow as molasses. She'd forgotten that she didn't need the complication men invariably brought to her life. She couldn't seem to shake the old ones—look at Liam—why would she want to bring somebody new into the mix?

Because she couldn't stop thinking about Luke Callahan, even when she could barely think. Because her heart had jumped when he called her. Because the man made her want to forget the lessons of her past and take a risk once again.

"I want you to stay with me, Luke," she said, peering through the bleary pool of tears swimming in her eyes. "I need you."

"Look, I have to leave. I have to track down Knucklehead. He got out of the truck when I went to your place."

"Then, come back after you find him."

Maddie didn't think she'd ever seen a man look so guilty.

"Rest your head, sweetheart."

"I don't want you to go, Luke. You've made a big step by coming here. Don't waste it."

What was that emotion she saw flitting through his eyes? Regret? Yearning? Confusion?

Then the headache and the stress got the better of her and Maddie drifted off to sleep, still waiting for his answer.

"She's right, you know."

Luke's spine went as stiff as a bois d'arc fence post. He glanced over his shoulder. His father stood just outside the doorway. "I thought you couldn't climb the stairs."

"I can do a lot of things if I'm motivated enough."

Except keep your youngest son from losing his head in the armpit of the world.

"Good." Luke took a step back from the bed. "Keep an eye on her, then. The nurse said to wake her every few hours and make her speak to you."

"I can do that." Branch moved into Luke's old bedroom and glanced around. "You're going after Jerry Grevas?"

"Yeah."

"You'll make sure he pays for what he did to Madeline?"

"I'll make sure the cops do their jobs." Giving Maddie one last look, Luke pushed past his father and headed for the stairs.

Branch followed him out into the hallway. "Something strange is going on here in town, son. I think Madeline's stumbled into more trouble than she realizes."

"Not my problem, old man," Luke muttered while he hurried down the steps and out of the house, as if saying it aloud might help him believe it. He climbed into his truck and spun his wheels as he shot down the driveway, just like old times. Running away, just like old times.

As he drove toward Maddie's neighborhood, his eyes sharp, looking for his dog, his thoughts drifted, snippets of conversations running through his mind like a recording. *Stumbled into more trouble than she realizes. I don't want you to go, Luke. Cuts and contusions and a concussion.*

And back on the boat with his brothers. *Just go, numb-nuts. Get her out of your system. Don't you dare let Branch's string tugging keep you away from something that could be good and right and just what you need.*

She wanted him to stay.

He'd told the DA they were dating. It would look a little strange if he rushed off while she was in her sickbed. He hadn't even had the chance to find out how Oscar was doing.

He could get a motel room tonight. Hell, he could stay at her place. Maybe that's what he'd do. He could straighten up for her, snoop around some. She'd certainly done her share of snooping on the *Miss Behavin' II*.

He didn't have to see Branch again.

He didn't *have* to leave. Not right now. Not before he got the answers he'd come looking for in Brazos Bend.

"Okay. Good. That'll work." With the decision made and the weight off his shoulders, Luke parked his truck at the curb outside Maddie's and started looking for his dog on foot. He walked up and down the street, calling and whistling, until a sporty BMW pulled up alongside him and said, "Sin?"

He recognized the voice before the man. "Austin."

"I hope you're not roaming the streets looking for Jerry Grevas."

"I'm looking for my dog." He gave a quick description of Knucklehead, then asked, "Have you seen him?"

Austin winced. "Actually, I have. Sorry, Callahan, but I called animal control on him. We're strict about our leash law here in Brazos Bend. They picked him up twenty minutes ago."

"Well, crap. Where do I go to spring him?"

"We have a new facility. Tell you what. Get in. I'll take you."

Luke sauntered around to the passenger side and climbed into the car. Always happy to multitask, he'd use this opportunity to grill the district attorney about the drug trade in this town. First, though, he asked about Jerry Grevas. "I trust that by now, y'all have him locked up where he belongs?"

"'Fraid not." Austin grimaced and jabbed at the car radio, switching it off. "Guy's disappeared. He's not at his house, not at his father's place. Not at any of the bars he's been known to visit. That's why I'm out. We don't have a lot of manpower to put on this, so I was hoping I might spot him."

Luke dragged a hand across his jaw. "That's not the news I was hoping to hear. Anybody try the lake place?"

"Yes. Chief Harper sent a car out there shortly after I spoke with you. No sign of him."

The DA turned a corner, and Luke caught sight of the animal shelter half a block ahead. "You might wish you'd thought this out better, Austin. This is a nice ride, and Knucklehead's . . . well, he has his name for a reason."

Rawlings laughed. "I'm a pet lover. In fact, once we pick up your dog, I need to go by Maddie's on a pet patrol." He jerked a thumb over his shoulder. Luke glanced into the back seat to see a goldfish swimming in a clear plastic bag half full of water.

"Is that Oscar?"

"Oscar Two. I'm afraid Oscar One didn't survive Jerry Grevas."

Hmm. Luke took a minute to digest this bit of news. "Since when is it the DA's job to resupply fish to crime victims?"

"Since he took said victim to the Valentine's Day dance at the country club."

Really. Well, wasn't that an interesting bit of news? Maddie hadn't mentioned Austin Rawlings in her rambling about the men in her past. Luke recalled that Austin was a widower, having lost his wife in a car accident a couple weeks before the Callahan brothers returned to Brazos Bend for John's memorial service.

Jealousy tweaked at Luke. Of course the Golden Boy would ask out the prettiest girl in town. Hell, nothing changes.

Knucklehead was sufficiently grateful at being rescued from the pound that he lifted Luke's spirits. Luke spent the ride back to Maddie's trying to save the goldfish from the hound, so he managed to slip in only a few questions about a drug problem in Brazos Bend before they turned onto Maddie's street. "There's my truck," he said, pointing toward the Ford. "Appreciate the ride, Rawlings."

"No problem. Although, I was hoping we'd have the opportunity for that talk."

Yeah, Luke wanted a conversation, too. However, first things first. "Tell you what. Let's get Grevas off the streets, then I'll buy you a beer."

"You planning to go looking for him?"

"Doing my civic duty."

Austin Rawlings leveled a stern look at Luke. "Look, Callahan, don't go acting cowboy. If you see Grevas, call it in. Don't try to apprehend him yourself."

"Wouldn't dream of it." Luke's idea was to beat him senseless, then haul him down to the police station and dump his ass on the cold, hard floor.

Luke followed Knucklehead into the truck cab and started the engine. Knucklehead stuck his nose into the air conditioner vent while Luke turned his mind to his former occupation and tried to think like a drug dealer. Then, applying his occupational knowledge to his hometown memories, he pulled away from the curb and went to work.

He visited a park in the older section of town, then a supermarket parking lot not far from the high school. He talked to teens and adults and even some children. No one could give him a bead on Jerry Grevas.

Hours passed and evening deepened to night. Sometimes he crossed paths with the cops; other times, they appeared to follow him around. Once an hour, he called the police chief for an update before phoning Callahan House to clip out his question regarding Maddie's status to his father. By God, if she wasn't up and on her feet by tomorrow, he'd hire someone to stay with her and answer his calls so he didn't have to talk to the old bastard.

Luke's investigation was slowed from time to time by a few friends and plenty of not-so-friendly acquaintances who stopped him either to welcome him back to town or to suggest he mosey on down the road. Brazos Bend citizens had long memories, and they'd yet to forgive him for his part in the boot-factory fire.

When thinking like a drug dealer failed to pay off, he tried to think like an accountant instead. He visited the library and a copy place without results, then abandoned logic and just went with his gut. Luke stopped by all the places he and his brothers used to hang out. He tried the bowling alley, the Dairy Princess, the liquor store where the owner used to misread their IDs.

The liquor store took him on a trip down memory lane, so when Luke left there, he instinctively drove out to the lake and the scenic overlook that served as Brazos Bend's version of Lovers' Point.

Surprisingly, he found the place deserted. He shut off his headlights and cut off his engine, then climbed from the cab and walked toward the edge of the rock cliff. Man, had he and his brothers had some wild times out here. Booze, sex, crap games in the dirt between the protruding roots of a sixty-year-old pecan tree. It had been party central for a time.

Some of the memories left him overcome with shame.

He'd been a jerk at fourteen. A full-fledged asshole by the time his father sent him packing at seventeen. What kind of man would he have become had his father not kicked him out? Would he be worth a damn?

Not likely.

A three-quarter moon rose in the night sky and was

reflected in the water below. Luke knew he should get back to town, return to his search. Still, the memories held him shackled.

Drunk and daring and downright stupid, Mark and Matt had damn near killed themselves here one day when they decided to play Butch Cassidy and the Sundance Kid and took a running leap off the cliff. Mark hit the water bad and it knocked him out. If Matt hadn't been right there, Luke's twin would have drowned.

Then there was the time they started shooting at beer bottles and damn near killed Susan Parker. Stupid, reckless, feckless boys. In moments like now, when he was being totally honest with himself, Luke could admit that Branch deserved a clap on the back and a handshake of gratitude for saving his sorry ass.

If not for John, he might have considered doing it.

Disturbed now, he turned away from the edge of the cliff and retraced his steps to his truck, where Knucklehead had fogged up the window. He didn't know where to search for Grevas next. Maybe he'd try the lake house again since he was out here. Then Gus's house. Jerry's. Maybe the bastard was on the move and felt himself safe once the cops had searched a place once.

Knowing small-town cops, he probably was safe.

Luke fired up his truck and made a big circle to turn around. That's when his headlights caught the shape on the ground.

A still shape. A bloody shape.

"Son of a bitch." Luke knew a body when he saw one.

He called the police chief and described the scene before him. Chief Harper instructed him to stay in his truck. Luke said he would, disconnected the call, grabbed a flashlight from the glove box, then climbed from the cab.

He had a sneaking suspicion as to what—or whom—he'd find when he approached the body lying on its side, facing away from him. He vaguely took note of the crickets chirping in the grass, the cicadas humming from the trees.

His attention was on the flies buzzing around the remains.

Luke circled the body. Shined a light on what was left of its face.

Jerry Grevas.

Luke dragged a hand down his bristled jaw and murmured, "What the hell is going on in Brazos Bend?"

Ten

By the time the ten o'clock news came on, Maddie was feeling better. What a day. Her headache had subsided for the most part, her aches and pains manageable through careful movement. She'd showered, removed the itchy Band-Aid from her forehead, and donned a smiley-face, seventies-era T-shirt and pair of gym shorts from Luke's dresser drawer. She made her way downstairs to the kitchen, where Branch had microwaved a Mexican casserole the Garza sisters had left for him in the freezer.

They settled into his living room just minutes before the hour. "Maybe the local news will have something about Jerry," Branch said. "Surely they've caught him by now, although Benny Taylor did promise to call me with news and I haven't heard a damned thing from him yet. That sumbich is too old to still be working down at the station. He forgets to return my calls half the time. I swear, I think he's got that old-timers' disease."

Maddie quietly sipped her water. She wouldn't think of commenting that perhaps Benny Taylor "forgot" Branch's calls on purpose. Since she'd started working for Branch, she'd noticed that while people seldom opposed him outright, they often asserted their independence and resistance through nonconfrontational ways. Like forgetting to return phone calls.

"So, which do you want to watch?" he asked. "Channel Six or Channel Three?"

"Whatever you ordinarily watch is fine with me."

He snorted. "I can hardly stand either of them. You got Mr. Good Hair and Ms. Perky-Pie on six, Ol' See My Teeth and his smarmy pal Big Nose on three. Doesn't matter which I watch, I end up throwing a slipper at them half the time anyway. They use this station as a training ground, you know. The announcers stay for six months or a year, then if they're any good they get shipped off to big cities like Waco and Wichita Falls. If you ask me . . ."

I didn't.

". . . they should leave us alone here and let hometown folk like Joe Brown do the news. Joe knows what's what behind a camera. He's been doing the 'Farm and Ranch' report for going on thirty years."

"I doubt a ten o'clock newscast would fit into Joe's schedule, since his farm report comes on at what, five a.m.?"

"Four thirty." Branch pointed his remote at the television, and Mr. Good Hair and Ms. Perky-Pie's beautiful, though somber, visages flashed on the screen.

". . . breaking news," Good Hair was saying. "Police have made a shocking arrest in the murder of longtime Brazos Bend citizen Jerry Grevas, whose body was found tonight up at Lookout Point. The man in custody is former Brazos Bend resident Luke Callahan."

Maddie's water glass slipped from her hand and spilled to the floor.

"What the hell!" Branch leaned forward in his chair, thumbing the remote's VOLUME UP button.

"Our reporter on the scene, Joe Brown, has the story."

As the phone started ringing at Callahan House, a skinny, rangy elderly man wearing a summer straw Stetson took the microphone from someone beyond the camera and grumbled, "I don't know what the hell is goin' on."

"You're on live, Joe."

"Oh. Well." He grimaced and rubbed the back of his neck with his free hand. "I was down here delivering a birthday present to my grandson—he's Patrol Officer Bobby Joe Brown. He's a good man, Bobby Joe is. His actual birthday is tomorrow, but his grandmother wanted him to have his gift first thing since it's a new electric razor and she figured he'd want to use it before the birthday party the family is throwing tomorrow night."

Maddie heard the cameraman say, "Joe! Get to Callahan!"

"Yeah!" Branch snapped at the TV, ignoring the trilling telephone.

"Get the phone, Branch. It might be Luke!"

"Oh. Yeah." He fumbled with the receiver. "Hello?"

He listened less than five seconds, then slammed the phone down. "Damn cemetery salesmen, calling so late. I think they're vampires. Only come out at night."

Maddie waved at him to be quiet and fixed her attention on the television. "Anyways, a few minutes ago Larry Henderson, that's Officer Henderson, brought Luke Callahan into the station with his hands cuffed behind his back. It was like old times, I'm telling you. Why, back in the day, not a week went by that one of those Callahan boys wasn't hauled into the station in handcuffs. This was the first time murder was involved, however, so everyone was pretty tense."

Maddie brushed absently at the water that had spilled in her lap while Branch threw a house slipper at the TV and shouted, "Idiot Joe Brown. Get to the point!"

"We're still trying to pin down just what happened," the "Farm and Ranch" reporter said. "Lots of hubbub, but not much real information. Hey, there's my grandson. Let's see if he has anything he can tell us. Bobby Joe? Hey, Bobby Joe, what's going on with Sin Callahan?"

"Hi, Grampa. I'm not rightly sure just what's going down. I hear somebody found Jerry Grevas with half his face shot off up at the lake. Callahan was close by and he'd been looking for Jerry all over town on account of how Jerry beat up Callahan's girlfriend. The lieutenant says that Callahan's been sneaking into town to date Maddie Kincaid, but no one really knows how long that's been going on. I know the DA is sweet on her, the librarian, too. They're gonna be upset to find out she's been stepping out with Callahan."

"Oh, my God," Maddie murmured.

"Goddamned small-town television station." Branch grabbed up the phone and shouted into it. "Hang up. I need to use the phone." Then he slammed it down, picked it up again, and called 911. When the operator answered, he said, "Janie, get me Chief Harper."

Since Branch held the receiver away from his ear to shout into it, Maddie could hear Janie's put-upon voice responding, "Branch Callahan, this line is for emergencies only."

"Good. Then get me the police chief."

A moment later, Chief Harper came on the line. "I knew I'd be hearing from you."

"What happened? Did my boy really fill that dipshit full of lead?"

Maddie's brows lifted. Surely he didn't think Luke really did the crime!

"A small-nose revolver, you say?" Branch repeated. "Well, that lets Luke off. My boy wouldn't carry a girly gun like that. You need to let Luke go."

Maddie closed her eyes at the realities of small-town politics and small-town justice. *Oh, Luke. What in the world happened? See, you'd have been better off not leaving me.*

"It's not the mushrooms," she murmured, thinking the matter through. Bet it was that mysterious box Grevas was so intent to find. Maybe that's what happened. He found it and somebody else wanted it, too. Wanted it bad. Bad enough to kill for it.

"This is just too much." First illicit drugs, now murder. This wasn't how Mayberry was supposed to be.

On the television, reporter Joe Brown promised he'd report back just as soon as he had more information, then he sent the broadcast back to the studio. On the phone, Branch continued to argue with the chief of police. Maddie wondered whether she should call a lawyer for Luke.

Branch let out a frustrated growl, then bellowed, "Listen here, Harper. There's an election coming up and you'd be wise to remember it."

Never mind that the police chief wasn't an elected official, Maddie took some comfort from Branch's harangue of the man. From what she could make of the conversation, the cops knew Luke wasn't guilty of murder. That, of course, begged the question, who was?

The front doorbell chimed and Maddie glanced over at Branch. He rolled his eyes as if saying, *What now?*

Rising, she made her way to the front foyer and glanced through the peephole. Surprise filled her as she opened the door. "Kathy?"

The older woman appeared frazzled as she stepped inside. "Hi, honey. I had to come see if you needed me."

"I'm fine. I—" She broke off, wincing, when her friend wrapped her in a big bear hug and held on.

"I'm so glad you're okay. I can't believe this happened. I went home not long after you left the Princess, and I spent hours gardening in the backyard. I didn't hear the news until Sally Jorgensen called to gossip about it. So Jerry Grevas was in your house when you went home? Right after you left my place? He attacked you?" When Maddie nodded, she added, "Oh, bless your heart." Then she burst into tears.

"Oh, Kathy," Maddie said, attempting to comfort her when the waterworks continued and her friend's agitation mounted. "It's okay. I'm okay."

"It's just the most awful—" Her sentence ended on a sob.

Maddie eased away from Kathy and said, "Come on in and watch the news with us. See if they have anything more about Luke."

"I can't believe they arrested him. I can't believe he's finally come home. What happened? Why do they think Luke is guilty?"

Maddie explained what she knew from the news. "That's all we know. Branch is trying to get more information."

"Of course he is." Kathy followed Maddie into the den,

where Branch was still on the phone. "That old coot will have his fingers all over this. He'll make sure his boy's not punished for something he didn't do." After a moment's hesitation, she asked, "He didn't do it, did he? I mean, Sally said he'd been hunting Jerry all over town."

"No, Luke didn't do it." Maddie moved too fast and gasped at the flash of pain. "If Jerry had been found beaten to a pulp, I might believe he was guilty. Luke wouldn't have killed him unless it was self-defense, and if that were the case, he'd have explained as much to the authorities."

"Look!" Branch interrupted, pointing toward the television. "Here's Joe Brown again."

He stood in front of a plain white wall. "All right, I've got the interview you all want." The reporter motioned to someone off camera, then to Maddie's surprise, an image of Luke filled the screen. "This here is Luke Callahan, one of Branch Callahan's boys. One of the twins."

"Good Lord," Kathy muttered. "That's no boy. He is all man."

Luke shoved his hands in his pockets and within the blink of an eye, his demeanor changed. He wasn't the stern federal agent or the solemn investigator. This Luke stood with his hip cocked, his grin a wicked challenge, his eyes full of attitude. He was Luke Callahan, badass.

What in the world . . . ?

"Luke, I think we'd all like to know what brings you back to Brazos Bend after so long, but first, why don't you tell us in your own words what happened tonight?"

"Jerry Grevas got his ass shot."

Maddie blinked, her mouth gaping open.

"Uh, this is live TV, Callahan," Joe Brown reminded him. "Maybe you could watch your language a bit?"

"Hey, you're the one who wants this interview. Me, I'm happy to head on back to my old man's place. I could sure use a drink right about now."

"Home? He's coming home?" Branch sat forward in his chair.

Joe Brown scowled at Luke, then asked, "Tell us what you know about Jerry Grevas's murder."

"He was dead when I got there. I don't know how it happened or why. All I know is that when I saw him lying among the rocks up at the lake, I did my civic duty and called the cops. They had no cause to haul my ass down here. Chief Harper did it out of habit."

"What brings you back to town, Luke?" the reporter asked.

"You can call me Sin. I'm back because I need a place to stay for awhile. Plus, I wanted to visit Maddie Kincaid. Met her in a bar in Dallas awhile back and we hit it off. Tell you what, Joe, if I'd known women the likes of Maddie were moving to Brazos Bend, I'd have come home long ago."

"What is he doing!" Maddie exclaimed.

"He's coming across as a real jerk, that's what," Kathy observed, now recovered from her earlier upset.

Maddie couldn't disagree. She might not know the man intimately, but she darn well knew him well enough to know he wouldn't be copping such an attitude and spouting such outrageous lies without a reason. She'd bet her favorite sandals that the reason had something to do with Jerry Grevas's death.

Maddie heard the doorbell chime in the entryway. On television, Joe Brown asked, "So, you're not home for good?"

"I'm home for no good," Luke replied, flashing a wicked grin. "Y'all know me. I haven't changed that much since I left Brazos Bend."

"Yes, he has!" Branch protested.

Yes, Maddie agreed, he had. He'd become a federal agent. A federal agent who worked undercover. That's the answer to her question. That's what Luke was doing.

Official or not, Luke Callahan had just gone undercover on local TV news.

A low-level fury hummed in Luke's blood, reminding him of how it felt to be sixteen and living in Brazos Bend again. Damned thick-headed country hicks. Wouldn't listen to a word he said. Hauled his butt off to jail just like old times until Austin stepped in and got him sprung. It'd pissed him off royally until it occurred to him that they'd handed him the perfect opportunity to connect with the underbelly of Brazos Bend society, with the added benefit of making Branch crazy.

Branch wanted his sons back in Brazos Bend. But he wanted them to return as the men they'd become, not the good-for-nothing boys who'd left. That didn't suit Luke's purpose. He needed to come across as his same old sorry self in order to connect with drug dealers and other low-life scum in Brazos Bend. That's how he'd discover the details of whatever trouble had led to Grevas's killing and whether Maddie might still be in danger.

So, Luke decided the time had come for Sin once again.

It was easy to slip back into the arrogant asshole mode. He'd done a version of it many times during his days in the DEA. This time he'd play the wealthy playboy, and Branch would live with it. If the subject wasn't so serious, if Maddie weren't mixed up in the middle of it, Luke just might have fun.

The patrolman taking Luke to get his truck peppered him with questions about the state champion football team of which he'd been a member his sophomore year in high school. Luke had relatively good memories of that year, so he didn't mind talking about it. A bit distracted, he didn't notice that the patrolman took the wrong road to the lake until the police car stopped in front of Callahan House.

"Not here. My truck's up at the lake."

"Sorry. Chief Harper told me to bring you here, and I'm to get right back to the station. I don't think he likes you very much. We did bring your dog back, though. The district attorney said to tell you he took the mutt home for the night."

Good. One less thing to worry about.

Luke strolled up the sidewalk toward the front door. He

lifted his foot to climb the first step, when a voice drifted from out of the shadows off to his right. "Luke? Is that you?"

Maddie.

Abruptly, he turned, stepped over a flower bed filled with begonias, and walked across the grass toward the gazebo. With the moonlight, the starlight, and the lamplight beaming from the windows of Callahan House, he was able to see her clearly.

She sat on the porch swing, the bandage gone from her head, wearing clothes that looked familiar. Her eyes gleamed like a cat's in the shadows. She smiled at him and some of the anger running through him abated. "What are you doing out of bed?"

"I'm feeling so much better. The headache's gone and as long as I move slowly, it doesn't hurt all that much."

"That's good." He took a seat beside her on the swing. "I've been worried about you."

Dryly, she replied, "I'm surprised you had time. I caught your performance on the local news."

Well, hell. He hadn't exactly counted on that. "Um, about that . . ."

"As much as I'd like to listen to you fumble around attempting to explain, I understand that it's part of your cover."

"You do?"

"You've decided to stay, haven't you?"

Luke fidgeted in his seat like a schoolboy. She'd think he was staying for her and that's not what this was all about.

Was it?

"You want to solve the murder, don't you?" she asked.

"I can't say I care all that much about the fact that Jerry Grevas is dead since I wanted to murder him myself."

"No, you didn't." Confidence rang in her voice.

Honey, if you only knew.

She took his hand in hers. "If it's not the murder, then it's the mystery. You want to know what's going on here in Brazos Bend."

Luke tried to recall the last time he'd sat in the dark holding hands with a woman. He couldn't. "You think you're pretty smart, don't you?"

"What I think—what I know—is that I'm relieved. I'm so glad I don't have to face this alone."

It was the perfect opportunity for him to tell her his stay was temporary, to explain that he'd leave Brazos Bend as soon as he'd satisfied his curiosity. Yet, all he did was ask, "Even if it means you have to hang out with the notorious Sin Callahan?"

She laughed, a soft, melodious chuckle that flowed over him like wine. "Hey, compared to some of the guys I've hung around with, Sin Callahan is a pussycat."

"A pussycat!" He stiffened in mock offense, his gaze zeroed in on her mouth. "You better watch what you say, Ms. Kincaid. As we say here in Texas, them's fightin' words."

"Nonetheless, it's true." She folded her arms, plumping up her cleavage. "Talk trash all you want, Callahan, but you're not the type to clean out my bank accounts and leave me stranded in Hong Kong. You're not one to make contributions to a terrorist organization in my name, with my money. You're darn sure not the type of man who'll turn me into his unwitting drug mule."

Talk about spoiling the moment. Luke stretched out his legs, crossing them at the ankles. "Are we talking about the previously mentioned Cade, Liam, and Rip?"

"You remember their names?"

Yeah. And what sort of a name was Rip, anyway? That should have clued her in from the first. "They were your boyfriends."

She paused a long moment before saying, "They were my lovers. The only lovers I've ever had."

Luke took a moment to digest that bit of news. *Three? Only three?* "But you're Baby Dag—"

She put her finger up to his lips. "Hush. Don't say that aloud, even when we're alone. You never know when someone might overhear. Didn't they teach you that in undercover school?"

"Three guys. And each one of them was a bastard?" When she nodded, he continued, "Jesus, lady. You need to keep better company."

Now her voice went smug. "I am now, aren't I?"

Luke shoved himself to his feet and moved to stand in the gazebo's doorway, staring out into the grounds of his father's estate. He needed to be straight with her. To be honest. Why was it so hard? In the past he'd had women who'd wanted more from him than he wanted to give, and he'd never had this problem telling them the way it was. He needed to spit the words out and be done.

His mouth was as dry as sand. "Look, Maddie, I don't know what you're thinking, but . . . hell . . . I don't know what I'm thinking, but I don't want . . . I can't . . . oh, hell."

"Do you know why you came to Brazos Bend?"

Crickets chirped and a bullfrog bellowed and Luke silently chastised himself. He came because he didn't do right by her the first time. He'd let her come back here alone, and she nearly got killed.

Maddie tried again. "Were you worried about me?"

"Yes. Yes, dammit, I was!" he snapped, rounding on her. "For good reason as today has clearly pointed out. I shouldn't have sent you back alone, Maddie. I'm sorry."

"Stop that. It wasn't your fault that Jerry went postal on me, Luke. Look at this from my point of view. You worried about me. You cared. You genuinely cared. And it didn't have anything to do with who my daddy is or how full my bank accounts are or the fact that I know the Bala Hissar bj technique."

"The *what*?"

"One of my dad's former lovers was into Eastern enlightenment. She'd been part of the Beatles entourage. She wasn't bashful about answering my questions. Here's the deal, Callahan. I know you and I don't have a future. Our goals are different, our hopes and dreams are polar opposites. I'm not looking at you as a long-term anything, so you don't need to be afraid about that. But right here, as of right now, I'm going to count you as my friend. All right?"

He had to drag his brain away from Bala Hissar. Friends? She wanted to be friends? Was this the conversation girls gave guys when they wanted to blow them off? Or did she mean real friends? True friends. Friends like Terry Winston.

"Not a good idea, Kincaid," Luke replied. "My friends tend to end up dead."

"*One* person. That happened once. Don't project it over the rest of your life." She offered her hand. "So, be my friend, Luke Callahan?"

Luke stared at her hand, all milky and soft in the moonlight, her nails natural and painted a pretty pink, and he silently admitted that he didn't want to be her friend.

He wanted to be her lover.

Unable to stop himself, he asked, "So, just what kind of friendship are we talking about, here?"

"What do you mean?"

"Is it one where we wave at each other as we pass on the street or is it a beer-and-ball-game friendship? Or, is it deeper than that? Would we pitch in to paint one another's houses?"

"Don't like house painting, Callahan?"

"Despise it."

"I see. Well, then, yes. I'm talking a two-coat friendship."

"Wow. Serious, then."

"Yep."

Luke rolled his tongue around his mouth. He should stop it here. *Don't go there, Callahan. Don't tempt the fates. You'll be sorry and she'll be sorry and it'll get ugly. For both our sakes, just shut the hell up.*

Instead, he popped the most important question of the conversation. "Is it a friendship with privileges?"

"Privileges?"

"Do I get to be number four?"

"Number . . . oh. *Those* kinds of privileges."

"Uh-huh."

"Hmm. Well, I have to think about that. Is it a deal breaker?"

A ball breaker. He wanted her so bad his teeth ached. "No. I'm not that big of a jerk, Maddie. I just think it's best to get everything out on the table, so to speak. Hey, you're the one who brought up techniques."

Damned if she didn't grin. "So, are privileges something you're in favor of?"

"I would say yes to that." Considering it was all he could do not to jump her right here and now. He wanted his hands on her. His mouth on her. He wanted to be inside her, to feel her wrapped around him, soft and warm and wet.

"As I consider this question, there's something you should know. I haven't had sex in over two years."

Whoa. That jerked him right out of his fantasy. No sex in two years? "You're kidding."

She shook her head. "Not since the night before Cade planted his pot in my purse."

Jealousy whipped through him. Hell. Maybe he'd be better off not knowing much about ol' numbers one, two, and three.

Luke rubbed the back of his neck. Two years. There'd be some pressure there. "Just curious, here. Does your, uh, dry spell make you more likely to go with privileges or less likely?"

She shrugged indifferently, but the gleam in her eyes gave him hope. "I'd say . . . probably . . . hmm . . . probably more."

Good. That's good. That's real good.

Okay, babe. What's the decision here? He wanted to start tapping his foot. Instead, he sat beside her once again. Closer this time. He couldn't stop himself.

"Although, I have to tell you, Luke, this conversation feels a bit like a negotiation, and that has solicitation overtones."

Conversation, negotiation . . . "Solicitation! Oh, for crying out loud. I'm not soliciting you for sex. I'm trying to communicate, to make sure we have no misunderstandings. I'm asking just how friendly you feel like being."

This time the sound of her laughter flowed through him like warm, intoxicating whisky. "Pretty friendly," she said. "Except, of course, that I'm in no shape to demonstrate. My ribs . . ."

Oh, hell. He'd forgotten. *God, I'm a pig.* "I'd like to dig Jerry Grevas up and kill him again." When she shot him a stern look, he added, "Jesus, I was speaking figuratively."

"I knew that."

"Besides, I couldn't dig him up. He's laid out like a salmon in the morgue."

"Okay. Right. Well, okay."

"Okay, what?"

"Okay, privileges granted. Now, how about we seal our friendship with a kiss?"

She didn't have to ask twice. He caught her hair in his hand and pulled her toward him. Her lips were hot and clever, and when her tongue made a lazy sweep into his mouth, he felt a strong jolt of pure, primal lust.

He'd kissed a lot of women in his time, but this time, this woman, was different. Scare-the-hell-out-of-a-man different.

Luke wasn't stupid. He knew this wasn't just lust. It was something else. Something too frightening to admit.

They both were breathing heavily when they finally broke apart. Luke moved away from her, scrambling for air, fumbling for words. "I, uh, whoa. I guess we'd better . . . I'd better . . . I need to go get my truck."

"Where is it?"

"Up at the lake. Lovers' Point."

"I hear it's beautiful up there. I've never been."

Luke trailed a finger down her petal-soft cheek. "I'll take you sometime."

She closed her eyes and drew a deep breath that called his attention to her breasts. His mouth literally watered.

"Tomorrow," she said. "How about we go tomorrow? At sunset. I'll drive you up to get your truck tomorrow night. You can use my van in the meantime."

That stopped him. "Your van? Your minivan? I'm not driving a minivan!"

She turned her face and nipped at his finger. "Lovers' Point seems like a good place to discuss Bala Hissar."

He shuddered. "Give me your keys."

Eleven

For appearances' sake, Luke slept at his father's house. He refused, however, to totally destroy his vow and sleep beneath his father's roof, so he spent the night in a lounge chair beside the pool, dreaming nightmares of hospitals and blood. He awoke in a sweat to birdsong as the sun peeked above the trees. His eyes felt gritty, his muscles stiff. He threw his arm over his eyes and let out a groan that ended abruptly when an intriguing thought occurred.

Maddie. It's tomorrow.

Suddenly, he felt downright chipper.

Luke rolled off the lounge chair and stripped off his shirt, eyeing the inviting water of the pool. With his duffel bag in his truck up at the lake, he had no change of clothes, so he shucked off his shorts and boxers, too, before diving into the deep end.

As he swam one lap after another, Luke couldn't stop the memories. He'd spent a lot of hours in this—to quote Matt quoting Jed Clampett—cement pond. Games of Marco Polo and shark with his brothers. Diving for the lost city of Atlantis. The traditional greased-watermelon scramble on the Fourth of July. God, that had been an all-out war.

Because Branch Callahan was Branch Callahan, he hadn't settled for a normal backyard-sized pool. He'd built an Olympic-sized pool to suit his Olympic-sized ego. Three times every summer—Memorial Day, Fourth of July, and Labor Day—he invited every family with kids at Fain Elementary to come for barbecue and pool games. The money scramble was a hit with the majority of the guests. Branch divided the children by age groups, then threw a thousand dollars' worth of nickels, dimes, and quarters into the pool and let the kids have at it.

Being the rich bastards they were, Luke and his brothers preferred the watermelon scramble. Once the pool had been stripped of its silver, ol' Branch brought out the watermelons and the jars of Vaseline. He greased up the melons and tossed them in the water, and then the battles began. Thrown elbows and kicks and punches to the gut—every year at least one of the Callahans scored a black eye in the attempt to be the one to hoist the melon from the pool and win the sweet summer prize.

Luke's mother claimed to hate the game. She'd fuss over their bumps and bruises, then cluck her tongue over the smears of Vaseline the pool cleaners invariably missed. Yet, she was the one who made a special trip out to Dennis Knautz's watermelon patch to pick out the perfect melons. Good summers, good times.

Luke plowed through the water, making racing turns at each end of the pool, pushing his body to clear his mind. Still, the memories came. Mom in her Katharine Hepburn sunhat, Jackie O sunglasses, and Doris Day swimsuit. His father doing backflips off the diving board. Matt holding John by the hands, Mark getting his legs, swinging the youngest Callahan, one, two, three, then into the deep end. All of them laughing. Laughing.

The laughter died with their mother.

Shit. Luke dove in the deep end, planted his feet on the bottom, then used every bit of strength in his legs to shoot himself upward. His head broke the surface, and he gave it a hard shake, flinging the water out of his eyes before he reached for the side and hauled himself out of the water.

He stood beside the pool, naked and dripping and grieving, until a towel hit him from behind and Branch Callahan's gruff voice said, "Put some clothes on, boy. There's women in the house. You'll give the Garza sisters heart attacks."

Great. Just what he needed.

Luke couldn't help but fall back into the rebellious patterns of old, taking his own sweet time to dry off. His father waited to speak until he'd wrapped the bright white towel around his hips and secured it. "That's an ugly-looking scar on your belly."

The knife wound was three years older than the bullet that had caught his shoulder in Miami. The South American doctor had done the best he could in the middle of the jungle, but the results weren't pretty. Luke didn't respond to his father, instead sauntering slowly over to his pile of clothes.

"Maria is making pecan waffles," Branch said.

Translation, *your favorite*. Luke still didn't speak.

"Since Madeline is in your room, I had Juanita put a shaving kit in Matt's bathroom for you. Stuff inside is all new. Didn't know if you used foam or gel when you shave so we gave you both."

The entreaty in his father's voice made Luke uncomfortable. It was pathetic, really, and were he any other man than Branch Callahan, Luke would take pity on him. But where his father was concerned, Luke remained fresh out of pity. That all died in a Balkan mountain village right along with John.

Luke broke his silence with a curt, "Look. Don't be reading anything into this situation that isn't there. I don't want to be here, and I'm not staying a minute longer than I have to. Things will go smoother if you just leave me the hell alone."

"I'd like to talk to you, son."

"Too bad. Talking's five years too late." Not pausing to pull on his britches, Luke stalked toward the house, emotion churning in his gut. Helluva way to begin a day.

At least he had "tomorrow" to look forward to.

That thought, along with the aroma of frying bacon and home-cooked waffles that greeted him when he entered the kitchen, managed to dispel the early-morning black clouds, and he paused beside the cook to give her a kiss on the cheek. "Good morning, beautiful."

"Mister Luke!" Juanita Garza swatted his hand with a spatula when he snagged a piece of cooked bacon from a plate. "*Dios mío!* If you don't have the nerve! No shirt, no shoes. No *shorts.*"

"No waffles!" piped up her sister's voice from the dining room.

Luke fired off some flattery in Spanish, then grabbed a cup of coffee before heading upstairs to shower, chased by the elderly women's laughter.

Outside Maddie's doorway, he paused, listening for signs of stirring. He rapped softly on the door. "Maddie?"

Nothing.

Setting his clothes and coffee cup on a nearby console table, he turned the doorknob and sneaked a look inside. Sleeping Beauty. Sleeping Black-and-Blue Beauty, he corrected with a frown. *Damn that Jerry Grevas.*

Luke stepped silently into her room, hoping that some of the color on her face resulted from shadows, not bruises. She let out a little snuffle and he smiled.

Luke moved to the window and adjusted the curtains, allowing in just a little more light. Then he approached the bed and sucked in a whistle. No shadows, those. *Poor thing. Damn that Jerry Grevas to hell.*

Unable to stop himself, Luke reached out and touched her, smoothing her hair away from a cut just above her right eyebrow. He wished he could lean down and kiss all those hurts away.

Her lashes flickered; her eyes opened. "Good morning," Luke said.

She smiled, slowly, sweetly. "It's tomorrow."

"Oh, yeah."

"I'm glad."

"Me, too. Didn't think it'd ever get here."

Her gaze flicked over him. "Nice towel."

"I had a swim. I'm headed for the shower. Wanted to check on you first."

"I'm—" She went to rise. Gasped a breath.

"Maddie?"

"Oh. Oh. Ow!"

"Maddie? Honey?" He tried to help her as she groaned her way to a seated position.

"Oh, wow. Oh, shoot." She panted like a tired puppy. "Jeez-o-pete, I hurt!"

That's when he had his Homer Simpson *D'oh!* moment. Where the hell had he left his brain? The second day following blunt-force trauma was always worse than the first. "Did the doc give you any pain meds?"

"I didn't think I'd need them."

"Tough girl." Foolish girl. "You can probably use a soak in a hot tub. Let me go run the water, then I'll help you to the bathroom."

He took it as a sign of just how badly she felt that she didn't argue with him.

As the tub filled with steaming water, Luke made sure any items she might need were placed within easy reach. His gaze snagged on a stack of magazines in a basket on the floor. *Hot Rod*, *Popular Mechanics*, *Playboy*. He checked the dates. Current. Then the address label. LUKE CALLAHAN. 3219 AVONDALE. BRAZOS BEND, TX. "He's still renewing my subscriptions?"

For God's sake. The man had too much money and lived in a fantasy world.

When he returned to the bedroom Maddie was struggling to her feet. "Hold on, there; I'll help."

"This is humiliating," she said as he slipped a supporting arm around her. "I wasn't near this sore yesterday."

"Today and tomorrow will be the worst of it. I know from experience. You'll feel better after your bath, but it'll be a few days before you feel like your normal self."

"But . . . ?"

"But what, honey?"

She sounded like a disappointed kid on Christmas morning as she said, "It's tomorrow!"

Tomorrow. Well, hell. "Yeah, Red. I know." Then, in a sad attempt to cheer her up, he offered an encouraging smile and crooned, "But it's only a day away."

She snorted and he winked, then retired to Matt's bedroom, where he brooded while he showered and dressed. The day that had started off bad hit bottom when he went downstairs. Juanita Garza had burned the pecan waffles.

And the cops had stopped by to haul him in for more questioning regarding Jerry Grevas's murder.

That afternoon while seated on the sofa in her living room surrounded by the flotsam of last night's attack, Maddie was not a happy camper. "Why did he have to dump all my pictures? I'm particular about my pictures. It'll take me weeks to get them back in order."

"I know it'll make you mad, but I can't say I'm sorry." Kathy held up a photograph of Maddie and her parents at the Hollywood Bowl. "These photos are a treasure trove. Look, there's one with your father and Keith Richards. These photos should be in a museum. I can't believe you've never shown them to me before. They're part of history!"

They were family and they were personal. Some things Maddie didn't want to share with the world. Her eighth birthday party was one of them. The fact that her old terrorist boyfriend had called twice today was another.

She was saved from any reply by a knock on the door. Kathy hopped up to answer it. "Well, Luke. We've been wondering when Chief Harper would get off his high horse and set you free. I don't know what's wrong with that man. Why did he want to talk to you some more? Did they discover something new about the killing?"

"No." He sauntered into the house and studied Maddie

with an intense look. "The police chief has a hard-on for me from the old days. He just likes to exercise his power. You doing okay, Red?"

She didn't bother correcting him about her name. He never listened, and besides, "Red" didn't sound so bad coming from his mouth. "Yes."

Luke glanced around. "I can see what you've been up to while I was otherwise occupied. Y'all have been busy."

"The Garza sisters did most of the work." Maddie cleared a spot on the sofa for Luke to sit down. "They had my kitchen and bathrooms put to rights before Kathy and I got here."

Kathy piped up. "I took Maddie by Tranquility Day Spa for an herbal steam. Thought it might loosen her up."

His eyes smoldered. "Did it help?"

"Not enough," she said with true regret.

He must have retrieved his truck at some point, because he wore jeans and a T-shirt she recognized from the *Miss Behavin' II*. Her gaze focused on the bulge of tanned muscle below the shirt's white sleeve and she had a hard time dragging her attention back to what he was saying as he answered a question of Kathy's she'd missed.

". . . drawn a blank so far. It's early yet, though. They're hoping forensics will tell them more."

"Like what?" Kathy asked.

"Trace evidence on the body. That sort of thing. Still, they'll need a suspect before that'll do them much good. I doubt forensics in Brazos Bend are exactly cutting edge. It may well take them months to figure out much of anything."

"That's what you intend to work on?" Maddie asked. "Finding a suspect?"

"I'm going to find his business associates."

"Drug dealers," Kathy surmised. "I'll bet they're the ones who did it. It's not too big a step from dealing to killing. Poor Gus. This would kill him if he weren't already gone. I wish you wouldn't get involved with this, Sin. It could be dangerous. I know it makes me sound hard, but after seeing what Jerry did to Maddie . . . well . . . he deserved what he got. What does it matter who killed him?"

Luke went serious. "I need to make sure Maddie is safe, that's why. I thought I'd protected her before, but just look at her. I'm not leaving anything up to chance. Not again. Kathy, I need your help with this. I know you're Maddie's friend. You've kept her secrets. I need you to keep mine, too."

Worry creased her brow. "But . . ."

"For her, Kathy."

She closed her eyes and nodded. "All right. Don't worry, Sin. My lips are sealed."

Luke spent an hour on the phone while Maddie and Kathy finished cleaning up the mess Jerry Grevas had made of Maddie's house. Neighbors and friends dropped by throughout the afternoon, fussing over Maddie, bringing casseroles and cookies and hunting for gossip. Each time the doorbell rang, Maddie watched in amazement as Luke dropped into the Brazos Bend bad-boy role.

"Did you watch a lot of James Dean movies growing up?" she asked him when they were finally alone after he shut the door behind the First Baptist minister's wife and Kathy, who'd left to work a shift at the Dairy Princess. "You've got that curled-lip sneer down perfectly."

"Thanks." Luke grabbed a Snickerdoodle from the church lady's plate. "I do try."

He broke the cookie in half and offered her a piece. Maddie shook her head, then watched him savor the sweet. She'd have squirmed in her seat had it not hurt to move that way. Good Lord, did the man have to ooze sex appeal with everything he did? She'd just about swallowed her tongue this morning when she woke up to see him wearing only a towel. That was understandable. He was built like a Greek god. But to get turned on by watching him munch down a Snickerdoodle? *Get a hold of yourself, Kincaid.*

She cleared her throat. "So, now that you've let Brazos Bend know that Sin is back in town, what's your next step?"

"I'll visit a few old haunts. Throw some money around. Let it be known I'm looking for a local supplier."

"I don't like this, Luke. Maybe Kathy was right and it's too—"

"It's my job," he said, putting a finger against her lips.

Maddie kissed it. She couldn't help herself. Instincts took over and besides, he tasted of Snickerdoodle. "Was your job," she corrected. "Unless you've rejoined the agency and neglected to mention it?"

"No."

Her gaze lifted to his, fastened on his, as she drew his finger farther into her mouth, stroked it with her tongue, and sucked.

Luke pulled in an audible breath. "Holy crap, Maddie."

She nipped the pad of his fingertip, then released him. "It's fewer calories having my sweets this way."

"Holy crap, Maddie," he repeated.

The heat in his eyes warmed her blood and Maddie tried to tell herself that the herbal steam had done the trick and her body didn't hurt all *that* bad. Nothing's broken. Right?

The sound of the doorbell settled the question for her. For now, anyway.

"I hate small towns," Luke grumbled as he rose to answer the door. "People here are just too damned friendly."

This visitor was simply doing his job, however. "Ron Harrison with Neiman's in Fort Worth, sir. I'm looking for Mr. Luke Callahan."

"That's me."

Harrison shook Luke's hand. "A pleasure to meet you, sir. I was able to fill every item on the order. I hope you'll be satisfied." The man handed Luke a folio.

"I'm sure it'll be fine. Go ahead and bring everything in here, if you would, please." Maddie's brows winged up in curiosity as Luke scanned the ticket, scrawled his name at the bottom, then handed it back. "And the car?"

"Right behind me. The driver stopped to fill the tank before delivery."

A short time later, Maddie's living room was once again filled with clutter, only this time it looked like the aftermath of Christmas rather than a break-in. Maddie fingered the soft, supple leather of a pair of Magli shoes. "I take it all this is for Sin Callahan to keep up appearances?"

"Dressing the part is the first thing they teach you in undercover school."

She glanced out her window, saw a fire-engine red Maserati pull up to the curb, then turned her attention to a black velvet jeweler's box. "A gold necklace? Luke, that is *so* not you."

Luke grimaced, then shrugged. "It's expectations. It's who they'll expect me to be." He turned his attention back to the boxes, exclaiming a moment later, "Finally!"

He handed a small box and a larger bag to Maddie. Both were as light as feathers. "Just some things I thought you could use."

Maddie eyed his casual mien with suspicion, then cautiously peeked into the box. It appeared empty. No, wait. She tugged the white tissue paper apart to reveal emerald scraps of fabric. "What . . . ?"

"Since you're staying at Branch's for a few days, I thought you should have a swimsuit."

She had a swimsuit in her bedroom dresser. A nice, modest one-piece. Not—she held up one scrap— "A thong?"

"I'm told they're really comfortable."

I just bet. The gift bag, though still lightweight, was packed full. Of silk lingerie. In a dozen different colors. "Grevas went through your panty drawer," Luke said as way of explanation.

"There is such a thing called a washing machine." She pulled a black lace demi-cup bra from the bag along with a matching pair of panties. A thong, of course.

"You want to try them on?" he asked, a note of hope in his voice. "Make sure they fit? If there's a problem, we can catch ol' Ron before he gets too far down the road and have them exchanged."

She could, but then they'd end up in bed and as much as the spirit was willing, the ibuprofen was wearing off and the body was weak. "I better wait until tomorrow."

He wanted to argue, she could tell. His gaze lingered on the lingerie with such yearning that Maddie couldn't help but be flattered. The man was hot for her. He wanted her for *her*, not for her connections or her money or her fame. It made her feel good.

"I was afraid of that." Now Luke focused on her lips. "I gotta kiss you, Red. Just a kiss. I won't hurt you, I promise. No hands. Just . . . ah, hell." He leaned forward and captured her mouth in a long, wet, intimate kiss that left her blood humming when he finally pulled away.

"I was afraid of that," he repeated.

Giving his head a shake, Luke got back to business and bundled up his packages to take to the car. "You're about through here, aren't you? Why don't I take you back to Branch's? You can take a nap there. I told Austin Rawlings I'd meet him for a beer later, and I don't want to leave you here alone."

"Austin? He doesn't quite seem Sin's type."

"He's all right. We have a common bond: overbearing, controlling assholes for fathers. Besides, I want to pick his brains about Jerry's murder."

"Who could have killed him, Luke? I'm trying to follow the logic, here, but . . ."

"I long ago gave up logic where drugs are concerned. It could have been his supplier, a partner, or a deal gone bad. Who knows? But until I learn the answer, I'm not letting my guard down where you're concerned, and as much as I hate Callahan House, you're better off there than alone."

Maddie didn't argue with him. Even though her house was back in order, she wasn't up to staying here by herself. Built in the 1940s, her place was small and intimate and perfect for her, but it made lots of noises. She'd worry over every creak and groan if she were here by herself. "That'll be fine."

While Luke loaded up his new sports car with his high-dollar costumes, Maddie stacked a couple boxes of photographs to take along to Branch's. While Luke went out on the town tonight, she'd spend some time with her own memories. She had pictures of Liam in here. Liam and some of his friends.

Just for the grins, she'd look through them, see if anyone looked familiar. See if she could figure out what her old lover wanted from her.

Maybe next time he called, she'd answer. Maybe she'd come right out and ask him if he'd followed her to Texas.

By midnight, Luke had enough evidence to get half the Brazos Bend High School football players kicked off the team before two-a-days started in August. Steroid usage by athletes was a problem all over the country, but this was Texas, where high school football was as serious as religion. He wasn't the least bit surprised that the kids were juicers. He wondered whether school administrators would even do anything about it if he phoned in an anonymous tip.

Hell, it'd be worth a try. Kids all over the country were killing themselves with this poison in order to be bigger, stronger, faster. Luke couldn't solve the country's problem, but he might be able to do some good here in Brazos Bend.

Luke sat at the bar at the establishment referred to by the locals as P-2, which stood for Pioneer 2, the second of six establishments owned and operated by the Terry family. P-1 was a downtown Tex-Mex restaurant, P-3 and P-4 home-cooking concerns on the main highway at each end of town to catch the tourists passing through. P-5 had blown away in the '79 tornado, and P-6 . . . well . . . it wasn't exactly a commercial establishment. P-6 was the lake house out at Possum Kingdom where the Terry boys went to drink and screw. Luke had spent some fine times at P-6 back in the day.

"Another red draw while you wait for the table, Sin?" a

bleached blond waitress asked, offering him the local specialty—draft beer and tomato juice.

"Think I'll hold off a bit," he responded. He'd barely been able to choke down the one he'd had for old times' sake. His high school palate hadn't been very picky.

He'd hung around here playing pool for three hours now, pumping the kids for information while he waited for the late shift at the plastics plant to let out. That's when he'd see some of his old running buddies, he'd learned. Bobby Hargett, Brandon Miles, and Scooter Westridge had gone to work there right out of high school, and they hadn't left. They still met here for beer and pool every Thursday night.

Scooter had been the grass supplier during their high school days. Brandon had a thing for chemistry and crime even in high school, so Luke thought he was a good bet to be a meth cook these days. Bobby had been the conscience of the group. He tried, at least, to keep the others from straying too far outside the law.

Well, all except for Luke and Mark.

The men arrived ten minutes after midnight and as he watched them shuffle inside, nostalgia washed over Luke. Except for his brothers and Terry, he'd been closer to these three than to any other people in his life. They'd gone to school together, raised hell together, and sworn they'd always have each other's backs. Luke lost contact with them completely when he left Brazos Bend.

Sometime during the past seventeen years, Brandon had lost his hair. Scooter had gained about fifty pounds, and tall, skinny ol' Bobby had grown some guns.

Hell, he'd missed these jerks.

Luke sauntered up to the table, plunked down an empty beer mug, and said, "Buy me a drink, assholes."

Scooter kicked back a chair and nodded toward the pitcher in the middle of the table. "Sit down and pour your own, Sin. Bobby's fixin' to tell us about the striper he caught up at the lake this morning."

It was as if seventeen years had never happened.

Bobby told his fish tale—be damned if Luke believed he caught a twenty-pound striper on a ten-pound line—then Brandon talked about their plans to attend a gun show in Fort Worth the coming weekend. Only after driving arrangements were settled did Scooter turn to Luke and say, "Heard about your TV appearance last night. Leave it to Sin Callahan to disappear for years and still manage to bag the second-prettiest girl in town."

"Second-prettiest?" Luke asked, taking a sip of his beer.

"Can't say she's better lookin' than my Laura. Wouldn't be right."

Laura . . . Laura . . . "Laura Wilson?"

"Laura Havens." Scooter tugged his wallet from his pocket and flipped it open. "We've got us two boys and a girl. I suspect my Peanut'll be the second-prettiest girl in town before long, but since she's still cue-ball bald, in all fairness, I can't claim the spot on her behalf."

Luke stared down at the family portrait, his mouth agog. Scooter reproduced? Three times? "Damn, Scoot. That's a fine-looking family. It's a crying shame they couldn't have done better than you, though."

"That's what they tell me." Scooter's smile was smug as he returned his wallet to his back pocket.

Luke glanced at the other two men. The absence of wedding rings on their fingers didn't tell him anything, since rings were a hazard in the factory. "What about y'all? You wearing leg shackles, too?"

"Two years to Penny Fenton," Bobby said. "No rug rats yet, but we're starting to think about it."

Brandon shook his head. "Not me. I was hitched to Samantha Parker for a year and a half, but that didn't work out."

"She wanted him to keep his dick in his pants when he was around other women," Bobby drawled. "Imagine that."

"It's reassuring to know not everything's changed around the old hometown since I've been gone."

"So where you been all this time, Sin? Whatcha been

doin'? I take it that's your high-dollar ride in the parking lot?"

Luke told them a mix of fact and fantasy intended to promote the reputation of fast-lane living that he needed to attract the element he intended to infiltrate. The fact his old friends obviously didn't approve shouldn't have surprised him or bothered him, but it did. In fact, it left him darn near speechless when ol' pot-pushing Scooter leaned back in his chair and said, "Hell, boy. Don't you think it's time you grew up?"

If you only knew, Westridge. If you only knew.

Luke decided to lay his cards on the table, so to speak. "I gotta say, I'm surprised. I figured there'd be a better-than-even chance that when I came back to town at least one of y'all would be in jail and the others cooking up meth or peddling blow. When Maddie told me about Jerry G's trailer house full of magic mushrooms, I figured he was probably growing 'em for Brandon."

The three men shared a guilty glance. *Bingo,* Luke thought.

Bobby looked downright miserable. "I might as well have killed the guy myself."

Luke leaned forward. "You in business with him, Bob?"

"Hell, no." Bobby Hargett shot him a mean look. "This isn't high school, Callahan. I'm no goddamned drug pusher or a sorry-ass user, so if you came here looking to score some of that shit off me you're a goddamned loser and you can just take your gay gold chains and fancy cars back to wherever the hell you came from and leave us the hell alone."

Luke drew back, his palms out. "Whoa, there. Your mama never did get you to clean up your mouth, did she? I didn't mean to hit a hot button. It was just a question. I've been gone a long time. I don't know what all you've been doing in the meantime, and you have to admit, the comment about killing him was a curious one."

Scooter drained his mug, then plunked it down hard onto

the wooden table. "Had nothing to do with drugs. We stopped messing with those ten years ago."

"It was gambling," Brandon said quietly. "A few of us started taking road trips to the riverboats in Shreveport awhile back. Jerry came along with us once."

"He was helping me with my taxes," Bobby confessed. "I invited him."

"He got hooked." Scooter rubbed the back of his neck and grimaced. "Got to be a real sickness with him. Apparently, it got him in some trouble."

"He told me a couple weeks ago that he owed some nasty people a whole lot of money." Bobby shoved back his chair and stood. "I'm whipped. I'm headed home. Good to see you, Sin."

Luke watched the others watch him leave, then casually observed, "Bobby always did feel responsible for stuff that wasn't his fault."

Brandon nodded. "He doesn't need to be working at the plant. Man should quit fighting the call and be the preacher he was meant to be."

Luke had never thought about Bobby Hargett that way, but now that Brandon had brought the idea up, he couldn't disagree. "Y'all think Jerry got taken out on a hit?"

"I'll bet Cowboys-Redskins tickets that he was growing those mushrooms to pay the bastards off."

"Cops know about this?"

Both his old friends shook their heads. "Nah," Brandon said. "We may have grown up, but Chief Harper hasn't. Old bastard still gives me grief every chance he gets. I'm not about to help him do his job. Grevas was bound to get it sooner or later, Sin. When you owe bad guys money, they collect." He paused, sipped his beer, then added, "Besides, since Gus is gone, it's not like it matters to anybody else why Jerry Grevas died."

"Well, now, that's not quite true. It matters to Maddie Kincaid. She's the one who ditched the mushrooms. It'd be nice to know that whoever offed Grevas won't come gunning for her next. If he had partners, they might look her way for some payback. I can't leave until I know she's not part of the collection process."

Scooter and Brandon shared a long look, then Brandon reached for his wallet and turned over a twenty-dollar bill to his friend, saying, "You were right."

"Of course I was right." Scooter pocketed the money.

Luke sensed he'd been had about something. "Right about what?"

"That you wouldn't have changed. I knew from the minute I heard what you said to Joe Brown last night on TV that you wouldn't leave it alone. Especially factoring in the hot redhead. I halfway expected you to show up at the plant asking your questions. Two things about you, Callahan." Scooter ticked them off on his fingers. "You never could leave a puzzle alone, and you have a streak of white knight about you as wide as the Brazos at flood stage."

"The hell you say." Luke sat back in his chair hard.

"What have you really been doing all these years, Sin?" Brandon asked. "Are you military? That's my guess."

Son of a bitch. "Now, why in the world would you think something like that?"

"Mark's military, isn't he? Mrs. McConnell spotted him getting off the subway in Washington, D.C., at the Pentagon stop. Said he was all dressed up in a uniform with lots of ribbons on it. She knew it wasn't you because he was chatting up some woman and he laughed. Mrs. McConnell knows his laugh. Anyway, I don't for a second think that your dad kept y'all apart like he said, and since Mark's your twin, since he's military, it makes sense that you would be, too."

"I don't think you're military," Scooter said. "I think you're a cop."

"You guys are a few melons shy of a bushel, aren't you?" Luke couldn't believe they'd pegged him so fast. Hell, he'd worked undercover in some of the ugliest neighborhoods, bars, and barrios for years and nobody saw through his cover. Why this pair, who hadn't seen him in seventeen freakin' years?

"We know you," Scooter said, answering his unasked question. "People don't change their bones."

"But I was a hell-raising badass son of a bitch!"

"Not until your mother died," Brandon allowed. "By then, you were already cemented."

"My father sure as hell didn't think so."

"He didn't know you. We did. Nah. You're here either to trace the drugs, catch the killer, or protect Marvelous Maddie. But what I really want to know, Sin, what we're all curious about, is this. Is it just part of the story, or are you really sleeping with the delectable Ms. Kincaid?"

Luke stared at the men sharing the table with him, noted the prurient interest in their eyes and the leering grins on their faces. "You fellas are something else, you know that? You may be 'grown up' with jobs and wives—"

"Ex-wives," Brandon put in.

"—and responsibilities, but you're still the immature a-holes you used to be. Are you sure you graduated high school?"

Scooter said to Brandon, "He hasn't bagged her yet. I'll take back that twenty."

Luke's chair scraped against the floor as he rose. He tossed a ten on the table for the beer and said, "Think I'll call it a night. See you around, boys."

Their laughter followed him out and Luke couldn't help but grin a bit. Coming home wasn't all bad, after all.

He whistled the old Brazos Bend High fight song as he headed for his car, but the tune died as he noticed the folded paper slipped beneath the driver's-side windshield wiper of his Maserati. He slipped the paper into his pocket without reading it, then started the car. His tires crunched on gravel as he pulled out of the P-2 parking lot and turned toward what once had been home.

He kept careful watch on his rearview mirror and only after he determined that he wasn't being followed did he pull over beneath a streetlight and open the note. He recognized Bobby Hargett's handwriting: *Fratelli's.*

Luke made the connection. Fratelli's restaurant. Marco Fratelli. The bookie they'd used in high school. Originally from Jersey.

"Jesus, Jerry. Not too smart getting in debt to the mob."

Twelve

Maddie awoke and for the first time in days climbed from her bed without groaning, moaning, or whining. Encouraged, she padded into the bathroom and stripped off her nightshirt, then stood before the full-length mirror to take inventory.

A little black, a bit of blue, a little more green, and plenty of yellow. Definitely not her best, but acceptable.

She twisted her torso. Touched her toes. Lifted her arms above her head and stretched. "Not bad," she murmured. "Definitely doable."

Man, was she doable.

She'd been thinking of this fling for days now. Having decided to go through with it and lounging around with little to do but think, she'd spent way too much time wondering how sex would be with Luke Callahan. Where would he take her? Would he be gentle or rough or a little of both? Would he make her laugh, make her sigh, make her scream?

She wouldn't mind screaming. It'd been a long time since she'd had a good scream.

She knew he'd be good. Men like him always were. She already knew he could kiss like a million bucks. It didn't make sense that he'd fall short in the rest of it.

Not that anything about him suggested short.

Maddie closed her eyes and gave her head a quick shake when doubts started to filter in. A part of her recognized that she was focusing on sex and Sin in order to avoid thinking about murder. About danger. About whether or not whoever killed Jerry Grevas also held a grudge against her.

Luke had some theories in that respect. He'd spent the last few nights haunting the bars in town for information about the local drug supply while Maddie stayed at Callahan House fretting about his safety. Not his physical safety—she had complete confidence in his abilities. No, Maddie worried about his legal status. Luke didn't have his badge anymore. What if Chief Harper raided wherever he was? The man was granite-headed where Luke was concerned. He'd never bend the rules, and Luke could end up at the Woodman unit just like Maddie had!

Well, not really, since the Woodman unit was women only and Luke would be smart enough and connected enough to get out of trouble, but it would take time and energy to solve. Time and energy he could better spend with . . .

No, warned her Wicked Inner Wanton. *Don't go there. There's no future there. That way lies heartbreak, and haven't you had enough of that from the men in your life? It's a fling, Maddie. No-strings sex. Getting your bell rung. Your chassis lubed. Do not try to make it anything more!*

In fact, it might not be anything at all. Maybe she and Luke simply weren't meant to be. Maybe they'd missed their chance. After all, she wasn't by nature a needy woman. She preferred standing on her own two feet to depending on others, especially when "others" had a Y chromosome. History had taught her the value of that. Now that she felt better, she didn't feel so . . . needy.

She glanced out the bathroom window toward the padded loveseat lounger beside the pool that Luke had commandeered as his bed. He lay sprawled on his stomach, wearing only a pair of boxers. *Liar.*

With her gaze lingering on his butt, warm, tingling need pooled low in her belly.

"This is stupid," she muttered, dragging her attention away from outside. Now that she could move again, she needed to move her way on down to Home for Now's office. Time to get back to reality. She wanted work, peace, and routine. She needed normality. Riding shotgun with a badass former DEA agent was not exactly normal.

Maddie bent over the bathtub and twisted the hot-water spigot. As water flowed, her thoughts turned to work and to Sandy Crawford. Sandy had been a lifesaver for her since this mess started, stepping in to do the office work while Maddie was away, but when she stopped by yesterday to go over the month's billing, Sandy had confessed how much she missed working with clients.

A new empty nester who needed an outlet to continue her mothering, Sandy was Home for Now's most requested representative and thus one of the business's greatest assets. Maddie wanted to keep her happy.

She also wanted to get back to work herself. Maddie missed her clients, too. She was curious to see whether the new medication was helping Mrs. Foley's memory. She fretted that Sam Perkins wasn't doing his exercises like he should. She feared that Harriet Quinn would go ahead and clean out that storage closet without Maddie's supervision and throw away family treasures that her children would want.

Steam rose from the filling tub, and Maddie added cold water to the bath, her mind busily making plans for the day. She needed to talk to Luke and see whether he'd learned anything new last night about Jerry Grevas's associates. She didn't want to act stupidly, but she couldn't put her life on hold forever. She wanted to go to the office this morning.

Surely by now Luke had a sense of whether or not it was safe for her to resume her normal life. He'd certainly been putting a lot of time and energy into discovering the answer, spending night after night in Brazos Bend pool halls and clubs. Chatting people up. Charming them. And, according to Sara-Beth during yesterday's visit, slow dancing and snuggling with short-skirted sluts.

Maddie dumped half a jar of bath salts in the water, then

scowled out the window at the sleeping stud. He'd claim it was all in the name of the job. She'd heard that one before.

Men.

Maddie reached for a loofah. Would Luke deny enjoying that part of the job? She'd heard that one before, too.

Annoyed, she abruptly turned off the water. Her gaze ventured poolside once again. How far did he take his research? Did he bring someone home with him? Was he out there alone? She couldn't see the whole pool area from this viewpoint.

Maybe she should check.

Maddie plunged her hand into the bath and opened the drain. As water gurgled down the pipes, she strode back into the bedroom and yanked open the dresser drawer. She fished among the lingerie for two scraps of emerald green. They matched her bruises, after all.

Maddie didn't ask herself why she didn't bother with a swimsuit cover-up. She didn't admit her plans might be influenced by the fact that this was Branch's morning to have breakfast with his cronies at P-3, so he wasn't around to see her. She refused to question why she felt the need to confront Luke Callahan in this manner, at this time. In fact, Maddie didn't think at all. She was running on feelings at the moment. Feelings that had festered since she'd been sprawled on the floor of the *Miss Behavin' II* staring up at a pair of pistols.

So to speak.

Luke didn't want to wake up. The sun warming his skin and the light seeping through his eyelids, shut tight and buried in the cushion's pillow, told him daylight had arrived some time ago. Nevertheless, he did his best to ignore it. He needed more than three hours bag time on a damned pool lounger.

Funny how quickly a man could get accustomed to peace and quiet and regular hours. And a regular bed. For years now, late nights and smoky bars and heavy perfume had

been his norm. He'd learned to function on too little sleep
and to sleep wherever he could rest his head. But a few
months of healthy living made this slide back into the fast
lane less than comfortable.

He missed his king-sized mattress.

He missed waking up ready to meet the day instead of
wishing he could shoot the bulb out on the sun.

I'm too old for this shit.

At least he was pretty much done with the Brazos Bend
bar scene. After spending the better part of a week connect-
ing with dealers, dopers, and dumb-asses, he was ninety-
nine point nine percent certain that Jerry Grevas's
connections had nothing to do with the local drug trade and
everything to do with owing money to a certain *familia* out
of the Northeast.

He figured tonight he'd do what he could to confirm that
piece of information. After that, he'd . . . well . . . he'd figure that out tomorrow.

The goddamned mob. Strung-out meth dealers were bad
enough, but when the big dogs from back East played hard-
ball, they played to win. Yeah, he needed to find out exactly
whether those were the folks Jerry Grevas was dumb
enough to run up a tab with.

He sighed, not really wanting to think about that, but in
his gut, he recognized that this situation could get real ugly,
real fast. If the mob had Maddie in its sights . . . Luke shook
his head. He'd have to call in the alphabet suits. He hated
dealing with the suits.

Hell. He wasn't going to think about the suits. He was
going to think about tomorrow.

Tomorrow.

Buried against the chair cushion, his lips spread in a slow
smile.

The sound of heels clacking against the pavement had
him wincing. Wait. He didn't bring anyone back here. Had
one of those bimbos from the party out at the lake last night
followed him home?

Jesus. When had country girls become man-eaters?

He rolled over and up onto his elbows, then pried open his eyes, ready to tell the female predator to get the hell out of here. But instead of a bleached-blond pool-crashing bimbo, he got an eyeful of the fiery-haired goddess Maddie Kincaid.

Luke damn near swallowed his tongue.

She wore his bikini and her take-me-baby heels. She walked toward him with her chin high, her shoulders back, and a strut to her step. Luke had to think to breathe.

She stopped just beyond his reach. "Good morning."

"G-g-g." He stopped, cleared his throat. "Good morning."

She glanced casually around. "It's quiet out here. Peaceful."

"You're out of bed."

"Observant guy, Callahan."

Oh, he was observant. He observed those hot pink toenails, the slender ankles. Legs that went up and up and up. That triangle of concealing-yet-revealing cloth—God bless Lycra. A navel that cried out to be tasted. Long waist. The swell of her breasts, the emerald-draped points of her nipples.

Good Lord.

Her long, graceful neck. The full mouth.

His watered.

Her supermodel cheekbones, dark honey eyes, and that hair. That glorious sunburst of color.

"You should be in bed." *I should be with you.*

"I'm feeling better."

Luke had a fever.

"I thought I'd take a swim."

She wanted to get wet. Oh, yeah. Wet and slick. Hot and soft.

"The exercise will be good for me; it'll give my muscles a good stretch."

He could name some muscles he'd be happy to stretch for her.

She kicked off one shoe. Then the other. Luke took it like a lick to the balls.

Then she turned away from him, faced the pool. The thong. *Holy Moses.* Her tattoo! *Lord, save me.*

Maddie dove into the pool. Luke broke out in a sweat. His dick was hard enough and long enough to hang a net on it and use it for a skimmer.

He was out of his seat and a step away from jumping in after her when his cooler head prevailed over his hot one and he stopped. She'd had a glint in her eyes, a tight expression as she dove into the water. "She's pissed about something," he murmured.

What the hell brought this on? Why was she angry? He hadn't done a damn thing but bust his ass to figure out who might be after hers. How did he get to be the bad guy?

He watched her graceful strokes as she propelled herself through the water. He'd told her he'd check in when he came home last night, but at four a.m., he'd decided not to do it. Maybe she'd been worried about him.

She made a racing turn at the far end of the pool, giving him another peak at her thong, and he sucked air past his teeth as he realized he wasn't entirely comfortable with the idea that she might have waited for him, worried about him. That suggested a relationship, and that was only one step away from commitment. He'd banished that word from his vocabulary long ago.

A taunting voice emerged from the recesses of his brain. *Might not be such a bad thing having a swimmer like that waiting for you every night.*

He blinked and shook his head to banish that insanity as quickly as it came. Luke Callahan might be a lot of things, but he wasn't a fool. Forever was for other people.

Right now, however, was something else entirely.

At the far end of the pool, the shallow end, she interrupted her swim. When she stood, the water hit her just above the waist. She lifted both hands to her hair and finger-combed it out of her face, her breasts lifting in luscious display during the process. The tease. The delectable, ornery tease. If she's going to play with fire . . .

He'd burn her, all right.

He'd have her. He'd have her soon and often, but not here and now. Not at Branch Callahan's house. No matter how much she tempted him or how badly he hurt. He could control himself.

Thank goodness the pool wasn't heated this time of year.

Luke jumped into the deep end. When his head broke the surface, he halfway expected to see steam rising from the water around him. Wouldn't surprise him too much if the water started boiling.

But at least he'd cooled off.

When Maddie resumed her laps, Luke made a beeline for the swim ladder. No sense being stupid about it. If he touched her now . . .

Well, he wasn't a fool, but he was human. There was only so much thong a man could take without breaking.

Luke waited until she swam three more laps, then, believing himself under marginal control, he stood beside the pool. When she went to make her turn, he reached down and grabbed her arm. "Maddie?"

She surfaced, flung her hair out of her face, splashing him in the process. "What is it?"

"Seven o'clock tonight. Italian food. Pack an overnight bag."

"What? Why?"

"It's tomorrow."

Fratelli's was located in a strip shopping center along Pecan Street, one of the main thoroughfares in town. The decor was Italian kitsch—too tacky for most places, just perfect for Brazos Bend. Hand-painted murals of the Roman Coliseum, the Leaning Tower of Pisa, and Tuscan vineyards decorated the walls. Plastic grapes hung from wooden arbors throughout the room. Bottles of olive oil sat on shelves next to photographs of Fratelli family members at the original restaurant in Jersey. And, because this was, after all, Texas, televisions hung within eyesight of sixty percent of the seats. On Saturdays in the fall, diners enjoyed their pasta with Big Twelve football. Sundays belonged to the Dallas Cowboys.

"Fratelli's opened when I was in grade school," Luke told Maddie as they walked toward his sports car, parked at the curb in front of his father's house. Five minutes earlier, he'd knocked on her bedroom door and asked whether she was ready for dinner. That, thank goodness, was a question she could answer. She was hungry, and while she'd delivered a client to a party at Fratelli's once, she'd yet to dine there. She'd heard their food was delicious.

Had he asked whether she were ready, period, she'd be less confident of her answer. She couldn't explain what had come over her this morning, playing the tease the way she had. She couldn't explain what she'd been feeling ever since.

She didn't know what she'd do when tomorrow arrived tonight.

The look Luke gave her when she opened the door wearing the new little black dress she'd picked up in New York had been hot enough to melt asphalt. Yet, his touch had been gentlemanly, his comments flattering, but not over the top.

And he'd looked so fine himself, dressed in his Italian designer suit.

"That was long before the big chain restaurants came to town and made it harder for an independent to survive," Luke continued. "I think it's a shame how America is becoming so homogenized. You see the same big box stores, same restaurant chains, in every town you visit. We've lost something along the way."

"It's one of the reasons I love Brazos Bend," Maddie said as he opened the passenger-side door for her. "Not every town is lucky enough to have a Dairy Princess."

"Kathy Hudson is one of a kind."

This felt like a date. Not a first date. A second date. Second dates had a sense of familiarity combined with a he's-still-a-stranger awareness. Second dates meant a lot of small talk. Which was why Maddie asked, "So, is Fratelli's food as good as I've heard it is?"

"It used to be. My mother loved the eggplant Parmesan. We'd eat there at least twice a month."

"I've seen pictures of your mother at Branch's house. She was a beautiful woman."

"Yes, she was. Beautiful, but stubborn as a two-headed mule. She said she took after her great-grandmother Jenny McBride, who was one of the first businesswomen in Fort Worth. Mom's idea of volunteer work went far beyond garden clubs and Junior League. She was a nurse and she took a personal interest in health care for low-income children. My brothers and I spent many a Saturday in rural health clinics handing out toys to bawling kids after Mom gave them immunization shots."

"She sounds like a special woman."

"She was. Mom loved her family, her 'kids,' as she called them at the clinics, her roses, and old Frank Fratelli's eggplant Parmesan."

After a moment's pause, his expression went grim and he added, "I haven't had a meal there since she died."

With that, the date atmosphere evaporated, and Maddie was reminded just why they were going to dinner there to begin with.

"You said the Fratellis' son was your bookie?"

"Yeah. I don't recall now how my brothers and I learned that Frank Fratelli's son, Marco, made book, but we liked to take advantage of the service. A lot of Callahan money flowed through his hands in those days."

"I don't think we have many Italian families in town. I wonder how they came to settle here."

"That I do remember. We were sophomores in high school when Mark asked Marco how a New Jersey family ended up in Brazos Bend, Texas. I'll never forget how he gave this nonchalant shrug and said it was a war within the family. His father had disagreed with someone who took exception to it, and since Frank had moved to the middle of nowhere, they thought he wasn't a threat to anyone any longer, so Frank was safe. His family was safe. It was my first clue that for the Fratellis, there was both the 'family business' and the bistro in Brazos Bend."

"Yikes." Maddie shifted uncomfortably in her seat. She knew that both she and Luke wondered how much the two businesses intertwined these days. Her life might just be riding on the answer.

Luke had told her he'd debated long and hard as to how best to approach Marco Fratelli about her situation. He considered a dozen different possibilities, everything from siccing the feds on the family to forking over a good-faith percentage of the losses from his own pocket. He'd decided that the feds had bigger fish to fry than the Brazos Bend chapter of Godfathers-R-Us, and while he had the money to burn, paying for drugs in any way, shape, or form went against his principles.

Maddie hadn't known whether to be horrified or flattered that he'd even consider it. None of her other boyfriends would have ever thought about it. And she hadn't even slept with Luke.

Yet.

"Tell me again why you think a direct confrontation is best?" she asked.

In front of them, a traffic light turned red and Luke braked the Maserati to a stop. "Now, I never used the word 'confrontation,' and I'm not committing to any course of action until after I witness Marco's reaction upon meeting you. That'll tell us a lot, Maddie."

"Yeah." She slumped back in her seat and folded her arms over her chest. "Like whether or not I'll be 'swimming with the fishes' in Possum Kingdom Lake anytime soon."

"Swimming with the fishes?" Luke snorted. "I thought only males quoted *The Godfather*. It's like the ultimate guy flick."

"Exactly. My most recent ex watched the *Godfather* movies every chance he got. I couldn't help but pick up a little bit of the lingo."

Luke sneered at the mention of Cade, then said, "Don't expect to find Don Corleone at Fratelli's. The last time I saw Marco he was wearing a rodeo championship belt buckle."

"Cowboys can be dangerous."

"That's true," Luke said as he pulled into the parking lot. He parked, cut off his engine, then reached over and squeezed her hand. "Red, you know I won't let anything happen to you."

She gave him a little sickly smile. "I've never done business with a mobster before."

He snorted. "Sure you have. I'll give you two words to prove it. Branch Callahan. In his own special way, Branch Callahan is the godfather of Brazos Bend."

He had a point. Sighing, Maddie climbed out of the car and sucked in a nerve-steadying breath. Then Luke opened his mouth and got her flustered all over again.

"So, you wearing my underwear under that itty-bitty dress?"

That fast, her knees went to water, but she fought to keep her composure. "Um . . . boxer shorts aren't exactly the right foundation for a dress like this."

He laughed. "Honey, your body is all the foundation a dress like that needs. So, which color did you choose? The blue? The green? Maybe the turquoise?"

She'd chosen the red because the shade he'd picked for her was surprisingly complementary to her coloring. She wasn't about to tell him that, though.

"You'll have to discover that on your own, Callahan."

He pulled her against him, captured her mouth in a hungry kiss that turned her mind to mush. When he drew away, his finger played her neckline, sending shivers racing across her skin. His voice was low and intimate as he said, "Ah, the Chianti. How appropriate."

"You looked down my dress!"

"Yeah." His smile was smug. "I did."

With that, he slid his hand around to the small of her back and escorted her into the restaurant.

The mouth-watering aroma of garlic and tomatoes and fresh basil hit Maddie the moment she walked inside. A teenager greeted them, asked their seating preference, then escorted them to the private table Luke had reserved.

Maddie glanced around the restaurant but didn't see any obvious godfather types. She spied a couple lotharios waiting tables and behind the bar, but neither of them was old enough to be Marco Fratelli.

Luke ordered a bottle of Chianti and they both chose the daily special. He told her about Knucklehead's latest neighborhood escapade while they waited for dinner—or the owner—to arrive. "Maybe you should enroll him in obedience school," she said when he finished his story. "Knucklehead has to learn he can't jump on people. You're lucky Mrs. McKendrick didn't end up in the hospital after he knocked her down."

"I know. Although I doubt obedience school would solve the problem. He's terminally friendly. The dog needs a brain transplant."

She rolled her eyes and the waitress arrived with their salads, at which point Luke asked, "Is Marco here tonight?"

Maddie gulped her wine as the young woman nodded. "Mr. Marco is in his office."

Luke slipped something from his pocket and handed it to her with a wink and a smile. "Would you see that he gets this, please?"

Once the girl was gone, Maddie leaned forward and whispered, "What was that?"

"I put five dollars down for the Rangers to win the Series."

Maddie just shook her head. "No wonder you said you'd sent a lot of money his way if you've always made stupid bets like that."

Luke sipped his wine and winked at her.

He appeared awfully relaxed, and it annoyed her, considering that she was a nervous wreck on two fronts, the whole tomorrow thing with Luke and the would-she-live-to-see-tomorrow situation regarding the Italian mafia, Texas style. She was seriously considering sticking out her tongue, when a voice boomed out in a thick Texas drawl, "Sin Callahan, you old reprobate."

"Hello, Marco."

Maddie blinked. He certainly looked Italian—tall, with thick black hair, olive skin, and dark eyes. He dressed Italian. She had no trouble identifying an Armani suit. But when he opened his mouth, he was rural Texas to a tee.

For some reason, that made her even more nervous than she'd have been if he'd spat out a mouthful of Jersey thug talk. She drained her wineglass.

The mobster refilled it. "I heard you'd rumbled back into town. Driving a nice car. Flashing some green around town. I wondered if I'd see you."

"I had to show my faith in my team."

Marco chuckled as he patted his jacket pocket, where Maddie supposed he'd stored Luke's bet. "You always were a dreamer, Callahan."

"Yes, well, sometimes dreams just come true. Speaking of which, Marco Fratelli, I'd like you to meet my date." He paused almost imperceptibly before adding, "Maddie Kincaid."

Marco Fratelli's smile was the picture of delight. "Ms. Kincaid of Home for Now. It's a pleasure to meet you. I've heard wonderful things about you and your business."

"Uh, you have?"

Oh, God. Would she have to pay protection now?

"My wife's sister's husband's grandmother's best friend is Lilly Taylor."

"Lilly Taylor was one of my first clients," Maddie replied.

"Lilly loves you. My in-laws aren't to the point where they need help yet, but they're already planning on giving you a call when they do."

Maddie's smile flickered to life. This did not sound like a man who was fixing to put a hit out on her.

Although come to think of it, did she really want to work for the mob? Would they allow her to say no?

Maddie took a sip . . . okay, another gulp . . . of her wine, then pasted on a smile. "That would be lovely."

She shot Luke a glare, looking for help. He studied her a moment, then said, "It's nice to hear that you have such a high opinion of Maddie. Rumors going around town suggested you might feel otherwise."

"Rumors?" Marco's brows arched. "Ah. Rumors." He studied Maddie with a narrowed gaze, then called out to a waitress. "Linnie, add an appetizer to this table's order on the house. Bring Ms. Kincaid here our grilled portobellos."

Maddie blanched, and Marco Fratelli let out a guffaw. "I'm teasing, my dear. Just teasing. Better to do that than berate my guests for believing me capable of such unpleasantness."

Luke swirled the Chianti in his wineglass. "I'm not all that interested in what you did or didn't do, Marco. I just need to know that Maddie is safe."

"Because she destroyed six million dollars' worth of the family's assets?"

"Oh, God," Maddie murmured, dropping her chin to her chest. When Marco laughed again, Maddie muttered in her mind, *Jolly fellow for a criminal.*

"Jerry Grevas and I had no business together, Luke," Marco said. "This is not my battle."

"He owed a gambling debt."

"A substantial one, so I'm told. But he didn't owe it to me. Not all Brazos Bend citizens are as loyal to their bookmaker as you were. He incurred his debt by other means. Besides, all I do is nickel-and-dime stuff anymore. My wife frowns on anything more."

Luke set down his wineglass. "I heard you married Terri Ruckerman."

"I did. We have three fine children. The two oldest are in school and play baseball in the Brazos Youth Organization. I expend my energies in that direction these days."

At that point, the waitress arrived with their appetizers

and the two men spent some time catching up. When Fratelli asked what he did for a living, Luke used the story he'd been giving all around town about his dot-com fortune and vagabond feet. Over a second bottle of Chianti, they heard all about seven-year-old Joseph Fratelli's fastball and the baby's problems teething and Marco's parents' retirement to Sarasota, Florida. While the men appeared to relax the longer the conversation lasted, Maddie reacted differently. By the time Luke brought the conversation back to the matter at hand, she was strung as tight as a six-string. "Who would you suggest I speak with regarding Maddie's safety?"

"No one." Marco leveled a serious look at Luke. "Something like this is better left alone."

Luke lifted his wineglass and swirled the ruby liquid as he clicked his tongue in regret. "See, that's a problem. I can't in good conscience leave anything alone until I know they're going to leave her alone. This wasn't a double cross, Marco. It wasn't a theft or a swindle or a betrayal. She's an innocent party in this."

Maddie tried to look innocent as she stabbed a bit of portobello with her fork. She'd lost her appetite for mushrooms, but she thought she'd best be gracious under the circumstances.

Marco drummed his fingers on the table for a long minute. Dinner arrived, offering even more delay. Maddie forced herself to take a bite of her meal, and despite its delicious taste, her stomach rolled with nausea. Stress was the best diet aid ever.

Finally, Marco Fratelli stopped drumming. "I haven't mentioned that I opened a second restaurant in Fort Worth. It's on a restaurant row on the west side. Next to my bistro, a family by the name of Murphy opened an Irish pub."

Maddie knew she'd had more than her fair share of wine when she had trouble negotiating the abrupt turn the conversation had taken. An Irish pub? The Murphy family? What does that have to do with the price of garlic in Tuscany?

If he says they have a son named Liam, I'm going to totally lose it.

"The Murphys are an interesting family," Marco continued. "A large family. Parents are very old school. Big on tradition. The father wants to pass his business down to his children. The problem is that one of his sons doesn't want to run an Irish pub. When someone asks him who he is, he doesn't say, 'I'm a Murphy' or, 'I'm an Irishman.' He says, 'I'm a Texan.' He's independent to the bone. Yet, he loves his family. Loves his father, his uncles. He doesn't want to alienate them."

And this has what to do with me and my mushrooms?

"Sounds like the Murphys and the Fratellis have a lot in common," Luke observed.

Ah-hah! The light finally burned through the stress and alcohol clouding Maddie's brain. A metaphor. The Murphys were Fratellis and the pub was the "family business" of vice, graft, drugs, and various other mob concerns.

All right. Now the story made sense. Though Luke and Marco were old friends, the restaurateur wouldn't want to admit too much. For all he knew, Luke could be a cop. Which he was. Or used to be. Maddie took another big sip of her wine.

"Over time, Murphy and his family reached a compromise," Marco continued. "He tends bar twice a month just to keep his hand in the business, but he does nothing more than serve drinks. He doesn't inventory the stock or mess with the menu or deal with vendors, because doing so would step on the toes of the siblings who are involved with the pub on a daily basis."

He paused, glanced at Maddie, and asked, "How is your penne con pomodoro, my dear?"

"Good. It's good." Though the taste didn't blend all that well with the coppery flavor of fear.

Luke took another roll from the bread basket. "So, this Murphy fella. He doesn't have a clue what's going on back in the kitchen?"

Maddie translated that question to be asking whether or not Marco knew what the family might have in store for Maddie.

"He's what you might call vaguely aware. He's careful not to get too curious, because a business like that, well, it can draw a man in. It can seduce him. He likes his life the way it is, and he doesn't want to risk it."

For crying out loud. He's afraid of being seduced to the dark side? What was it about men? Had they no strength of will at all? With that, aided by nervousness and too much wine, Maddie's patience slipped. She set down her fork and snarled, "He can look at the daily special chalkboard, though, can't he? Surely he can tell if"—she flicked a long auburn curl over her shoulder—"red snapper is on the menu."

Luke winced. Marco furrowed his brow and asked, "Red snapper in an Irish pub?"

"Served up with magic mushrooms, no doubt." Maddie swiped her napkin across her mouth. "Let's quit dancing around the red sauce, shall we? Mr. Fratelli, are your relatives going to come gunning for my hide?"

For just a moment, shocked silence reigned. Then Marco Fratelli threw back his head and let loose with a long, loud laugh. He wiped tears from his eyes before turning to Luke and saying, "You have your hands full with this one, Callahan."

"You're right about that."

Maddie sniffed. *As if he'll get his hands anywhere near me now.*

Fratelli patted Maddie's shoulder. It was all she could do not to turn her head and nip him. "Murphy doesn't need to check the chalkboard, my dear. He knows the vendors who service the restaurant. He knows the family's menu philosophy. Rest assured, Maddie. Murphy knows his family would never count red snapper as pub grub."

Maddie's heart caught. Hope joined the doubt and fear swirling within her. Would she be a fool to believe this?

"Any chance he could confirm that?" Luke asked, casually dipping a hunk of his bread in olive oil.

"It's not necessary."

Luke jerked his head toward Maddie. "She'll sleep better.

The better she sleeps, the more energy she has when she's awake. I like her energetic."

"I can see where you would." Marco sighed with gusto, then said, "All right. I'll see what I can do. Besides, I owe you one for the win over Cedar Dell High. I still get preferential treatment at the barber shop because of catching that touchdown pass to win the district championship."

"Hey, you don't owe me for that. I just threw the ball." When Marco walked away, Luke explained, "The boy had Vaseline hands. He was forever dropping passes. Somehow, though, I knew he'd catch that one."

"Forget football," Maddie began.

"Forget football! What kind of Texan are you?"

"Is he saying what I think he's saying?"

"That it's conceivable that Grevas was killed by the hood he owed money to, but Marcos doesn't know for sure? That he's not about to ask? That he does know the family well enough to be certain they won't hold your actions against you?"

"Yes. Can I believe him, Luke? Am I safe?"

Luke didn't answer because Marco returned and asked them to join him in his office. "My father wants to speak to you, Luke."

Maddie caught her breath. Was this good news or bad news?

They followed Marco through the kitchen to a well-appointed office at the back of the restaurant. Luke held the receiver to his ear. "Mr. Fratelli? Yes, this is Sin Callahan."

After that, it was ten long minutes of old home days as Luke caught up the elder Fratelli on the affairs of friends, family, and acquaintances of times gone by. Then Luke said her name and Maddie's ears perked up, but all she heard were a series of yes sirs, no sirs, and interminable silences while the other man spoke. Maddie couldn't tell a thing by Luke's expression. It was all she could do not to rip the phone from his hand and talk to Frank Fratelli herself.

"Yes, sir, she threw them away."

The mushrooms. Oh, God. They *were* mob mushrooms.

A soft but wild giggle escaped her. A new variety—shiitake, portobello, chanterelle, and now, mob.

The wine in her stomach did a roll.

"Yes, sir," Luke continued. "I will. Yes, sir, she is. Yes. Yes." Then Luke broke out in a slow, sexy grin and finally made eye contact with her. "I sure as hell hope so."

Okay. It's okay. Everything will be okay. He wouldn't be smiling otherwise.

"Thank you, sir. I will. Good-bye." To Marco, Luke said, "Your father asked that I remind you about your great-aunt's upcoming birthday."

Marco slapped his forehead with his palm.

"And . . . ?" Maddie demanded.

Luke's grin turned sly. "Mr. Fratelli also said that Marco explained how beautiful you are." He took Maddie's hand and pulled her to her feet. Then he bent her backward over his arms and captured her mouth in a long, lusty, theatrical kiss that had Marco Fratelli snickering.

Luke released her mouth and steadied her on her feet. "That's from Mr. Frank. He said to tell you that next time he visited Brazos Bend, he'd claim a kiss personally."

She blinked in confusion. "I don't understand."

"Because you don't know my father," Marco said.

"He'll take payment for the mushrooms in kisses?"

Marco barreled out a laugh. "Heavens no. My father enjoys kissing beautiful women."

Again Maddie blinked. "Your mother must just love that."

"Oh, she's accustomed to it. You see, my father thinks every woman is beautiful. Old, young, fat, thin, it doesn't matter to Pop. Plus, he's very old-fashioned. He'd never betray my mother. He'd never harm a woman in any way." Marco paused, then added, "He'd never transfer one person's debt to another's account."

"He wouldn't?"

"No, he wouldn't."

Luke spoke up. "Something else, Maddie. Something important. Mr. Frank told me Jerry Grevas had no outstanding debts in the Shreveport casinos. Apparently, he paid what he owed months ago."

Shock had her reaching for an office chair's back for support. "He did? How?"

While Luke shrugged, Marco propped a hip on the corner of his desk. "Who knows? The family wouldn't care where he got the money as long as he paid his due."

Maddie slowly absorbed the information, and a joyous sense of relief washed through her. She faced Marco Fratelli and confirmed, "So I didn't throw away mob mushrooms? I'm safe?"

"Please. A different term." Then the restaurateur pursed his lips. "As far as your safety is concerned, judging by the look in Sin Callahan's eyes, I'd say the answer to that question depends on your definition of danger."

Maddie gazed at Luke, drank in the sight of him, savored the taste of him in her mouth, the scent of him clinging to her skin. Her head buzzed from wine and delight and Luke Callahan's kiss. "I'm not worried, Mr. Fratelli."

She made a slow circle of her lips with her tongue. "That kind of danger, I can do."

Thirteen

She was back.

That siren who'd seduced him at the pool. That temptress who'd taunted him on the *Miss Behavin' II*. The woman who'd made him want her with every fiber of his being.

Maddie Kincaid was a live wire as they exited Fratelli's, high on a little Chianti and a whole lot of relief. Her smile lit the dusky evening sky. Her laughter floated on the gentle breeze like a song. She bubbled and bounced and beamed like a hundred-watt torch on an inky night.

She obviously hadn't thought of the downside of the news they'd just received. If the mob hadn't killed Jerry Grevas, who had? And why?

And would they be after Maddie?

Luke was back to square one with his investigation, but when she grabbed his hand in the big fat middle of the parking lot and yanked him into her arms and kissed him—long and lustily and lavishly—he couldn't find it within him to care. Not at that moment. Not when he thought his eyes might remain permanently crossed.

Twenty minutes. It'd take twenty interminable minutes to reach the Victorian bed-and-breakfast owned and operated by Sara-Beth's cousin Annie. Earlier that day, stirred up by Maddie's swim and hoping that dinner at Fratelli's would put an end to the worry about her safety, Luke had decided a celebration was in order. He'd rented the entire B and B for the night. The situation hadn't quite turned out like he'd hoped; he still had cause to worry. But what the hell. He could take one night off from bar crawling.

The time had come to do his crawling across Maddie's luscious body.

He'd take tonight. He'd put killers and mysterious money sources out of his mind for twelve short hours. Okay, maybe fifteen. Eighteen, but no more. Then, back to work.

He'd filed away the comment Maddie had made back on the houseboat about never having been romanced, and this morning, after her little pool performance, he'd decided that romance would be the perfect payback. The woman wanted romance? Well, she was fixing to get it. Lots of it. More romance than he'd ever given a woman before.

When she ran her hand down his torso, then copped a quick feel below his belt, he mentally added, *Unless she gives me a heart attack before we get there.*

"Come on, big boy," she teased. "Get in the car and take me . . . somewhere private."

"You're a menace," he grumbled, taking off his suit coat and tossing it in the trunk.

"True." She settled back into the sports car's leather seat and dropped her head back, her face lifted toward the sky, exposing her long, graceful neck.

Luke wanted to bite it.

"Just call me Dracula," he muttered beneath his breath as he yanked his necktie loose.

"I'm so relieved!" Maddie said, closing her eyes and smiling. "I feel like I've been wearing a full-length coat made of lead and I've just thrown it off." She waited a beat or two, then gave him a sidelong look as she added, "And I'm naked beneath it."

"Good Lord." Luke gunned the engine and spun his tires as he fishtailed out of the strip center's parking lot. "Look, Madeline, we have a twenty-minute drive to get where we're going, so you need to just bring it down a notch."

"Madeline? You've never called me Madeline before."

"I've never been this serious before."

The blasted woman laughed. Laughed!

Then she started to tease him. She shifted sideways in her seat so that she faced him. She kicked off one shoe and folded her leg up under her. Her dress rode up on her thigh.

Luke's smile went grim and he promised himself he'd keep his eyes on the road as he pressed the gas pedal harder.

"So, where are you taking me to Sin?" she asked, her tone full of innocence.

He shook his head at her play on words, then answered. "There's a bed-and-breakfast up at the lake. We've got a reservation."

"I don't have any reservations," she said, leaning toward him, trailing her finger down his arm. "I'm high on life and ready to live."

She unbuckled her seat belt, leaned across the console, and licked his neck. Luke shuddered. "Stop that. Put your seat belt back on. It's against the law not to wear your seat belt."

"So handcuff me."

Luke inadvertently jerked the wheel. *Hell, if she keeps this up I'll kill us both.* She pouted playfully and he let loose a menacing growl. Maddie laughed at it, laughed at him, then settled back into her seat, thank God.

"Oh, Luke," she sighed in her normal-Maddie tone when they passed the edge of town and hit the open road. "I've been so on edge. I don't think I realized how bad it was until now. Life's been a roller coaster and I needed to get off."

Luke knew all about needing to get off.

"Of course," she continued, the teasing note back in her voice, "now I'm ready for another hard ride."

His foot slipped off the gas pedal.

"That's enough," he told her.

"What?"

"You know what."

"No, I don't." The false innocence in her tone said she knew exactly what she was doing.

He gave her a sidelong, disbelieving look and she laughed again. "You know, it's been a long, long time since I set out to seduce a man. They always seduce me."

She stretched languidly. "I've decided I like being the one in charge. The one in control. You wouldn't know what it's like to be out of control, would you, being a big badass DEA guy and all?"

"Former DEA," he corrected automatically, the slim hold he had on his famous control slipping with every second that passed.

"Former, current, future, whatever." She lightly trailed a finger up his arm. "You guys are all the same. Big ego, big attitude . . . big gun."

He couldn't deny any of it. His gun had grown to an all-time size. "You have seduction down pat, Maddie. You haven't lost your touch."

"That would be awful. For both of us. I'm told my touch can be . . . quite nice."

The speedometer inched upward. So did the tent in his pants.

"I've been dreaming about touching you, you know," she purred. "Daydreaming. Night dreams. The daydreams were fantasies. Things we'd do and places we'd go once 'tomorrow' finally arrived. It was a lovely way to pass the time. Now, my dreams at night were different. At night they tended to be more erotic. Some nights I'd wake up breathing hard, the covers kicked all the way off. One night I dreamed of you and woke up wet and ready."

His mouth was as dry as West Texas in July.

"My nipples were tight. Throbbing."

A shudder rippled down his spine.

"I felt hollow inside. I needed to be filled. Kind of like I'm feeling right now."

"That's it." Luke braked and steered the Maserati onto the shoulder of the road in a move that had Dale Earnhardt smiling from above. He shoved the gearshift into park, wrenched open his car door, and paced the side of the road. Jesus. He had to get control of himself. He was on the verge of going off like a schoolboy.

"Luke?"

He glanced back toward the car. Holy crap. She'd hung her thong from his rearview mirror.

He heard the snick of the passenger-side door opening. "Don't! You stay in that car, Maddie Kincaid. You're the one who wanted romance. I didn't make all those arrangements at the bed-and-breakfast just to end up taking you in the backseat of a car."

"Um . . . your car doesn't have a back seat."

She ignored him, of course. She slipped her shoe back on and unfolded from the low-slung Maserati. In the hazy twilight, she glowed like a Titan goddess as she approached him. "What sort of arrangements, Sin Callahan?"

Sin. Hah. If he was Sin, then she was pure Temptation. In a black dress. Sans panties.

"Candlelight?"

"Yeah." He turned away from her.

"What else? Satin sheets, maybe?"

"Yeah."

"What color?"

"Green. Emerald green." It was her color.

Delight rang in her voice. "And I'm wearing a red bra. I'll be your Christmas present to unwrap."

No. He wouldn't live that long. She was killing him. He was gonna have a heart attack and die right here beside the road.

"The bed-and-breakfast, the holiday, is so far away."

He heard the snick of a zipper. "Want to take a sneak peak?"

That did it. He could take no more. Luke grabbed her around the waist and lifted her off her feet. He carried her to the hood of the car and set her down, cursing his high-dollar sports car. Where was his pickup with its flat bed when he needed it?

"You play dirty, Maddie Kincaid."

"I play to win."

He kissed her hard, leaning her back on the hood. "Is it too hot?" he whispered against her bottom lip.

"Burning." She rocked her pelvis against him.

He groaned as his mouth moved in to nibble her neck. "I mean the car. The hood."

"It's a little warm, but my engine is hotter. Do something about it, Luke. Do me."

With another helpless groan, Luke kissed her again, harder this time. He feathered kisses down her neck, over her collar bone. Biting, licking, tasting, he let her scent wash over him until Luke knew he'd drowned.

Her hands were all over him, pulling at his shoulders, delving into his hair. Christ, he was only human. Raw sex with a gorgeous woman on a car hood? What red-blooded man would walk away from that?

Yet still, he fought it, looking deep inside himself for some of that vaunted control. They were on a little-used country road, true, but a car could drive by at any time. He didn't want to be caught with his pants down. Literally.

"Tell me you don't want me," Maddie teased, licking the sensitive skin beneath his chin. She tugged at his belt buckle, pulled at the strap until she released it. He sucked in a breath as her fingers found the button of his fly.

Luke swallowed hard and pressed his forehead against hers. It was taking every ounce of strength he had not to let loose and bang the living daylights out of her.

"Tell me you don't want to take me, right here, right now." Making quick work of his zipper, Maddie took him in hand and caressed the tip of his straining penis in a slow circle, then another. With sensual innocence, she looked up and met his gaze while gently squeezing his shaft. "Tell me you don't want . . ."

Running her tongue over her lower lip, she finished, "More."

He tried counting to ten.

He gave up at three. "Dammit, Maddie."

Slanting her body back, she parted her legs a notch. "Take me, Luke Callahan."

Okay, maybe he didn't care so much about where he bared his ass.

His head spinning, Luke reached for the wallet in his back pocket. Tearing into it with one hand and nearly blind with need, he found the condom, ripped the packet open, then rolled it on.

He pushed against her steamy folds and answered her demand, taking her with one strong stroke. God, she was tight. Tight and sweet. He knew he wouldn't be able to hold on long. Nothing in his life had felt like this.

With a throaty moan of abandon, Maddie's head lolled back, exposing her long neck to the moonlight. "Luke," she breathed.

With a primal urge of possession, Luke cupped her bottom and found his rhythm, his thrusts deep and desperate. He tried to hold on, hold back, wanting her pleasure, but captive to the demand of the need her actions had stoked to a raging inferno.

He couldn't talk. He could barely breathe. Feeling his release creeping down his backbone, he reached down for the stiff little nub that topped her wet, swollen flesh. Circling it, plucking at it, Luke urged her up. He wanted her with him. He wanted her wild.

She whimpered, gripped his shoulders for purchase, and cried out his name. Luke answered by giving her what they both needed. He moved hard and deep, feeling the first tremors of her release tingle around him.

Maddie's body tightened and her back arched and she cried out toward the moon.

With a guttural groan, Luke gave over and pumped himself into her until the night went black.

As the Maserati roared down the road, Maddie closed her eyes, enjoying the sensation of wind blowing through her hair as she wondered why she wasn't embarrassed. She'd never acted so wildly before. Her Wicked Inner Wanton had taken over and she'd not even tried to stop it. Oh, she could try to blame it on the wine or the heady sense of freedom she'd felt upon leaving the restaurant, but the truth was, her Wicked Inner Wanton had wanted a taste of Luke Callahan since the moment she'd spied his naked magnificence aboard the *Miss Behavin' II*.

Now, she thought smugly, she'd had her taste. Her appetizer, so to speak.

She couldn't wait for the next course. From tidbits he'd dropped, she believed he had a banquet planned, and be hanged if she'd let inhibitions or cautions or concerns about the future deny her this one night of sensual delight.

"Tomorrow" had arrived, but it would last only tonight. Maddie intended to enjoy it.

A three-quarter moon rose in the eastern sky as they turned into the drive leading up to Cottonwood Cottage Bed and Breakfast. A Tiffany lamp shone in the front window of the two-story Victorian. Charming lanterns illuminated the front porch. It was a doll's house, complete with gingerbread and a turret and a huge old magnolia tree perfuming the air.

Maddie took one look at the place and fell in love.

With the house. Just the house. Don't go and be a fool and fall for the man.

"It's lovely," she said, trying to distract herself.

"I thought you'd like it."

Luke retrieved their overnight bags from the trunk, then took Maddie's elbow and escorted her up the stone steps to the front porch. There he reached beneath a ceramic garden gnome and retrieved a key. "Annie is staying at a friend's place in town, so we have the whole place to ourselves."

"You know the owner?"

"Yeah. She and Mark were high school sweethearts. He was head over heels for her, then she up and moved away. Not her whole family, just Annie. She broke his heart. Mark couldn't find out why she left. That was about a week before the fire."

"But she moved back."

"About a year ago. I ran into her at P-3 yesterday at lunch. She told me about her place and I thought it'd be perfect for tonight."

"I like a man who thinks ahead."

"I've been thinking about 'tomorrow' constantly."

Luke opened the door and soft music greeted them as they stepped into Cottonwood Cottage. Maddie smiled with delight.

The room was right out of a magazine, furnished with an overstuffed sofa and two chairs in a cabbage-rose print, mahogany tables and an antique rocker placed before the fireplace, where votive candles placed inside the hearth provided summertime romance. Irish lace curtains adorned the windows, and antique yellow roses arranged in milk-glass vases perfumed the air. Maddie fingered one of the many crocheted lace doilies decorating the room and decided she had to have some of the same for her place. "This is lovely, Luke."

"Girly," he said, glancing around.

· "Romantic," she said on a sigh.

He lifted her chin with a finger and pressed a quick kiss to her lips. "I'm glad you think so. Now, we have our choice of bedrooms. Do you want to pick one or"—he winked at her—"shall we just use them all?"

Suddenly, despite everything that had happened before, despite her wicked, wanton behavior beside the road and her determination to retain her free spirit tonight, Maddie grew a bit nervous. A bit shy. She guessed it was one thing to abandon her inhibitions in the heat of passion, but something else entirely to do it in the calm, romantic atmosphere of Cottonwood Cottage.

This was the kind of place couples visited. This was the kind of place where people created memories, the kind of memories Maddie didn't dare envision. Careful, she told herself. This is a dangerous place.

"Let's not get ahead of ourselves," she suggested.

"I think we already did." He gave his brows a leering waggle, which coaxed a laugh from Maddie.

Luke ended up leaving the bags at the foot of the stairs, then he crossed the room to a tea table, where champagne chilled in a bucket set beside a plate of chocolate-dipped strawberries. Ice rustled as he lifted the champagne and checked the label. Moments later, the bottle opened with a soft pop.

The sound jerked Maddie out of the romance of the moment and back to the day she'd been released from jail. Kathy, a teetotaler, had met her at the gates with a horribly sweet bottle of sparkling grape juice and two paper Dixie cups. Unsettled, she blurted out, "Where is the strangest place you've ever drank champagne?"

"Hmm . . ." Luke considered the question while he poured two flutes. "That'd be a toss-up between Times Square on New Year's Eve and an emu pasture in West Texas."

"You drank champagne with a bunch of smelly birds? Why?"

"Well, there was this woman . . ."

"Never mind." She truly didn't want to hear about Luke and other women. "Why did you say Times Square on New Year's? That's a pretty normal place to drink champagne."

He handed her a glass. "There is nothing normal about Times Square on New Year's. The stuff you see . . . the very definition of strange."

"Okay. I can't argue if you look at it that way. I was there for the millennium."

"So was I. Was that a crazy place or what? Between the people convinced it was the end of the world and the ones who thought the mother ship was going to land in Gramercy Park, it's a wonder Dick Clark didn't walk off the set. So, what brought you to the madness that year?"

"I was at a party with a couple of girlfriends, but things got a little wild for me. I went down to Forty-second Street by myself and watched the ball drop, resolving to make better choices in the new century. I met Cade a week later. So much for resolutions."

"So you got off to a slow start." Luke shrugged. "Looks to me like you've made some very good choices since then. You're a survivor, Maddie. You've taken the odd lot that life's cast your way and made it work. Sure, you've made mistakes, but who hasn't? Look at me. It wasn't all fun and games growing up a Callahan, but I'll bet it was a helluva lot easier than being the child of a rock icon. I think you've done pretty damned good."

Maddie didn't know how to respond. No guy she'd been with had ever given her any credit before. They never realized she was partly a victim of circumstance. They, like her father, always laid the blame at her feet. Blame Baby.

Luke, God bless him, was different.

He lifted his glass. "To you, Maddie Kincaid. To your beauty, your courageousness, your fire. The day you boarded the *Miss Behavin' II* was definitely my lucky day."

Maddie couldn't speak past the lump in her throat. She wasn't certain her watery knees would keep her upright. So she sipped her champagne and sank onto the sofa. Luke crossed over to a bookshelf where a selection of CDs sat beside a stereo. He flipped through them and slipped his choice into the player, and moments later Frank Sinatra started singing "I Get a Kick Out of You."

Her favorite. "I love Sinatra. How did you know?"

"I drove your minivan, remember? Of course I snooped through your CDs. Strange collection for a rock princess, I might add. Only two artists and not a steel guitar among 'em." He met her gaze and confessed, "I wanted to set the right mood for you tonight, Maddie, but I had to draw the line at Barbra Streisand."

Affronted, she demanded, "What's wrong with Barbra?"

"Oh, she can sing. I'm not denying that. It's the cheesiness of her songs that . . . never mind." Luke set the plate of strawberries on the coffee table, then sank down onto the cushion beside her. He held a strawberry in front of her mouth, saying, "Let's not argue over ol' Babs."

As Maddie bit the juicy, sweet strawberry, Luke nuzzled

her neck. "Mmm . . . I do love the way you smell. Chanel and spice. The fragrance seeps into my blood and makes me hotter than hell. Only thing better is the way you taste."

He stared down at her, his eyes heavy lidded and so hot they made her tremble. His warm breath feathered across her skin. "Let me taste you, Maddie. Now."

Maddie offered her mouth and he took it. His lips brushed hers, as soft and light as a butterfly's wing. Gentle, coaxing, he rewarded her acquiescence. His firm, warm lips molded to hers, his tongue soft but insistent, sliding into her mouth. It dipped and delved and danced. His tongue stroked hers, prodded it, coaxed it into his mouth, where he gently nibbled the tip, then sucked. She closed her eyes and lost herself in the pleasure of Luke Callahan's kiss, forgetting her nervousness altogether. She swirled her tongue around his, wanting the moment to never end.

He captured her nape in the cup of his palm, and as a growl of delight rumbled deep in his throat, Maddie admitted that she wanted him. Again. Still. She wanted him, period. It had never been this way for her before. So intense. So consuming.

Danger, Maddie. Danger. You could get used to this. You could get used to him.

The kiss took on a life of its own, lasting long minutes, maybe even hours. Days. It was wet and warm and wonderful, exhilarating. He kissed her until she could barely stand. Barely breathe. It was all-encompassing. Thrilling.

Frustrating. She needed his hands on her. Where were his hands? She arched against him and her own hands streaked across his back. She rubbed her chest against his, seeking contact, seeking relief.

Instead, he released her and moved away. Bereft, Maddie met his gaze.

"Gotta slow down," he murmured. His eyes smoldered. His jaw was set, his breathing heavy. "You are the most delicious thing I've ever tasted. Before this night is over, I'll know the flavor of every inch of your body."

Oh, my. She ached, tightened, and tingled. She was being seduced. Thoroughly and completely. She liked it very much.

Luke rose from the couch. She halfway expected him to sweep her into his arms and carry her up the stairs à la Rhett Butler. Instead, he dimmed the lights in the room, then held out his hand. "Dance with me?"

"Dance?" She all but melted on the rug.

"Sinatra is singing about summer wind. A man needs to have a beautiful woman in his arms when a song like that is playing."

Maddie took his hand and he pulled her close. They slow danced to Frank through "Summer Wind" and "That's Life" and "Strangers in the Night." While Luke softly sang "Night and Day" into her ear, Maddie's blood hummed with a heady sense of pleasure and anticipation.

"This is a first for me," she confessed as he nuzzled her hair.

He nipped her earlobe, then drew back. His eyes gleamed hotly. "What sort of first, Red?"

"I've never danced in a man's arms this way."

"Oh?" His brows arched. "You don't like to dance?"

"Oh, no," she was quick to say. "It's wonderful. *Wonderful.* It's just . . . I hung around with rockers. European rockers at that."

"Your mistake."

"Oh, yes. Most definitely yes. The fact they didn't know how to dance was but a very minor part of it."

The tempo picked up and Luke spun her around. Maddie laughed, then their eyes locked. Desire sizzled in the air between them and for a long moment, Maddie thought Rhett time had arrived. Except she wouldn't be like Scarlet. She knew that while tomorrow was another day, there wouldn't be another tomorrow like tonight for her and Luke. She wasn't about to let herself fall into the trap of believing that this was a fairy-tale romance.

Instead, he clasped her tighter and continued the dance. "I learned to two-step early because it was a good way to get my arms around a girl. It's still a good way."

"Always thinking, aren't you Callahan?"

"I'm always thinking of you, it seems." The hand at her waist took a lazy stroke up her back, then down across her hip to curve on her buttock and bring her closer still. She felt his erection against the aching part of her. "You get in a guy's mind, Red. In his fantasies. I've imagined dancing with you a number of times."

Her heart stuttered. "You have?"

"Oh, yeah." The song ended and the hand on her bottom dropped away. Luke took a step back, then drew her hand up to his mouth and kissed her knuckles one by one. "I've dreamed of dancing with you beneath the stars. Naked."

Oh my oh my.

He kissed her again, once, then twice. The silken heat of his tongue dipped into her mouth again with irresistible tenderness that caused Maddie to sigh against his lips.

After that, she waited expectantly, but still no Rhett. Instead, in a rough, husky voice he said, "Come to the kitchen with me?"

The kitchen! Her knees almost buckled as she pictured him taking her on the table. Or the counter. A tile floor.

"And actually, we're going through the kitchen onto the deck. I want to make dessert for us."

She blinked. Food? Now? Whoa. Earlier when she'd pondered an upcoming sensual banquet, she'd been thinking metaphorically. Now she wondered whether she'd been wrong. "Does it involve whipped cream?"

His eyes flickered and flared, then Maddie watched with disappointment as he deliberately banked the fire. "No whipped cream. Bananas."

"Bananas?" Hmm. That took her a bit aback. Wasn't it a little early in their relationship to go kinky?

"Bananas Foster. A great New Orleans recipe. Have you ever had it?"

The intent light in his eyes made her answer, "No, I don't believe I have."

"Then you're in for a treat. It's the most sensual dessert I know. Bring the champagne, Red, and watch a maestro at work."

How could she do anything else?

The kitchen at Cottonwood Cottage was cozy but well equipped. Luke paused long enough to remove a tray from the Sub-Zero refrigerator and a large bowl of vanilla ice cream from the freezer. The man had certainly planned ahead.

"When did you do all this? How did you do it?"

An enigmatic smile flirted with his lips. "Maestros don't share the secrets of their . . . recipes."

Recipes for seduction, she thought, her knees going weak yet again. At this point in the evening, it was a wonder she could still walk.

He opened the back door, and Maddie preceded him outside, where the star-filled sky nearly took her breath away. "Isn't it beautiful."

"Exquisite." His gaze was on her, not the heavens.

Pool lights and a pair of tiki torches helped the moon and stars provide soft illumination of Cottonwood Cottage's backyard. As Sinatra crooned from outdoor speakers, Luke motioned for Maddie to take a seat on a quilt spread upon a lush lawn. Big square pillows and another champagne bucket sat at one end.

Unless the B and B owner had a special romance package listed in her brochure, Luke had gone to quite a lot of trouble to set this scene. How did she feel about that? How would she feel once the night was over and the reality of daylight set in? Would she want to— Nope. She wasn't going there. Tonight was nothing more than an interlude. A time to make a memory. This place was made for memories, after all. The stars, the night sounds, a drop-dead sexy man who wanted her. It was perfect.

It was temporary.

Enjoy, but don't forget it.

Since she wore a dress, Maddie would have preferred to sit in one of the teak chairs that sat beside the pool, but

Luke was directing this play and he'd done an excellent job up until now. She kicked off her shoes and stretched out on the blanket while Luke set his tray on the stone countertop of the outdoor kitchen and went to work. Within moments he had butter and brown sugar melting in a chafing dish.

The stars, the moon, the music, relaxed her. The man had her on edge. Giving in to the sensuality of the moment, Maddie lay back and made a long, languid stretch.

Luke dropped his fork and had to get a clean one.

She watched him sauté bananas, then sprinkle them with cinnamon before dousing them with banana liqueur and rum. Her mouth watered, not for the man's concoction, but for the man himself.

"All right, here's the fun part. Watch." He lit a fireplace match and set the stuff afire, grinning like a schoolboy until the alcohol burned off. What was it about men and fire?

Luke poured the banana mixture over the vanilla ice cream, then, with a bowl in one hand, a spoon in the other, sat down beside her. He stared deep into her eyes as he held a spoonful of dessert to her mouth and said, "Taste."

The rich blend of flavors exploded on her tongue. "Mmm. That's wonderful."

He took a bite. Frowned. "Good, but not perfect. It's missing something."

Luke filled the spoon again, fed her another bite. "What do you think?"

It was perfect. This was perfect. The music, the man, the moment. She sat smack-dab in the middle of a romantic fantasy. "Delicious."

"But it needs something else." He tossed down the spoon, then dipped his finger in the bowl and held it to her mouth. "See?"

Following his lead, she sucked the ice cream from his finger. "Mmm . . . it's fine just the way it is."

"I don't know . . ." Slowly, deliberately, Luke tipped the bowl. Cold ice cream dribbled onto her bare skin just above her neckline. Then he dipped his head and his soft, rough tongue licked it off. "Yeah. That's the spice that's missing. It needed a dash of Maddie."

And so began a sensual assault the likes of which Maddie had never imagined. With clever, teasing hands he stripped her down to her underwear, then rocked back on his heels to relish the sight. The hard, hot glint in his eyes was enough to curl her toes.

Deft fingers made quick work of the fastener between her breasts, and when he pushed her bra away, his hand brushed her nipple. Instantly, it puckered, begging for attention.

Luke accommodated. He dipped a finger in the ice cream, then painted her with slow, sensuous motions that left her tingling and needy. "Luke . . ."

"Patience, Madeline," he said, smiling. "I like to savor my dessert." He played Picasso on her breasts until she whimpered with frustration. Only then did he give her what she wanted.

Luke kissed the valley between her breasts. His tongue lapped, then flicked over her nipples, scalding her sensitive skin. He licked her like a cat, murmuring his pleasure low in his throat. "Mmm . . . butter and brown sugar, cinnamon and spice. Cinnamon and you."

Days later, his mouth finally closed around her hot, throbbing peak and suckled. It was heaven and pure sin tied up together. Maddie arched her back as pleasure jolted through her, and she gasped and curled her toes and forgot to breathe. A surge of hot anticipation pooled between her thighs.

He took his time at this, too. Once he had her writhing, Luke embarked on a culinary tour. His large hands smeared her with the cool, creamy treat. His hot mouth followed, cleaning up his mess. His earlier promise kept, Luke went about tasting every single inch. He tasted, devoured, consumed. He supped his way across her shoulders, her neck, then down between her breasts to her navel, where he used the very tip of his tongue to retrieve the sweetness. He licked the tender skin of her thighs, nibbled the back of her knees. He even sucked her toes.

When Luke's breath fanned against the filmy triangle of her thong, her nails curled into the quilt.

"Red is my favorite color," he murmured, his finger slipping beneath the elastic, scorching a path from hip bone to hip bone. His thumb brushed across the filmy silk covering her curls, and Maddie's entire body clenched.

He rolled back on his heels and tugged her panties down her long legs, then past her ankles and feet. He feasted on the sight of her, his eyes heavy lidded and blazing hot, glittering like jewels. "My very favorite color."

He lifted the bowl and poured melted ice cream over the delta between her legs. Maddie half expected steam to rise from her skin as he added, "My very favorite taste."

Her bones melted when he gave her the most intimate of kisses. Pleasure bolted through her as his tongue touched the small aching bud and Maddie cried out.

"Mmm . . . delicious."

Maddie's breaths came in pants as he worked his magic between her legs. She clutched handfuls of the quilt, her head thrown back, her blood pounding and pulsing. He slid his hands beneath her, lifting her for better access. Steadying her when tremors raced up and down her nerves and shook her to her soul.

Her blood burned, her body tensed and trembled. She thrashed beneath his attentions, the pressure within her building. Building. A searing, brilliant promise hovering just beyond reach.

He lifted his head. She whimpered. "Give me your flavor, Maddie. Give it to me now."

He put his mouth to her and feasted hungrily, and Maddie cried out his name as her body convulsed and she came in a hot rush of exquisite pleasure.

He stayed with her, coaxing the tremors to continue, to build again, until she shuddered and shook and screamed, then finally went limp.

Only then did he stop what he was doing and roll to his feet. He looked down at her, his eyes twin flames, as he yanked off his shirt and shucked out of his slacks and shorts, then tossed them toward the side of the pool. She lay there weak with satisfaction, watching him, wanting him again.

Naked and aroused, Luke Callahan was just about the most magnificent sight she'd ever seen. His bronzed, broad shoulders were thickly muscled. His wide chest tapered to an abdomen ridged with muscle. A wedge of brown hair narrowed to his navel, then arrowed down to his sex, which jutted toward her, huge and thick and ready.

He made her mouth water.

Luke reached out. "Give me your hand, Madeline."

She wasn't sure she had the strength to move. "Why?"

"I promised you a dance."

"Come down here and dance."

His lips quirked in a smile. "Patience, Red."

He beckoned her with a wiggle of his fingers and she reached for him because she couldn't help herself. Then he wrapped his arm around her waist and pulled her against him, heated skin to heated skin. Hard to soft. His penis pressed against her belly, triggering a hollow ache deep within Maddie.

Luke waltzed Maddie across the lawn beneath the silvery moonlight to the soft, sultry jazz now drifting on the air. Thick grass tickled her feet. A warm, gentle breeze kissed her bare skin. She breathed in Luke Callahan's musky male scent and tasted him and herself in his kiss.

It was the most sensual experience of her life.

"I feel wicked," she told him.

"Wicked works for me." His big hand stroked down her spine, then cupped her buttock. "You work for me."

Then he kissed her again, wetly, deeply, and their waltz ended, as a different kind of dance, a dance as old as time, took control.

Maddie rubbed herself against him, her hips moving slowly and sensuously. When he made a growling sound low in his throat, she indulged her hunger to touch him. She spread her fingers against his chest, then scraped her thumbs across his flat nipples, and his muscles went as taut as a drum. Then she trailed her hands lower, following that tantalizing trail of hair that pointed the way to the part of him her body ached to know again.

His hot, heavy shaft filled her hand, both as soft as velvet and as hard as steel. When her fingers closed around him, Luke shuddered and groaned. "Madeline."

She smiled and licked her lips, then leaned forward and licked him.

He growled a laugh and said, "Not yet. Not here."

Then Luke scooped her legs out from beneath her and lifted her into his arms. *Now* he'd do the Rhett Butler thing.

But he surprised her again by carrying her not into the house but toward the pool. "I've been thinking about this all damned day."

He carried her down the pool's steps until they were submerged in the cool water up to their waists. He paused just long enough to kiss her senseless before reaching for his pants beside the pool and the condom in his pocket. Releasing her, Luke quickly dealt with necessities, then he was moving, pushing her back against the pool's wall. Maddie clung to his shoulders and allowed her legs to float up around his waist.

He supported her with his hands on her bottom, then with one quick thrust he was inside her, stretching her, filling her. "Do you know how hard it was for me to leave you alone this morning? You're a fantasy, Red. My fantasy."

Then he was taking her, plunging into her over and over in a pounding rhythm that swept her into a maelstrom of sensation that turned her bones to water and set her blood afire. She lost all sense of time.

Maddie vaguely heard herself sobbing his name as she hurtled toward the peak. He accelerated his movement, driving into her with a series of fierce, deep thrusts. Then she shattered, crying out as intense pleasure exploded within her.

"Maddie," Luke groaned, his teeth nipping at the tender hollow where her neck and shoulder met. He buried himself in her shaking body, grinding against her as he found his own release. Holding her tight until his shudders finally eased. "Maddie."

For a long, lovely moment they held one another. Then he kissed her with such tenderness that it made her heart weep. "You are a special woman, Maddie Kincaid."

"You're pretty special yourself."

They drifted apart and Maddie floated, totally replete, stretching languidly. Luke ducked beneath the water, then surfaced once more, flinging water from his hair as he gave his head a shake. "The water feels good. I've been hot since I woke up this morning, and it's all your fault."

She smiled smugly as she climbed the steps out of the pool. "You're all cooled off now?"

His eyes glittered like a cat's. "Let's just say I'm surprised I don't see steam rising off the water."

As Maddie reached for a towel, she couldn't remember ever feeling so feminine.

"God, I love that tattoo."

Feminine but earthy. Sensual.

Powerful.

She'd been content to let him direct this play since they'd stepped over the threshold of Cottonwood Cottage, but now, as she watched him watching her, she decided her turn had arrived once again.

She wanted to torture Luke. She wanted to torment him. She wanted to make him howl at the moon.

She wanted to make the big, bad, tough former federal agent lose control again.

She dried herself slowly, teasing and tempting and taking her time, expecting to find her task more difficult now that he'd sated himself twice already this night. However, judging by his condition as he rose from the water, she had more power than she'd realized.

She tossed him her towel, then as he absently dragged it

across his body, stepped into her high heels and nothing else.

"Wicked," Luke murmured.

He retrieved her panties from the blanket, then tossed them to her. Surprised, Maddie arched a brow.

"You promised me Christmas."

Oh. The green satin sheets. She turned away from him, stepped into the thong, then glanced over her shoulder and began walking away toward the house.

She'd covered half the distance before he let out the howl she'd wanted. Then he was there, lifting her. Throwing her over his shoulder.

As he climbed the stairs with her, Maddie nipped at his shoulder blade. "Luke Callahan?"

He cupped her bottom with his large, hot hand. "What?"

"Just so you know. You're even better than Rhett."

Fourteen

Luke opened his eyes. Maddie lay spooned against him, her sweet little ass snuggled up to his lap, her legs entwined with his, her hair tangled and tickling his nose. He considered lifting a hand to shift the hair out of his face, but that would mean giving up his grip on her breast. He wasn't stupid.

Or was he?

Maddie Kincaid was every bit the firecracker in the sack that he'd suspected. When he'd set out to give her the most romantic night of her life, he'd never considered how it would affect him.

He'd had good sex before. Hell, he'd had great sex a time or two in his life. But last night with Maddie . . . damn . . . he didn't know how to describe it. Fantastic? Mind-blowing? Off the friggin' charts?

Still, Luke wasn't one to be led around by his dick. He'd never formed an attachment with a woman because she'd proved to be a good lay. He'd always been able to say good-bye and forget.

This time, he feared it might be different. Hell, he knew it would be different. He'd never be able to look at a dish of vanilla ice cream again without getting a hard-on.

Forget her. Right. Like that was going to happen. He'd have better luck forgetting his own name. He might be able to say good-bye, but he'd never forget.

But he was a short-timer in Brazos Bend. He couldn't forget that, either. As soon as he solved the mystery of Jerry Grevas's murder or found another way to prove her safe, he'd be out of here. The thought of saying good-bye had his gut clenching.

Why? Luke wondered. In the past, he couldn't find his pants fast enough. But Maddie Kincaid was different. She wasn't an easy lay or a one-night stand. She wasn't that kind of woman.

She was . . . special.

Special. Great. Just great. He hadn't been able to forget her before he'd taken her to bed. How the hell would he put her behind him now?

Special.

Yeah, well, she is. You can't deny it. And she's got you all tied up in knots. Question is—how do you untangle yourself?

He eyed the sun-kissed curve of her shoulder, recalled her potent beauty as she'd stood naked in the moonlight. He inhaled her fragrance, a heady combination of Chanel, sex, and Maddie's own spice. He listened to the soft snuffle of her breathing as she slept and remembered how she'd whimpered out his name at the height of their passion. The sound had made him feel as powerful as his Maserati.

Now he just felt anxious.

Maddie stirred, rolled over, and settled against him, her head pillowed on his chest, her hand resting on his hip. His heart did a funny little catch and a whisper of temptation floated through his thoughts.

He could stay in Brazos Bend.

Luke closed his eyes. He could stay in Brazos Bend. He didn't have a job to get back to. Didn't have responsibilities to meet. He had the money to live wherever he wanted.

But he didn't have the stomach to live in Brazos Bend.

His mouth flattened into a grim line as he eased out from beneath Maddie and climbed from the bed. He went into the bathroom and turned on the shower. While he waited for the flowing water to turn hot, his gaze focused on a basket of lavender-scented bath salts sitting beside the tub.

Without any effort at all, he could see Maddie's shampoo in his shower. Imagine her pink-handled razor sitting beside his blue one. Her girly doodads would be spread all over. Before he knew it he'd have pantyhose hanging over the shower rod.

Along with that red bra.

Hmm . . .

Strange words flitted through his brain. Relationship. Commitment. Family.

Home.

"Shit."

Luke wondered whether too much sex affected a man's brain. Had he just considered the ultimate, unforgivable act of actually living in the shadow of his old man? Giving up his boat for heart and . . . oh, God . . . hometown? What the hell was the matter with him? No way would he stay in Brazos Bend! That'd make his father as happy as a pig in a peach orchard, and he'd rather go metro in a pink shirt and tie to P-2 on a Saturday night than please his father that way.

But even aside from that, he wasn't sure he could give Maddie what she wanted. What if it didn't work out? He'd only disappoint her, and God knows, she's had enough of that in her life.

So why the hell did you take what she offered last night?

Conscience stung like a bull nettle as he realized that loving and leaving made him no better than those other dickwads she fell for.

Luke stepped beneath the tepid shower spray. But what was the alternative? Brazos Bend? Christ.

No, what he had here was a case of postcoital brain freeze. What was he thinking? He'd already broken his vow by stepping foot in this town. He wasn't going to obliterate it based on a couple weeks' acquaintance with a woman. His brothers would kill him. This situation wasn't like Matt's, whose land purchase would be a thorn in Branch Callahan's side. Hell, he couldn't forget that Branch had sent Maddie to him to begin with.

No, he by God wouldn't hang around Brazos f'ing Bend. He'd find the killer and ensure Maddie's safety. Then, he'd sure as hell leave this sorry-ass place.

Luke soaped and rinsed and reached to turn off the water when another thought struck. *Maybe Maddie could leave with him.*

His heartbeat picked up as the idea turned in his head like a roulette wheel. She could come with him, move onto the *Miss Behavin' II.* They could take a few months, maybe float along the coast and spend the winter on the South Texas coast. Did that sound like heaven, or what?

Hmm. Luke had never lived with a woman before. Did he want that? Was he ready for that? It'd be a commitment. It wouldn't be fair to ask Maddie to give up her life here in Brazos Bend if he didn't intend to make the situation long-term.

He grabbed a towel and dried off. Tried to separate his wants from his shoulds. He *should* remember that the time the two of them had spent together didn't qualify as normal, and who knew if they'd even like each other on an everyday basis?

But he wanted her.

He *shouldn't* forget the turmoil of the last few months and recognize that now probably wasn't the best time for him to be making life decisions.

But he wanted her.

He *should* remind himself that she had a life here that she said she loved and had desperately wanted to protect. Then there was the little detail of her family connection. He *shouldn't* forget just who this woman was.

But, dammit, I want her.

He wrapped the towel around his waist and went downstairs to retrieve their bags. When he entered the bedroom, Maddie was awake and sitting up against her pillow, the sheet covering her breasts. With her hair tousled and her eyes heavy with sleep, she offered him an uncertain smile. "Hi."

"Hi." Luke felt awkward, something unusual for him the morning after. Ordinarily, he'd pull out smooth and debonair. Today, his debonair well had run dry.

Maddie pulled her bottom lip into her mouth and started to chew on it. Watching her, eyeing the graceful curve of her shoulder and the creamy swell of her breasts rising above the sheet, he wondered why he'd ever left the bed.

"I . . . um . . . guess I'll . . . um . . . take a shower," she said.

Luke felt himself start to go hard again, and he opened his mouth to tell her not to budge, but only a single word emerged. "Okay."

She rewarded him briefly with an excellent view of her delectable ass and legs as she shifted off the bed before covering herself with the sheet. Now, why did she have to go and do that? Had he not just spent the night doing a whole helluva lot more than looking at every square inch of her body?

Again she gave him one of those unsure smiles. "My bag?"

"Oh, yeah. Here." He thrust it toward her.

When she disappeared into the bathroom, Luke raked a hand through his hair. Hell. He felt as awkward as a three-legged dog.

Needing something—anything—to do, he yanked on clothes, then went downstairs to make coffee. While the water dripped, Luke stared blankly at the slowly filling pot and tried to wrap his brain around the notion of what to do next.

Breakfast. He'd fix breakfast.

Luke looked into the fridge for the breakfast casserole Annie had promised to leave for them. Finding it, he read the directions taped to the glass, then stuck it into the microwave. While he set the table, poured juice and milk, he decided that after their meal, he'd talk to Maddie about her situation and clue her in to the fact that she wasn't safe yet. Then he'd go back to work. The sooner he found Jerry Grevas's killer, the sooner he could head back to Louisiana.

Alone.

Well, hell.

Maddie entered the kitchen just as the microwave dinged. She wore white capri pants, a black-and-white polka-dot top, flat black sandals, and that damned hesitant smile. "The coffee smells good."

Luke opened his mouth to ask her to pour them both a cup, but the words that emerged were different. "Come with me."

She glanced around the kitchen. "Where?"

"To the boat. My boat. I'm thinking we could take the *Miss Behavin' II* to South Padre, winter along the coast."

Maddie grabbed the back of a kitchen chair and her face registered shock. "You're asking me to take a vacation? Now?"

"Uh . . . well . . . sort of."

She drew a deep breath, then let it out slowly. Regret laced her tone as she said, "Luke, I appreciate the thought, but I need to get back to work. You know that. While it sounds lovely—truly it does—I can't afford another week away from Home for Now."

"All right. Okay. Except . . . you see . . . a vacation isn't exactly what I had in mind."

"It's not?"

"No."

Her brow creased with a frown. "Then I don't understand."

"I, uh, I thought . . . I want . . ." He blew out a breath. "I'm talking something longer than a vacation."

Awareness dawned slowly in her expression. "You're asking me to what? To live with you?"

No. His stomach rolled. "Well, yeah. I am."

Time hung suspended as he waited for her response. He waited so long that he could have run up to the corner convenience store and bought a six-pack of beer. Then yearning filled her eyes and a smile flirted with her lips. Luke's pulse rate tripled.

Then Maddie gave her head a shake. "Luke, that's crazy."

Well, yeah. He knew it, but still . . . "Why do you think it's crazy?"

She ticked off on her fingers. "For all intents and purposes, we only just met."

Okay, he'd thought of that.

"Plus, the time we've spent together has been completely out of the ordinary. We know how we get along under stressful circumstances, but how would we deal together when life is ordinary?"

So, he'd hit on that one, too. Doodads and pantyhose in the bathroom. He smothered a sigh.

"On top of that, you've just had a major life change, what with losing your partner, quitting your job. Now isn't the time for you to be making such a huge decision."

Hell, they were three for three.

"That doesn't begin to address my issues." Now her toes began to tap. "I've told you how important my life in Brazos Bend is to me. Do you think I'd just walk away from it? Because a man asked me to? It isn't like I haven't had that lesson shoved down my throat before."

He tried not to scowl. "I thought you'd do it because *I* asked you. I'm not one of the assholes in your past, Maddie."

Not exactly, anyway.

"Oh? And how are you different, Luke?" She braced her hands on her hips. "You're asking me to run away and shack up on a boat, for God's sake. How irresponsible is that? I finally have my life on track and you're asking me to give it up? At least when I ran off with Rip and Liam and Cade, I didn't leave anything but trouble behind."

Ouch.

"Can't you see how important all this is to me? My life here in Brazos Bend? My job? It's normal, Luke. I want normal. I *need* normal. I can't just pack up and leave because a man crooks his finger at me. That's something Baby Dagger would do. Well, Maddie Kincaid won't. Not this time. Never again."

His jaw clenched, Luke looked away. Dammit all, she had a point. This hadn't exactly been his finest moment. He didn't think it through; he let his emotions—and, admittedly, his dick—prompt him to speak precipitously. He couldn't give Maddie Kincaid normal. He barely knew what normal was. Normal, safe, comfortable—that had all died with his mother.

"All right. Okay. I hear you. I guess you're right."

Her eyes widened with frustration. "You *guess*?"

He folded his arms. "It's probably not a good time for me, either. I'm at a crossroads. I don't know what I'm going to do with the rest of my life. Now is probably not the time to make a long-term decision."

She lifted her face skyward and shook her head.

"And yet . . ." He rubbed the back of his neck. "Last night was . . . dammit, it was the best. It seems a shame to walk away from it. Are you sure you can't carve out a few weeks for a little vacation?"

She dropped her hands to her sides, and the wistfulness that played across her face served to soothe his ruffled feathers a bit. "It's tempting, Luke. You don't know how tempting. Ten years ago, I'd have gone along in a heartbeat. Five years ago, I'd have taken a minute to think, then I'd have jumped at the opportunity. But I'm not the same person I was five and ten years ago. Life has changed me. Men have changed me."

"This is about those dickwads you dated."

"Well, yes. Some."

Luke's lips tightened. God, he hated being lumped in with those assholes.

"I trusted them, Luke. I loved them. Foolishly, it turned out, but I gave each of those men a piece of my heart. I've learned to guard the pieces I have left."

Luke didn't like hearing that she'd given away pieces of her heart to men who damned well didn't deserve it. Not that he'd deserve it, either, but still . . .

Needing something to do, he grabbed the hot casserole from the microwave and set it on the table.

Maddie took a step toward him. "Luke, neither one of us has even floated the L word. Why would either one of us think it's a good idea to jump off and do something so reckless at this time?"

He had to admit she had a point. He'd always shied away from using that four-letter word. "Is that what you want to hear, Maddie? The L word?"

An emotion he didn't want to name flickered in her eyes, and he warned himself of dangerous ground. He wasn't going to say it. Never had said it to a woman. Probably never would. He didn't want to hurt her, but he wasn't about to lie to her, either.

Once that word was spoken, there was no taking it back. Luke wasn't about to commit the mortal sin of morning-afters and use the L word without thought to the consequences. Sex might have confused and rattled him a bit, but it damn sure didn't fry his last coherent brain cell.

As the silence between them dragged out, he realized that she wasn't ready to say it, either. Good. That was good.

He tried hard to mean it.

"Look, last night was wonderful," she finally continued. She didn't meet his eyes. "It was honestly the most romantic, exciting night of my life. You ended my two-year sexual drought in a blaze of Bananas Foster glory, and I will never, ever forget it. But it would be stupid of me to make a life decision on a sexual high."

Sexual high? Dammit, did she have to always think the exact same thing he did?

And why did it make him feel so empty? What had he been expecting her to say? That she might, just might, have deeper feelings for him?

You're a fool, Callahan.

He raked his fingers through his hair and tried to tell himself he was glad somebody made sense. That it was nice to hear he'd rung her bell—not that he'd had any doubt about that. That he should be glad he was off the hook. Yet, he felt damned lousy. How crazy was that? After a night of the absolute best sex of his life, he felt like his own heart had been chopped into tiny pieces and auctioned off.

One fact especially stung. "You don't trust me."

"I trust you with my life, Luke. But to trust you with my heart . . . to put the little I have left at risk . . . ? Maybe we *could* make it. You could be the answer to all my prayers and worth giving up my life in Brazos Bend. But this has all happened so fast. Too fast. I need more time to be sure, but our time is up, isn't it?"

Unable to deny it, Luke simply shrugged, and after that, there didn't seem to be much to say. In the end, she was right. It was time for her to return to her life, and for him to figure out what the hell he was going to do with his. "You, uh, want a cup of coffee?"

Her smile went bittersweet. "Yes. Let me get it. After all, you cooked breakfast."

They ate their meal in an awkward silence. Maddie's gaze kept flicking toward him, then away. Finally, she sipped her orange juice, then confessed, "I lied to you last night."

He looked up from his plate. "Oh?"

"Last night wasn't the first time I tasted Bananas Foster."

He set down his fork. "Really."

"I didn't want to spoil your surprise. I had it once in the French Quarter at Brennan's restaurant."

"Really?" he asked, his mind elsewhere. So she wanted to shift back into neutral, did she? Maybe that wasn't such a bad idea. There'd been too much, too fast. Both of them needed to coast for awhile.

They each had scars to deal with. Scars of a different kind, but scars nonetheless. If he could say something—anything—to make a difference, he'd do it, but there simply wasn't anything left to say.

The reality of that made him downright sad.

Enough. Just stop it. Don't ruin the time you have left.

He wanted to end their "tomorrow" on a good note. He wanted her to be able to think of him and smile. But how to go about it? Luke drummed his fingers on the table.

Maddie set down her glass, dabbed daintily at her lips with a napkin, then slowly, sultrily, licked her lips. "Yes, really. They served dessert at breakfast."

Good Lord, she'd done the thinking for both of them. *Maddie Kincaid, you are one special woman.* A smile played on his lips as he asked, "So, how's your sweet tooth this morning, Red?"

She got up and sashayed to the freezer. She withdrew the gallon of ice cream and said, "How about I show you?"

Founded in 1858, Mossman Market remained the premier grocery in Brazos Bend despite the influx of national chains, so when Maddie said she wanted to pick up a few personal items before returning to Branch's house, Luke charted a path to Mossman's. "I'll go in with you," he told her as he switched off the engine. "The Garza sisters don't stock my brands of junk food."

Inside the store, Luke grabbed a shopping cart, then proceeded to trail Maddie around. Spying a fresh stack of Parker County peaches, she veered into the produce department. They'd made it no farther than the tomatoes before being reminded of the realities of small-town shopping.

"Luke Callahan," came the crisp, superior-sounding voice of Miss Mirabelle Fontaine, a recently retired teacher at Fain Elementary. "While I'm happy to note that you're buying vegetables, I'm disappointed to see that you've no more common sense than you had as a ten-year-old. Do not stack the peaches on top of those tomatoes."

"Hello, Miss Fontaine," Luke said. "Yes, Miss Fontaine."

When she'd passed by, Luke leaned toward Maddie and murmured, "Fourth grade was the longest year of my life."

In the shampoo aisle, a thirty-something blonde batted

her eyelashes at Sin and recalled the time the underage teen shoplifted a bottle of Boone's Farm Strawberry Hill on her behalf because the girl simply couldn't stand the taste of beer.

"You stole a bottle of wine?" Maddie commented as Luke steered her toward the cookies.

"Strawberry Hill. Nasty stuff. Cost me a night in jail."

"For stealing?"

"Nah. Fighting. Matt and me. He was a wine snob even back then. Said the least I could have done was swipe her a white zin."

Maddie laughed. Tooling around Mossman's with Luke had a distinctly domestic feel to it, and despite her better instincts, she couldn't help but enjoy it. This is what life might have been like had she taken him up on his offer. Little mundane chores accomplished together. Or maybe, she'd do the shopping and he'd help with the unloading and putting away. She'd reward him, of course, for his efforts, and they'd end up atop the kitchen table with . . .

Stop. Don't go there. You'll only cause yourself more grief.

They tarried in the baked goods, then moved on to ethnic foods. Distracted by the selection of hot sauces, Luke failed to pay attention to where he steered the shopping cart. He ran right into Austin Rawlings.

"Sorry about that," Luke said in answer to the district attorney's yelp. "I was distracted by the picante. You ever try Mrs. Renfro's brand?"

Austin ignored his question. "When I saw your car in the parking lot, I decided to stop. Where the hell have you been?"

"Well." Luke arched a brow. "Looks like somebody got up on the wrong side of the bed."

Austin gave them both a good once-over, then his lips flattened as a knowing look entered his eyes. "You should have stolen a couple moments to check your messages. I've been trying to call you two since yesterday."

"What's wrong?" Maddie asked. "It's not Branch, is it?"

"No." Austin offered her a quick, reassuring smile. "We've had a break in the Grevas case and I need to ask you a few questions."

"What break?" Luke demanded, morphing into all-business cop mode.

"The Dallas police called yesterday afternoon trying to retrace the movements of a stiff found at White Rock Lake. Vic's name was Bartolo. He was muscle for a Dallas-area loan shark with ties to Louisiana."

"Shreveport?" Luke asked.

"Yes. He had a receipt from the Dairy Princess on the day Grevas was killed, and his prints matched some we found in Grevas's truck. It's not positive proof that he was the killer, but the circumstantial evidence is enough to satisfy me."

Luke shot his words like bullets. "How did he die?"

"Execution-style shot to the head. Body was dumped in a park at White Rock Lake."

"Huh." Luke absently loaded three varieties of Mrs. Renfro's hot sauce into Maddie's cart. Maddie could all but see the wheels turning in his head. "Have the Dallas cops brought in the banker?"

"Yeah. They didn't get anything from him."

Maddie tried to catch up, working to put together the pieces of information Austin Rawlings had imparted with those that had been hovering on the edge of her consciousness since the alcohol-and-sex haze had faded from her brain. "Austin? Let me see if I have this straight. You think this Bartolo guy killed Jerry Grevas?"

"I don't have definitive proof, but yes, I do."

"And you're surmising that Jerry borrowed money from a loan shark to cover the gambling debts he ran up in Shreveport." Money he owed the mob. Talk about robbing Peter to pay Paul.

"Yes."

"And when he couldn't pay, the loan shark had his minion, Mr. Bartolo, kill Jerry."

"That's my theory."

"Then why kill the minion? That makes no sense."

Luke tossed a bag of tortilla chips into the basket as Austin said, "I don't know the answer to that. It's one of the reasons I wanted to talk to you. Maddie, have you run across anything in Gus's stuff that strikes you as curious? Anything unusual at all?"

Maddie considered the question. Much of what she'd removed from Gus's house could be considered unusual. His collection of plastic turtles certainly fit the bill, but she doubted Austin needed to know about those. She recalled Gus's gimme caps and his Matchbox cars, but she didn't think . . . wait—the box. She recalled how Jerry screeched about needing some box the night he attacked her. She didn't know anything more about any box now than she had then and she'd already told the police about Jerry's demands. "No. I can't think of anything, Austin."

"This Bartolo guy's death ties up the case in a nice pretty bow, doesn't it?" Luke observed. "No need to keep looking for Grevas's killer. No need to keep digging here in Brazos Bend."

Something about his manner was a little bit off, Maddie thought. He'd said it as if he didn't necessarily believe it.

"That's the way I see it," Austin agreed. "So, your job here is basically done. Maddie is safe. You can leave town."

Maddie startled. Her heart dipped to her knees and she turned a sharp look toward Luke. He gave Austin Rawlings a tiger's smile and drawled, "I'll think about it."

Austin looked disgusted with Luke's noncommittal tone. He turned back to Maddie, asked her a few more questions regarding the mushroom stash. He promised to call her if he learned anything else from the Dallas police, then took his leave.

Maddie mulled over Austin's news while she finished her shopping, shaking her head in amazement at the amount of food Luke loaded into the cart. She wondered whether the bags would all fit in the sports car's little trunk.

It turned out she'd been right to wonder. Luke arranged then rearranged the bags in the back of the Maserati, grumbling all the while about missing his truck. Maddie's musings returned to Austin's comments and she asked, "You don't think the Fratellis had anything to do with this Bartolo fellow's death, do you, Luke?"

"As in offering him up to protect Marco's continued forays into the family business?"

She nodded. "Exactly."

"No." Luke rescued a loaf of bread from certain squishing by handing it to her. "I made some calls, checked some sources since I've been in town, and I simply don't believe our Fratellis are involved in anything more than nickel-and-dime business. No drugs. Certainly no murder."

He slammed the trunk shut and added, "I couldn't ignore it if I did, Maddie."

No. He was too much a federal agent to do that. "Do you think Austin is on the right track? That there was another loan shark involved?"

"It's possible. He had to get the money to pay off the Fratellis somewhere. My hunch was that he'd already sold at least one crop of mushrooms and got the money that way, but who knows?"

Maddie stared at a mud splatter on the Maserati's back bumper. Something about that statement bothered her, too, but she couldn't figure out quite what it was. "And you think Bartolo's death has nothing to do with me?"

"Could be. I'd like better proof—especially given your involvement—but sometimes the bad guys kill each other and save the cops the trouble. In my experience, drug dealers are always popping each other off, and the DEA can't necessarily tell who did what to whom when the bullets stop flying."

"How can we find out if that's the case here?"

"I don't know that we can." Luke rubbed the back of his neck. "Bottom line, we may never know what happened. Rawlings might be right on in his deduction. Bartolo could have had loans of his own that got him offed or he could have run afoul of his boss some way. Hell, an angry husband could have taken him out. I'm glad Rawlings is confident of his theory, but . . . I don't know, Maddie. This news makes me feel better than I did an hour ago; however, something still smells fishy to me."

Luke's instincts left Maddie uneasy, but before she could comment, they were treated to yet another show of small-town reality when one of Branch's neighbors, Margaret Swan, stopped to comment on the fact that she'd seen Maddie and Luke depart in the Maserati last night, but the car never came home. "It was bad enough that you told the whole town on television that you had the hots for our Maddie, but to flaunt your affair that way . . . it's not right. You're still the same irresponsible scalawag you were years ago, aren't you?"

As she huffed away, Luke glanced at Maddie. "You have to appreciate someone who uses both 'the hots' and 'scalawag' in the same breath."

"Not to mention her talent with binoculars. I can't tell you the number of times I've seen her standing in her window with a pair of field glasses trained on your dad's house watching that cute guy clean the pool."

Luke grinned as he gentlemanly assisted Maddie into his car's passenger seat before climbing behind the wheel. They didn't speak much during the drive. Maddie's thoughts churned with the day's revelations, and she tried to capture the idea that fluttered just beyond her grasp.

Preoccupied, she didn't note their direction until Luke pulled into her own driveway. "You brought me home? Not to Branch's?"

"If Rawlings is right, there's no need to go back there. Besides, I need to sleep in a bed and not on a pool lounger."

"What if he's wrong?" Maddie asked, a bit perturbed by his high-handed decision making.

"Then I'll be here to deal with it."

She almost asked him what made him think he was invited to stay, but better sense prevailed. Under the circumstances, she'd be stupid to turn away his protection. "I'll go open the garage door and we can carry the groceries right into the kitchen."

Luke switched off the car but didn't make a move to leave his seat. Maddie climbed her front steps, then opened the door, and the soothing scent of home surrounded her as she took a moment to enjoy. Her happy-to-be-here gaze made a quick sweep of the living room as she dropped her purse onto her desk. She loved her house. Loved the friends who'd helped her put it to rights after Jerry Grevas tore it to pieces. "It's good to be home," she murmured aloud. Next, she made her way through her kitchen to the garage, where she slapped the garage door opener button.

Luke's feet came slowly into view as the door rose, but while she looked at him, her mind wandered elsewhere. Something nagged at her, but she couldn't place it. With a brown bag in each arm, Luke ducked his head beneath the lifting door and strode into the garage. "After we put the groceries away, let's make a run to pick up Knucklehead and your things."

"All right." In her kitchen, Luke set the bags on the table. Maddie began putting the groceries away, rolling her eyes at some of Luke's choices. She set a bag of corn chips next to her cereal in the pantry, and the sight of a jar of spaghetti sauce allowed the truth niggling at the back of her brain to finally work its way to the forefront.

Last night between the liquor and the lust, she'd managed to avoid the reality the dinner at Fratelli's revealed. Had she given it any thought, she'd have realized that the danger wasn't over, after all.

Luke, G-man that he was, had certainly thought about it. *That's why he asked me to leave with him.*

Maddie chewed her bottom lip, her emotions beginning to seethe as she worked through the timing of the events of the past eighteen hours or so and belatedly put the clues together. She'd been high on wine and a sense of safety, but Luke'd had his wits about him.

Oh, yeah. That sorry, sneaky son of a Callahan. He didn't really want her to "vacation" with him aboard the *Miss Behavin' II*. He was just trying to get her out of town so he didn't have to stay there!

Maddie's foot took to tapping. He'd lied to her. She despised being lied to, especially by a man. To think she'd actually considered having a Baby Dagger moment. She'd actually contemplated throwing caution to the wind and following him off to the bayous.

She'd seriously thought about offering him her heart.

A shudder ran through her. Good Lord. What a mistake to think that Luke Callahan was any different from Cade or Rip or Liam. What a close call she'd had!

She'd believed him. She'd believed he'd wanted her, had felt the special connection she felt. His hesitation when he'd asked her to leave with him had been evident, which made him even more convincing. Had he jumped off and declared his undying love for her, she'd have known he was blowing smoke. Instead, he'd fooled her.

The lying dog. The scheming skunk. The prevaricating pig.

The pig.

"The pig!" She twisted her head around toward the living room. The cereal box in her hand fell splat on the floor.

"Red?"

Without responding, she hurried to the living room. Her gaze focused on the bookshelf and the silly little pig figurine that Sara-Beth Branson had given her during the cleanup three days ago. It had been a gag gift, given with plenty of jokes about the pig gene men were born with, and they'd set it on the shelf with great ceremony.

They'd set it backward. Now it faced outward.

"What's wrong, Maddie?"

"Have you been over here without me?"

"No."

"Has anyone?"

"Not that I know of. What is it, Maddie?"

"My pig. Someone . . ." She looked carefully at the bookshelf, then around the room. Nothing but the pig appeared brazenly out of place. The knickknacks on her coffee table could be lined up a little too straight, and the books on her shelf were certainly out of order. But Kathy had been the one to return the books to the shelf following Jerry's destructive visit. Maybe *she* hadn't put them in alphabetical order.

Her bedroom. A dozen paces took her to the doorway. "Maddie, what the hell is wrong?"

"I think . . ." She moved to her lingerie chest, unease swirling inside her. She'd put her clothes away herself, so she knew exactly how she should find them. Sliding her panty drawer open, she glanced inside and drew a gasping breath. *Someone has been here.*

A shudder of fear snaked through her. She checked her closet. Her shoes. They might look a mess, but she had a system.

Her system had been obliterated.

She considered the timing. It couldn't have been Bartolo. She had been here since his death. Was Austin wrong? Was someone still out to get her? What other explanation could there be?

"Goddammit, Maddie!"

She glanced over her shoulder. "It's wrong, Luke. Things aren't where they belong, where they were when I left here day before yesterday."

"You think someone has been here?"

"I'm certain of it." She blew out a long, harsh breath. "Luke, somebody has searched my house."

Fifteen

"Hold on a minute." Luke spoke in a soft, menacing tone. "You're telling me someone's been through this place since Jerry?"

"Yes! They were careful about it, but I can tell. I know how I leave my underwear!"

Luke marched over to her lingerie chest and peered at her panties as if he'd find answers inside the open drawer. Worry sat in his gut like a bad piece of fish as he thought his way through this new development. What the hell was going on here?

Methodically, he inspected the windows and doors for signs of forced entry. "Who has keys to your place? Kathy?"

"No. No one. Not even my landlord."

Unusual, but this was Brazos Bend. "Do you keep a house key at your office?"

"No."

"Maybe you forgot to lock up."

"No!"

Hmm. Either somebody had a key she didn't know about or whoever got inside here was really good. Burglars, maybe?

He flipped open the inlaid wood jewelry box sitting atop her dresser and peered inside. A flash of diamonds and a Rolex watch confirmed his fears. Crap. Of course it wouldn't be that simple.

Maddie plopped down on the edge of her bed and rubbed

her temples with her fingertips. "This is crazy. Nothing makes sense. I've had a smooth, uneventful life since I got out of jail. It's been wonderful. It's been stable. It's been just what I wanted!"

"What are we missing, Maddie? What's going on here that we're not seeing?"

"I don't know!"

"Think about it," he said, feeling grimmer by the moment. "Help me out here. Think beyond the mushrooms. Beyond Jerry Grevas. Could this have something to do with Baby Dagger?"

"I can't imagine . . . oh." She dropped her hands to her lap and shut her eyes. "Hmm. He couldn't do this. He wouldn't."

He? "Who's 'he'?"

"What?"

"Who wouldn't break into your house, Maddie? You obviously have an idea."

"Yes, well, I do have one idea. It's possible . . . oh, I hope this isn't the case."

"Maddie, if you don't spit it out I swear I'm going to—"

"It's Liam."

Liam. One of the exes. "Tell me."

"We had dinner when I was in New York."

She's dated a dickhead? Since she met me? The idea pissed him off, but that would have to wait until he found out why she thought the jerk might have broken into her house. "How did that happen? Did he come looking for you or did you call him for old times' sake?"

"I didn't call him!" The annoyance in her eyes faded to amazement. "Are you jealous? For heaven's sake, Luke."

He set his teeth. All right, maybe he was acting stupid, but hell. "Tell me why you think he's been snooping in your panty drawer."

She folded her arms, visibly bristling. "You don't need to take that tone with me, Luke Callahan. I'm not the one lying about vacations."

"What?"

"Oh, never mind." She waved a dismissive hand. "Look, Liam somehow ran across my father during his trip to Alaska, and Liam convinced him I'd want to see him. I actually dropped my purse when I saw him instead of my father at our reserved table at dinner."

Luke tried to recall what details she'd given him about the old boyfriend named Liam, but he came up blank. "Who is he and what did he want?"

She narrowed her eyes. "If you'll give me a chance, I'll tell you."

Maddie pushed off her bed and sashayed past him, headed for the kitchen. What the hell had put the burr beneath her saddle? He's the one who'd just had another man thrown into the mix, one who she suspected of breaking into her house and rifling through her things.

In the kitchen, she took a large sun-tea jar from a cabinet and began to fill it with water. "I was with Liam about eight or so years ago. I left him when I discovered he'd used my bank account to provide funds to some friends of his in the IRA."

"Good God. You dated a terrorist?"

"Liam wasn't a terrorist," she defended. After a brief pause, she added, "His brother was."

"Jesus!" He glanced around her house. Christ. Terrorists? In Brazos Bend? What the hell has she stepped in? This could go beyond mushrooms. Had her Irishman hidden something on her or given her something to hold? "When you saw him in New York, what did he want? Did you take anything from him? Anything at all? Did he tell you anything? Think, Maddie. Those guys don't play around."

Maddie's teeth worried her bottom lip. "Liam didn't give me anything. He made up this elaborate story about a possible reconciliation between us, and since Blade and I don't talk about my love life, he didn't know any better. My father is a romantic at heart, and he liked the idea of furthering the course of true love."

"With a terrorist."

She chastised him with a look. "I didn't want to make a scene, so I stayed and listened to what he had to say. It appears he's gone on to new schemes. He actually thought I'd be willing to finance one of them. I turned him down and ditched him after dinner, but I think he might have followed me. I thought I saw him on the street a time or two, and then later at the airport. He's called me a couple of times since then."

A terrorist was stalking her and she hadn't bothered to mention it before now? Luke's anger went hot. He couldn't believe that with everything that had been going on, she'd kept this information to herself. In a grim tone, he asked, "What does he want the money for?"

"Who knows?" Maddie dangled two family-sized tea bags into her jar. "He spun some story about a nursing home investment, but the man—like so many of his kind—is a liar. Liars and users. Always trying to take advantage. Women often don't see past that kind of charm. I might have fallen for it in the past. Shoot, I *did* fall for it in the past. But now I see. I've earned bloody bifocals when it comes to men like . . . well, men."

Luke might be slow sometimes, but he wasn't stupid. That had been a dig at him. Why? *What the hell did I do?*

And why the hell did it even matter at this particular moment, when they ought to be worrying about who rifled her house and why?

"Look, I don't know what's put this bee in your bonnet, but whatever it is will have to wait. I need every scrap of information you can give me about this creep so that I can check him out." He stalked to her desk and removed a notepad and a pen. "Start with his full name."

"Liam Michael . . . wait."

Luke could see in her expression that a new thought had occurred to her.

"With Liam, it's always been about money. I'll bet that's it. Money." Maddie snapped her fingers. "Money. I wouldn't give it to him, so he figured out another way to use me to get it. I'll bet you anything he tracked me down in order to sell Baby Dagger out to the tabloids."

Hmm. She might be on to something there. "The paparazzi come to Brazos Bend."

Maddie groaned. "It makes sense. I bet he came here looking for me and when I didn't come home, he snooped around a bit. That'd be just like him. I wouldn't take his calls so he came to blackmail me in person."

"Blackmail?"

"I can see it now. With one phone call, the vultures would descend, shoving microphones in everyone's faces, taking pictures. The bastards." Maddie paced the room. "Except first, he'll try to get me to pay him off. Pay him to keep my secret. Well, I won't do it!"

Then she stopped abruptly, looked at Luke, and asked, "Or should I?"

That pissed him off all over again. The idea of paying blackmail went against everything Luke believed in, but, hey, it wasn't his call, was it?

All Luke's anger and frustration and worry went into his reply as he drawled, "It's your decision, Maddie. Your life. And an exciting life it is. Terrorists, rock stars, magic mushrooms. Not to mention rap sheets and run-ins with the mob and loan sharks and—"

Maddie slammed the jar's plastic lid down on the countertop. "Stop it. Just stop it. How dare you make fun of my life!"

"You don't have a life, Maddie," he snapped right back. "You have a fucking soap opera!"

She gasped. Her eyes flashed. Color flushed her cheeks as she walked up to him and poked a finger at his chest over and over as she said, "You just be quiet, Luke Callahan. You don't know what it's like. You have no idea. You can't! You think I want to have a life like this? You think I wanted my mother to die baking me brownies? That I set out to fall for jerks and end up in jail and get tangled up with mushrooms and murderers and men that beat me up and tear apart my house and—and—and—kill my fish! Well, that's not the way it happened. All I ever wanted was a home. Somewhere to belong. Well, I belong here, and now, through no fault of my own, it's being taken away from me. I didn't do anything wrong. I just tried to be normal. Of all people, I thought you might understand. I thought you might help me. Instead, all I hear are snide remarks. Blame Baby. Same old song, just one more verse."

Every poke was a bullet to his heart. She was so damned beautiful. So damned vulnerable.

God, Callahan, you're an ass.

"Maddie, look. I didn't mean . . ." Hell, he didn't know what to say. She whirled away from him, returned to her jar of tea. Luke watched her swipe tears from her cheek and he said, "I guess I'm just another dickhead."

"I won't argue with that."

"I'm sorry." He approached her, took her hand in his. "I didn't mean to blame you or poke fun at your life. I know you've had it rough. But let's get one thing straight. I want this crystal clear between us. Maddie, I've never lied to you."

The doubt he saw in her teary brown eyes cut like a knife. "I didn't say . . ."

"Yeah, you did. Explain why, Red. What did I say? What do you think I lied about?"

Hurt mingled with the doubt. "I thought that you . . . that we . . . you knew that the danger wasn't necessarily over, Luke. You wanted me to leave Brazos Bend."

He absorbed that. Didn't understand the problem. "Yes. And this was bad because . . . ?"

"I thought . . ." She looked away from him. Pulled away from him. Hurt and anger and pain rang in her voice as she exclaimed, "I fell for it! I thought you meant it!"

"I did mean it." He reached for her, but she shrugged him off. "It wasn't a lie, Maddie. Don't compare me to the others in that respect. Yes, I want you safe, but that's not the reason I asked you to leave with me."

"Then, what was?"

The question stumped him. Confused him. He didn't know the answer.

"Why did you ask me to leave with you, Luke?" she asked again, her eyes big and round and teeming with emotion. With pain. With fear that he was going to hurt her, to let her down like everyone else.

Suddenly, the words were there on his tongue. *Because I love you.*

Whoa. Luke's world changed in that moment. He hadn't planned on this. Never guessed it would happen.

He didn't have a clue what to do about it now.

Except instincts told him to keep the news to himself. Not because he was afraid to say the words, but because he didn't think she was ready to hear them. So he told her something close. "I'm not ready to let you go."

"But you won't stay here," she declared flatly, her words at odds with the hint of hope in her eyes.

"No, not forever. And that'll be a problem we'll have to tackle at some point. But right now, I think we need to put our energies into confirming who broke in here and why. If you think I'm going to walk out now and leave you vulnerable to your old boyfriend's machinations, then you've got another think coming, Maddie Kincaid. I'm not going anywhere until everything is settled."

A smile flirted with her lips. "Oh, really?"

"Really." He stroked his knuckles down her cheek. "You're important to me, Red. You're special. I need you to believe that."

She looked at him long and hard, her gaze searching his. When the last vestiges of doubt melted from her eyes, Luke felt like he'd won the lottery.

He bent his head and kissed her, taking that last step to move his body against hers. His kiss was tender, loving, conveying his emotions in a wordless poem. It was a kiss like none other he'd given before.

He loved her. He did. And he didn't have the faintest idea what he was going to do about it.

He didn't fall in love. It was irresponsible. Pointless. Wrong. Weren't those the lessons life had taught him? Love hurt. Love damaged. Love didn't last.

But all those reasons didn't mean squat when Maddie curled her arms around his neck and pulled him closer.

He was toast. Finished. Done for. When finally he stepped away, he knew that fundamentally, life would never be the same. He loved her.

And some a-hole was stalking her.

Luke cleared his throat. "Now, tell me more about this Irish dipshit so I can find him and kick his ass."

At the Home for Now offices on Magnolia Avenue just south of downtown a week later, Maddie sat down at her desk with a glass of iced tea and her employees' work schedule. At her assistant's desk in the outer room, Luke was on the phone again. For the past week he'd spent long hours speaking with various contacts in government and law enforcement in his efforts to find Liam Murphy.

He'd blown the one contact they'd managed to make with the man. On Luke's instructions and with him listening in, Maddie had returned Liam's call and tried to pump him for information to either confirm him to be her stalker or eliminate him from suspicion. Maddie had thought she'd been doing a good job, but when Liam started flirting and made a few rather personal comments about the sex life they'd enjoyed, Luke lost it. He'd grabbed the phone, and the threats flowed hot and furious. Liam hung up on him and canceled the cell phone number.

Luke's subsequent efforts to locate Liam had met with little success. Each day Luke got a bit grumpier.

Maddie didn't care. She was enjoying every moment of playing house with Luke. She invariably awoke in the mornings to his lovemaking. They'd cook breakfast together, then head off to the office. He'd tagged along on a couple of her client visits, but mostly, he left her to do her everyday business while he worked the phones and pestered Austin

Rawlings and Chief Harper about any new developments regarding Grevas or Bartolo. In the evenings they'd take Knucklehead for a run, fix supper, feed Oscar, do a few chores, then head to bed early. Maddie couldn't recall a time when she'd enjoyed life this much.

Life was normal, just like she'd always wanted. If only it would last.

Liam hadn't called again. She'd seen no sign of him in or around Brazos Bend. Had her guess about blackmail been correct? Or would he even bother to hit her up first? Maybe he'd decided to go straight to the tabloids.

She was getting tired of looking over her shoulder all the time for a photographer's flash.

"Hey, beautiful," Luke said from the doorway. "I'm hungry. Do you want something from the Dairy Princess?"

She ordered a chef salad and listened to him make the call, flirting with Kathy, as he did daily. Twenty minutes later, lunch arrived by way of the Dairy Princess owner herself. "I decided you need a lecture about your diet, Sin. You've ordered onion rings for lunch every day this week. I'm worried about you. Have you had your cholesterol checked? I expect Maddie has told you that your father has high cholesterol and that's something that runs in families."

"I take after my mother," Luke declared before changing the subject. "So, is the Dairy Princess short of delivery kids today? How is it we rated the owner to bring us our cheeseburgers?"

Kathy's gaze whipped toward Maddie. "I thought you ordered a salad."

"I did. Just ignore Luke."

She frowned at Luke and clicked her tongue, but something about the light in her eyes, perhaps the absence of their usual twinkle, caused Maddie to give her friend a closer look. Kathy appeared a bit ragged. Definitely tense. "What's wrong?"

Kathy opened her mouth, then hesitated. Maddie's concern deepened. "What happened?"

"I'm worried," her friend finally said after emptying the sacks on the worktable Maddie used as a place to eat. "I don't like it that Luke can't find Liam, and I'm worried that he's up to something more than siccing the tabloids on you. I think Luke was right, Maddie. I think you should leave town, if only for a couple of weeks."

Kathy turned to Luke, her eyes pleading. "You could do that, couldn't you? You could take her away just for a little while until it's over?"

"Until what is over?" Luke asked, eyeing the onion rings. "What do you think the jerkface might be planning?"

"I'm afraid he'll try to kidnap her and hold her for ransom. Like those criminals did to your poor brother. Blade would pay. He's not an American citizen and he wouldn't let any government policy stop him."

"Unlike my father." Bitterness seeped into Luke's tone as he widened his stance and folded his arms across his chest.

"That's silly," Maddie said, shaking her head. Luke's reaction told her this was a dangerous subject, and she didn't want him to have to think about it at all. "Liam wouldn't do anything like that."

"How do you know what he'd do? It's been years since you've spent time with him. He could very easily be as crazy as his brother by now."

Luke nodded. "I don't think your idea is silly at all, Kathy. I've learned a bit about the brother—mean SOB. Part of a nasty IRA offshoot. Is there a particular reason why you suspect your scenario might be true?"

"I don't know any more than you do, but it just makes sense to me."

"To me, too," Luke replied, his mouth grim. "The same thought had occurred to me, too. That's one reason I don't let Maddie out of my sight."

"Oh, for crying out loud," Maddie muttered. She hated seeing her friend so worked up, so upset. Kathy loved Maddie like a daughter, and considering that she'd already faced one tragedy involving a daughter, no wonder she looked ragged.

Luke wasn't helping things, either. He refused to listen to Maddie's arguments that Liam wasn't a terrorist, but rather a pain in the butt. The Irishman just wanted her money. Maddie was certain of it. Why couldn't Luke accept it?

Because he's a cop at heart, that's why. The kind of cop who won't stop digging until the last stone is turned.

"There is one other thing." Kathy's gaze fluttered between Maddie and Luke. "A stranger came into the Princess today. I've only seen pictures of Liam Murphy a couple of times and I don't recall what he looks like, but this man was just about the right age and he did have an Irish lilt to his voice."

"Did you talk to him?"

"I tried. He wasn't very friendly."

"What kind of car was he driving?"

"A Taurus."

"Popular rental car. I don't like this. I don't like it at all." Luke pinned Maddie with a severe look. "Maybe you should think about doing as she says."

Maddie wasn't a stupid woman, and if she honestly thought she was in danger from anything more than a camera shot, she'd pack her bags in a heartbeat. "I have responsibilities here in Brazos Bend. I can't walk away from them, not again. Have you forgotten that Mrs. Charlton comes home from the hospital today? I promised her family I'd be there every afternoon this week, and they're counting on me."

"Send a substitute."

"I don't have any more substitutes," she pointed out. "Every employee I have is already working maximum hours."

Kathy piped up. "Hire more help."

"I've tried. Please, Kathy, you're a business owner. You know how difficult it is to find good help, and you have a large pool of teenagers to choose from. My choices are much more limited, and I refuse to send anyone but the best to my clients' homes. Right now, the only 'best' on my availability board is me.

"I've thought about this long and hard, and I've decided that I can't keep running. I've been running, hiding, and making the wrong decisions most of my life. For once, I'm standing my ground. If Liam does show up with extortion in his eyes, I'm turning him down. I'm standing my ground. If he wants to sell me out and call in the vultures, then there isn't much I can do about it, is there? I am who I am. I'm Baby Dagger. But I'm also Maddie Kincaid and I'm proud of that. I'm not backing down. I'm not quitting. Some of my clients will do without help if they can't have me, and while Branch Callahan's daily letters aren't a matter of life and death, Sue Ellen Parker's physical therapy is."

"What letters?" Luke demanded. "You've mentioned them before."

Maddie hesitated, wishing she hadn't revealed that particular detail. Yet, maybe it was time. Maybe knowing about the letters would spark Luke's curiosity and finally bring about some communication between father and son.

From what Maddie could tell, Luke hadn't spoken to Branch since picking up Oscar and Knucklehead from Callahan House a week ago. Branch's hopes that the closer proximity might lead to a reconciliation were fading fast. In fact, his frequent calls demanding her help in the area were quickly becoming a nuisance. So far this morning, he'd called every hour on the hour.

Luke pretended he didn't hear the conversations.

Maybe his question about the letters showed a crack of curiosity in his wall of resistance.

"The letters are the reason your father hired me in the first place. Up until this mushroom mess interrupted us, every weekday he would dictate three letters—one to Matt, one to Mark, and one to you. I filed them by date with the others. He's written to you all daily since you left Brazos Bend. You'll find boxes with your name on them in that wall of built-in cabinets in his study."

It took him a good ten seconds to respond. "You're lying."

"He still writes a letter to John on holidays and your

brother's birthday. I think it's cathartic for him. You should read your letters, Luke. I think you'd be more forgiving toward your father if you did."

His eyes flashed. "I don't give a damn about forgiveness and you're changing the subject. If Liam Murphy has followed you to Brazos Bend, I need to know why."

"I won't argue with that."

"But you won't leave town."

"No, I won't." She turned to her friend. "Kathy, you know I love you dearly and I appreciate your concern, I truly do. I'm not dismissing your advice out of hand. I've weighed the pros and cons of any decision I might make. If I believed Liam was a danger to my person, I'd leave in a heartbeat. I do believe he's a danger to my happiness, and while I'm hoping Luke can help me avoid the paparazzi pitfall, if I end up on the cover of the *Globe* or *National Enquirer*, I've decided it doesn't have to be the end of my world here. Life might be uncomfortable for a bit, but except for recently, I lead a pretty boring existence. After the initial brouhaha, the excitement will die down. The photographers will eventually go away. I've decided that if I have to, I can wait them out."

"People here won't like the notoriety," Luke cautioned.

"A few of them will," Kathy replied.

"Nevertheless, I've decided to have some faith in the people of Brazos Bend. Even if the worst happens, I'm going to trust that they accept me for who I am now, not who I was in the past."

Kathy stared at her for a long moment, then sighed. "I'm not going to be able to change your mind, am I?"

"No."

Kathy pushed wearily to her feet, for once looking every day of her fifty-nine years. "I feel in my bones that you're in danger, Maddie, but at least you've been warned. I want you safe. Luke Callahan, you'd better stick to her like syrup to a countertop. I think she's filled her quota of stubborn with this decision to stay, so if she tries to give you any grief, well, I'm the closest thing she has to a mama, and you have my permission to deal with her however you think best."

Maddie glanced at Luke, expecting to see amusement gleaming in his eyes. Instead, she spied a slow-burning anger, not just in his gaze, but in the set of his jaw, the line of his mouth, and the clutch of his fist against his thigh.

Liam, if you are in Brazos Bend, you'd best beware. My man looks ready to kill.

Luke used Maddie's house key to unlock the door at Callahan House, then stepped aside for her and Knuckle-head to enter first. He slammed the door behind him. He didn't want to be here, didn't want to come within a half mile of the man, but Maddie had surrendered to Branch's repeated requests and promised to give him two hours this evening to supervise his exercises and work on his damned letters.

Letters. As if anyone wanted to read anything the old bastard had to say. Trying to lessen your guilt, dear old Dad? Won't work. Not with him. Not with his brothers, either. They knew exactly what went down, and they didn't need anything in writing to make it any clearer.

"What a freakin' waste of time," Luke muttered as Knucklehead made a beeline for the kitchen. "You know, Maddie, we could be home making love right now."

Her eyes twinkled devilishly. "You know what they say about anticipation, don't you?"

"No."

"It makes the . . . heart . . . grow longer." She waggled her brows. "Works for me."

"Very funny. My heart is plenty long enough, as you well know."

"Braggart." She rose on her tiptoes and bussed his cheek. "Behave, Luke. You don't have to stay, you know. This is the safest house in town."

Since they'd already fought this fight, he didn't waste his breath replying to that. The latest news he'd uncovered about Murphy had him worried. According to a report out of Langley, Kathy might not be as far off the mark as Maddie liked to think. In the past two years, Liam had been spotted in his brother's company on four different occasions.

"All right, then," Maddie continued. "Why don't you see if your dog has left you anything to snack on. I checked the schedule and saw that the Rangers are playing the Yankees tonight. You can watch it in Branch's study. We'll be working in his exercise room tonight."

He waited for her to go upstairs before taking her suggestion. He was pleased to find a note from Maria Garza and a snack tray in the fridge. Knucklehead lay stretched out on the cool tile floor feasting on his own snack—a ham bone the cook had left lying in his favorite spot just inside the back door at perfect tripping distance. Luke snagged the tray and a beer and headed for the plasma TV in the study.

He sprawled in the leather recliner, commandeered the remote, and settled in to watch baseball. But his gaze kept drifting toward the cabinets lining the far wall.

So the old bastard still wrote letters, did he? Luke had to admit, that one caught him by surprise. That first year after Branch sent him away from Brazos Bend, Luke would have given his left nut to get a letter from his father. He'd tried to act tough, to tell himself he was doing just fine working the offshore rigs in the gulf, but underneath he'd been scared yellow. He'd been kept in the dark about his brothers' locations. Had never felt so utterly and completely alone. It'd been hell.

But not hell enough to keep him from continuing his destructive ways. It'd been toward the end of that year when hungover and at risk of the clap, he'd entered the knife fight that changed his life. Terry Winston had decided to return the favor after Luke had saved his life, and before Luke quite knew what had happened, Terry got him off the rig and in college.

His father's first letter arrived the same day as his first history exam. Luke marked it *Return to Sender* and dropped it in a mailbox. Once a week for the next four years, he repeated the procedure. When Luke graduated and began his training with the DEA, the letters stopped.

Or so he'd thought.

His gaze drifted once again to the cabinets. Lots of years worth of letters. If he actually did write to all of them . . . No, Luke didn't believe it. "Probably came up with the idea to keep Maddie hanging around. Dirty old man."

Luke turned his attention to the Rangers, and his attention didn't drift until the perennially poor Ranger pitching gave up five runs in the third. At that point, while reaching for another nacho, his gaze skidded across the cabinets once again.

Well. Hmm. He guessed he could check it out. Just so he could prove to Maddie that Branch was blowing smoke. The cabinet hinges squeaked as he opened the door. He spied row after row of cardboard file boxes with white labels written in his father's handwriting. *Matthew, 1990 & 91. Luke, 1996 & 97.* Boxes for Mark and for John, too, just like Maddie had said.

He touched his younger brother's box and a memory of the last time he saw John flashed through his mind. They'd had a celebration dinner at a steak house in D.C. right after John received his latest promotion at the State Department.

Luke's eyes momentarily closed. Better he'd grown up to be a dogcatcher than a diplomat.

Luke located a box marked with his own name and the year 2002. He pulled it from the shelf, lifted the lid to reveal the stack of neat white envelopes, and chose one at random.

Dear Son,
    I hope this letter finds you well. I was proud to learn of your success in Target Bravo. The agency earns high marks for shutting down such a vicious ring of criminals. I'm sure the commendation you earned as an undercover operative was much deserved.

"I'll be damned," Luke murmured. How had Branch wrangled the details of that one? Target Bravo was still a classified operation.

Branch had kept track of his sons. Luke had figured that out the day Maddie arrived on his boat deck, but he hadn't realized the extent of his father's snooping. It surprised him, intrigued him—how *had* he learned about Luke's undercover work?— and stirred a deep sense of satisfaction within him.

All of Branch Callahan's sons grew up and showed him. They all turned out to be fine men. And they did it on their own, without Branch Callahan's help.

Luke returned the letter to its envelope and the envelope back to the box. As he returned the box to the stack, his gaze fell upon a file labeled *John, 2006.*

Slowly, curiosity getting the better of him, Luke reached for the box. For some strange reason, his heart began to pound as he lifted the lid. Inside, he found four letters. Dates were penned in Maddie's hand across the front of the envelopes. *January 1, New Year's Day; March 2, Texas Independence Day; March 17, St. Patrick's Day; April 16, Easter.*

Luke chose the March 2 letter. Luke's mother had brought the McBride family tradition of celebrating Texas Independence Day to the Callahan family. The day had been second only to Christmas on the enjoyment scale for Luke and his brothers because Mom had made a party of it. Every year, rain or shine, their family would load up and travel to the old dogtrot cabin on ranch land that had come to Mary Margaret Callahan through her grandfather Billy McBride. They'd spend the night playing pioneers, and their mom would tell stories of old-time Texas, including family tales that had been passed down through the generations. Luke would never forget the time she'd brought an heirloom wedding gown with her and worn it while she and his father danced beneath a silvered moon across a field awash in bluebonnets to music only they heard. That night had been the first time he and his elementary school–aged brothers heard their parents having sex in the room across the dogtrot. They'd been horrified, scandalized, and though none of them would admit it, just a little bit titillated.

Luke grinned at the memory as he unfolded his father's letter and read:

Dear John,
  It's Texas Independence Day, and I'm recalling one of my most favorites. You'd have been in first or second grade. We arrived at the cabin early in the day and you and I and your brothers propped fishing poles on our shoulders, grabbed a pound of bacon, and walked down to the creek to catch crawdads. Halfway through the morning, your brother Mark got distracted by some tadpoles and he lay on his belly over the creek bank, his head getting closer and closer to the water until a big old granddaddy crawfish reached up and pinched his nose.

Luke laughed aloud. He'd forgotten all about that. His twin had screamed like a girl when the crayfish grabbed him.

  Later that night, your mama put on her great-great-grandmother's wedding gown, and she and I danced beneath the stars. It was a magical day. One I'll never forget.
  I wonder if up there in Heaven, you and your mama are remembering it, too.

                                          Love,
                                          Dad

Luke's hands trembled as he folded the letter. He was shaken. Those were not the words of a coldhearted bastard.

"I've kept writing the letters because I don't want to give up hope that someday you and your brothers will go through your boxes."

Jerking his head around, Luke spied his father standing

just inside the study. Well, crap. He hated getting caught in the act of snooping.

"I think they'll help you understand," Branch said.

Luke summoned his anger to repair the soft spot in his defenses battered into being by the contents of the letters, then attacked. "Understand? No way in hell, old man. None of us will ever understand how you could sit back and let John die."

"I didn't do that!" Branch shot him a furious look.

"Bullshit."

"You watch your mouth, boy. You're not going to talk that way to me in my own house."

"Sure I will. I don't owe you my respect. You gave up that right seventeen years ago when you kicked my ass out the fucking door."

"Did I? Let me ask you something. Where do you think you'd be, what kind of a man do you think you'd be, if I hadn't done what I did? I can answer that. You'd be a no-good bum instead of the fine man you became. Remember how worthless you were? A rich kid with no discipline, no goals. No compassion. Do you remember what you said to me the night y'all burned the boot factory down? You said, 'It's no big deal. They'll find other jobs.'" Branch grimaced with disgust. "I should have kicked your ass from here to Dallas."

Luke shut his eyes. He couldn't argue with that. He *had* been a shit back then.

"Now, I'll take the blame for your lack of character in those days. After your mama died, I didn't do my job. I let you boys down. Once I realized what I'd done wrong, I tried to fix it the best I knew how. If you think sending y'all away was an easy decision for me, you're flat-out wrong. Second to burying your mother, that was the hardest thing I'd ever done. But I stand by my decision then and the ones I've made since. I'm so damned proud of you boys. Even if I die before you can find some understanding in your souls, I'll be able to go to my grave knowing I made it all right in the end."

"Really?" Luke shoved John's box of letters into the cabinet, then rounded on his father. "So, you're good with seventy-five percent? Three out of four? That's what you have here, you know. Three out of four. Goddamn you for letting John die!"

Branch staggered back a step and gripped the doorway, his expression stricken. "No . . . I didn't . . ."

"That's right. You didn't." Luke prowled around the room like an angry mountain cat. "You know, Branch, it's possible I could get past how you handled things after the fire. You're right; being tossed out did make men of us. I believe you could have achieved similar results in safer, less traumatic ways, but—"

"Y'all were safe," Branch interjected. "I had people watching out for each of you. They'd have stepped in if any of you managed to get into too much trouble."

Luke recalled some of the trouble he'd landed in during those first few years and snorted. "You think? Wonder how your"—he sneered the word—"people defined trouble. Apparently getting knocked off an oil platform into rough seas didn't qualify. Nor did fighting for my life in a Mexican alley."

"The rig accident was a case of your being in the wrong place at the wrong time. That's karma. The other thing . . . well . . . what makes you think my man wasn't in that alley?"

"Nobody was there but me and Terry and the sons o' bitches trying to kill us," Luke scoffed.

Branch waited a moment, then said, "I know."

The implication of that rolled over Luke like a cement mixer and sucked the breath right out of him. "No. Terry Winston wasn't . . ."

"He wasn't my man on the oil rig, but he pitched in when you took some of your side trips."

Luke slumped back against the desk. Betrayal left a sick weakness in his muscles. Terry reported to Branch? "We were partners."

"I hated hearing about his death. He was a good man. A damn fine friend to you."

He was like a father to Luke. He lied to him for a dozen years. *Holy crap, they're all alike.*

Luke cleared his throat. "How much did you pay him?"

"Not a cent. Not after that first meeting, anyway. Terry was better than that."

Luke shoved his fingers through his hair. He needed to lock all this away. Now wasn't the time to think or react to this bit of news, not in front of Branch. He could chew on it later. "So where was John's guardian angel when he was snatched off the streets of Sarajevo?"

Branch's complexion washed white, and he sank into a leather wingback chair. "He was taken, too."

"Should have hired better help, Daddy," Luke drawled meanly.

"The ambassador told me it was a relatively safe posting. John wanted to go. You know that. He spoke the language like a native and he felt he needed the experience. In time, I believe he'd have become a great diplomat."

"Well, he didn't have time, did he? His time ran out because you failed to act."

"I *did* act!"

"You call that acting?" Luke let loose the rage that had seethed inside him since his brother's death. "You turned to that good-for-nothing good old boy from West Texas for help. What the hell did he do? I'll tell you. He got my brother killed."

"Congressman Parsons tried to cut the red tape—"

"Like I said. Good-for-nothing. All Parsons is good for is making sure Texas crude gets top dollar on the market floor. Bunch of corrupt old men in Washington." Luke shook his head. "You had us—your blood, your sons—and instead you trusted an old oil-field buddy who wouldn't know a terrorist's motives from a goddamned coyote's."

Branch gripped the armrests and pushed to his feet. "I'm gonna say again what I tried to tell you at John's funeral.

Listen to me this time, Luke. Do you honestly think I didn't do everything I could to see your brother released? The government was telling me I couldn't pay the ransom, and they were throwing roadblocks in my way so I couldn't do it on my own. I had to have help. I didn't know who else to go to other than Parsons."

"And that's what's unforgivable!" Luke exploded, finally saying words he'd wanted to say for years. "You didn't know who else to go to? Goddammit, Dad. You never called us. It was bad enough before I knew just how close tabs you kept on us, but now . . . hell! You knew! You knew the uniforms we wore. You knew Mark was in the army, but you must have known he's army intelligence. I'll bet you knew Matt was a spook, too. I'm sure Terry must have told you about my special skills. For God's sake, old man. Why didn't you come to us?"

"You don't understand. The ransom—"

"Fuck the ransom. It's never been about the ransom. I actually agree with the government's policy not to pay. But Mark and Matt and I, we could have gone after him. We had the skills and the balls and the motivation and the responsibility to go after John. He was our brother. The best of us. The *best*."

Luke's throat threatened to close, and he strove to maintain the control that he held on to by a thread. Johnny. He'd paid for his brothers' sins all his life. He'd been a kid when the boot-factory fire happened. Luke and Mark and Matt had been old enough to know better, but Johnny had just tagged along. Look what had happened. Guilt all but knocked Luke to his knees.

Guilt should have knocked his father flat. "He didn't deserve any of it, Branch. All he had was you, sorry as you were after Mama died, and us. I won't argue with your decision to kick us out of town, but to send Johnny away, too? To send him to military school? Christ.

"But you weren't finished yet, were you. You helped him get that job, and then when he really needed us, you turned your back. You didn't even tell us until it was too damned late."

Luke recalled his return to Brazos Bend. John's coffin. The helpless sense of rage—at his father, at himself—that had eaten him alive.

"Maybe we wouldn't have saved him, but we could have tried. We damned sure would have done better than anything Barney Parsons put together. You should have trusted us, Branch. Damn you for not trusting us to attempt to rescue our baby brother. That's why we'll never forgive you."

Branch appeared to have aged ten years in the past ten minutes. He looked old and pathetic, but Luke couldn't pity him. He was too filled with anger. With betrayal.

Damned if the old bastard didn't have tears in his eyes.

"I guess I'll have to live with that, then," Branch finally said. "Look, son, I have to go to sleep every night knowing it's my fault. I'm the one who put John in that military boarding school where he discovered his talent for languages. I'm the one who paved his way into the diplomatic corps with my money. I'm the one who called the State Department when the ransom demand arrived. Yet the one thing I can feel good about when I close my eyes is the decision I made regarding you and your brothers."

"Feel good? Are you crazy?"

"No, I'm your father. I was John's father. I know in my heart that he wouldn't have wanted me to risk his brothers' lives on a suicidal mission against Croatian warlords. Losing John was bad enough. I couldn't bear losing you three, too."

"Wait a minute." Luke's voice came as soft and cold as a snowfall. "Are you saying you didn't tell us because you were trying to protect us? Try again, Daddy."

"I tried my level best to effect a rescue for John, but I couldn't, I *wouldn't*, risk the lives of the boys I had left. It's what John would have wanted. What your mother would have wanted. You can hate me for the rest of your life, but you'll be alive to do it. And for that, I'm thankful."

"Fuck," Luke muttered.

"I'll ask you this, Luke, and then I won't say another word. What if it had been you being ransomed by a warmonger? Would you have wanted your brothers to sacrifice themselves on the razor-slim chance they could get you out safely? You think about that."

Having said his piece, he turned to leave, shuffling slowly toward the door like the old, broken man he was. Then he stopped and made a liar of himself by speaking some more. "And don't you ever let me hear you say the F word in your mother's house again."

For a long moment, Luke stood frozen in place. His heart pounded; a metallic taste coated his mouth. He couldn't think about what his father had just said. He couldn't. He wouldn't. He didn't want to think about his brothers dying because of him. He wasn't going to be manipulated by Branch Callahan. Never again.

What if it had been you being ransomed . . .

He wasn't sure he could draw a breath. The old man might have controlled the past, but he sure as hell wasn't controlling the future. Luke wanted to get away. Far away. He couldn't deal with all this. He wanted to run. He wanted Maddie. He wanted her to take the pain away.

His gaze fell upon the letters, the lies. The betrayal. Be damned if he'd try to see his father's point of view.

It was just too much. Terry, now this. His mind spun like a top. "I gotta get out of here."

Taking long, powerful strides, he crossed to the doorway, brushing past his father without glare or glance or comment. In the entry he shouted up the stairs, "Maddie! Come on. We're leaving!"

"I'm right here, Luke," she said calmly, gently. Compassion filled her eyes and she smiled with understanding. She knew. She's read the letters, wrote many of them. She'd been standing there all along. She'd heard it. Heard it all.

"Knucklehead! Here, boy." Luke's hand grasped Maddie's and held it hard. "We're leaving. Right now." His voice was shaking and he hated it.

"All right." She brought his hand up and kissed it. "Take me home, honey. It's been a long day."

"Hell. It's been a long life."

He brooded as they walked out to his truck, then as he opened the door for Maddie, he glanced over his shoulder to see his father's silhouette framed in the dining room window. All his anger and his pain and his guilt came roaring back. For a good five minutes, Luke ranted; he raved; he cursed and kicked his tires. He railed at Terry, even blamed Maddie for recording the lies his old man told for posterity. "Those lies should die with him. Soon. I'll burn 'em. I swear, that's what I'll do. I'll cremate them right along with his sorry, lying hide."

Maddie listened to him go on, silent and supportive, waiting until his temper faded, his voice went silent. Then she said, "You may have your chance sooner than you know. He's an old man, Luke. An old man who isn't well. Maybe he isn't perfect. Few people are. Few fathers are. Look at my dad. He blamed me for my mother's death and it went platinum!"

"That had to be hard."

"It was, but you know what? I forgave him. Why? Because everyone makes mistakes. I've certainly made my share. Nobody's perfect. Not me, not my dad, not your dad, and not you. Where would we be without forgiveness?"

"You're wasting your breath, Madeline."

"Right now, I probably am. But maybe someday you'll give a little and you'll remember what I had to say. Forgiveness isn't easy, I know, and I'm not suggesting you should forget what happened. But Luke, he *is* your father. The only one you'll ever have. In his own, admittedly misguided way, he loves you. All of you. And he's already paid dearly for the mistakes he's made with you and your brothers. Don't make him continue to pay to the grave. I truly believe you'll grow to regret it. Maybe not right away, but someday."

Her words made sense; Luke knew that. He even felt a measure of guilt for the hard-ass stance he was taking toward his father. But forgiveness? No. He couldn't do that. He just didn't have it in him. He tried to explain why.

"When my mother died, all the good times in our family died with her. When we lost Johnny . . ." His voice broke, and he gave up trying to talk.

Maddie reached for him, hugged him hard. "You need your father, Luke. So do Mark and Matt. Hopefully, you'll realize that in time."

He shrugged and looked away. She went up on her tiptoes and pressed a kiss against his cheek. "Until then, let's just go home."

Luke's gaze rested on Callahan House once again and he snorted. "Home? Where the hell is that?"

"Wherever you want it to be, Callahan. You'll know it when you get there."

Sixteen

Luke didn't speak during the ride back to Maddie's, but when they retired for the night, he made love to her with a quiet desperation she'd never seen from him before, one that left her sad and unsettled, even in the afterglow of really good sex. Maddie lay awake long after he'd fallen asleep, considering what she'd learned about the man who lay beside her.

Luke might be a tough, smart, ex-supercop with a hide as tough as Kevlar, but inside beat a soft, vulnerable heart. A heart damaged by the losses of his past. A heart far from healed.

Poor Luke. Poor Branch. They'd come at the problem from opposite directions and she could understand both ways of thinking. Of course Luke wanted to rescue his brother. Of course Branch wanted to keep his other sons safe. From her viewpoint, they'd both been right. She feared that unless Luke could let go of some of his anger and his guilt, he'd never be able to accept his father's actions. Branch would never achieve the goal he longed to see before he died—a reconciliation with his sons.

Would Matt or Mark be more understanding? Or would their heads be made of granite, too? Was there anything Maddie could do to help this family?

Not unless they wanted to help themselves. Wanted to heal. So far, she'd seen no sign of that.

Maddie sighed into the darkness. She wished she could help the Callahans. A caregiver by profession, it was in her nature to do so. But she couldn't force them to forgive, and without that main ingredient, the cause was most certainly lost.

No, the best she could do was to be there for Luke, to be there for Branch, and offer whatever support they'd accept from her. Because this wasn't a mere misunderstanding that kept this family apart. Not simple hurt feelings and family history. This family had death and betrayal and years of loneliness to overcome.

"Forgiveness, Callahan," she whispered. "Work on it." With that, she cuddled up to Luke and eventually fell asleep.

The br-r-ring of the telephone pierced her sleep. Her eyes flew open to the red numerals of the clock: 2:58. Oh, no. Nighttime phone calls were never good. One of her clients? Not Branch. Please. Not after the confrontation. Luke would never forgive himself.

She grabbed the receiver. "Hello."

An electronic voice said, "Get out of your house now. You have one minute before it explodes."

"What?" She jerked up. "Who is this?" The connection clicked dead in her ear. "Oh, God."

"What is it?" Luke asked.

Her voice trembled as she scrambled from the bed repeating what the caller had said. "God, Luke. Hurry! We have to get out of here."

He reached for his boxers, firing questions at her as she grabbed her robe and slipped it on. "I don't know who it was! Oh, God. Hurry!"

Luke lifted his head like an animal on the scent. "Smoke. Something's burning." He stepped toward the window and yanked it open. "Go out this way, Red."

Her pulse pounding, her heart lodged in her throat, Maddie didn't hesitate. She scrambled over the windowsill and fought her way through the wax-leaf ligustrum into the yard, expecting Luke to follow on her heels.

He didn't. Luke was still inside!

"Luke!" she screamed as facts bombarded her consciousness. Seconds ticked away too fast. Red and yellow flames licked through the roof in at least three places. Gray smoke billowed into the starlit sky. "Luke Callahan!"

She'd taken a step back toward the house when Knucklehead appeared at the window and she saw Luke's arms lifting him through. "Hurry!"

Smoke burned her nostrils and heat stung her eyes. She couldn't believe her eyes when Luke disappeared from the window once again. *Where is he going!* "Oh my God oh my God oh my God."

Knucklehead barked. Fire crackled and wood creaked and crashed. Then Luke was there again, diving through the open window; just then a loud whoosh erupted from the house as fire burned through the roof above the kitchen. He flew over the shrubs and landed on his belly, his arms outstretched.

He held Oscar's bowl in his hands.

Sirens roared as fire trucks approached. Luke scrambled to his feet and ran toward her, grabbing her hand as he passed and pulling her along behind him. Rocks and sticks poked Maddie's bare feet, but she hardly noticed. She heard another roar of fire behind her, but the promised explosion never occurred.

Her house. Her home. Gone. Why? Who? Liam? Was Luke's terrorist theory on the mark, after all? Who else would do such a thing? Why warn her? She didn't understand!

By now, neighbors had joined them outside and the fire lit the night like a sun. Luke didn't stop until they were two doors down from hers. When he released her arm, he set Oscar on the ground and bent over double, his hands propped on his knees as he coughed hard and long. Maddie watched him, breathing hard, trying to catch her own breath. Thank God Luke and the dog were safe. Oscar was safe.

Oscar?

She looked at the fishbowl, then at Luke on his hands and knees coughing up a lung. Her relief turned to fury and Maddie lost it, just flat out lost control and started screaming like a fishwife. "You went back for a goldfish? You risked your life for a stupid goldfish? I can't believe you did that! Do you not have a scintilla of sense, Luke Callahan? You could have died! Our minute was up!"

"Calm down," he told her when he could breathe again. "Once our minute was up, I figured there wasn't a bomb."

"You figured? You figured!" She doubled up her fist and hit his bare chest. "You fool!"

She cried. She screamed. She pitched a redheaded fit. "How dare you do something so . . . so . . . idiotic. I swear if you'd died I would have killed you!"

He caught her forearm, pulled her to him, and wrapped her in his arms as Maddie sobbed against his chest. "Hey, now, it's all right, Red." He stroked her hair, trying to calm her down. "If he'd wanted to kill us, he wouldn't have called. Our minute was up, Red. When the house didn't blow, I made an educated guess that it never would. I couldn't leave Knucklehead behind."

"But a goldfish?"

"Hey, Oscar's a living thing."

"Yeah, well, so is the mold on your leftovers in my refrigerator. Did you stop for those, too? How stupid could you be, Callahan? It's not even Gus's Oscar, either. I know you've replaced the silly thing at least twice."

He frowned. "You noticed?"

"Of course I noticed! I can't keep the blasted things alive."

"Oh."

A loud crashing sound came from her house and Maddie turned to look. Red and yellow flames engulfed the entire structure. The fire hoses blasting water on the conflagration appeared to make little headway. "My home," she moaned.

"Shush, honey. It's okay. You're safe. Everyone is safe. That's all that really matters."

He was right. She knew that. They were safe for the moment, at least. But what about after that? Who was doing this? Why? Liam? That didn't make sense. It didn't fit.

As an ambulance and a news truck arrived on the scene, Maddie's neighbors approached. They fired questions about Maddie's and Luke's physical well-being and how the fire started and how the couple escaped. Someone handed Luke a robe. Knucklehead nudged his way through the small crowd and rubbed up against Maddie's legs. She took the hint, dropped to her knees, and hugged and petted the dog, not minding the dog slobber as he licked her face.

She lost track of how much time passed, but when a firefighter told Luke the blaze was under control, she could tell it was too late to matter. Her home was beyond salvage.

Another fireman walked up to them as a car came speeding up to the curb. Branch jumped out, and Maddie watched the relief wash across his expression as his gaze locked on Luke. Then he looked at her, gave her a quick once-over, and smiled. "You all right, honey?"

"I'm all right. It was awful, though, Branch. I was so scared. The phone rang and a man said there was a bomb in the house."

"What man?"

"I don't know. I swear I didn't think Liam had changed that much. Blackmail makes sense. Setting fire to my house doesn't."

"What were the caller's exact words?" the firefighter asked.

"What?" Maddie glanced up blankly. "Who are you?"

"Sorry. I'm Robert Thompson, arson investigator with the BBFD. Can you elaborate a bit on what Luke Callahan told me? He said you received a warning call?"

"Yes. He said . . ." She braced herself, shuddered a little, then repeated, "He said to get out of the house now, that we had one minute before it exploded."

"Did you recognize the voice?"

Maddie thought back, tried to recall. "No. The voice sounded weird."

"Electronic?" Luke asked.

"Yes, that's it."

"He must have used a voice changer," Luke told the investigator. "And probably a pay phone, is my guess. He didn't want Maddie to die and he didn't want to be recognized. She knows whoever did this."

Liam? she wondered once again. Would he do such a thing? *Why* would he do such a thing? She couldn't conceive of a motive. Unless Luke was right and he had joined his brother's madness. But that still didn't answer why they'd target her. What had she done? Why would terrorists target her? Did it have something to do with her father, maybe? Had he gone and gotten involved in something stupid?

The investigator fired question after question her way until Luke put a stop to it. "That's enough. We're not going to solve this thing tonight, and Maddie needs a bath and some sleep. Why don't you give us a shout tomorrow. Maybe by then you'll have found some answers in the rubble."

The investigator hemmed and hawed for a minute, but gave in when Maddie pleaded exhaustion. "Where will you be staying?"

Maddie and Luke shared a grimace. Their wallets, IDs, keys—everything but Luke's cell phone, which he'd left in his truck, had been inside the house.

Branch stepped forward. "Come home, son. For Maddie's sake. She needs more comfort than a hotel room can provide, and you both left some clothes at my place."

Luke's reluctance was evident, so Maddie rose and took his hand. "Please?"

She held her breath, knowing that on the heels of his fight with Branch, this meant more than a bed and clothes. After a long moment's hesitation, he said, "Why not. I couldn't sleep any more after this anyway."

A policeman handed Oscar's bowl to Maddie as Branch gave his phone numbers and address to the BBFD official. Meanwhile, Luke used a hidden door key to retrieve his phone before escorting a weary Maddie to his father's Lexus sedan, where she set the fishbowl carefully on the backseat floorboard. Luke whistled for Knucklehead and let him into the front seat, then grinned at his father's wince at the muddy paw prints on white leather. "Hope he doesn't throw up," Luke observed, climbing into the backseat with Maddie. "Smoke inhalation on top of chili for supper could be a problem."

Maddie rolled her eyes. Dr. Phil would have a field day with this family.

"You okay?" Luke asked as his father pulled away from the curb.

"I'm still mad at you," she said, snuggling up against him.

"That's fine by me, Red." He tilted his head back against the seat and his hand stroked her hair as he let out a sigh. "As long as you're safe, that's all that matters."

"Me and the dog and the fish?"

His eyes closed, he grinned. His smile widened when he heard his father tell Knucklehead to stop slobbering.

"How many Oscars have I killed, Luke?"

"Counting the one Sara-Beth replaced, you're up to five."

"Sara-Beth's in on this?"

"It was her idea. Apparently the first Oscar didn't live past Tyler. Bee was afraid of your mental state, so she did the first live-for-dead fish switch."

Maddie slipped her hand beneath the vee of his borrowed bathrobe and placed her palm against his warm skin over his heart. "I've never been so scared. You were right the other day. My life *is* a soap opera."

"Nah. You haven't had a single case of amnesia, and you don't have a secret baby or an evil twin." He cocked open one eye and added, "Do you?"

"No baby. No twin. I pretended having amnesia once or twice, but that was when I was with Rip and I didn't want to face the truth about the kind of man he was." Her thoughts then followed the old-boyfriend path, which brought her right back to tonight. She bit her bottom lip, then added, "Why would Liam want to burn down my house?"

"I don't think he did." Luke pressed a kiss to her hair. "I think it's mushroom related, Maddie. Think about it. All your troubles—your recent troubles, anyway—started when you cleaned out Gus Grevas's lake house."

He was right, but . . . "I don't want to think anymore."

They didn't speak the rest of the ride to Callahan House, listening instead to Branch's near-constant griping at the dog. Maddie melted against Luke as he carried her up the stairs. She clung to his hand when tucked her into bed. "Don't go," she breathed when he turned to leave.

"Maddie, I—"

"Just hold me? 'Til I fall asleep?"

"I need a shower and some clothes and a cup of coffee and a big plate of ham and eggs."

"I'm frightened, Luke."

"Oh, hell." He lay beside her and took her in his arms. Maddie drifted off to sleep thinking, *Here's where I belong. And where he belongs, too.*

Luke woke up angry. He'd fallen asleep. Beneath his father's roof. He'd broken his vow.

He let out a string of curses that had Maddie lifting her head and glaring at him before burying her head beneath her pillow.

Where she slept safely.

Okay, so maybe sleeping at Callahan House wasn't that big a sin in the scheme of things. While he admittedly had a stubborn streak when it came to his father, he wasn't stupid. Maddie was a helluva lot more important than the vow he'd made. She'd been frightened for good reason last night, and she'd asked him to stay. How could he have said no?

But he didn't have to like it. Luke rolled from the bed and strode toward the bathroom, stopping long enough to check the bureau. Gym shorts should fit okay. He wrinkled his nose at the tighty whities; the Brazos Bend Wildcats T-shirt would be snug, but it would do.

His mood didn't improve in the shower as his thoughts returned to the events of the previous night. For the first time, he allowed himself to feel the fear he'd held at bay during the crisis, and his knees went a little weak. Maddie could have been killed. They both could have burned to death. Luke closed his eyes and ducked his head beneath the shower spray. *I'll find the bastard who's doing this if it's the last thing I ever do.*

He tried to set the emotion aside and think like a cop. Why the phone call? Why warn them? What was he missing here?

Frustration rumbled in his blood as he went downstairs a few minutes later and turned to head for the kitchen. His father's voice stopped him in his tracks. "Good. You're up. I was about to send Maria up to wake you. Come into the study, please, Luke. I thought about what you said to Maddie last night in the car, and I have a couple of thoughts about who is behind these attacks. In fact, I think I might just know something that could explain part of it."

"Sure you do," came Luke's automatic response. More likely the old bastard had seized the opportunity to attempt to manipulate him. However, considering that Maddie's safety was at stake, Luke couldn't afford to ignore his old man. Branch did have his thumb on the sleepy pulse of Brazos Bend. He might actually know something. "Let me get some coffee first."

"There's coffee in here. And some of Maria's breakfast biscuits."

When he entered the study, only to see the district attorney, the chief of police, the county sheriff, the county commissioner, and the mayor, he let out a weary sigh. Golden Boy and a quartet of aging Barney Fifes. They'd probably spend an hour talking about their cholesterol and lumbago before getting around to arson.

Luke's gaze met Austin's weary one. He didn't look any

happier to be here than Luke. How did he stand working in this town? "Someone called an AARP meeting?" he drawled as he sauntered toward the coffee service.

"We haven't started yet." Branch took his usual chair behind his desk. "Austin just arrived and I thought it best to wait for you."

"Lucky me." Luke filled a china cup with the rich, aromatic brew, wishing for a mug. He snagged a sausage-and-egg biscuit, then moved to stand beside the window overlooking the front lawn. He propped a hip on the windowsill and took a long sip of coffee. Next door, Mrs. Swan stood in an upstairs window with a pair of binoculars aimed his way. The sight amused him and he relaxed a little. He finger-waved, then took a bite of biscuit.

Branch said, "Gentlemen, if you'll take a seat, we can get started. Luke, I'd intended to allow you to give us a summary, but since you're eating, I'll give it a try. Let me know if I miss anything, and pay attention to what I say. I've a detail or two you are unaware of."

Luke's ears and his bullshit meter perked up as Branch addressed his visitors. "You're all aware of the difficulties Madeline Kincaid has encountered in recent weeks. Maddie has suspected an old boyfriend of hers might be behind the trouble. Fellow's name is Liam Murphy, and he's an Irishman with ties to the IRA."

The county commissioner choked on his biscuit. "A terrorist in Brazos Bend?"

Sheriff Drake shaped the brim of the tan-colored felt cowboy hat he held in his lap. "Kathy Hudson thought he might have come into the Dairy Princess, and my men followed up. Found his rental car parked in Hoss Wilbarger's driveway. Turns out he's a fellow from New York who's sweet on Hoss's girl. Met her at that fancy college she goes to back east, and he came to town for a visit."

The commissioner, a sixth-generation Texan with a drawl as thick as cold molasses, snorted. "Bet Hoss has a clod in his churn over that. Bad enough he's got a Yankee sparkin' his daughter, but a Yankee fereigner? He should have listened to me. I told him he was making a mistake by not sending her to the University."

"Back to business," Branch said, frowning at the commissioner. "My boy here brought up a good point. It's possible this trouble has nothing to do with old boyfriends. Since Maddie's troubles started when she cleaned out Gus's lake house, we must consider that the villain's interest may lie in that direction. When one questions his possible motives, one answer comes to mind. He's after the box."

"What box?" asked the county commissioner, slathering butter on his fourth biscuit. He let out a loud belch that had Austin grimacing.

Branch responded, "When Jerry Grevas attacked Maddie on the night he died, he was desperate to find 'the box.' Subsequent to that, her home and probably her place of business and her car were searched. Then, of course, last night her home was destroyed. It makes sense that our villain was looking for the box and, when he couldn't find it, set out to destroy it."

"Why?" asked Austin. "Why is this possibility any more likely than the old-boyfriend theory?"

"It's what was in the box that's important," Luke clarified.

Branch nodded. "I agree. I suspect Jerry Grevas used whatever was in that box to blackmail someone. Based on history, I suspect the box contained pictures."

"History?" Chief Harper asked.

"Jerry Grevas once attempted to blackmail my son Matthew with photographs he took of Matt and one of his lovers, a married woman in town."

Well. This was news to Luke. He managed, just barely, to keep his surprise from showing.

"Who was she?" the sheriff demanded.

"Bet it was Sparkle Hudson," the commissioner said, brushing biscuit crumbs from his bushy white mustache.

"She was a wild one, running off the way she did. It's criminal what she put her mama through."

"Nope, I'd bet it was Billy Jean Wilson," the sheriff declared. "Heard she made one of them porno films. Billy Jean and three men and a goat."

"Yeah?" the commissioner asked.

"I've seen it," the police chief piped up. "In the course of duty, of course."

Austin shot a glare around the room. "For heaven's sake, he said a *married* woman. Sparkle wasn't married. She was fifteen when she disappeared. Billy Jean isn't married, either. Aside from that, this was when? Back in high school? Who would care about something that happened twenty years ago?"

"I'm not saying it happened twenty years ago." Branch scowled at the DA. "What I'm saying is that a blackmailer doesn't usually reform. Especially one who's growing dope on the side."

"Can Matt verify all this?" Luke inquired.

"Ask him who the married woman was," the commissioner demanded.

"Yes." Branch glanced at Luke. "You'll want to contact your brother to see if he recalls more details than I, but yes, apparently Grevas was on the yearbook staff and carried his camera everywhere. He had a nice little extortion business going when he tangled with Matt. I'll bet if you ask around, you'll find some of his other victims might be willing to talk."

Austin shook his head and addressed Luke. "This sounds too far-fetched to me. I still think the terrorist boyfriend is a better bet."

"Maybe, maybe not. It'd help if somebody could track him down so we could question him. Since that doesn't seem to be happening very fast, I agree that we should pursue this line of investigation. There's a logic to it. Grevas wanted Maddie to turn over the box before he got clipped. Something could very well be in that box. Something important enough to burn. My guess is that it's evidence of some kind. And, if history is repeating itself, that evidence might well be pictures. Pictures that our perp wants bad enough that he killed Grevas because of them."

"No . . ." Austin shook his head.

Chief Harper sneered. "You're wrong as usual, Callahan. Jerry Grevas was killed by a loan shark. The Dallas police proved it."

"And we know they never make mistakes," Branch said snidely. "I think Luke is right. I think that this mystery box is dangerous enough to somebody that they're willing to kill for it."

The mayor grimaced and rubbed his brow. "You're trying to say we have a murderer in town?"

"Guess that's better than a terrorist," observed the sheriff.

"Wonderful," the mayor continued. "How am I supposed to keep this from turning into a panic? Aside from Grevas, the last person shot in this town was Otis Purcell, and that was because his wife found out he'd been wearing her bras."

"Good thing she shot him." The commissioner reached for yet another biscuit. "Can't have that kind of thing going on in Brazos Bend."

"Don't forget we're also dealing with an arsonist," warned Chief Harper. "You'd best be careful, Branch. Someone might try to burn Callahan House if you've got that girl staying here."

Austin stood with his arms folded, his fingers drumming his arm. "People in town are going to be nervous." Distractedly, he muttered, "Damn Grevas."

Luke hated participating in this conclave. The mayor and the commissioner were worthless, the sheriff and the police chief only slightly better. However, both his father and Austin had sharp brains. They might be able to help him think this through.

He finished his biscuit, drained his coffee, then went to refill his cup. "The arson is the key."

He glanced toward Austin, then his father, as he said,

"Our bad guy probably thinks he's in the clear since Maddie's house is gone, but he can't be sure. What if someone else found the box? What if someone else has the pictures and he's waiting for the right time and place to use them? I'd hate to think there's more trouble on the horizon for this town. Better we deal with this now. Deal with him now."

"How can you be so sure it's pictures?" Austin asked. "It could be drugs. Remember, Jerry was a doper. He could have been looking for his stash."

"I didn't turn up any info that he was involved in the drug scene here in Brazos Bend."

"What drug scene?" protested the mayor. "We don't have a drug scene."

Luke ignored him. "I think Grevas was looking for his meal ticket. Blackmail provides money and that's what Grevas needed more than anything else. Now that Grevas is gone, his victim wants to ensure that no one picks up where Jerry left off."

"Your theory is plausible, I'll admit," said Austin. "However, I deal in evidence, and the only hard evidence we have is that last night's fire was intentionally set. It's just as likely her boyfriend saw you staying overnight at her place and decided to burn away his heartbreak."

"Either way," Branch said, "I want him caught. I want our Madeline to know she's safe here in our town. So, you boys think you're up to the task or should I hire me some outside help?"

Luke already had plans to call in a couple freelance guys he knew, but he wouldn't turn down Branch's help. Keeping Maddie safe was the first priority.

Chief Harper declared, "We'll find him. We don't need outside help."

"He's right," Austin agreed. "We've got good men here in Brazos Bend."

The men all nodded their agreement, then Branch dismissed them by saying, "Then, git 'er done, boys. Go git 'er done."

When the last of the visitors departed, Luke turned to follow. His father stopped him by saying, "Luke? About yesterday. There's something else—"

"Does it involve Maddie?" Luke interrupted.

"No."

"Then I'm not interested." He strode out of the study and saw Maddie on the stairs. "Want to go for a walk, honey? Knucklehead is scratching at the door."

"Coffee first?"

"Bring it with you. I need to ask you some questions, Red, and there's no time to waste. I have an idea to run past you."

"All right."

"I'll grab the dog's leash and wait for you out front," he called after her as she headed for the kitchen.

Outside, Knucklehead dragged Luke over to an oak tree and started sniffing the ground happily as Luke's cell phone rang. He dragged the slim phone from his pocket and checked the number.

Mark. Luke thumbed the CONNECT button. "Hey."

"I found your man," his brother said without preamble.

Luke went still. "The Irish laddie?"

"Yep. I also found out why your connections couldn't turn him up."

"He's dead?" Luke asked, hope in his tone as his gaze shot back toward the house.

"Not exactly. He's left the dark side, Skywalker. He apparently had a religious and political conversion. He's working for the good guys now, although you won't find his name on anybody's official payroll."

"What! Where?"

"Somewhere in the States. I haven't been able to pin him down yet."

Luke drummed his fingers against his thigh. "Brazos Bend, maybe?"

"It's possible, I guess, but probable?" Matt let the question hang for a beat. "I seriously doubt he's working a blackmail scheme on your lady, Luke. He's earning a nice fat paycheck from Uncle Sam. Plus, I'm told he's serious about the religion thing now. I honestly don't think he's your guy. I wouldn't spend all my time looking for an Irish bomber, if I were you."

"Hadn't planned to," Luke assured his brother as the front door opened and Maddie stepped outside. His spinning thoughts halted as she paused on the front steps to take a reverent sip of her coffee. Damn, she was beautiful. A warm wave of possessive, lusty love washed over Luke.

The sound of his brother clearing his throat yanked Luke back to the conversation. Mark said, "Uh, I hate to be obvious, but have you considered that he might have been shooting straight?"

"What do you mean?"

"Maybe he wants her back."

Maddie started toward Luke, her smile shining like the sun. "If that's the case, then the luck of the Irish has taken a turn for the worse," Luke spoke into the cell phone. "She's mine now and he can't have her. Let me know when you get a bead on his location. I've a mind to tell him so myself."

"Luke and his bright ideas," Maddie grumbled that afternoon as she plopped into a lounge chair beside the pool. Earlier, on their walk, he'd outlined his grand, foolish plans. The man intended to draw out the killer by pretending to have found the box. And no amount of arguing with Mr. Big Badass Ex-Superagent convinced him otherwise.

Worry and concern had her in a snit. Luke intended to play hero, to put himself in harm's way on her account by acting as bait, while her part in the plan was to remain holed up in the Callahan castle like a princess.

Not that she necessarily wanted to go out and be her own detective. She wasn't a heroine in a mystery novel; she was the owner of a senior care business in Brazos Bend, Texas. She was fine with the idea of letting a professional do the dirty work.

Under ordinary circumstances.

When she wasn't sleeping with said professional.

"Idiot." Whether she referred to the professional or the princess, she couldn't say.

She heard the kitchen door open, then shut behind her, but she didn't turn to look. She'd hoped he'd just leave without speaking to her. She had so much emotion churning inside her that she feared she wouldn't get through two sentences without starting to blubber. While she might not have the courage of a mystery-novel heroine, she certainly had her share of pride.

She reached into the basket of new pedicure supplies she'd brought from the house and pulled out cotton balls, which she slipped between her toes. Next she grabbed polish-remover pads and clear base coat before hesitating over her color choice.

"I vote for that hot-pepper red," Luke said from behind her.

Maddie sniffed and picked up a bottle labeled Petulant Pink.

"You're a tough act, Maddie Kincaid."

No, she wasn't. That was the problem. She wasn't tough at all. She wanted to throw her arms around his neck and beg him not to put himself in danger for her sake. She wanted to beg him to stay with her, to build a life with her. She was as soft as the cotton between her toes, but she wasn't going to let him see it.

He walked around in front of her and sat at the end of the lounge chair. He lifted her foot into his lap, and when she tried to yank it away, he held tight. "Calm down."

"I'm calm."

"No, you're not."

"Sure I am."

"You're pissed at me."

"No I'm not."

"You are."

"Fine." She relaxed her leg, folded her arms, and lifted her chin. "I'm pissed. Happy?"

He grinned, tore open one of the polish remover packets, and went to work on her toes. "I finally got hold of Matt. He gave me a half dozen names of people to talk to about Jerry Grevas's extortion hobby. He's also sending a buddy to help keep an eye on things around here."

"I don't need a babysitter."

"It's for my peace of mind more than anything. Callahan House is undoubtedly the safest place in town for you. Branch's security system is top-of-the-line. And I can trust you not to do anything stupid, right?"

"You mean like going around town asking people if they've been the victims of blackmail?"

"Maddie," he said in a chastising tone, "I know what I'm doing. I promised you I'd be careful." Finished removing the polish from her right foot, he exchanged it for her left. "And what did you promise me?"

She wrinkled her nose. "I've already talked to Sandy. She's agreed to cover my appointments for me today."

"Good girl." He put his thumbs in the arch of her foot and massaged her muscles. "You have the sexiest feet. I'm liable to be fantasizing about them all afternoon."

"About my feet?"

"Uh-huh. In fact . . . what size shoe do you wear?"

"Seven. Why?"

"Howard Jackson is one of the names on Matt's list."

Howard Jackson managed the shoe store on the town square, Maddie knew. "Seven narrow," she clarified.

He reached into the nail polish bucket and pulled out a bright red. Dangling it in front of her, he said, "I read in *Cosmo* that red is the hot color this summer. Bet I can find something strappy and expensive in a hot-pepper color."

She sniffed. "I can't be bought, Callahan." But if he came home with red shoes . . . *I'm only human.*

"You break my heart, Kincaid." Standing, he leaned over to kiss her. "Don't worry, Red. I've done a lot of undercover work and this doesn't rate on the danger scale."

"Yeah, well, neither did sleeping in my bed last night, and that almost burned your bacon."

He gave her one more quick, hard kiss. "Once you finish your pedicure, I have something to occupy your mind so you don't worry yourself to death." He picked up an item from the ground behind her chair.

A book. Maddie read the title aloud. "*The Goldfish: An Owner's Guide to a Happy, Healthy Pet.*"

"Necessary reading for a serial goldfish killer."

She couldn't help but laugh. It was hard to stay mad at Luke Callahan.

"Now I'm off. Matt's friend should be here within the hour. His name is Steve Barrington. If you simply have to go somewhere, take him with you, okay?"

"I'm not going anywhere. Kathy's supposed to come by after the lunch rush to help me with my list for the insurance guys. She remembers what I had in the house better than I do."

He squeezed her shoulders, then said, "I'll call."

"Just be careful, Luke. Promise?"

"My word on it, Red. And remember, I never lie to you."

Maddie thought about that as she painted her toenails with the clear base coat, and she finally admitted to herself that she did believe him. Luke Callahan didn't lie to her. He wasn't like Rip or Liam or Cade. She could trust him.

It was a big step. A leap of faith, one she'd never thought to take again, but there it was. She trusted Luke Callahan's word. She trusted he wouldn't betray her. Trusted he'd never play her false.

And what of your heart? Can you trust him with that? Not hardly.

Her hand trembled, making a mess of the polish she applied to her toes. Luke Callahan was a good, honest man. A hero. He'd saved her life. Saved her goldfish's life, for heaven's sake. But an honest man, a hero, could break a woman's heart as easily as a liar if she let him. A good man could do bad things to a woman without malice or meanness if she put herself at risk.

Maddie knew she could trust Luke with her life, but could she trust him not to break her heart?

She was a strong woman. She knew that. She'd proven that to herself. She could and she would deal with just about anything life had to throw her way.

But she honestly didn't think she could survive another broken heart.

"Well, no sense fretting about it now. He hasn't asked for my heart, has he? All he's asked for is red nail polish. Maybe that's as deep as we'll ever get. As deep as I'll have to think."

Maddie stared blindly at the sparkling blue water of the pool. Maybe red nail polish was all he wanted, but what about her? What about what she wanted?

She wanted the whole spa treatment, that's what.

Maddie groaned and wiggled her hot-pepper red toes in the afternoon breeze, then firmly put those questions aside. She had matters of life and death to dwell on.

"I've killed my last fish," she said to Knucklehead, who was rooting for something beneath her chair as she picked up the book on fish care. When the dog came up with a weathered yellow tennis ball, knowing her place, Maddie threw it for him. The game of catch lasted a good ten minutes before the dog's attention switched to something rustling in the flower beds next to the house and Maddie settled down to read.

Despite her best intentions, by Chapter Two her interest waned and her mind began to wander. Where was Luke? What was he doing? Whom had he told about the box? Was he even now speaking to the man who'd burned down her house?

"Callahan! Callahan, are you back here?"

"Austin?" Maddie said, recognizing the voice. She rose from her chair to see the district attorney dashing through the back gate, a wild look on his face. "Austin, what's wrong?"

"Maddie, where's Luke? I rang the doorbell but no one answered. I need help. His dog . . . ?"

"Knucklehead?" She stepped forward. "What about Knucklehead?"

"He ran right out in front of me. I couldn't stop in time."

"You hit him!" She started running toward the gate.

"I need help with him, to get him into the car so I can take him to the vet. He's hurt bad, I think. Can you help me?"

Maddie's heart was in her throat as she sprinted into the front yard. Her stride faltered and she gasped when she spied Knucklehead lying in the middle of the road. Completely still.

"No! Oh, no!" Maddie cried. "Luke will go crazy if something happens to this dog."

"Oh, hell," Austin muttered.

"Hurry!" Maddie ran faster than she'd ever run before, her gaze locked on the dog's chest, praying to see some sort of movement.

Austin reached Knucklehead first. "He's breathing. He's still alive. God, I'm so sorry. At least he's still breathing. Maybe he's just passed out. For now, anyway. Quick, Maddie help me get him into the car."

"Okay. Yes. Okay."

"Let's put him in the backseat." Austin slipped his hands beneath the limp animal and hefted him into his arms. "I'll take him to Doc Hander. He's closest."

Maddie climbed into the backseat. "Here, set his head in my lap. If he wakes up he'll need comforting."

"I don't want him to wake up and bite you."

"He won't.

Austin laid the dog on the seat, then quickly climbed behind the wheel. "We were playing catch just a little while ago," Maddie explained. "I saw him digging in the azalea beds. How did he get out? The gate should have been closed."

"It was open when I saw it," Austin said as he put the car in gear. "That's why I came around back when nobody answered the door."

"That doesn't make any sense, either. Branch and both the Garza sisters are there. Did they not hear the doorbell?"

"I don't know. I even tried the knob, but the door was locked."

Maddie stroked the dog's fur. "He's not bleeding. That's a good sign, don't you think, Austin? Maybe you just knocked the wind out of him."

Austin didn't answer, and Maddie told herself that was because he was concentrating on his driving. She turned all of her attention to Knucklehead. "It's okay, boy," she crooned. "You'll be okay. You're a tough puppy dog. You'll get through this. You'll be up chasing the tennis ball in no time at all."

She wished he'd make a sound, a whimper, a mewl, anything. This silence frightened her. "I need to call Luke but I don't have a phone." She hadn't even paused to put on shoes.

"You can use mine when we get to Doc Hander's. Although, maybe you should wait to call him until we know something. Don't worry him yet."

"Okay. That'll work. That's good." *Oh, Knucklehead.* Had she been the one to leave the gate open? She'd used it this morning when she went out to cut roses for Maria's favorite kitchen vase, but she'd have sworn she latched it behind her.

Killing goldfish was bad enough, but if she'd left the gate open . . . if it was her fault Knucklehead got loose . . . and if he didn't make it . . . oh, no. Luke would never forgive her. Maddie shut her eyes and tears overflowed and spilled down her cheeks.

Suddenly, the car swerved wildly. Maddie's eyes flew open as Austin exclaimed, "Dammit! What did I hit now?"

He steered the car to the side of the road and threw it into park. "Stay where you are, Maddie. Let me just see . . ."

He opened the driver's-side door and walked to the back of the car. Maddie heard him curse. "What is it, Austin?"

"It's okay. I just have to . . ." He reached inside and popped the trunk. "This will just take a second."

The seconds ticked by like minutes. Couldn't have been

more than ten of them, but it felt like a hundred times as many.

Knucklehead let out a long shudder.

"Hurry, Austin!"

"Yeah. I'm almost . . ." He opened her door. She looked up and saw regret gleaming in his eyes just as the fume-soaked cloth pressed against her face. "Done," Austin said.

Maddie's world went black.

Seventeen

Luke exited Wagoner Oilfield Supply in downtown Brazos Bend and checked off another person on the list of blackmail victims his brother had given him. Of the thirteen people Matt had named, eight of them still lived and worked in Brazos Bend. So far, Luke had visited four of them and came away with six new names to investigate. Quite a secret little business Grevas had going back in high school. "No wonder he grew up to be an accountant."

On Luke's fifth stop of the afternoon, he perused the heeled-sandal display as he waited for Howard Jackson to finish with his customer, debating between a pair of slip-ons and one with a strap behind the heel. Both styles were sinfully sexy, but he leaned toward the ones with the strap. It'd drive Maddie crazy for him to tug down that strap with his teeth.

"Can I help you, Sin?" Jackson asked.

Luke indicated his choice. "I need that in red in a seven narrow."

The shoe salesman made a point to eye Luke's feet. "You sure of that size? You look more like a twelve or thirteen."

"Very funny."

Luke glanced out one of the store's big plate glass windows toward the Dairy Princess across the street as he waited for Jackson to return with the shoes. Kathy Hudson was out front dressed in a tie-dyed T-shirt and jeans washing the windows. When she gave her butt a good old bump and grind, he grinned and wondered what music she had playing on her jukebox at the moment.

"Here you go."

Luke turned. "Fancy box for a pair of shoes."

"Goes along with the fancy price you're paying."

Luke checked the price tag on the end of the box and his brows flew up. "They made of gold or something?"

"Italian design doesn't come cheap."

"Hmm." Luke handed Jackson his credit card and waited until he was in the process of ringing up the sale to casually say, "Speaking of shoe boxes, I ran across one of interest a few weeks back. It was in a stack of stuff Maddie Kincaid took from the Grevas house. A shoe box full of pictures. I do believe there's some of you in the mix."

Howard Jackson snorted. "So photos of my bony bare butt are still around for posterity, hmm? I know it's not polite to speak ill of the dead, but Jerry Grevas was a first-class jerk. He blackmailed me with those pictures back in high school. I should have guessed he kept a copy for insurance." The electronic register clicked through its calculations. "I've always wished I'd stood up to him, but hell, I'd have been humiliated if he'd passed those pictures around the girl's gym class like he'd threatened. I wasn't built like you and your brothers, Callahan. I put the 'skinny' in skinny-dipping in those days, that's for sure." He handed Luke the receipt and a pen.

"You think he continued to dabble in extortion after high school?" Luke asked as he signed his name.

"Who knows?" Jackson shrugged. "He quit carrying his camera around all the time—I heard your brother had something to do with that—but I wouldn't have put it past the bastard to peep in windows at night."

"I have no intention of keeping the pictures," Luke told him. "What would you like me to do with yours?"

"Doesn't matter. I'd just as soon you toss 'em. I'd rather not see 'em up on the Internet, though. Not something I'd want my daughters to run across."

"Not a problem. Consider them history."

"Thanks. And thanks for the purchase, too. Tell Maddie if she has any trouble with the shoes to give me a holler."

"Will do." The door chimes dinged as he exited the store and his cell phone rang at the same moment. "Five for five," Luke murmured as he fished in his pocket. So far, no one on his list had cared that he'd supposedly found the box or their pictures. Yet, his time wasn't wasted, because word of his visits was bound to get around.

He flipped the phone open. Matt's number. "What's up?"

"We got trouble, Luke." Matt's tone was all business. "I'm in Brazos Bend. After I spoke with you this morning, I called Barrington and told him not to come, that I'd watch your back. I just arrived at Callahan House. Your Maddie's gone missing."

Luke went icy inside. "What!"

"The dog is gone, too, and the gate's wide open."

Luke's stomach clenched with worry and a heavy feeling of dread. *Wait . . . don't panic. Think it through. If the dog was gone . . .* "She's probably chasing after Knucklehead. Where the hell is Branch? What does he say? Or the Garzas?"

"They're clueless. Didn't hear a thing. Didn't know she wasn't out by the pool any longer."

Luke took off running for his truck. "The neighbors. We need to ask Mrs. Swan. Nothing gets by her. Hell, maybe Knucklehead chased after her cat again and Maddie ran after him."

"Could be," his brother agreed. "What bothers me is the pair of shoes beside the lounge chair. Wherever she is, she appears to have gone barefoot."

Luke closed his eyes and pictured the area around Callahan House. The aggregate sidewalks were a bitch to go barefoot on and the asphalt streets would burn her feet in this heat. Maddie would know that. Even if she'd gone chasing after the dog, she'd have grabbed her shoes on the way.

His worry morphed into fear. *Goddammit! I screwed up again. I shouldn't have let her out of my sight. Hell, I*

thought she'd be safe in the backyard in broad daylight.
"I'm on my way, Matt."

Matt hesitated a second before asking, "She's different, isn't she?"

Luke sucked in a trembling breath. "Yeah. Yeah, Matt. She is."

"We'll find her, bro," Matt said. Luke seized on the confidence in his brother's voice as Matt added, "In fact, I'll probably find her next door sipping sweet tea with Mrs. Swan. I figured you'd want to know, first."

A picture of Maddie's bare feet flashed through Luke's mind. "Yeah. Thanks. I'll be there in five."

"I'll call if I find her," Matt replied, then disconnected.

Luke tossed his package onto the floorboard of his truck and started the engine. As he wheeled the vehicle around to leave the parking lot, he caught sight of Kathy once again and changed directions.

With Matt covering the neighborhood, Kathy would be a good place to start. Maybe Maddie called her. Maybe this was all a big mistake. He'd wring her neck if it was—then he'd take her in his arms and never let her go.

He pulled into the lot in front of the Dairy Princess and shoved the gearshift into park. He hopped out, leaving the truck running. "Hey, Kathy?" he called above the pounding sound of the King singing "Blue Suede Shoes" blaring from outside speakers. "Have you heard from Maddie in the last hour or so?"

"No. Why?"

He motioned for her to cut off the music, and while she did so he debated just how much to tell her. If Maddie were in bigger trouble than dog chasing, he'd need somebody to help him filter through local personalities and issues, so he decided to tell the older woman everything. He briefly recapped the day's events to Kathy, noting her growing pallor. He finished with, "I hoped I'd get a bead on the arsonist with my questions, maybe even flush him out. However, I thought he'd come after me, not Maddie."

Kathy's hands trembled as she brought them up to her mouth. Tears welled in her eyes and she began rocking back and forth. "Oh, no. Not Maddie. Not my Maddie, too! I knew last night that it had gone too far."

Then she grabbed Luke's shirt. "Now she's disappeared off the face of the earth, just like my Sparkle. Today's her birthday, you know. Sparkle's. Oh, no. Not Maddie, too. Please, no."

"It's okay, Kathy." Luke gave her shoulder an awkward, comforting pat, wishing he'd never stopped. Sparkle's birthday. Damn. Had he known that, he'd have kept on driving. "I'm sure she's fine. Bet Knucklehead took off after something and she took off after him."

"The homecoming king needed another queen," Kathy murmured. "Maddie's the prettiest girl in town. Oh, I can't do this. I can't go through this again."

She's lost it. Luke felt bad for having caused Kathy such trauma. Now that he thought about it, she always went a little crazy on days special to her daughter. However, Luke didn't have time to deal with Kathy's grief at the moment. He motioned to the wide-eyed teenager watching from behind the counter inside.

"I love Maddie," Kathy wailed. "This can't be happening."

"I know. I love her, too. I'll find her. I'm sure she just lost track of the time."

"No. Maddie's not like that. Sparkle's not like that, either. They're responsible girls. Sweet girls. Oh, dear. Oh dear oh dear oh dear."

Feeling like a heel for having set Kathy off and yet beyond anxious to leave, Luke handed her over to the bewildered teenager. He'd make it up to her later, but right now finding Maddie required all his attention. "I'll have her call you. I promise."

"Sparkle," Kathy sobbed on the boy's shoulder. "So long. It's been so long. I just need to know."

"Take her inside, son. Get her something to drink." Then, to Kathy, "It'll be all right, honey. I'll find her and I'll call you, okay?"

Luke got back in his truck and headed for Branch's place, working the phone as he drove, notifying the police, the sheriff's office, and even the Texas Rangers of Maddie's disappearance. He arrived at Callahan House just as Matt exited Mrs. Swan's house. His brother saw him and shook his head.

Five minutes later, the two Callahan brothers studied the scene beside the pool where Maddie had been sitting. "She didn't just disappear off the face of the earth," Luke said to Matt. "Somebody took her. Somebody has her stashed somewhere. We have to find her."

When his phone rang, he leaped to answer it. "Maddie?"

"No, Luke. It's Sara-Beth."

He shut his eyes, dropped his chin. "Hey, Bee. I don't suppose you've seen Maddie."

"No, but I have your dog."

Now Luke's head came up. "Where?"

"At Doc Hander's. Luke, I found him lying in the parking lot at Edgemere Park. I was pushing the stroller and there he was, poor thing."

"But no sign of Maddie?" Luke met his brother's concerned stare.

"No. What's going on, Luke? Doc Hander thinks Knucklehead has been drugged. He's coming around, but he's groggy."

Drugged. Luke blew out a long, hard breath. This was confirmation.

"He says he'll be all right, though. You needn't worry."

Oh, yeah, he did need to worry. He recalled what Kathy had said earlier in front of the Dairy Princess. *She's disappeared off the face of the earth, just like my Sparkle.*

Luke's stomach took a nauseated roll. He cleared his throat. "Bee, I'll be right there."

Maddie awakened slowly, shying away from the pounding in her head. Her hair hung in her eyes and she attempted to lift a hand to shove it away.

Her hand didn't budge.

"What the . . ." She pried up her eyelids and tried to focus through blurry eyes and fuzzy thoughts. She lay on something soft and leathery. Something brown. A six-point buck hung on the wall above her.

Maddie blinked twice, staring at the animal's glass eyes. Ick. It smelled bad and she hated the stuffed-animal theme in decorating.

Wait. She didn't know anybody who used the stuffed-animal theme in decorating.

With that, her thoughts cleared and the events of the day came rushing back. That stink wasn't the deer head on the wall. The stink was the scent of the chloroform. Chloroform that had coated the rag Austin Rawlings had held to her face.

The district attorney drugged me!

She levered herself up, twisted her head around. "Where am I?"

"My father's river house." Austin Rawlings sat in a rocking chair in front of a stone fireplace replacing line on a fishing reel.

Maddie struggled against the rope binding her ankles and wrists. "Austin? What in the world have you done?"

He looked at her then, his eyes cold and hard and a little wild. "It's not me. It's him. Your boyfriend. Everything could have stopped. It could have been over, but no."

His gaze darted toward the window. He gave the fishing line a jerk. "Sin Callahan had to come back to town. Screw everything up."

"I don't understand. I thought you two were friends."

"Friends. Hah. Right." Austin sneered. "He's always been jealous of me. We both came from prominent families, but I was this town's favorite son. He was the screwup. I took over as quarterback in the Mineral Wells game our senior year when he went out with a hamstring pull. Team was down fourteen to three in the fourth quarter, and I threw for three touchdowns and ran for sixty-eight yards. I won the game for us. Made him spittin' mad. He never got over it."

"This is about *football?*"

He acted as if he'd not heard her. "I was smarter than he was, salutatorian of our class. I was more popular. I was elected class president and homecoming king. And I took Sara-Beth away from him our junior year. She didn't like his drinking and fighting. The street racing. She didn't like the way he talked to his father."

He's crazy, Maddie thought. *He's snapped. He's reliving his youth.* "Austin, hello? You're not in high school anymore."

He dropped the fishing reel into his lap. "No, I'm not. I've come a long way since high school. UT undergrad, SMU law school. I've been the district attorney for Palo Pinto County for seven years now. I'm active in state politics and I've set my sights on the governor's mansion. Everything is in place, just like my father and I planned. I won't let any extortionist get in my way."

Blackmail. Of course. "So you're the one who's been after Jerry Grevas's box? You're the one who set fire to my house?" Her mind clicked, putting the facts and suppositions together. "He had compromising pictures of you?"

He shoved to his feet and began to pace the room. Maddie surreptitiously struggled against the bindings on her wrists as another thought occurred. Jerry. Oh, no. Was Jerry Grevas's killer five feet from her right this moment?

"Sin Callahan hasn't changed, you know. He used people back then and he's using you now. You led him to Jerry Grevas and Jerry Grevas led him to the pictures. That's why he killed Jerry. He wanted Jerry's box of pictures."

"Luke didn't kill Jerry Grevas."

"Sure he did. Sin Callahan wanted to have a hold on me, and he couldn't afford for anyone to know it. I figure he planned to sit on them until I was in office. Then he'd spring 'em on me. Demand the big bucks. That's the way he thinks, you know. Sin Callahan is sneaky."

Maddie's mind raced. Wait a minute. If Austin didn't kill Jerry, then who did?

"He made a mistake, though. He just had to show his

hand, didn't he? Had to brag. Had to let me know that burning down your house wasn't enough. I considered letting it go until I found his little gift in my mailbox, you know. After all, who would believe the likes of Sin Callahan over me? Nobody. But he had to go and lord it over me, first with the notes, then the necklace, and finally with his smart-ass attitude this morning. 'What if someone else found the box? What if someone else has the pictures, and he's waiting for the right time and place to use them?' I got his message and now he's getting mine. I didn't want to have to kill anyone else, Maddie. This is his fault. Not mine."

Kill anyone else? Whom did he kill? Anybody? Or was Austin mixing everything up?

"Wh-wh-what do you plan to do, Austin?"

"I figure I'll wait awhile to contact him. It'll give him time to get good and worried. He cares about you, you know. I can see it." Regret seeped into his eyes. "I'm really sorry about this, Maddie. I tried to think of another way, but I simply couldn't see one."

Maddie's blood went cold. "You're wrong, Austin. I swear. You've gone after the wrong person. Luke didn't kill Jerry. He doesn't have any pictures. He doesn't have any proof. It's not too late. You don't have to do this. You can let me go and I give you my word I won't tell anyone."

He sighed sadly. "He fooled you, Maddie. He lied to you. He always does. Uses women like a tissue, then throws them away. Too bad for you. You could have had anyone."

"He absolutely did not lie to me!" Maddie declared. "If you do this, Austin, you'll be making a huge mistake. Your problems with the pictures won't be over, and you'll have my father to deal with. Believe me, you don't want that."

"Your father? Why should I care about your father?"

"He's rich and he's famous and he'll turn this town upside down if something happens to me. Austin, my father is the rock star Blade. I'm Baby Dagger."

Austin looked at her for a long minute and Maddie's

hopes swelled. Then he laughed. "Good try, Maddie. You have an unusual imagination, I'll give you that." Chuckling, he shook his head. "Baby Dagger."

"It's true."

"I ran your name, Madeline."

"I changed my name. I was Madeline Connaught. I am Baby Dagger. I'll prove it. Ask me any question about Blade or Savannah and I'll answer it."

"You're best friends with Kathy Hudson, the world's biggest rock-and-roll fan. Of course you know rock music trivia."

Frustration surged through her and she wiggled and fought and tugged on the ropes. "I guess I have that coming, don't I? I guess this is what I get for running away, for hiding who I really am."

"Calm down. Quit struggling. I'm an Eagle Scout. I know my knots and you won't work them loose." During her efforts, her shirt had crawled up her torso, baring her midriff. Austin's stare locked on her skin and he said, "You know, I've had a thing for you ever since our date to the Valentine's dance. You're not the political partner I need in a wife, but we could have enjoyed ourselves for a time. It's too bad you decided to date that loser instead of me."

Maddie went still. That was a spark of lust she saw in his eyes, and a woman's fear of rape washed over her. *Stop it, Maddie. Keep your wits about you. There are worse things than rape.*

Burning to death. Being shot to death. Bleeding to death. Death, period.

Rape. *Lord, help me.* All right. Okay. She could deal with that if she had to. Could she use it?

Possibly. She needed a plan, though. At the rate her luck was going, Austin Rawlings had a thing for bondage, in which case she'd be screwed in more ways than one.

In order to develop her plan, it'd help to know his. She knew the big picture—she and Luke both dead. Maybe she could find salvation in the details.

"I'm telling you, Austin, you're making a mistake. If

Luke turns up anywhere with a bullet in him, Branch Callahan won't rest until he finds the killer."

"You're wrong. He's not hunting down John's killer, is he? Besides, that's not the way this is going to happen."

That's it, Austin. Spill the beans.

"Once I have the pictures in hand, it only takes a phone call for me to set into motion the plan my father put in place years ago to frame Mark Callahan should it become necessary. My father despised Mark ever since he cheated to snatch the valedictorian slot right out from under me in high school. Considering that Mark and Luke are identical twins, it took only a few tweaks from me to substitute one brother for the other in the plan. Once the 'truth' is revealed, not even Branch Callahan will doubt that Luke died by suicide."

"Truth about what, Austin? What do those pictures show?"

He met her gaze. His mouth worked but no sound emerged.

From the direction of the kitchen, another voice spat a single word. "Murder."

Austin's eyes went wide and he and Maddie both whipped their heads around. Kathy Hudson stood in the doorway, the gun in her hand pointed right at Austin, the look in her eyes deadly. "Murder," she repeated. "My Sparkle didn't run away. Austin Rawlings killed her."

Maddie gasped. Kathy grinned evilly. Insanely. Sparkle was dead, and Austin killed her? Is that what . . . Why? "Is it true?"

In a flash of movement, Austin pulled a gun of his own and held it against Maddie's temple. "Yeah, I did. So don't go thinking I won't kill again now."

Eighteen

Luke careened into the veterinary clinic's parking lot and slammed on the brakes. He shoved the gearshift into park, and leaving the truck running, dashed for the front door. "Doc?" he called as he entered the crowded waiting room. "Bee?"

A black lab reacted to Luke's agitation with a loud woof as the vet called out, "Back here, Callahan."

Sara-Beth gave Luke a worried smile as his stare focused in on Knucklehead, who still lay on an examining table. Luke's heart gave a wrench. Grimly, he asked, "His condition?"

"I see no sign of injury," Doc Hander said. "Still waiting on the blood work, but I suspect that'll tell the tale."

Luke patted the dog's belly, reassured by the steady up-and-down movement. "He'll be fine?"

"I expect so, yes."

Luke gave one sharp nod, then turned to Sara-Beth. "I need you to show me where you found him. Exactly."

"You gonna tell me what's wrong, Sin?"

"On the way."

Ten minutes later, they parked at the entrance to Edgemere Park and Sara-Beth led him to the spot where she'd found Knucklehead. Luke made a careful inspection of the surroundings, looking for anything and everything that could provide a hint of who may have orchestrated the events. He came up dry.

"He picked a good spot," Luke said, observing the surrounding trees. "No clear line of sight. A casual observer would have a tough time noting anything unusual. When you stopped, Bee, did you see anyone at all in the park?"

"No, and I did look. I could have used some help lifting him into my car, but the place was deserted. This is an older neighborhood, Luke. Not many kids around to play."

"Not a place a visitor to town would just happen to stumble across, either. This wasn't one of the dickheads."

"Who?"

"Her old boyfriends. One of them has been bothering her, but my gut tells me this is all about that godforsaken box." A hollow sense of worry expanded in his gut. Damn. He'd hoped to find something out here, anything. "There has to be something I'm missing," he muttered. "I know this town. I know the people. I'm a trained investigator. I should be able to see the clues. There are always clues."

"Maybe," Sara-Beth agreed. "However, I'm not so sure that even with your training, you'd be the one to see them. Sin, you've been away a long time. You don't know this town and its people. You don't know the secrets. Maybe you should talk to people who do."

She had a point. "All right, so where do I start? You work for the newspaper. You must have your finger on the pulse of Brazos Bend. Who has something to hide?"

"Half the people in town," she replied. "I'll tell you who you should talk to and that's Kathy Hudson. She knows—"

"Nothing," Luke interrupted. "I talked to her right when I learned Maddie had disappeared. She flaked out. Apparently today is her daughter's birthday and having Maddie turn up missing sent her over the edge. She started sobbing, didn't make any sense. I felt awful for her."

"She never has gotten over Sparkle's disappearance. She still makes huge deals out of all the anniversaries— Sparkle's birthday, all the holidays. She even makes a homecoming mum every year with a picture of Sparkle wearing her crown and—"

"Homecoming? Sparkle was homecoming queen?" Kathy's strange statement flitted through his mind. *The homecoming king needed another queen.*

"Don't you remember? There was such a to-do in town that year because no seniors were voted onto the homecoming court. It was the week before she disappeared. Everyone expected Janis Plummer to get it, so it was a big surprise when they announced Sparkle's name. I can't believe you don't remember. Mark was up for king."

"But he didn't win," Luke said, sifting back through his memories. He hadn't cared about that sort of stuff at the time, and he hadn't thought of it at all in succeeding years. "I can't recall who did."

"Austin Rawlings."

Rawlings. Hmm. Luke's heartbeat accelerated. Maybe. The man had power, position he valued. Worth checking into, anyway. "Do you know where he lives?"

"He's in his dad's old house in Country Club. Randolph built a new place on the north side of town. Luke, surely you don't think Austin is behind this. He's no arsonist."

"It's a place to start." Luke desperately needed that.

Since Branch's house was on the way, he swung by there to collect Matt for backup and leave Sara-Beth in a safe place. Then, for the first time in years, he asked his father for a favor. "In case Maddie's not at Austin's, I need a list of every piece of property the man has a stake in. Could you work on that for me?"

"Be glad to, son. Although, if your hunch is right and Rawlings is behind this, then I have a really good idea of where he'd take her."

Matt and Luke shared a look. "Where's that?" Luke asked.

"His old man had a place on the river, up north of the lake. He's owned it for years. He used to take his women there. It's isolated. Hardly anybody knows about it. It'd be a perfect place to hold somebody hostage."

"Y'all are crazy." Sara-Beth shook her head. "This is

Austin Rawlings we're talking about. The district attorney. There's never been even a hint of scandal attached to his name. Do you really think he'd go to these lengths just because he wants to be governor?"

"Governor!" Branch snorted. "Hell, Sara-Beth. Randolph Rawlings has had a written political plan for Austin since the boy was in elementary school. He always had his sights set higher than the governor's office."

"Washington?"

Luke's father nodded. "My boys think I'm bad. At least I never expected them to grow up and become president."

In the great room at Austin Rawlings's river house, Kathy Hudson cocked her gun and said, "Let her go, Rawlings."

Austin's hand tightened on Maddie's arm. "Put it down, old woman."

Maddie sat frozen, afraid to move, as her mind tried to piece together the puzzle. Austin killed Kathy's daughter. Oh, poor Kathy. Poor, poor Kathy. She'd waited all these years.

When had it happened? Back all those years ago when she went missing? Why? How did Kathy figure it out? Was Jerry Grevas blackmailing Austin? Was the proof in the missing box? Did Austin kill Jerry? "Um, since I'm up to my neck in trouble here, would one of you please explain why? If I'm going to die, I'd like to know why."

"You're not going to die!" Kathy's voice went shrill. Tears flowed down her face. "I'm sorry I got you into this, Maddie. I never intended for you to get hurt. I trusted Luke to keep you safe. I never thought Austin would burn down your house or go so far as to do this. I never would have sent those notes, sent the necklace, if I'd known. I just want . . . Tell me what happened. Tell me why. Tell me *where.* I need to know where my baby is!"

"You?" Austin snapped. "You're the one who sent the stuff? Not Callahan?"

"Sin doesn't know anything."

Austin spat a curse and raked his free hand through his hair. "Great. Just great. Now look at the mess we're in. How did you find out? Grevas?"

The gun in Kathy's hand shook wildly and Maddie held her breath. Too much emotion. Too much anger and pain and despair. Kathy shook with it. Austin vibrated with it. *Someone's going to get hurt.*

"I thought he was the one who hurt my baby!" Kathy cried. "Maddie gave me jewelry from Gus's house and I recognized Sparkle's necklace. She was wearing it the last time I saw her. So I went to Jerry to get answers."

"He gave you the pictures?" Austin asked. "Where are they?"

"I don't know. I've never seen them."

"Pictures of what?" Maddie asked.

The barrel of Austin's gun nudged her skin. "That day. Me and Sparkle. He's kept them all this time. I didn't know they existed until Jerry was arrested for growing the shrooms. He told me about them then, said he was in the woods that day, saw what happened. Took pictures of me and Sparkle, me and my dad."

"Your dad! What did your father have to do with it?"

"When I realized Sparkle was . . . well . . . that she was gone, I didn't know what to do. I went to my dad for help. He helped me bury her body in the woods."

His *father* did that?

Austin paused a moment, then mused, "That must have been when Grevas found her necklace. I noticed it was missing, but I was afraid to tell my dad."

Maddie couldn't believe what she was hearing. Her father would do just about anything for her, but he'd draw the line at covering up a killing.

Austin cleared his throat. "Jerry promised me the pictures if I let him out of jail. But they were gone. You did something with them. That's when he attacked you."

"I never saw a box of pictures!" she protested.

"Jerry told me that he'd hidden them inside videotape

sleeves," Kathy told them. "That's what was in the box. VCR tapes. You told me you threw a bunch of videos away, remember, Maddie?"

"Yes." Maddie's mind raced. Only she hadn't thrown them all away. She'd sent a stack of movies to her dad. She doubted he'd even opened the box yet. Could the pictures be in with those videos? Maybe she could bargain with them now.

While Maddie debated the questions, Austin asked Kathy, "Grevas told you this? When? Right before you killed him?"

Maddie startled. "A loan shark had him killed."

"No." Guilt rippled across Kathy's expression. "I did, but it was self-defense. He attacked me."

"Oh, wow," Maddie muttered. Her head was spinning. She couldn't believe this. Any of it. The district attorney and her best friend? Both of them killers? *And I thought my boyfriends were bad.*

Kathy's worried gaze pleaded for Maddie to understand. "I didn't mean to kill him. He rushed me. We struggled. It was an accident!"

"Yeah, well, so was mine," Austin declared. "But that doesn't make any difference. Dead is dead."

"Do you mean Sparkle?" Kathy brought a hand to her heart. "It was an accident? How? Tell me how she died. Was she in pain?"

In her peripheral vision, Maddie could see the gun barrel shake from the tremble in Austin's hand. "No. She was angry at me. Yelling. I didn't want the baby."

Kathy gasped. She swayed on her feet.

"I wasn't going to lie about it," Austin continued. "We didn't have a future. I told her that from the beginning. My father would never have allowed me to marry a girl named Sparkle who didn't have a father and whose mother was an ex-hippie who ran a hamburger joint." He paused, and his expression turned a bit wistful. "She was so sweet, though. Funny. She made me laugh. I loved that about her. I loved her."

Kathy let out a little mewling sob.

Austin's voice hardened. "But I needed a wife who'd be a political asset, not a liability. My dad had already picked her out. So Sparkle and I kept our relationship secret. We couldn't get married, so I told her to get an abortion."

"Oh, Sparkle," Kathy moaned.

"She got hysterical. She hit me." Austin shook his head. "Again and again. She kept coming after me. Finally, I'd had enough. I shoved her away. Not even that hard, just a little push."

His voiced faltered then and he cleared it before adding, "She stumbled. Cracked her head on a rock. All the blood. It was awful." He swallowed hard. "Awful."

Across the room, tears streamed down Kathy's face. Moisture pooled in Maddie's eyes, too. Such a sad, tragic tale, and it had led to so much grief.

Yet, the fact that it had been an accident gave Maddie hope. "Austin, you don't want to do this. You're not an evil person. Kathy, neither are you. Put down the guns, both of you. Let's not make this a bigger tragedy than it already is."

Austin didn't speak. He didn't so much as move.

"She's right," Kathy said. "Nobody has to know. Let Maddie go, and tell me where my Sparkle is buried, and this can be the end of it."

"I'm not telling you anything." Austin went as taut as one of Blade's guitar strings. "Put down your gun, old woman, or I'll pull the trigger here and now. Maddie's like a daughter to you, isn't she? You want to lose her, too?"

"Do you want to die, Mr. District Attorney?"

It's a standoff, Maddie thought. Neither one will give up or give in, so we're all liable to get hurt. *We need a distraction.* If Austin would shift the gun away from her, then maybe she could fling herself at him. Knock him down. Knock the gun away. Kathy could make a grab for it.

Or maybe . . .

A new thought occurred to Maddie. How did Kathy get out here? How did she know about this place?

Maybe she didn't come alone. Maybe she brought the distraction with her and somebody—like Luke—waited outside to play knight in shining armor at exactly the right moment.

Now is good, Callahan. No need to wait. Feel free to rush right in to the rescue anytime now.

At that moment, to Maddie's amazement, the front doorknob began to turn. Her heart leapt. Her hopes took flight. Luke! He'd come to save her. Finally, she'd hooked up with a hero.

She drew a deep breath. A huge, welcoming smile waited to burst forth.

Randolph Rawlings stepped into the river house carrying a sawed-off shotgun. "Well, boy. What sort of trouble do I have to get you out of this time?"

Maddie's heart sank. *Randolph. It's over now.*

Then everything happened at once. Movement above her caught her attention. Matt Callahan launched himself from the staircase onto Austin Rawlings at the same time that Luke rushed in through the front door behind Randolph. A gun discharged and Kathy screamed.

As if in slow motion, Maddie saw the shotgun come around as Luke took the old man down. Sunlight beaming through a window glinted off the shortened barrel.

Maddie never heard the shot.

At first, she felt no pain, just the suffocating surprise of not being able to breathe. Then the pain came, a wave of hot, intense agony that pulled her down . . . down . . . down into the dark.

The last things she saw were Luke Callahan's eyes, his beautiful, guilt-laden, terror-filled eyes.

The Careflight paramedic told Luke his first aid had saved her life, but he didn't believe it. Nor did he believe the nurse who showed up in the waiting room to report that the surgery was going well. He had a little more faith in her word when she showed back up and mentioned complications.

Luke sat by himself in the waiting room, warning off with

a glare everyone who attempted to approach him. He was vaguely aware of his brother running interference in that regard. Matt knew him. He didn't want to talk to anyone, see their sympathetic stares, listen to their platitudes. Bottom line was, he'd fucked up and Maddie had paid for it. Same as with Terry.

And Terry was dead.

The waiting room grew crowded as word spread. Friends, neighbors, and clients congregated to worry and whisper together, the shock of the story they'd learned etched across their expressions. Despite his efforts, Luke heard snatches of conversation. *The Rawlingses under arrest. Kathy's daughter, Sparkle, dead. Kathy sedated. Sin Callahan a federal agent of some sort.*

They sneaked glances at Luke, their faces alive with curiosity, but he ignored them.

Except when they started talking about Maddie. Those bits of talk he strained to hear, because they made her seem closer. Vibrant. Alive. They talked of how nice she was, how kind. How she'd made a place for herself in Brazos Bend so fast. How much everyone loved her. What a good job she did for her clients. How pretty she'd kept her yard before the fire. That she deserved better than the likes of Sin Callahan, federal agent or not.

When the surgeon walked in with a smile on his face, Luke didn't believe that, either. Terry had survived the surgery, hadn't he? Nevertheless, he rose from his seat and approached the man, the crowd parting like the Red Sea before him as he claimed the right of next of kin. "Maddie?"

The doctor rattled off details of the surgery, and Luke's patience grew short. "Bottom line, Doctor," he interrupted.

The surgeon frowned at Luke's impertinence, but said, "She should make a full recovery."

The gathering erupted with exclamations of relief and joy. Luke's knees went a bit weak and he felt a hand clasp his shoulder. Matt.

Luke was waiting in her room when she was moved to

ICU and his first glimpse of her nearly brought him to his knees. So pale. Pale as death. Tubes and bandages everywhere. Thank God for the steady, reassuring beat of the heart monitor.

He lost track of time. At some point a nurse arrived with a stack of clean clothes his brother had provided, giving him an ultimatum to change out of his bloody clothes or leave. He refused until she said that Maddie would be awakening soon and the sight of him would scare her. Rather than leave, Luke stripped right where he was, heedless of the admiring glances of the nurses at the desk; then he continued his vigil.

Luke didn't spend the hours chastising himself. He didn't replay the events of the day or second-guess his actions and decisions. In fact, he didn't think at all. His mind was a blank, his emotions frozen. Nothing would change until he saw for himself life and clarity of thought in her beautiful brown eyes.

Finally, his patience was rewarded. Her lids flickered. Lifted. She blinked a couple times, then looked at him. His heart lifted. *Red.*

Then tears pooled and pain dimmed her eyes. Her lips moved. She croaked, "Luke."

"It's okay, Red." He stood over her, tenderly took her hand. "You're going to be okay. The doctors promised."

Her eyelids drooped and she fell back asleep. Luke stood beside her bed, holding her hand for a long, long time. Now he allowed the thoughts to come. He relived the horrific events of the day. Her disappearance, the search, the tense drive up to the river cabin. Those horrible minutes inside. The Careflight helicopter lifting off. The interminable drive back to town.

He should have seen it coming. He should have suspected Austin. Should have had better radar. This was Terry all over again. Another fuckup, courtesy of Luke Callahan. And this time, Maddie paid the price.

For that, he could never forgive himself.

*   *   *

Somebody set my chest on fire. Maddie tried to shy away from the pain, but movement made her feel as if they'd taken a poker to her to stir the embers. She whimpered, felt completely sorry for herself. She cracked open her eyes, and the sight of Luke sitting beside her bed reassured her. She fell back asleep.

She drifted in and out of consciousness repeatedly until finally, she awoke for the most part clearheaded. First came the questions. *What happened? Where am I?*

Then the answers. *I was shot. I couldn't breathe. I'm in the hospital. I can breathe again.*

She remembered waking up before. Luke was here. And a banker? Or had that been a dream?

She opened her eyes to see the clean-shaven man with a military haircut dressed in a Brooks Brothers suit seated in a chair reading a copy of *People* magazine. No dream. She shifted her gaze. Luke stood with his back to her, staring out a window. She was so glad to see him. "Luke?"

He turned and Maddie frowned. He looked awful. Tired and worn and in pain. Had he been hurt, too?

He studied her with a laser gaze before clearing his throat. "Hey, there. You with us this time, Maddie?"

"Have I been somewhere else?"

"In and out for a couple of days now."

So that's why she felt as if a significant amount of time had passed. It had. He picked up a cup of water from a bed-side tray and held the straw to her mouth. Maddie drank greedily, then asked, "What happened?"

"Do you remember anything?"

"Bits and pieces."

He set down the water, then moved back toward the window, away from her. He never touched her. Didn't stroke her hair. Didn't kiss her. What was wrong?

"You took a hit from Randolph Rawlings's shotgun. Your lung collapsed and you hemorrhaged on the operating table, but the doctors pulled you through. They said it'll take some time, but you should make a complete recovery."

"What about you? What happened to you?"

He looked surprised. "Me? I'm fine. Not a scratch."

Maddie didn't believe it, but she decided to wait until they were alone to press it. She tried to sit up, and Luke showed her the button on the bed railing for adjusting the bed. Once she'd tilted up her head, she had a better angle to see the room. The Brooks Brothers stranger had set aside his magazine and he stared at her anxiously. It took Maddie a moment, but she finally recognized the eyes. "Daddy? Is that you?"

"Hi, Baby. You've rejoined the living." Those familiar eyes teared up and he added, "Hallelujah!"

"How did you get here?"

"Rowboat," he quipped, obviously trying to lighten the mood. "How do you think I got here? I flew, of course. Left within fifteen minutes of this fella's call." Blade hooked a thumb toward Luke, then brushed his lapels with his knuckles. "Like my disguise? Callahan here insisted on it when he called me to come. Said we had to protect your life here in Podunk, Texas."

"I've never seen you with short hair and without a beard. You're handsome, Daddy."

"Nobody recognizes me. It's amazing."

The wonder on her father's face made Maddie smile, and she turned her head to share it with Luke. He didn't smile back.

A tear slipped from Blade's eye and rolled down his cheek. "Oh, Baby, I've been so worried about you. Are you feeling better? They've been giving you some good drugs. I've been here half a day now, and every time you woke up you were flying."

Her father was here. Maddie couldn't believe it. Blade had come to Brazos Bend. Kathy would . . . "Kathy!" Maddie's stare flew to Luke. "Is she okay? Was anyone else hurt? Matt?"

"Kathy is fine. Matt is fine. You were the only person hit," Luke replied, his lips settling in a thin, grim line.

"So, Baby," her father said, "tell me, now. How are you feeling? Should I call the doctor?"

"I'm . . . okay." Actually, she was worried because Luke wouldn't meet her eyes.

Blade rattled off the tale of his arrival, stressing his fear and concern and desire that she'd come home to England with him upon her discharge from the hospital. "Your doctor told me it'll be a month or so before you can travel, so I've rented a house here in town for the duration of your recuperation. I understand your other place burned down."

Maddie waited for Luke to say he was taking her to Branch's place, but it didn't happen. Luke didn't react to her father's suggestion in any way, and Maddie's consternation grew. Unable to stand it any longer, she interrupted her father. "Daddy? I'm awfully glad you're here, but could I have a few minutes alone with Luke, please?"

"You sure, Baby D?"

"I'm sure." *Oh, I'm sure, all right. What the heck is going on, Callahan? What aren't you telling me?*

Or are you telling me exactly what I don't want to hear?

Blade shot Luke a warning glare, straightened his tie, then departed the room. Maddie expected Luke to come to her then. To kiss her. At least to touch her. To connect with her as lovers do.

He didn't budge from his stance beside the window.

Peeved now, she asked, "Luke, what's the deal here? What did I miss?"

He deliberately misread the question. "The Rawlings are both in jail, for one thing, on charges of kidnapping, arson, and attempted murder to start. Judge denied bond for them both. The old man called in some high-powered attorneys out of Dallas, but before they arrived, Austin folded like a cheap tent. Sheriff's office recovered Sparkle's remains yesterday. They're still working on the exact charges they want to bring for that crime. That office has been turned upside down by this whole thing. It helps their case that your father found the infamous pictures in with a John Wayne video.

The most damning one shows Austin and his old man lowering Sparkle Hudson's body into a grave."

Distracted by the information, Maddie shook her head. So many people hurt. So much grief. All because of one man's thirst for power. "Randolph Rawlings is an evil man. What about Kathy? Is she in trouble because of Jerry Grevas?"

"Kathy told her story, and forensics backed her claim of self-defense. She won't get off scot-free because of the obstruction charge, but I doubt her punishment amounts to much. Probation, maybe. Community service. No time, I would bet. She has public sympathy on her side, and the deputy DA has stated that she's recommending lenience."

"That's a relief." Maddie tried to shift her position and the effort had her grimacing in pain. Yet, the pain helped her focus. What was going on with Luke? Why was he acting so distant?

And then, suddenly, she knew. It was over. The mystery was solved. He was leaving, going back to the bayou. That's why he summoned Blade. He'd always told her he wasn't hanging around Brazos Bend, hadn't he? And Luke Callahan never lied.

"Oh," she murmured.

"Are you hurting?"

"Yes." Oh, yes. Her heart was breaking in two.

"It's probably time for your pain meds again. I'll get the nurse."

Luke wouldn't meet her eyes. The cad. He all but ran out the door. It was the last time she saw him for a week.

Oh, he stayed in Brazos Bend. She didn't ask about him, but her visitors told her that much. Sara-Beth made sure to tell her how Luke was overseeing the furnishing of the house her father had rented. Branch let it be known that Luke called her doctors twice a day to check on her progress. Her own father went out of his way to make sure she understood that Luke was pestering the prosecutors to make certain that Austin and his father received their just rewards.

Even Kathy got into the act. Out of jail on bond funded by Luke, Kathy arrived at the hospital bearing a peace offering in the form of Maddie's favorite ice cream sundae. After an awkward apology, she begged for Maddie's forgiveness, and hardly believed it when Maddie said there was nothing to forgive. Once that was out of the way, she spent the rest of her visit talking up Luke and the lawyers he'd hired to help her. The man certainly had turned his reputation around in town.

Wasn't that special?

They all knew he was a short-timer. That much was obvious. As the days passed and Maddie waited in vain for him to appear at the hospital, she began to wonder whether he'd even show up to say good-bye. He'd better. He owed her that much.

Twice she picked up the phone to call him, but pride prevented her from dialing the number. She vacillated between being hurt and being angry. Sometimes she considered throwing away her pride and begging him to stay, but she knew that would be the wrong thing to do. If he turned her down, she'd have sacrificed her pride for nothing. If he stayed when he didn't truly want to, he'd eventually come to resent her. She didn't want to live like that.

Finally, upon her discharge from the hospital, the rat arrived to take her home. "You ready to go?" he asked from the doorway.

She eyed the plastic water pitcher on the tray table and seriously considered throwing it at him. But Maddie had her pride, so she smiled instead. "Hello, stranger."

If she'd scored a hit, he didn't react. "Wow. Looks like a jungle in here. You taking all those flowers home?"

The fact he hadn't sent her flowers when just about everyone else in town had hung in the room like skunk spray. "No. I'm giving them to the nurses, except for the daisies from your father and the basket of roses from Liam."

She followed his gaze to the white wicker basket and its two dozen stems of beautiful yellow roses. His lips thinned.

Didn't like that, hmm? Good. "Liam visited me yesterday. It was really nice to see him. We had a nice talk and I do believe he's a changed man. We've decided to be friends. I understand you and he have spoken?"

Temper fired in Luke's eyes, and when he opened his mouth, Maddie thought she'd finally pushed him far enough. She sat up a little straighter, more than ready for this confrontation, but then a nurse pushed a wheelchair into her room and spoiled the moment. Luke grabbed her suitcase. "I'll head on down and bring the car up to the entrance. I borrowed your father's Lexus. Thought it'd be easier for you to get in and out of than my truck."

"What about your Maserati?" the nurse piped up. "That is the neatest car in town."

He flashed her his friendly smile. "It's not in town anymore, I'm afraid. I sold it."

"No!" said the nurse. "Why would you do that?"

Luke shrugged. "Didn't need it anymore."

"He's good about getting rid of the things he doesn't need," Maddie added as the nurse walked away.

That one did score a hit, judging by his flinch.

On the short drive to the house Blade had rented, Maddie waited for Luke to speak. He turned up the music instead. She drummed her fingers on her knee. He whistled beneath his breath.

She bit the inside of her mouth to keep from crying. How had they come to this? She'd truly thought he cared. How could she have been so wrong?

He never said he loved you, Maddie.

Luke Callahan never lied.

He pulled into the driveway of a pretty two-story colonial. "Is that my father? The man in a golf shirt? With a five iron in his hand?"

"He's taking to this new lifestyle." Luke switched off the engine as her father finished his practice swing, then waved. "I think Blade would rather have been an actor than a singer."

Knucklehead came bounding out around the side of the house barking a welcome, and Maddie was glad to see for herself that the dog had recovered from his ordeal.

"Welcome home, luv," Blade said, grasping her hands and giving her a thorough once-over. "You look marvelous. Your bed is all ready, and the cook has been at it all day making your favorites. Shepherd's pie and fish and chips. Cream custard. Strawberries and lemon curd."

Maddie smiled, knowing they were her father's favorites, but he'd honestly believed they were hers. "That sounds wonderful."

"Your friend Kathy is bringing pecan pie. She made one the other day and it was so good it made my eyes roll back in my head. I told her I'd sing 'September Loving' for her if she'd bring another one."

"I'm sure that thrilled her to death."

"I admit I'm enjoying this anonymity, but it's nice having one person in town who knows who I am."

"Especially a fan like Kathy." Maddie went up on her tiptoes and pressed a kiss to her father's cheek. She still couldn't get over how smooth it was.

"So, she's not married?" Blade asked, throwing his arm around Maddie's shoulder and escorting her toward the front door.

Luke followed them inside and set her suitcase on the floor. He made a second trip to bring the flowers inside. Setting them on the entry hall table, he stuck his hands in his pockets and rocked back on his heels. "Well," he said, "I, um, I guess I'll be going."

Maddie braced herself and turned. "Away from here or away from town?"

He looked away, hardened his jaw. "I'm leaving Brazos Bend."

Even though she knew better, she hesitated, waiting for an invitation to join him. When the moment stretched on in silence, she nodded. "I'll walk you out."

"No. That's all right. You need to rest."

"I'll. Walk. You. Out."

Luke gritted his teeth, then nodded once.

Magnolia trees shaded the front walk, their blossoms perfuming the air as Maddie and Luke walked side by side toward Luke's truck parked at the curb. She wanted to touch him. She wanted to throw her arms around him, to have him hold her in return. It took the last vestiges of her control not to throw herself at him.

Spying a bench beneath the tree off to the right, she made a detour and took a seat, saying, "Five minutes, Callahan. I think you owe me that."

Again one of those short, sharp nods.

Knucklehead nuzzled up beside her and she made a show of petting and scratching him, telling him good-bye, that she'd miss him, that he was the very best of dogs. Luke watched for a moment, then turned away.

Words bubbled up on Maddie's tongue, questions and accusations and even that declaration neither one of them had ever said. Yet, only a single word escaped. "Why?"

"Because I have to."

Peeved, she repeated, "Why?"

Finally, he looked at her. "I've thought about it a lot. You were right before, Red. Brazos Bend is where you need to be. You love it here, and Brazos Bend loves you. It's home and hearth and the promise of family. I can't give you that. It isn't in me to give that to anyone. All I have to offer is a boat and Buffett tunes by sunset. It's not enough. You deserve more. You certainly deserve better than me."

Better than him? He saved her life. He was her knight in shining armor. Her hero.

Her love.

She closed her eyes. She loved him. From the bottom of her heart, with every fiber of her being. "Luke, I—"

He touched her for the first time in a week by putting his finger against her lips, saying, "Shush, now. Don't. Don't make this any harder. It isn't good for your lungs to get all worked up. It's okay. This is the best thing for both of us,

Red. I need to take some time and figure out what I want to do with my life. I'm obviously not cut out for law enforcement any longer. I have to apologize for letting Randolph get off that shot. I should have figured that old bastard was involved somehow. You paid for my mistake and I'll regret that for the rest of my life."

"No, Luke. Please, just listen—"

"I think what I need to do is take some time to decide what interests me," he interrupted, his eyes not meeting hers. He was obviously anxious to escape. "You're lucky, you know? You've found a place that fits you, found an occupation that suits. I think I'll take your example and see if I can't find the same for myself."

Pride came to Maddie's rescue. "More than anything, I want you to be happy, Luke Callahan. Whatever it takes. Now, since you foolishly felt you had to apologize—"

"Maddie," he protested.

"I need to thank you for saving my life. You were my hero when I needed one, Luke, and for that I'll always"— she swallowed the words "love you" and finished—"be grateful."

He looked down at the ground, rubbed the back of his neck. She saw his chest expand as he drew a deep breath. "Good-bye, Maddie Kincaid."

Tears pooled in her eyes, but determination prevented them from spilling. "Good-bye, Luke Callahan."

He leaned down, captured her lips in a swift, hard kiss, then walked away.

Maddie didn't watch the truck pull away or follow its path down the street. She stared blindly at a pair of mockingbirds pecking at seed in the grass spilled from a bird feeder and tried not to bawl like a baby. He left. He really left. Just drove off into the sunset like a cowboy in a bad B movie.

Good Lord, she'd done it to herself again. She'd given her heart to someone who didn't want it, and he'd handed it back to her in pieces. A million of them. A billion aching, painful pieces. Maddie couldn't see how she'd ever put it back together again.

She heard a screen door bang behind her, then footsteps on the porch. Brooks Brothers Blade took a seat beside her and put his arm around her. After a moment of silence, he began to hum the Beatles tune "Hey Jude."

Maddie managed a watery smile and rested her head on her daddy's shoulder.

Nineteen

In the local archives section of the Rosenberg Library in Galveston, Luke took one last note about the island in the 1890s, then set down his pen and called it a day. He rose from the hard wooden chair where he'd spent most of his day, put his hands to his lower back, and stretched. It felt good. He felt good. He'd accomplished a lot of work today.

Work, he'd found, provided a good distraction from the hollow feeling in his heart.

Luke stuck his notebook and supplies into his backpack, then returned his books to the stacks. He paused to flirt with the librarian before leaving the building. "You mind if I bring in my La-Z-Boy with me next time, Mrs. Wilmington?" he asked, snatching a peppermint from her candy jar. "Sure would be more comfortable than those oak torture devices you have in here."

A spry seventy-eight, Mrs. Wilmington grabbed a folded newspaper and whacked him on his thieving hand. "Only if you bring a recliner for me while you're at it. Unlike yourself, I'm all bone in the bottom. I can use some padding."

"Mrs. Wilmington! Have you been checking out my butt?" he asked with a wink.

"People-watching is one of the great joys of my job."

Laughing, Luke leaned over the desk and kissed her cheek. "You better stay out of trouble while I'm gone,

Mrs. W. You're my best girl here in Galveston. I don't want any young hard-butt carting you off while I'm away."

"So your research is done? You're leaving town?"

"I think I have everything I need," he replied. Everything the library can provide, anyway. "I'm going to take the *Miss Behavin' II* south and winter in Mexico. See if I can't get the first draft of the book done. Want to run off to Cozumel with me?"

The librarian's eyes twinkled. "You wish. I'd be too much for you to handle, too much of a distraction for you, boy. You'd never get your book done, and that won't do. I'm anxious to read it. I love a good pirate book, and your family connection to Jean Laffite gives the story an added élan."

"He was a character, all right."

"Which makes you the perfect person to write this story. If you'd been born a few hundred years earlier, I could see you hanging with ol' Jean and his brother on the island. So, you go to Mexico and write your book, Callahan. You can dedicate it to me."

"I might just do that, sweetheart. I might just do that."

Luke slung his backpack over one shoulder as he left the library. The first cold front of the season had moved in while he'd been indoors, and he hunched his shoulders against the chilling north wind as he walked toward the bay. It was definitely time to head south. He needed warm sunshine to battle the coldness that had plagued his soul during the months since leaving Brazos Bend and Maddie Kincaid.

He missed her. Missed the joy in her laugh, the spark in her temper. The natural sensuality she oozed with every breath. He recalled the last time they'd made love the night of the fire and the pagan-goddess look of her as she rode him to completion. So beautiful. So sexy. So—

"Hell." His prick had gone as hard as a tire iron. Damn, but he needed to get laid. He hadn't been able to bring himself to date since saying *adiós* to Red. Maybe for old times' sake he should visit one of the whorehouses on the border on his way down south, no matter that the idea left him cold.

Truth was, he couldn't imagine being with anyone but Maddie.

It had been a long, lonely few months since he saluted Brazos Bend in his rearview mirror. He'd been at loose ends at first. Spent his days getting the boat in tip-top shape and his nights playing pool in the sleaziest honky-tonk in southwestern Louisiana. Some nights he drank to forget her. Other nights he drank because he couldn't forget her.

The time wasn't wasted, because while he swabbed the decks and polished the brass and recovered from bad-beer hangovers, he did what he'd told Maddie he'd do. He'd found a place that fitted him and an occupation that suited.

He'd moved his boat to Galveston and begun research for a thriller idea he'd played with for years based on the old McBride-family tales his mother had liked to tell. His had a treasure-hunt plot with an unlucky hero, lots of adventure, a murder or two, some drug-runner villains, and a happy-ending romance with a hot, redheaded heroine.

Maybe the hero didn't have such bad luck after all.

Maybe happy endings didn't happen in real life, but he was writing fiction, wasn't he? Fiction didn't always have to imitate life. The hero didn't have to end up lonely and alone.

Shoving aside the memories, Luke whistled a Buffett beach tune as he stopped by the post office to pick up his mail, which included a copy of the *Brazos Bend Standard*. He'd been keeping track of the legal developments in the Rawlings cases and was frustrated, but not surprised, by the delaying tactics their high-dollar lawyers had employed. Twice he'd read snippets about Maddie in the newspaper and he'd been pleased to see that her famous father had managed to maintain his disguise during the six weeks he'd spent in town during her recovery. According to Sara-Beth's gossip column, he'd even gone so far as to finance the construction of a small synagogue for weekenders up at the lake. Had to like generosity in a man.

That thought brought to mind his own father. Branch had been on a spree of charitable giving around town of late, and

Luke couldn't help but wonder the reason behind that. Because Branch Callahan most definitely had a reason that went beyond a simple act of kindness. He always did.

Luke had left Brazos Bend without any final confrontation or communication with his father. He hadn't known what to say to the man. Branch obviously loved Maddie and he'd been of help when she went missing, thus poking a hole in Luke's defenses against him. However, Luke hadn't been ready to forgive and forget, so he avoided. Not exactly mature of him, he admitted, but with his emotions already so raw over Maddie, he simply couldn't face a scene with his father.

Maybe over the winter he could come to grips with any changes in his attitude toward Branch in the wake of his weeks in Brazos Bend. When he could bear to think about Maddie again, he'd think about her arguments on his father's behalf. She'd been right about one thing. His old man wasn't getting any younger. It'd be good for Luke to have everything straight in his head so he didn't suffer regrets when Branch Callahan kicked the proverbial bucket.

Luke set all that aside as he paid a call at the vet's office to pick up Knucklehead following the mutt's checkup prior to the Mexico trip. A stop at a barbecue place for take-out was the last of Luke's errands before he headed toward the pier where he kept the *Miss Behavin' II* berthed. Knucklehead had his nose to the ground on the scent of who-knew-what, until suddenly, his head came up and he sniffed the air. Luke followed suit. "Mmm . . . fried chicken. Mrs. Hardy must be cooking for the captain tonight aboard the *Wind Whistle,* and her chicken is the best. Maybe we could talk her into trading some beef for her bird."

He could use some company tonight, maybe shake this sense of loneliness that had hung over him all day like a rain cloud. But even dinner with the Hardys, nice as they were, probably wouldn't do the trick. Only a certain redhead could do that.

Yeah, well. Dream on. Only way you're getting your hands on breasts and thighs is batter-dipped and fried.

Knucklehead let out an excited bark, then suddenly took off running. But instead of padding across the gangplank to the *Wind Whistle,* he leapt aboard the *Miss Behavin' II* and disappeared inside.

I left it locked. I know I did. Somebody's inside.

Probably Matt or Mark come to try to talk him into going back to work again. Neither of his brothers could understand that he'd lost his fire for the job. They worried about him. Matt was the worst. And if he started in about Maddie again, harping on about how Luke was being a fool for walking away, well, Luke'd just toss his lecturing ass overboard.

Glad at the prospect of company despite the price he'd invariably pay, Luke smiled as he stepped aboard the houseboat and moved toward the open doorway where his dog had disappeared.

The sound of Frank Sinatra singing "The Best Is Yet to Come" stopped him in his tracks. Luke's smile died. His pulse sped up. *I don't own that CD.*

He stepped inside and the scent of Chanel teased his nostrils. Maddie's scent. Luke's mouth went dry.

Whoa. Wait a minute. Could it be . . . ? Was she really. . . . ? Holy Moses. Why? Why had she come? He wanted to rush forward to find out. He wanted to turn and run away and never know the answer.

He didn't know whether he had the strength to face her.

It took every bit of courage Luke possessed to take two more steps inside. All the breath whooshed from his body when he heard the familiar voice say, "Hello, Luke."

Luke turned around. Maddie stood in the master bedroom doorway, her feet bare, wearing shorts and a T-shirt and an uncertain smile. She stood there petting Knucklehead, looking so beautiful, so healthy, so . . . whole.

No thanks to you, jackass. She got shot on your watch, remember?

He remembered her lying in a hospital bed hooked up to

tubes and machines. His stomach clenched and all his defenses went up. "What are you doing here?"

"We need to talk."

No. They absolutely didn't need to talk. Luke took a step backward, though every instinct urged him to rush forward, to take her into his arms and hold her tight. "Look, Maddie. There's no need for that. I don't—"

"You shut me out before," she interrupted. "You walked away. From me. From us. I let you do it because I wasn't strong enough to fight you. I have my strength back now, Luke. And I'm ready."

"Well, I'm not." He'd never be ready for this. He couldn't fight Maddie. He didn't want to, even though he knew he should. His arms ached with the need to hold her. He was the weak one. Just looking at her hurt enough to nearly bring him to his knees.

"I've done a lot of thinking since you left Brazos Bend. There is something you need to know. Something you need to understand. I talked to my father about you. I even talked to your father. I even called Matt. He'd left me his number in case of an emergency."

Emergency? Luke's senses went on point. He glanced down at her flat stomach, wondering. Well, crap. *That* would certainly constitute an emergency.

To his guilty surprise, he actually hoped that maybe . . . was she?

"I'm so angry at you, Luke Callahan. More furious than I ever was with Rip, Liam, and Cade. In fact, if I lump all those feelings together, it doesn't come close to the amount of mad I feel for you."

"That's why you're here?" he asked slowly. "To tell me that you're pissed?"

"You bet I'm mad. In fact, mad doesn't even come close to what I feel for you."

"Are you pregnant, Maddie?"

That stopped her. Her mouth gaped while her eyes widened with shock. "No!"

Well, hell. Luke looked away, his gaze falling on Knuckle-head, whose brown eyes stared at him as if to say, *Dumb-ass. Why is she busy petting me instead of you?*

He cleared his throat. "All right, then. I can't blame you for being angry, Maddie. I'm pretty pissed at myself, too. I let you down, and I'm damned sorry for it."

"Just so I understand, how did you let me down?"

"A gunshot wound for starters. Need I go on?"

Disgust flashed in her eyes as she folded her arms. "Well, I'll be. Wouldn't you know it? Branch Callahan was right on the money. I should never have taken that bet. Your father knows you better than you'd like to think."

"I don't want to hear about Branch!"

Ignoring him, she continued. "He told me you felt guilty about what happened. So did my father. So did Matt. But I argued with them. I told them they all were wrong. I thought you wanted fishing and freedom and Buffett at sunset, but I was the one who was wrong, wasn't I? I was too hurt and too blind to see what was plain to everybody else. You felt guilty."

"Of course I felt guilty. I didn't do my job. Again. And you paid for it." His voice trembled with emotion as he declared, "It's just by the grace of God that you didn't end up dead like my last partner!"

Maddie's brown eyes glowed with determination. "Is that what I was to you, Luke? Your partner?"

Ouch. She wasn't going to make this easy, was she? And damned if he didn't deserve every last blow. He stuck his hands in his pockets and turned away. "Let's not do this."

"You left me."

"I made sure you were going to be okay."

"Did you?" She laughed without amusement. "You thought I'd be okay? Why? Because my dad was there. Because you left me in Brazos Bend and thought someone would take care of me. Someone other than you? My lover. The man I thought . . . Yeah, well. It's funny, Luke. I didn't feel okay. You broke my heart, Luke Callahan." Her eyes filled with tears. "You shattered it."

Don't cry, Red. Please. If she cried, he'd lose it, and he had to keep it together. Him leaving had been the best thing for her. Didn't she see that? "I did what I thought was best. You belong in Brazos Bend, Maddie. I saw it firsthand when you were in the hospital. You have friends there. People who are closer than family. You've made a place for yourself. You've made a home."

"What good is a home if I'm living there alone?"

Luke didn't have an answer for that, and when he didn't reply, she continued. "It's lonely, Luke. I'm lonely."

He knew all about being lonely. Being . . . split in two. Being . . . lost. But this wasn't about him. It was about her and what she needed. "Maybe you should . . ." He cleared his throat again. "You need to find someone. Someone who deserves you."

Just don't let me see him with you, Red. Not ever.

"Oh, for crying out loud." Maddie advanced on him then, her hands braced on her hips, her eyes flashing. "You have as much nerve as a broken toe. Find someone? How dare you say that to me, Luke Callahan."

She snorted with disgust. "Is that the best you can come up with? Honestly. Admit it. You don't want anyone else to have me." She poked him in the chest. "You love me!"

Everything inside him froze. "I never said that."

"Yes you did. You said it to me in the hospital."

"You were unconscious!"

"Doesn't matter. Women are attuned to such things. We hear those words when they're said. I heard them. And guess what else? I know that unlike the Terrible Trio, who said them to my face and lied about it, you told the truth. You said it and you meant it and then you walked out on me. Damn you." She poked him once more, then added, "And, curse your sorry hide, I love you, too!"

He took it like a punch to the gut. "Maddie . . . I—"

"Shut up. You're going to stand there and listen to me, Callahan. I didn't come all this way for you to talk your way out of it, either."

"I wasn't going to—"

"You fell in love with me. *Me*. Maddie Kincaid. Not Baby and her entourage. Not the rock princess with a past and a big bank account. You wanted me. You loved me. How could you leave?"

I was an idiot. I'm still an idiot. Because he couldn't think about anything but her saying those three little words that just changed the universe. Those three little words that he desperately needed to hear again. "You love me?"

"Yeah. Isn't that pitiful? I swore I'd never do this again; three strikes and I'm out and all of that. I was never going to bat again. Little did I know that Rip, Liam, and Cade were little league. But you . . . you're the blessed World Series! How does a girl battle that?"

"Uh . . ." She really loved him? Well, damn.

"I have one question, Luke, and I want an answer. If it wasn't for your misplaced guilt, would you have pulled away from me? Would you have shut me out? What would you have done if I'd told you I loved you and asked you to find a way to stay with me in Brazos Bend? Hmm? What if I'd laid it all out right then and there under my father's rented magnolia tree? What would you have done? Would you still have run away? I never took you for a coward, Callahan."

She'd blindsided him with that one. Luke turned away from her and paced the room. He raked his fingers through his hair. "What kind of question is that, Maddie? I'm not a coward. A coward would have stayed, because let me tell you, Red. It was a class-A bitch to walk away."

"Then why did you?"

"Because I had to."

"Not good enough, Callahan. Answer the question."

Frustration rumbled up and burst forth in his words. "The answer doesn't matter! I left! I can't live in Brazos Bend. I can't give you the life you want. Your question is irrelevant."

"I don't care. Answer it anyway."

"Fine." He threw up his arms. "I don't know what I'd have done. That's the damned truth."

"Don't lie to me, Callahan. You're no good at it."

He snorted and rolled his eyes. "Honey, I worked undercover for almost ten years. I can lie like a rug."

"Not to the woman you love, you can't. Now, one more time. If you hadn't been wracked by guilt, would you have stayed in Brazos Bend for me?"

"Maddie, my father—"

"This isn't about Branch. I know the two of you are still a long way from kissing and making up. I'm asking about me. What would you do for me? Would you have stayed for me?"

Well, hell. He couldn't lie to her. He broke, cracked like a pecan at pie time. "Anything. I'd do anything for you, Red."

Her eyes shined behind watery tears. "I knew that. I knew that because I know the kind of man you are. The bad boy of Brazos Bend? Hah. You're the best of Brazos Bend, Luke Callahan. The very best."

Staggered, he could do no more than shake his head. "Hell, Maddie."

She put a finger up to his mouth. "Hush, now. I've come a long way to say this, so let me. I love you, Luke. I love your honor and your honesty. I love your heart. I even love your humor. I'm a strong woman, and I can survive without you, just as you can survive without me. But we shouldn't have to live that way just because we can. We're good together, Luke. We're better together."

Her words left him humbled but hopeful. "But what about your white picket fence?"

"Since I was a little girl, I've wanted a home. I dreamed about that white picket fence and I thought my life wouldn't be complete without it. Well, I was wrong. I don't need a fence. I don't need brick and mortar. I need you. Just you."

"I don't understand."

"Here."

As she walked across to pick something up from the coffee table, he noticed a new addition to the living room. "An aquarium?"

"Oscar does better with friends." She handed him a folded newspaper. "Read this."

The masthead said EXTRA TO THE BRAZOS BEND STAN-DARD. Luke gave Maddie a quick glance. He'd never known the paper to run an extra. Then his gaze fell to the date. "Tomorrow?"

"Just read it."

A two-inch headline proclaimed, WHAT A SURPRISE, BABY! just above Sara-Beth Branson's byline. Luke skimmed the first paragraph. *Maddie Kincaid, owner of Home for Now senior care . . . Baby Dagger . . .* "Ah, no. You've been outed. Why would Bee do such a thing?"

"I asked her to," Maddie said calmly.

"What!"

"I'm not as nice as you, Luke. I'm not as honorable or honest. When I play, I play to win and to hell with the rules. I set fire to my bridge, Callahan. By noon tomorrow, the pa-parazzi will be interviewing Mrs. Swan about what we did in Branch's backyard. I can't go back. So, what are you going to do about it?"

Luke's heart pounded. He had a hard time sucking in a breath. Good God. She did the one thing he'd have never banked on. "You threw away your home? Your life? To be with me?"

"No, Callahan. I want my home. I badly want my home. But home isn't a place out"—she waved her arm toward the northwest—"there."

Maddie lifted his hand and placed it against her breast, over her heart. "Home is in here. Home is you and me to-gether. Together, we can carry it with us anywhere. Every-where. That's what I want. What I need."

She dropped his hand and took a step back. Her voice held the slightest tremble, and her eyes shimmered with vul-nerability as she asked, "So, Cap'n, what do you say? You gonna let me and my fish stay aboard?"

Emotion had wrapped a noose around Luke's neck and his heart swelled as big as Texas. If he didn't take control of himself, in another minute he'd be blubbering like a baby. She loved him.

Maddie loved him.

It was more than he'd ever hoped for. Ever dreamed of. Certainly more than he deserved.

He drew a deep breath, then said, "You're the one for me, Red. The one and only. I know I don't deserve you, but you're here now and damned if I'm turning you loose. You're mine, Baby."

Her smile bloomed like a daisy. "You've never called me Baby."

"I'd rather call you Mrs. Callahan. Marry me, Maddie."

Her eyes widened, and he took her hands in his, holding them tight. "Make a home with me, Maddie. Here and everywhere. Make a family with me. Maybe a couple little redheads with bouncing curls. I want that. I want you. No one will ever love you the way I do. If they try, I'll gut 'em and pitch 'em overboard."

"How romantic," she said between laughter and tears, her expression alight with love and happiness.

He grinned his pirate's grin. "That's me. Suave and debonair. So how about it, wench? You willing to be my first mate?"

"First and only mate," she warned.

"Works for me." He lifted her off her feet and spun her around. Their lips met and clung, a sweet promise, a solemn vow. In that moment, in the miracle of their kiss, Luke's heart overflowed. Finally, he had a home, they both had a home—in each other's arms.

He loosened his grip on her just enough to let her slide slowly down his body until her feet touched the floor. The physical need that had simmered inside him since he'd walked away from her demanded its due, and the rogue in him gave her fanny a swat. "Now, off to the bedroom with ye, Maddie me mate. I'm of a mood to hunt for hidden treasure."

Mischief lit her eyes. "In that case, it's a good thing I brought rations. We might get hungry."

"Rations?" He reached for her shirt. Tugged it up and off. Black lace. Beautiful.

"Bananas. Ice cream. Chocolate sauce."

He dragged his gaze back to her face. "What?"

She dipped a finger into his waistband and tugged him toward the galley, circling her mouth with her tongue. "Whipped cream, too."

Luke damn near tripped over his own feet. "Well, blow me down."

"Don't worry, Callahan. I'd planned on it. In fact, I brought enough chocolate sauce to do it twice."

Read ahead for a peek at Matt's story
Coming from Signet Eclipse in October 2007

If they caught her, she'd die.

Torie Bradshaw's pulse pounded with fear as she forged her own path through the island's dense tropical foliage. In the dim, dappled sunlight, she pretended she didn't see the snake coiled around a low-hanging branch on her right or the huge ball of termites hanging from a high branch on her left. Razor-sharp palm fronds sliced at her exposed skin, and thorns pierced the negligible protection of beach shoes on her feet. *If I'd known fleeing for my life was on the afternoon's agenda, I'd have worn something more than a string bikini and flip-flops.*

Torie fought to keep panic at bay. So she was in a spot of trouble. She'd been in trouble before, hadn't she? What about the time she got arrested by the French gendarmes for taking photographs in the Louvre? Or that time when the *federales* nabbed her because of a shot that included a government official frolicking on the Mexican riviera with a woman who wasn't his wife? It hadn't been pleasant, but she'd found her way out of those scrapes, had she not? She could make her way out of this one.

Maybe. Possibly.

If they caught her, they'd kill her.

Oh, Lord.

Ironically, the trouble was not of her doing for once. Her work had nothing to do with her being on the wrong beach at the wrong time. She'd come to this godforsaken island as a favor to her sister. Helen had wanted her to see firsthand that Collin Marlow wasn't the snake Torie suspected him of being.

Torie had seen, all right. She'd seen the bastard in action and had the pictures to prove it, the digital camera's memory stick tucked snugly between her swimsuit top and her breast. Now all she had to do was live long enough to prove to Helen that her brilliance in the laboratory once again failed her in the real world. This wouldn't be the first time Torie had bailed her sister out of romantic trouble. When it came to men, Helen's instincts sucked.

From Torie's left came the haunting cry of a howler monkey. At least she hoped that's what it was, and not the cry of some other poor sap who'd gone out for a swim and stumbled across a murder.

Torie swallowed a fearful whimper and forged ahead, breathing hard in the heavy, humid air. Every few minutes, she paused a moment to catch her breath and listen beyond the cacophony of birdsong for the sounds of human pursuit. On her third such rest break, she heard it. Sure enough, something or someone—multiple someones—thrashed through the forest behind her.

She shuddered in fear, praying they weren't as close behind as they sounded. Weird things happened to sound in the rain forest, right? The canopy above messed with acoustics. The killers could be a long way away instead of right on her tail.

Oh, God. I don't want to die.

She still had dozens of items on her To Do list. She hadn't skydived yet. She hadn't seen the Great Wall of China. She hadn't had sex with a man she loved in broad daylight on a secluded tropical beach.

Torie started when a bird let out a shrill shriek right above her. Her heart no sooner calmed from that bit of excitement then the tiny hairs on the back of her neck rose.

She wasn't alone.

She lifted a foot to take off running just as a hand shot out of the shadows and clapped hard over her mouth, muffling her scream. Simultaneously, an arm gripped her waist and yanked her back against a hard body. Startled, scared to death, Torie froze stiff as a rough voice whispered in her ear, "Quiet. I'm here to help. You need to follow me."

Not believing him, she struggled, trying desperately to get away. His grip tightened.

"Stop it. Your father sent me."

Dad? Hope rose within her, and she shuddered as her thoughts came in a flurry. Was the general here on the island? Had the cavalry arrived? Was the island surrounded by a small army or marines waiting for the signal to attack? Would they sweep onto shore and arrest the bad guys and free the damsel in distress?

Except nobody would consider her a damsel. Most people—her father included—lumped her in with the wolves of the world, predators who prey on the innocent. They didn't understand that 80 percent of the time, the innocents weren't innocent at all. But, then, they were rescuing Helen, weren't they? Not her. She wasn't supposed to be here.

Maybe this wasn't a rescue at all. Maybe he wasn't U.S. Army, but Killers-R-Us instead. Maybe he was leading her back toward the house, where he'd turn her over to Marlow for interrogation, torture, and execution. Maybe by going with him, she'd be acting as naive as her sister.

After all, danger radiated from him in waves. His physical strength overwhelmed her. This man was a *real* predator. The prey in her sensed it. By throwing her lot in with him, she might be condemning herself to the very fate she tried to escape. Yet what choice did she have? She knew the other guys were bad guys. Marlow's minions would kill her if they found her, and she'd had no luck shaking them so far. Mystery Man here might just be the answer to her prayers.

Behind her, the sounds of pursuit grew closer. The stranger's arm tightened around her waist as Torie nodded her agreement. The hand over her mouth moved away, but he tapped her lips with his finger twice, signaling the continued need for silence.

She nodded and swallowed her need to drill him for information. Despite the surge of patriotic gratitude she felt at the idea that the army had come to her rescue, now was not the time to break out into "The Star-Spangled Banner."

The arm around her waist fell away. She turned and got her first good look at him. Holy hell. He wasn't dressed in fatigues, but in the dark slacks and white shirts the scientists on the island tended to wear to work. And dress shoes! All he was missing was a lab coat. He was no more suited for jungle running than she.

Nor did he have the rough-and-ready drill-sergeant look she expected in one of her father's minions. He looked like . . . hmm . . . James Bond. The man was a gorgeous combination of Sean Connery in *Diamonds Are Forever* and Pierce Brosnan in *Die Another Day* salted with Roger Moore in *Live and Let Die*. Under other circumstances, Torie would have asked him how he liked his martinis.

Not regular army then, but army intelligence. A soldier-spy. She was good with that. As long as he was a good guy, she didn't care what uniform he wore.

He clasped her hand in his and stepped forward at an angle to the direction she'd been traveling. He moved like a jungle cat, Torie thought. Silent and graceful. Deadly. She really really really really hoped he was truly on her side.

Plants scratched and sliced at Torie's skin, but she hardly noticed the discomfort. It took all her concentration to keep up with him while making only minimal noise. He must have considered her efforts inadequate, because he stopped abruptly, scooped her up, and tossed her over his shoulder in a fireman's carry. With his hand on her bare butt, holding her.

Well. This was . . . interesting. Her instinct was to struggle, but she forced herself to remain still.

His big hand felt like a branding iron on her cheek.

With him carrying her, they moved much faster than they

had when he'd dragged her along behind him. For the first time in a long time, Torie was happy that she didn't have the tall, statuesque build she'd always coveted in other women. Petite was a positive thing today.

She startled at the sound of a torrent of angry Spanish coming from a short distance away off to their left, and she burrowed her head against her rescuer's back. He smelled of salt and sea and healthy sweat. She figured she must reek of fear.

With her head down, her eyes closed, and her heart pounding, flung over the broad shoulders of a stranger, Torie tried not to feel like a wuss. Ordinarily she wasn't a coward. A coward wouldn't dangle from a helicopter to get the primo shot at a celebrity wedding. A coward wouldn't sneak a miniature camera into a courtroom to capture the moment a Hollywood star learned his sentence after his conviction for a drunk-driving homicide. A coward certainly wouldn't have crept into the locker room at the Super Bowl to get the money shot of the quarterback lip-locked with the team owner's wife.

Yet here in the inky darkness of a rain forest jungle on a tropical island, bouncing on the shoulder of a stranger and armed with nothing more than her own besieged wits, the only thing keeping Torie from peeing her pants was the fact that her legs were draped over a government agent. Death was preferable to the humiliation of peeing on James Bond.

"We're here," he murmured. He eased her effortlessly forward, but rather than set her on the ground, he stopped when they were chest to chest. Instinctively, her arms wrapped around his neck and her legs around his torso. "Get ready. It's cold.'"

"What's cold?"

"The cenote."

The cenote? He'd brought her to one of the caves that dotted the island and gave access to the underground river?

"We're going in."

"What!" she said with a yelp.

Rather than respond, he stepped forward. Torie loosened her death grip around his neck long enough to yank the memory stick from her bikini top and toss it onto dry ground even as her feet sank into the icy water. The cold sucked her breath from her lungs, and she inadvertently squealed until the G-man shut her up.

By kissing her.

All your favorite romance writers are coming together.

SIGNET ECLIPSE

Penguin Group (USA) Online

What will you be reading tomorrow?

Tom Clancy, Patricia Cornwell, W.E.B. Griffin,
Nora Roberts, William Gibson, Robin Cook,
Brian Jacques, Catherine Coulter, Stephen King,
Dean Koontz, Ken Follett, Clive Cussler,
Eric Jerome Dickey, John Sandford,
Terry McMillan, Sue Monk Kidd, Amy Tan,
John Berendt…

You'll find them all at
penguin.com

*Read excerpts and newsletters,
find tour schedules and reading group guides,
and enter contests.*

Subscribe to Penguin Group (USA) newsletters
and get an exclusive inside look
at exciting new titles and the authors you love
long before everyone else does.

PENGUIN GROUP (USA)
us.penguingroup.com